Full Marks

Neal James

PNEUMA SPRINGS PUBLISHING UK

First Published in 2013 by:
Pneuma Springs Publishing

Full Marks
Copyright © 2013   Neal James
ISBN13: 9781782282631

Neal James has asserted his/her right under the Copyright, Designs and Patents Act, 1988, to be identified as Author of this Work

British Library Cataloguing in Publication Data. A catalogue record for this book is available from the British Library.

Illustrations by Rachel Beardmore

Pneuma Springs Publishing
A Subsidiary of Pneuma Springs Ltd.
7 Groveherst Road, Dartford Kent, DA1 5JD.
E: admin@pneumasprings.co.uk
W: www.pneumasprings.co.uk

Published in the United Kingdom. All rights reserved under International Copyright Law. Contents and/or cover may not be reproduced in whole or in part without the express written consent of the publisher.

This is a work of fiction. Names, characters, places and incidents are either products of the author's imagination or are used fictitiously. Any resemblance to actual events or locales or persons, living or dead, save those clearly in the public domain, is purely coincidental.

Dedication

To the staff at Maple Leaf House in Ripley, Derbyshire.

With thanks for all the kindness shown to Joyce.

Acknowledgements

Once more it falls to me to extend thanks to a range of individuals whose efforts have eased the flow of 'Full Marks' to its conclusion as a published novel.

Robert Eldridge, my editor, and a fierce adherent to the art of English grammar. His attention to the minutest of detail amongst the 100,000 words has been the boon which all authors would give their right arm to enjoy.

Ian Robertson (BA, FCIS). Thank you for being the Reader of Full Marks, and also for scrutinising and correcting the legal inconsistencies in the text. Evenings spent trawling through the intricacies of the English legal system have given me a fresh insight which will be of immense value in the future.

Rachel Beardmore for the drawings in the text. This talented young lady is at the threshold of a promising career, and it has been my pleasure to work with her in the detail of the eleven wonderful images which illustrate the novel. Also, Tracey Mosley in particular, and the Heanor Gate Science College Art Department in general.

My wife, Lynn, for the snippets of advice and 'word gems' which have been constantly demanded from her during the year which it has taken to get 'Full Marks' to its finished state.

Pneuma Springs. What more can I say that I have not already said? You took a chance, and now I'm right here. For all of the support, artwork, promotional material, and advice, a simple 'thank you' just doesn't seem enough.

List of Illustrations   **Page**

George Groves was in his fifties and stood just over six feet in height	26
Dave Monk was a big man, standing just over six feet two	61
"Listen, Mr Detective Inspector Marks, that Miles Thomas was one dirty operator	81
"Take a seat, Barry. There's something I'd like you to take a look at."	117
The sudden cold made Goldblum shiver involuntarily	129
Picking up the whisky once more, Staines drained the glass and checked the time	146
"Back to the lab then?" said Spencer	182
"Yes, can I help you?" She had a voice which could charm the birds down from the trees	196
"Mrs Yates?" The question came from a man in his fifties	222
"You can't just walk out on me, you pencil-pushing little weasel!" Shaw yelled…	262
"What did I tell you?" Groves beamed	275

Friday, 17th March 2006

Dennis Marks' professional world was about to fall apart. Today had, so far, been one of those run-of-the-mill episodes in the life of the typical Detective Chief Inspector in the Metropolitan Police. Now in his mid-fifties and married for thirty years, he had just about seen and done it all in his career. From the verge of a nervous breakdown in the not too distant past, he had recovered to be a much more pragmatic and open-minded individual.

The sessions had been hard, very hard at the outset, and the catalyst of Solomon Goldblum served only to expose all of the frailties inherent in the human psyche. Years of solid, factual police work had simply left him unprepared for the world inhabited by the old Jew. He had been sceptical, very sceptical, at the outset of the psychiatric techniques which laid his mind bare. The near collapse brought on by the case had been the least of his worries at the time. June, his wife, had been a rock, but the nightmares, when they came, had pulled her into the darkness which had started to drag him down. The eyes - Goldblum's burning, demonic eyes - lay in wait for him each night he tried to sleep. The treatment, in the end, had been a clear instruction from those above – it had been an ultimatum, and one which he had tried in vain to ignore.

He was five feet ten, of medium build, and, for a man of his years, took pride in the fact that he could still run a mile in under eight minutes. The glasses, which he wore for effect in meetings (though they were strictly for reading only), lent him an air of authority to which younger officers deferred without question. He had progressed through the Met in the old way of pounding the beat, and earning promotion by virtue of deed rather than word.

All of that was about to change with the arrival of the man now making his way down the office. Like the Red Sea before Moses, those officers present stood aside. Marks never saw him coming.

Eric Staines – a name to strike fear into any copper operating within the Metropolitan Police. With the rank of Superintendent, he ran his own Professional Standards Department within the Independent Police Complaints Commission with an iron fist forged in the controversies surrounding the appeals of The Guildford Four in 1989 and The Birmingham Six in 1991. As an inspector in his mid-thirties at the time of both scandals, he had been involved at a senior level, and his name had become synonymous down the years with a determination to root out corruption whatever the cost. A number of high-ranking officers had suffered the ultimate penalty as a result of his work.

He had read the file on Dennis Marks, and although the DCI seemed, on the face of it, to be a typical hard-working senior officer, there was no room for sentiment. A number of issues had been raised, and there were some inconsistencies in the man's record. It would not be the first time that a top-ranking detective had fallen foul of the rules.

He walked into Marks' office unannounced - it was always the best way.

"Detective Chief Inspector." He flashed the dreaded ID card before Marks' face. "Eric Staines - IPCC."

It was customary for anyone approaching a private office to at least knock before entering, but not these boys. Staines was held in a combination of repugnance and fear by anyone operating at New Scotland Yard. Since the days of the original trial of the Birmingham Six in 1975, police forces up and down the country had operated under the increasingly powerful shadow of anti-corruption squads from within. The Stephen Lawrence Inquiry of 1998 had laid a charge of institutional racism right at the Met's door, forcing radical changes to operations. Marks could not suppress the involuntary shudder which ran up and down his spine. He tried to outstare the man – he failed.

"Yes, sir. What can I do for you?" The DCI's tone was brusque and businesslike. It was always advisable to be upfront with IPCC investigations. Anything else was apt to be treated as a weakness, and thus be seen as suspicious.

"Your warrant card will do for the moment. You are suspended from all duties with immediate effect, pending an inquiry into your record."

The flat, impersonal statement hit Marks like a dagger to the heart. He had known of colleagues falling foul of the internal discipline routine in the past, and even those few coming out of it exonerated were never the same coppers as before.

"Suspended? What are you talking about?" Marks scowled. " What is it that you think I've done?"

"Just the card for now, Chief Inspector. Any charges will be notified to you through the usual channels. You will be escorted from the premises and driven home, but do not attempt to leave the area. You will be sent for if we need you, but I would advise that you contact the Police Federation... and get yourself a good solicitor."

Behind Staines stood Marks' boss, Superintendent Gordon Davies; he was shaking his head almost imperceptibly, and nodded in the direction of the office door. The look on the man's face told the DCI that there was more to this than met the eye. They had been colleagues for a number of years, and the body language was a clear indication that more information than Staines was revealing would be divulged in private. Picking up his coat, and throwing the warrant card down on the desk, he walked out.

Back at home, Marks slammed the front door behind him and threw his coat over the newel post at the bottom of the stairs. June heard the noise and came from the kitchen to see her husband, in a state of ill-concealed despair, sitting with head in hands on the hall chair.

"Dennis, what's the matter?"

"The bastards!" He growled. "They've suspended me!"

"Suspended?" She followed him into the lounge. "What for? What have you done?"

"If I knew that, June, I'd be as wise as they are!" He saw the hurt on his wife's face at the last remark. "Sorry, love; they dropped it on me suddenly, and I haven't a clue what's behind it."

They were interrupted by a knock at the front door, and the grave face of George Groves greeted June as she opened it.

"Where is he?"

"In the lounge, George. You'd better come in." She closed the door, and returned from the kitchen with a bottle of wine and three glasses.

"Dennis, I just heard. What on earth's wrong with them?" Groves sat down.

"You could be in trouble just for being here, George. I don't think anyone's supposed to be talking to me while the suspension's in operation."

"Doesn't affect me." He shook his head. "I work for the Home Office, not the Met. Have they told you why you're on garden leave?"

"No. I probably won't find out until Monday. I got the impression that Davies knows more than he's letting on, though. All they've said is that I'll be sent for. I'm going to ring the Federation rep today, and find myself a good solicitor. No-one's doing this to me."

"If there's anything I can do, you only have to ask."

"I know that, George, but until I can see what's behind it all and what's been said, it would probably be better for you to remain on the sidelines."

Marks was acutely aware that, by the very reason of their close working relationship, whatever allegations had been made against him could also have a serious effect on Groves' reputation. Not only that, all of the officers in his CID team might also suffer the same penalties meted out to him, should those allegations be substantiated.

"There's no way they can find any case to answer against you. I've never come across a straighter copper in the Met. This is an absolute disgrace!"

"Steady, George, it's my head on the block. Don't be in too much of a hurry to join it. You said it yourself; you work for the Home Office. The IPCC can't touch you unless you stick your neck out for me. I'm going to try to set up a meeting with the Police Federation representative and my solicitor on Monday; let's leave it until then."

Saturday, 18th March 2006

Gordon Davies paused at the front door of the Marks home, index finger of his right hand poised over the bell push. It had been twenty-four hours since the suspension of his DCI, and this was an encounter to which he was not looking forward. He, and the department, had been given no advanced warning of the sudden appearance of Eric Staines, and he was as shocked at the action taken as Dennis Marks himself. He took a deep breath and pressed. The door opened.

"Gordon. How nice to see you." The voice of June Marks was heavily laden with sarcasm, as she fixed him with a stare which could have frozen the Sunday roast.

"June. How is he? May I come in?"

"In the lounge." She nodded over her left shoulder. "You won't be wanting tea, will you?" It was a statement, not a question, and was delivered with not a little venom.

Davies swallowed and smiled thinly. June Marks was no respecter of rank, and his status carried no weight in her eyes. He walked past her and into the first room to the right. Marks was sitting in a leather chair, coffee in one hand, TV remote in the other. He glanced to one side as his boss entered the room, but made no attempt to switch off the set. He waved the Superintendent to a chair. Davies sat down.

"Dennis." This was a greeting, and one which the Superintendent hoped would thaw the icy atmosphere which surrounded him. Marks swung the chair around on its pedestal, finally muted the TV, and stared silently at the man opposite.

Detective Superintendent Davies was a career policeman. This terminology, used widely by other ranks within the Metropolitan Police about those of higher status, set him aside from those within the force whose purpose in life was to apprehend and punish members of the criminal fraternity. He had been a detective of average ability who had learned the knack of climbing the ladder to his current rank. He knew the key acts and phrases, and was driven not by a desire to enforce the law but more to further his own position. He had thrived under the Labour government and its obsession with 'box ticking' and the achievement of targets. In Marks' opinion, and that of those of similar rank, he was nothing more than a highly paid pencil-pusher.

The DCI put down his empty mug, crossed his legs, folded his arms, and sat in silence.

"Look, Dennis, this is no easier for me than it is for you…"

"What?!" Marks bristled at the throw-away comment, and could feel the hackles on the back of his neck start to rise. "You haven't a clue how I feel! How could you possibly sit there and say that?"

"I had no idea that Staines was involved. It came as much out of the blue for me as it did for you. This reflects on the department as well, you know. It's not just you that's under the spotlight."

"You arrogant…" Marks stopped himself before the words had time to form. Davies was still his superior, notwithstanding the situation which was staring him in the face. He took a deep breath. "I've served the Met for more years than I care to remember, and I've never stepped outside the rules."

"Yes, yes, I understand that, but you have to see that there is a procedure to go through now that the IPCC are involved. We can't simply dismiss the matter with a mere wave of the hand. Don't forget what happened after the Stephen Lawrence Inquiry – we were all branded with that charge, and I for one do not like being regarded as a racist."

Marks had to concede that Davies had a point. The failings of the Metropolitan Police to bring to justice the killers of the young man, despite the names having been freely published by the tabloid press, had tarnished the reputation of what had been regarded as an example to every other force within the country.

"Alright, sir." The title was heavily laboured. "Where do I go from here?"

"As a matter of fact, I have something which may be of interest to you and your legal team." The Superintendent reached into his inside pocket and withdrew a folded piece of paper. He handed it across to Marks. "That is a list of the cases which the IPCC are reviewing as part of the complaint which has been made against you."

Marks took a few moments to study the contents, and then looked up at Davies. He was on the point of speaking when a raised hand silenced him.

"I'm sorry, but there's nothing more that I can tell you. The list has been cleared by Eric Staines, and I've no idea who else is involved in the procedure. That will come from your legal team as he said at the time. I have to go now, and I won't be able to help you any further."

He was on his feet, sensing that this was the time to take the opportunity of a strategic exit.

"I'll see myself out, and please express my sympathies to your wife. I am on your side, despite what you both may believe at the moment."

Hearing the front door close, June Marks came out of the kitchen where she had taken refuge. Her opinion of the man who had just left was very much in line with that of her husband. They had both attended police events over the years, and had witnessed first-hand the political manoeuvrings which had propelled Davies to his current position. It was a widely held belief within the force that the man was destined for much higher things. He left her with a very unpleasant taste in her mouth.

"Gone then?" She came into the lounge where Marks was still staring at the list given to him by the Super.

"Mmm?" He looked up. "Oh, yes. Just."

"What's that?" She leaned over his shoulder, frowning over the top of her glasses.

"A list of cases that Staines has under review. Davies left it. Here, take a look."

She sat down opposite with the piece of paper. It contained a series of names, some of which were familiar to her, others which were not.

"Solomon Goldblum? Wasn't he the one who...?"

"Yes. The old Jew who apparently made a deal with the devil. It was the one that landed me with the psychiatric assessment. His father was killed in the aftermath of the Battle of Cable Street in the thirties, and there was simply no evidence to use against the guy he supposedly held responsible. I'm still not certain what happened in the end, but the case is on the list, so we'll have to come up with something to convince the IPCC that I'm alright."

June shook her head at the situation that had surrounded her husband. In the force for thirty years, and not a blemish to his record – now a seemingly ridiculous investigation was set to ruin his career, and probably deprive him of the pension which he had been earning all that time.

"So, what do we do? Just sit it out and wait? Is there no-one you can talk to at the Met?"

"No. All contact with squad members is strictly out of bounds, and anyone trying to get in touch with me could end up on the wrong side of a disciplinary hearing themselves. I'll just have to wait until Monday, and the first meeting with the Federation rep and my solicitor."

Marks ran down the list of case files once again, and shook his head. He would need access to the complete records before any kind of a defence could be *mounted, and that was not about to happen today. A further twenty four hours would elapse before the first meeting with his representatives, and Sunday was looking like one hell of a long day. He looked at Davies' list once more, and an idea elicited a wry smile on his hitherto stern features. Crossing the room to his bureau, he sat down and drafted out a copy, sealed it in an envelope, put on his coat and made for the door. June called from the kitchen where she had begun to wash the glasses they had used.*

"*Off out, Dennis?*"

"*Won't be long, dear. Just have to post a letter.*"

Despite earlier misgivings, this was a serious favour which Marks was about to ask. If this came off, he might just be in a position to launch a counterattack before things got out of hand.

Sunday, 19th March 2006

Peter Spencer had picked up the plain envelope when he arrived home late on Saturday evening at the end of a very long series of shifts at the Yard. Dennis Marks' suspension had placed all of the team in a precarious position, and the DI was acutely aware of the possible impact that the matter might have on his own career, should the investigation into his boss go sour.

With his wife at the home of her parents, looking after her mother following a fall, he was left to fend for himself for a while. Consequently, he was able to read the contents openly, and tore the seal at the top of the envelope. Two pieces of paper dropped onto the kitchen table, and he picked them up as he made himself a cup of tea. The handwriting was that of Dennis Marks - the message brief and to the point.

'Peter,

See what you can dig up from these case files and destroy the letter as soon as you've read it. Someone's after my blood, and I need to know anything that may link them together.

Dennis.'

He flipped to the second sheet, where a series of names, all of them familiar to him, were listed. It would be relatively easy to acquire the files, and no-one would question his having possession of them as long he remembered to return the lot to the archive without delay. Photocopies would suffice, and he could keep them away from prying eyes.

The department was quiet when he arrived at New Scotland Yard later that day, and his instinct that requests for the files would not be questioned proved to be correct. Spencer was able to pore over their contents undisturbed for the entire morning, before photocopying them and returning the originals to central records.

"You're keen, Peter. After Dennis's job?" Sam Wright, the duty sergeant, and friend of Spencer's, pulled his leg as the files changed hands for the second time that day.

"You must be joking with what's been happening this week." Spencer laughed, and returned to the squad room.

A little more pretence at clearing up paperwork would be sufficient to cover his tracks for now, and taking the copied material home would give him a much better chance of finding whatever it was that Marks was looking for.

Towards the middle part of Sunday evening, the Spencers' lounge resembled the state of the floor of the Stock Exchange prior to its computerisation. Papers were strewn around, some in piles, others awaiting scrutiny. He sat back against the sofa with the latest of innumerable cups of coffee, and rubbed his forehead in exasperation. Marks had been certain that somewhere amongst this forest of data lay the answer to his problem, but Peter simply could not see it.

"Think, man, think!" Spencer steepled his arms on his knees, pressing the tips of his fingers against his forehead as he sat before the sea of paper. "What could someone have on the boss that could make the IPCC take this seriously?"

The Weston file lay before him and just to the right. That case had propelled Dennis Marks from Detective Sergeant to the rank of Chief Inspector when Michael Roberts had been exposed as a spy by MI5. It had been before Spencer had joined the squad, and Marks had related the story to him many times. Peter sat for what seemed an age, mulling over the facts of the entire matter. Like a bolt of lightning, it hit him.

"That's it!" He grabbed the file, rifling through the sheets, searching for a name, and there, as a mere footnote, was one which both he and Marks had come across before. Martin Ponsonby – solicitor known to those of a less than lawful background.

It appeared, not as a material fact within the case, but simply as that of a known associate of Roberts. More than that, further digging around unearthed the fact that Ponsonby was also the brother of Roberts' wife. What better motive for wanting revenge on the man who the family held responsible for the death of one of its members?

Ponsonby - there was something else about the name that set alarm bells ringing. Spencer smiled as he realised that the solicitor had crossed swords with Marks prior to his promotion to Chief Inspector. If memory served, he had also received a disciplinary warning from the Law Society after one run-in with the Met. Now things were beginning to fall into place - he looked through the rest of the files again.

"There is no link. The rest are just a blind to hide the real motive." Speaking out loud served to convince Spencer that he was now heading down the right track.

It did, indeed, seem that the other cases were there merely to reinforce a charge against the DCI – one which would 'expose' not just a corrupt copper scaling the ladder, but also a man whose psychological problems in the wake of the Goldblum issue should have seen him pensioned out of the force.

"Not enough, though. Just because I see it, doesn't mean that it's proof. I need someone further up the chain to take an interest." *He prowled the lounge, racking his brain for an idea.*

Spencer was acutely aware that, not only would he need the clout of a much more senior officer, but that he would also be, inevitably, putting his own career on the line simply by getting involved. Nevertheless, Dennis Marks had been an extremely fair and loyal boss, and now was not the time to shy away from what was a clear attempt to set him up and remove him from the Metropolitan Police.

"Colin Barnes." *Spencer nodded his head.*

Marks had mentioned the man's name on a number of occasions. The Superintendent was widely regarded as the best that the Met had on its books. Getting his attention would be quite another matter, but the following day was to bring Peter Spencer just the opportunity that he was looking for.

Monday, 20ᵗʰ March 2006

Aware of his boss's meeting in a closed office with legal representation, Spencer made his way to the car park. Barnes was just arriving as he turned the corner, and with the place empty, Peter made his move.

"Excuse me, sir, but there's something very important that I'd like to discuss with you."

"Peter Spencer, isn't it?" Barnes smiled. "Don't worry, son, I make a point of knowing most of the ranks in CID." He paused then, and frowned. "You're Dennis Marks' DI, aren't you?"

"Yes, sir." He shuffled his feet uncomfortably but, recovering his composure, continued. "That's what I was hoping to talk to you about."

"You do realise that DCI Marks' case opens today, don't you?" His eyes narrowed – this could be tricky.

"I do, sir, but there's something not quite right about the whole thing, and it's probably best dealt with in private."

"Are you after a transfer? You wouldn't be the first officer to see the writing on the wall and jump ship."

"No, sir!" Spencer paused – his voice carried too much anger. He sighed. "I know my career could be on the line for just approaching you, but it's vital that you hear what I have to say."

"Very well." Barnes glanced around the car park and, seeing it empty, beckoned Spencer to follow him.

They made their way up to his office on the third floor. Barnes' secretary, Charlotte Williams, was waiting with his morning mail.

"Thank you, Charlotte. Could you get two teas, please, and then why don't you pop off into town for an hour or so? I'll hold the fort." He smiled.

"Very good, sir. You'll be alright on your own, will you?" She pointedly looked directly at Peter Spencer.

"I will. Thank you." They sat down. "She's the soul of discretion, and no-one will even know that you as much as stepped into the outer office. We're safe from prying eyes in here."

"I see, sir." Spencer nevertheless felt less than completely comfortable in the circumstances.

"Now then, Detective Inspector, what's on your mind?" Barnes was a model of politeness, and Spencer was keenly aware of the man's skill in disarming those in his presence. This would have to be handled very carefully.

"Sir, you'll be aware of the issues surrounding DCI Marks." Peter shifted nervously in his chair.

"I am, and, before you go any further, I would remind you again that those matters are under the control of the IPCC. Your involvement could be seen as an attempt to influence the outcome."

"Yes, I know that, sir, but I may have unearthed something which the investigation could miss."

"Alright then, let's have it. What is it that you think you've found?" Barnes leaned back in his chair and folded his arms.

Spencer took the next half hour to carefully outline his findings from the previous day, and the deeper he went into the data the more interested Barnes became. He too recognised the name of Martin Ponsonby, and had been aware of Marks' involvement in the man's appearance before a committee of the Law Society.

"How confident are you of this?" Barnes frowned.

"DCI Marks simply isn't the kind of copper to be involved in a series of fit-ups. It's just not in him. He's as straight as they come, and yes, I know that my career is tied up with his, but if he does go down I go with him; it's as plain as that."

"Willingly?" Barnes frowned again. There was depth to this young detective, and it reminded him of the loyalty of David Willis at the same rank. He leaned back.

"Yes." The reply was instantaneous, and in that single moment Spencer placed his entire career on the line. The silence from Barnes was nerve-wracking, as the Superintendent weighed up the situation.

"Very well." The words jolted Peter out of his trance. "Let me have copies of all of the files under review, and I'll take a look through them. Place your own notes in with them, and I'll see what I make of it all."

"Thank you, sir." Spencer sighed with relief.

"Don't be too quick with that. You've crossed your own personal Rubicon now, and you're going to have to trust me. I have to say, though, that if this comes out as you'd like, Dennis Marks should count himself one of the most fortunate senior officers here. I wish there were more like you around."

Marks' meeting with Ron Greenaway, his solicitor, and Jim Pierce, the Police Federation representative, was taking place in another office only one floor down from that now vacated by Peter Spencer. Pierce smiled ruefully and shook his head.

"Never thought I'd be sitting in on one of these sessions with you, Dennis."

"Have you heard what Staines is up to?" It was a loaded question, Marks' meeting with Davies having already prepared him. The original list copied to Peter Spencer still in his pocket, he needed to see if it corresponded to the files in Greenaway's hands. At this point he was not prepared to trust anyone.

"You're kidding. These people would shop their own grannies if they had to. The IPCC don't report to anyone below the level of the Chief Constable."

The atmosphere was suitably tense, and Greenaway started the proceedings by placing a batch of folders onto the table.

"They're charging you with misconduct, Dennis, and those are copies of the case files currently under review." He indicated the manila folders which Marks had begun to leaf through. The DCI started making a series of notes.

"So, who's behind this, then?" Marks looked up, and came straight to the point.

"Does the name Harold Shaw mean anything to you?"

"Shaw? He was a drug dealer we nailed in 2003. It was an open and shut case."

"Well, it would seem that his solicitor doesn't share that opinion. He's filed an appeal, and has alleged that his client was fitted up, as he put it. There's also another, related, matter surrounding the conviction of Giorgio Gasparini at the same time."

"Gasparini!" Marks spat out the name. "He was Shaw's enforcer, and we put him away in connection with the killing of Roger Preston. He wouldn't testify against Shaw in court, and cut himself a deal. He did give enough, though, to get a search warrant on Shaw's premises."

"Yes, and he's claiming that you falsified evidence, specifically..." He checked his notes, "... the DNA trace which linked him to Preston's body."

"This is outrageous! George Groves handled that, and he'll testify in my favour. I did nothing wrong – Gasparini's conviction was as clean as a whistle."

"Well, that's what we're here, hopefully, to prove." Greenaway took out a notebook, and started writing. "Mr Pierce is here to ensure that all procedures *are followed correctly, but it'll mainly be down to you and I to present a defence. They've given us twenty-eight days."*

"A month? Is that all?" Marks looked incredulous.

"I'm afraid so. These matters do tend to be something of an inquisition, and the Met like them wrapped up pretty quickly."

The DCI snorted. He had seen enough of the operations of the IPCC to know that no-one came out of one of their inquiries smelling of roses. The normal rules of being innocent until proven guilty did not seem to apply once they had their claws in you. Ron Greenaway continued.

"The Shaw issue is only one of two of the more serious matters which have been raised, and it might be a good starting point to pick up on the second one first. It would appear that Staines' group is more than a little concerned with the circumstances surrounding your rise from Detective Sergeant to DCI. They've been looking into your relationship with the now deceased Michael Roberts."

"Roberts? My God, that man was a spy!" Marks jabbed a finger through the air. "Listen, I've earned all my promotions! Are they saying I bribed him in some way?"

"It might help if you calm down, and we could go over the circumstances of your dealings with the man. Things may then be a little clearer."

"That was the Weston case." Marks began, once he had regained his composure. "I was a DS at the time, and Roberts led me down the garden path until I rumbled what it was that he was really after. By then, I'd been dragged into areas where the police have very little influence."

"And the bribery issue?" Greenaway raised his eyebrows.

"Roberts said that he could influence my promotion, but I find that very hard to believe. No-one leans on the Met, and Roberts was taken down by MI5 in the end. Why don't you ask them?"

"No. The security services cannot be drawn into this on your word alone." Greenaway shook his head. "We have to stick to purely police issues."

"In that case, George Groves is my only corroborating witness. Roberts had agents remove evidence in the Weston case from his lab." Marks sighed in frustration; if this was to be the standard of his defence he doubted very much whether he had a future in the force.

The involvement of Michael Roberts in the Weston Affair had propelled Marks into a murky world where the police had very little leverage. It had all started so simply – a fairly routine murder case. He shook his head at the now familiar details which lay in the case file before him.

Metropolitan Police

Case No. 600439782
Name: Weston, T.
Date: 2-11-2000

Extract From Autopsy Report

The body is that of Thomas Weston, an eighty-eight year-old male. All internal organs display signs of chronic abuse. The heart is enlarged, and arteries leading to and from all main chambers are almost closed.

The liver shows signs of advanced cirrhosis and would, in itself, have been the cause of death within two months.

Only one of the kidneys is capable of functioning routinely, and samples of blood taken reveal low levels of oxygenation.

Skin is waxy and pallid, and the extremities of hands and feet are blue and stiff, suggesting poor and deteriorating circulation.

None of these factors were the reasons for the death. A single wound to the centre of the forehead was the cause, and the bullet extracted revealed the weapon to be a Beretta 92FS Parabellum.

There are no signs of any other injuries on the body, suggesting that Weston was not conscious when the fatal shot was fired...

Neal James

The Weston Affair

1

The stench was almost overpowering, and it hit them as soon as they had forced open the front door of the house. Detective Sergeant Marks recognised it immediately – the smell of death and decomposition. He had experienced body discovery before but nothing as bad as this, and they were yet to locate the source. Ten years earlier, as a uniformed PC, he had been called to a house on the local council estate where neighbours had reported an unpleasant odour coming from a property at the end of their street. They had noticed rats going in and out of the place, and hadn't seen the occupier, a single woman in her late fifties, for some time. It had been down to him as the neighbourhood policeman to gain entry and assess the situation.

You never forget the smell of decomposing human flesh once you have encountered it, but the body hanging from the stairwell by a piece of curtain wire was something which PC Marks hadn't anticipated. He ran back outside and was violently sick, retching until the pain in his stomach was almost unbearable, and its contents lay on the ground for all to see. He slumped against a wall as his legs gave way, having strength only to instruct one of the now gathering crowd of onlookers to call for an ambulance and police back-up. When his colleagues arrived, he could not hide his embarrassment at being unable to deal with the situation, but the sergeant just patted him on the back, told him to forget it, and sent him home.

Standing here, on another doorstep, and what seemed like a lifetime away from that incident, DS Marks braced himself for what he suspected he was about to see. Covering his mouth and nose with a wet handkerchief, he proceeded methodically through the house until he reached an upstairs sitting room. There, slumped backwards in a chair and surrounded by piles of newspaper, empty beer cans, and the remains of what must have been his last meal, sat the occupier. What grabbed Marks' attention was the single bullet hole in the centre of the man's forehead. With no apparent evidence of a suicide, this was looking like a murder enquiry.

The arrival of the medical examiner, summoned following an update of the situation to CID, provided Marks with an approximate time of death of two to three weeks, based on the state of decomposition of the body. Following completion of the preliminary examination and the removal of the body to the mortuary, the scene was sealed off in preparation for a more detailed forensic examination, and the team commenced a room-by-room search. Initial evidence revealed the man's name to be Thomas Weston, aged eighty-eight, and a retired bus driver. There was no information in the house relating to a Mrs Weston, and all evidence was labelled, bagged, and tagged for transport back to Headquarters.

The removal of the material took the rest of that day and all of the following morning, and a uniformed guard was stationed at the place overnight. It wasn't until the afternoon of the second day that one of the DCs reported finding more items in the back corner of the loft. They had been overlooked in the first instance due to falling darkness and the fact that the package containing them was wrapped in black cloth. Once brought downstairs and unwrapped, the contents had the CID team scratching their heads in amazement. Individually wrapped in tissue paper, and each within its own box, were a collection of medals the like of which Marks had rarely seen. Apart from awards from a number of high profile campaigns since the start of the Second World War, there were individual honours including the Victoria Cross, the Military Cross, the Order of Merit, the Distinguished Conduct Medal, and the Military Medal.

This man had obviously been a highly decorated soldier during one of the most turbulent times in recent history, but it wasn't until Marks came to the bottom of the parcel and picked up the final item that all his senses went to high alert. There, in a large plain envelope, was a buff file stamped in large red letters "TOP SECRET", together with several passports and sets of ID cards. He dropped it as if his fingers were on fire, cleared the room, sealed it, and called in for DI Harris, his boss. Harris arrived thirty minutes later together with an anonymous figure who bore all the hallmarks of MI5. They asked him if he had read the file, and upon receiving a reply to the negative, told him to complete the examination of the house, secure the premises, and resume normal duties.

That Thomas Weston had been murdered was beyond doubt. When door-to-door enquiries had been completed, Marks noticed comments from several neighbours that, although visitors to the property were rare, there had been a middle-aged man who called some weeks prior to the discovery of the body. Descriptions were sketchy at best, and no-one could agree on the type of car he used, let alone the registration number. They were all certain of one fact, however; he was smartly dressed and seemed completely out of place for the area. Marks frowned after reading the reports – he needed to get back to the forensics lab to find out more about the body.

George Groves had been the area Chief Pathologist for over twenty years, and Marks knew him to be methodical and meticulous in his work, and honest and forthright in his opinions. He was in his early fifties and stood just over six feet in height. The slight stoop always made him appear shorter that he actually was – a trait he attributed to years spent leaning over autopsy tables. Thin as a rake, and with sharp, aquiline features, the horn-rimmed spectacles perched at the end of a beak-like nose gave him the air of a wise old owl. His eyes missed nothing.

George Groves

The two of them had always worked very well together. The cause of death, not surprisingly, was a single gunshot to the forehead from fairly close range. The bullet retrieved was a 9mm, and tests showed it to be from a Beretta 92FS Parabellum pistol. Striations revealed the likely use of a silencer, which accounted for the fact that there had been no reports of gunfire or similar noises from the house where he had lived. This was an assassination, the killing of a man in his eighties - but for what? The file removed by MI5? And what about the other sets of documents? What was going on here?

A full report from Groves' office would not be available for 48 hours, but at present there were simply too many questions and too few answers. Marks returned to base to find out more from the property removed by CID and uniformed officers. He was disappointed to discover that, apart from piles of accumulated rubbish, there was very little to indicate any more than the facts they already knew. The man was Thomas Weston, he was 88, lived alone, had no family, and kept himself very much to himself. So why kill him? There had to be more to it than this. He had been a soldier so the Ministry of Defence should have a record of him, particularly bearing in mind the collection of special awards amongst the array of medals. Initial calls to the relevant department went unanswered, and it wasn't until Marks contacted a friend in the ministry that the pieces of a puzzle began to fall into place.

He was informed that the records relating to his enquiry were not available as they had been removed from the file, and when he pushed harder a senior official told him that he did not have the required level of security clearance for any further information. Marks' instincts told him that he was on to something way above his head, but he persisted and went back to see George Groves. The pathologist was not available, and one of his junior staff told Marks that an urgent telephone call concerning a family illness had compelled him to take an unexpected leave of absence. When he asked about the body of Thomas Weston, the same junior informed him that two officers from Special Branch had removed it together with all items relating to the case, and he was told that no further action would be required by his department.

So, there was now no body, no forensics, and no records at the Ministry of Defence. When the DS returned to the house where Weston's body had been found, all traces of police activity were gone and the place had been boarded up – neighbours seemed to know nothing about it. Sitting at his desk back at the station, Marks sipped his coffee as the events of the past few days were replaying in his mind. He detested loose ends, and this case was littered with them – apparently the same two men from MI5 (he assumed) had confiscated all contemporaneous notes made by officers at the scene. As senior SOCO he had not taken any – he was left with no hard evidence at all. His telephone rang, and a call from the PA to the Detective Superintendent requested his presence at a meeting upstairs in fifteen minutes.

He had been up there on occasion before, but this gathering was unlike any of the previous ones. Present were Detective Superintendent Johnson, Detective Inspector Harris and a suit with a briefcase. It was the suit who addressed him.

"Take a seat please, Detective Sergeant Marks. I would like you to read and sign this."

He placed a document headed 'Official Secrets Act 1989' before Marks, and indicated a space for him to append his signature. The DS frowned and looked up at him questioningly. The suit turned to the other two detectives.

"If you gentlemen wouldn't mind, I'd like a few moments in private with Detective Sergeant Marks, please."

Johnson and Harris looked at each other and then made their way out of the office. After a suitable interval, the man turned back to Marks and introduced himself.

"You may call me Michael Roberts. You'll not find my name on any official contact list, and you may not even believe that it's my name at all, but that's not the reason for your being here. You'll be aware, by now, that all trace of the man you know as Thomas Weston has been removed from circulation. As far as you're concerned he never existed, and any other people with whom he has been in contact have been, shall we say, 'persuaded' likewise."

Marks signed the document, and listened intently as Roberts explained the penalties for breach of the 1989 Act, and also the reasons necessitating his signature. The man, Thomas Weston, was indeed a highly decorated war hero, and his name had been mentioned in a number of despatches from a variety of front lines across the globe. This, however, was not his true identity, and the additional documents which Marks had not had the opportunity to scrutinise painted the picture of an undercover operative working secretly behind enemy lines in a variety of scenarios, none of which were relevant to the police.

"I'm telling you all of this, DS Marks, because the documents you retrieved from the house where the body was found could have had serious repercussions for Her Majesty's Government and the security services had they fallen into the wrong hands. We're very grateful to you for your professionalism and expediency in the matter. They've been returned to the appropriate authorities, and we've noted your application for promotion to Detective Inspector – this will be receiving suitable attention in the coming weeks."

Marks stood up and turned to leave the office, assuming that the meeting was at an end, but Roberts held up a hand to delay him a little longer.

"There is just one further thing; I can reveal to you, off the record of course, the identity of Weston. We're alone in this office, and the information will be of no use to you outside of our conversation which, of course, never happened. His real name was Gordon Marks, and should you wish to check what family records are freely available to you as a member of the public, you'll discover that he was in fact your grandfather. The dates of his birth and marriage are of no interest to us and his death, should you wish to check that too, was recorded under the heading 'Missing in Action' during Montgomery's part in the Ardennes Offensive during January 1945 – there will be nothing to arouse suspicion amongst the general public. You may wish to hold on to these though."

Roberts handed a package to Marks, and watched as he opened it and smiled to himself. Beyond the fact that his grandfather had lived and died, his own father had told Marks very little, presumably at the insistence of whatever government agency the man was working for at the time. All the war and campaign medals, together with the original individual citations, were there in a black box along with a single black and white photograph of a middle-aged man in the army uniform of a Captain. Marks looked up at Roberts and thanked him for the gesture.

"Finally, Detective Sergeant, we'll never meet again, and your two superiors outside have also appended their signatures to the Act, so no discussion of any of the material facts of this case will be permitted. Is that understood?"

Marks nodded in agreement, and Roberts (if that was his name) closed his briefcase and left the office. The two returning officers shuffled their feet as parting pleasantries were exchanged, and shortly afterwards Marks and Harris returned to their normal duties. Six weeks later he was called once more to the office of the Detective Superintendent, but this time there were smiles on all their faces as congratulations were expressed on his promotion to Detective Inspector. There would, of course, be relocation to another area, together with a significant increase in salary and all moving expenses. The new position would be as head of homicide, with his own team of detectives. He was never provided with the location of the remains of Thomas Weston, but felt sure that his detective skills would furnish him with all that information in due course. Marks hated loose ends, but perhaps there would be opportunities for tying them up in the future.

2

Dennis Marks closed the file and smiled. Another serious criminal removed from the streets of Britain and looking at a ten to fifteen year stretch in one of Her Majesty's maximum security establishments. Since his promotion from DS to DI eighteen months ago, his job satisfaction index had risen significantly. He had his own team of detectives, a budget which was the envy of every other Inspector in the division, and a clear up rate which made him the area's top man. This last case had been particularly challenging, involving a triple murder following on from a serious fraud. It had taken them five months to unravel the complicated sequence of events leading to the deaths, but a combination of dogged determination, dedicated police work, a few strokes of luck, and access to George Groves (the best forensic pathologist Marks had come across) had finally wrapped up the case. All that now remained was to send the file off to the Crown Prosecution Service and let them do their work.

He unlocked his top left hand drawer and pulled out a brown A4 envelope, emptying the contents out onto the desk in front of him. The case of Thomas Weston (AKA Gordon Marks) was still niggling away at the back of his mind. He had been given a clear hint by the man calling himself Michael Roberts that any investigation into the circumstances of Weston's death would not be welcomed, but there had been no specific instruction not to proceed in that direction. He sat, elbows on the desk, drumming the tips of his fingers together whilst he stared out of the window into the fading light of a November afternoon. Looking down at the black and white photograph of his grandfather in army uniform, he knew that he would be unable to resist the temptation to dig deeper into the man's history. He was roused from his reverie by a goodnight call from DC Wallace and, replying in similar fashion, he put the contents back in the envelope and returned them to the drawer, locking it afterwards.

During a holiday the previous summer, Marks and his wife, June, had journeyed to Belgium and found themselves in the town of Roermond near the German border. In a corner of the town cemetery stood half a dozen war grave memorials, one of which bore the name of his grandfather. As he stood there, the DI wondered just whose body was six feet down in the coffin where history recorded that his ancestor lay. It would not have been too difficult, in the heat of battle, for someone working covertly to exchange dog tags with a fallen comrade and simply become that person. In the confusion of one of the most bitterly fought battles at the end of World War II, Gordon Marks became just one more of the 1,400 British casualties suffered in the Ardennes Offensive. None of this could be revealed to June of course, who merely believed this to be something which her husband felt he needed to do.

That was then. Back in the present, Marks put on his overcoat and, before departing, left a message on George Groves' mobile, ostensibly to set up a meeting finalising the case he had just closed. He had one more call to make, and pulling a scrap of paper from his pocket, dialled the number of eighty-four year old Walter Price, Sergeant in the same regiment as his grandfather during the Battle of the Bulge in Belgium in 1945. He had obtained the information relating to the man's whereabouts from the Royal British Legion, and after assuring the old soldier that he was merely trying to track down a relative, arranged to call on him on the way home. Marks' distrust of the facts given to him by Michael Roberts compelled him to check them out with an independent source, and who better than an eyewitness?

The old man, although sprightly, was living with his daughter on the other side of town, and it took half an hour to reach the place. He was made very welcome, and having shown his ID card, sat down to a welcoming hot drink with Walter and Susan, the aforementioned daughter. He came straight to the point - that he was trying to locate the resting place of his grandfather, and believed that he and Walter had served in the same regiment in the push against the Germans in late 1944 and early 1945. Marks said he was aware that Gordon had fallen during the fighting, but that the precise location of his grave was not known. Walter frowned at this information.

"That can't be right. He survived the battle, and I know that for a fact because I saw him after it was all over. There was a lot of confusion with units becoming separated, but I'm as sure as I can be that he was still alive when Montgomery announced the allied victory."

Marks tried to look suitably stunned at the news, and asked Walter if he had any information as to what happened to Gordon afterwards.

"No idea, son. I tried to find him, but you must understand that it was the duty of all of us to report back to whatever remained of our companies. After I'd done that I tried again, but he seemed to have vanished into thin air."

"So, you're absolutely sure that he wasn't killed then? What about dog tags, weren't they supposed to be collected from the dead to help with identification?"

"Dog tags!" He snorted. "Listen, if you wanted to go missing for whatever reason, how difficult do you think it would be to swap with a corpse and take its identity? Things were pretty crude in those days."

Seeing her father becoming agitated at the memories, Walter's daughter stepped in at this point and informed Marks that she believed there was nothing more that her dad could tell him. Thanking them both for their time and hospitality, he left for home. Just as he was getting into his car, a call from George Groves to his mobile voicemail stopped him in his tracks. He would not go into detail, and his voice sounded strained, but he needed to see Marks at the office first thing in the morning. It was on a matter of some urgency, but a return call revealed that Groves' mobile was now switched off. The mystery deepened when he arrived home to be told by his wife that an unnamed man had called at the house only thirty minutes earlier. He left a telephone number which, he said, would be manned around the clock – Marks decided to speak to Groves in the morning before taking any further action.

George Groves was one of those men who never seemed to age, but his expression the next morning was grave and careworn. He was at the station when the DI walked in, and had been there for a good half hour. Marks looked at his watch.

"You're early, George. What's the matter? Can't sleep?"

"Not funny, Dennis. We can't talk here – come on, we'll take my car."

He ushered Marks back through the door and round to the car park at the rear of the building. They drove a couple of miles to the Common, where Groves said they should take a walk to avoid being overheard. Marks was intrigued – he had never seen George so engrossed and concerned, and was impatient to hear the man's information.

"Okay, less of the melodramatics, George. What's going on?"

"You are. It looks like you're getting too close to something or someone. I got a visit yesterday, when the rest of my staff had gone home, from two 'gentlemen' from MI5. It could have been them that removed the body and effects of Thomas Weston after I was called away from the lab. Don't be concerned for me, there was no threat of violence, but they made it plain that your activities are causing concern at a fairly high level. What exactly have you been doing?"

Marks told him of the visit to Belgium, the churchyard at Roermond, and the subsequent trip to see Walter Price. Groves had also been making his own discreet enquiries concerning the whereabouts of the body of Thomas Weston after its removal eighteen months ago, and had been down several blind alleys until he received a Home Office memo concerning the man. He could only assume that he had been copied in to the e-mailed document in error, since it was marked up as 'Confidential'. The text of the note was brief, but led him to believe that there was more to Weston than had originally been divulged. Marks took a deep breath. He needed to trust George; after all, they had been colleagues for a number of years. They sat down on a bench.

"Thomas Weston was my grandfather. His real name was Gordon Marks, and he was some kind of special agent working undercover for the government. I've signed the Official Secrets Act, so telling you this could land me in trouble. Nevertheless, you seem to be involved now anyway, so one way or another that doesn't worry me at present. I need to find out where he's buried, and it's not in Belgium because one of his army buddies swears that he survived the war. I've already had a visit from what I believe was a spook, and no doubt I'll be contacted again. It's up to you whether you want to pursue the matter any further, but I'll be damned if I'll let them get away with burying him in an unmarked grave somewhere."

Groves sat silently throughout Marks' revelations, and taking a small envelope from his inside pocket, passed a photograph over to him.

"Don't ask where I got that, but the man in the middle is, I believe, Michael Roberts. He runs an independent agency within the security services, and the two men with him are the same ones who removed Weston and his effects from my department. I suspect they're also the two who cleared up your crime scene for you."

Marks put the photograph into his wallet, thanked George for his help, and they returned to the station. He called in at home on his way there, and handed his wife a plain brown envelope from a locked drawer in the study. He told her to post it if he should fail to return home at the normal time that day. The address was that of the editor of one of the daily newspapers – a personal friend of his. June looked very anxious and asked him what it was about, but he explained that the less she knew at this stage the better it would be for both of them. Thirty minutes later, he was back at his desk going through the next set of files which had landed in his department. There was no time for any detailed review however, as a call from the front desk informed him that there were some gentlemen to see him.

He was politely requested to accompany them to a meeting with Mr Roberts, but was left in no doubt that he could not refuse. Getting his coat, he informed his sergeant, Peter Spencer, that he would be out for a while but that he was expecting to be back in the afternoon. The car was fitted with windows tinted so that it was impossible to see where they were going, and there was a screen separating the rear from the front seats. One of the men sat in the back with him, but it was clear from the outset that conversation was not on the agenda. The vehicle pulled up about half an hour later outside a house with a gravel drive, and Marks stepped out to be greeted by Michael Roberts himself.

"Good morning, Inspector Marks. It seems that our paths were always destined to cross again. Would you come with me, please?"

They walked up the steps of a large country house and into a drawing room furnished in late Edwardian style. Marks was invited to sit down, and tea was poured by a butler.

"Thank you, Jones. That will be all for now."

Roberts smiled as he walked over to the table and picked up his cup. He looked across at Marks and shook his head slowly.

"I understand your motives for persisting in this search for Thomas Weston, but you must let go of the matter. There's more at stake here than merely a lost relative, and unless I can find some way of dissuading you in what's become a quest, there are matters of national security which could be seriously compromised."

He walked over to the large bow window and gazed out into the impressive grounds. Pausing only momentarily, he turned back to Marks who was, by now, staring at him intently.

"What will it take for you to abandon this search? I have a certain amount of influence in a number of circles, and I'm sure that we can come to some sort of arrangement. I see from your records that you've become one of the force's most effective detectives, and it would be a shame for such a talent to be wasted."

Marks thought he detected a carefully veiled threat in this statement, and the change in his demeanour was not lost on Roberts.

"We are prepared, if it's your wish, to divulge the location of the interment of Thomas Weston, and no-one will prevent your visiting the site. However, nothing must be left at the grave which could possibly associate him with you or any member of your family – is that clear?"

Marks nodded, sensing that he could come out of this whole matter completely unscathed if he played his cards right. There did seem to be more to the package however, and he delayed his reply, choosing instead to sit back in his chair and sip his tea. Roberts laughed, and at last sat down.

"We have a lot in common, Inspector Marks, and I've been watching your career with some interest. In the eighteen months since our first meeting you've become something of a star, and certain faces high up in the force would like to see you progress further so that your talents can be used more effectively. How would the position of Chief Inspector suit you?"

Marks tried hard to conceal his clear surprise at this statement, regarding Roberts with a deadpan stare before returning his cup to its saucer. He stood up, walked across the room to one of the bookcases where he feigned interest briefly. Turning quickly around, he addressed Roberts.

"Very nicely if you can pull it off. I will, however, require the services of some of my existing staff and one or two of them are overdue for promotion themselves."

"That will not be a problem – simply provide me with a list of names and we have an agreement. I must reiterate though, that any thoughts of your continuing an extracurricular search must stop right here, and right now."

Marks arrived back at his office early in the afternoon and immediately telephoned his wife - he would destroy the letter himself that evening. A call to George Groves set up a late lunch at one of the local pubs, where Marks brought the curtain down on the Weston matter. Groves was himself curious as to the location of the remains, and they travelled to the cemetery indicated by Roberts. Dennis placed a small pebble on the headstone of Thomas Weston's final resting place, and George looked at him curiously.

"Something I picked up from a friend – it means that I was here. Roberts specifically said that nothing was to be done which could link Weston back to me, but you'd have a tough job interpreting a stone as a bunch of flowers. It would be better, though, if neither of us were to discuss him in public again."

At a celebratory gathering four weeks later, Detective Chief Inspector Marks, Detective Inspector Spencer, and Detective Sergeant Wallace, all newly promoted, took their leave of the remainder of the station staff before commencing duties in a neighbouring division, heading up a new serious crime squad. Marks smiled and wondered who exactly was watching over his career and its sudden climb into the stratosphere.

3

It had been two years now. Two years since the facts about Thomas Weston had finally been revealed to Marks by the man calling himself Michael Roberts. A shadowy figure operating in the background of the security services, Roberts exuded an air of menace with the subtle smile of the predator about to consume its prey. They had crossed paths on a couple of occasions, and each time the detective had come away from their encounters unscathed, but with the uneasy feeling that he was treading upon very thin ice. Their last conversation had revealed the location of the body of Weston who was, apparently, Marks' grandfather, Gordon, and Roberts' parting remarks left him in no doubt that the case should now remain firmly closed. However, he was a detective, and his natural instincts told him that the jigsaw puzzle was one piece short. He had no idea what shape it was or any clue as to its colour, but it was missing; a loose end, and he hated the damned things.

He had visited the graveside on a number of occasions, and each time had placed a pebble upon the memorial. Taking the tube of superglue from his pocket, he fixed another alongside those already there – glued so that weathering would not remove them, and also so that a permanent record would be made of each visit. The wording on the headstone was simple and to the point:

Here Lies Thomas Weston
Born 14th January 1912
Died 2nd November 2000
Rest in Peace

Until Dennis Marks stood back, he didn't notice the additional inscriptions which had been appended at the bottom right hand corner of the headstone since his last visit. He couldn't read the text and moved closer to get a better look. It was not in English, and although he had suffered a year of Latin at school, very little of it had sunk in. Nevertheless, Latin it was, and taking out a scrap of paper he wrote it down word for word. There was only one person he could trust with the information, and that was George Groves, chief pathologist and known Latin scholar. A call to his office was enough to set up a private meeting that evening. It was 8.30 when he rang the doorbell at Marks' home. June answered the door.

"Evening, my dear." He smiled. "Is the old devil at home?"

"Yes, come in, George. Let me take your coat; he's in the front room."

Groves had built up a familiarity with the Markses, and this had developed into an easy friendship between them, built on mutual trust and understanding. Dennis had been compelled by circumstances to put his wife in the picture regarding Thomas Weston, and knew that it would go no further. They sat down to dinner shortly after George's arrival, and the talk moved almost immediately to the inscription on the headstone.

"I didn't notice it last time, so there's no telling when it was put there, but here it is."

Marks passed over the piece of paper bearing the transcription of the two phrases, and Groves put on his glasses. He studied the note for a moment, and then replaced the spectacles in his pocket.

"Well, what is it, then?"

"Not very good Latin, I'm afraid, but the first phrase, '*Peto quod vos vadum reperio*', roughly translated means 'Seek and ye shall find'. The second is a little better – '*Non solus es*' comes out as 'You are not alone'."

"What does *that* mean, and why in Latin?"

"No idea my friend, but it looks to me as if somebody's trying to tell you something. As for the Latin, it's anyone's guess, but probably to prevent the casual observer from suspecting anything. Anyway, you're the detective and I'm the pathologist; it's over to you, I'm afraid."

They passed the rest of the evening in more general and non-work-related conversation, and when Groves' taxi arrived just after 11.30pm, the mood was considerably lighter. After they had tidied up for the night and gone to bed, June asked her husband what he intended to do about the subject of their earlier conversation. He had to admit to being confused but intrigued by the message, although he hadn't a clue how to make contact with whoever had left the inscription. Despite a pleasant dinner in George Groves' company, he spent a restless night tossing and turning, with those involved in the Weston affair flitting in and out of his mind. As it turned out, he didn't have too long to wait for an answer to the riddle of the Latin message.

The team had been working on the case of a young woman found in a patch of woodland. She had been robbed and strangled, and the body had been left with no identification at all. Marks was in the office early to find documents from the forensic lab already on his desk and, after a visit to the coffee machine, he commenced his usual scrutiny in search of anything to point them in the right direction. His gaze was drawn to the brown foolscap envelope protruding from the pile about half way down. It was almost as if it had been deliberately placed in such a way so as to attract his attention and he withdrew it, pushing the rest of the documents to one side. There was nothing on the back or front to indicate a destination, and it was completely out of place amongst the remainder of the paperwork, which bore the meticulously presented style of George Groves' department.

Uncertain whether or not to treat the package as suspicious and summon the bomb squad, he nevertheless carefully examined it and, taking a deep breath, carefully slit the top edge with his letter opener. It contained a single sheet of paper bearing a photocopied section of a street map. There was a red cross at the intersection of Ramsey Road and Norris Street, with a message which read 'Tonight, 10.30pm – come alone'. There was no-one else in the office at that time of the morning, and the desk sergeant downstairs had not seen anyone unfamiliar on the premises since the start of his shift. Marks rang George Groves.

"George, the forensics you sent over, anything odd about them?"

"Odd? I don't know what you mean. What's wrong?"

"I don't know. Can't talk now, but I'll see you later – same place as last time."

This was a coded message of the type to which Groves had become accustomed since the death of Thomas Weston, and he knew exactly where and when to meet. The park bench was empty, not surprisingly during the winter, and guaranteed them complete privacy. Marks showed him the envelope and its contents, and asked for discreet tests to be carried out for possible DNA traces, with comparisons to staff in each other's departments. Someone had clearly intercepted the batch of documents between the lab and CID, and that someone must have known of Marks' connection to Weston. Groves bagged the envelope and its contents, and told Marks that he would have the results the following day.

Back at the office, the rest of the team had assembled and Peter Spencer was conducting the morning briefing on the current case. He stepped aside as Marks entered the room, making way for his boss to take over.

"No, it's okay, Peter, you carry on; I've already been through the file."

He sat down, ostensibly re-reading the forensic reports delivered that morning whilst listening to Spencer's briefing, but his mind was focussed on the message in the envelope, and the day seemed to drag as time wound slowly around to the appointment that night. The crossroads of Ramsey and Norris is marked by the presence of a telephone kiosk, and as Marks approached on foot from his car three streets away, the phone inside was ringing. Entering and picking up the receiver, he was greeted by a distorted and impatient voice.

"I said 10.30, it's now 10.35. Where've you been?"

"Traffic." said Marks in a matter-of-fact manner. "Who are you, and what do you want?"

"Never mind that, just shut up and listen. There's a key taped underneath the shelf in front of you. It opens a locker at the railway station. Take the contents away with you and don't hang about. Roberts is not the man you think, and the contents will prove that. You're in danger, and this thing is bigger than you could possibly imagine."

With that the line went dead, and in the distance Marks heard the sound of footsteps receding into the darkness. The person, whoever it was, must have been watching from a concealed position, and the detective was still no closer to getting to the bottom of the Weston matter than he had been eighteen months ago. No, that was not true; he now had a key - a key to who knows what information about Michael Roberts - and there was no telling where it would lead. He decided that there was no time like the present. Retracing his steps back to the car, he headed for the town centre and one of the NCP car parks – the railway station was only a short walk away.

The station left luggage lockers were at the end of the entrance hall and to the left. It was now 11.15pm and the place appeared to be empty. Marks made his way casually to the unmanned locker room and inserted the key into its lock. He half expected that it would not work, and a sense of nervous anticipation ran through him as the door opened to his touch. Inside was a large, plain, unmarked white envelope and, looking around like some schoolboy stealing an apple, he slipped it inside his coat and walked away, leaving the only evidence of his visit, the key, still in its slot ready for the next customer. He had, of course, wiped it clean. Trying to remain anonymous, he returned to his car and drove home, arriving there shortly before midnight.

He had made no attempt to examine the contents of the envelope at the station, but now, in the privacy of his lounge and behind closed curtains, he tore it open. The contents took him by surprise, for there, before him, was the very same file which had been recovered from Thomas Weston's house on the day they discovered his body. Marks was certain of that fact, as it still bore the small cross which he had put on the back cover before handing it over to Harris and the suit that afternoon. The 'TOP SECRET' stamp stared defiantly out at him as it had done before, but this time he had no qualms about opening it; after all, someone had taken the trouble and the risk to put it into his possession.

The contents were old, dating back to WWII, and it was a while before the names rang any bells with him. When they did, he sat down in amazement – 'Lidice', 'Heydrich', 'assassination', and 'Ravensbrück' all flew from the pages like thunderclaps. Reinhard Heydrich was one of Adolph Hitler's closest allies, and Reichsprotektor of Bohemia and Moravia. He was assassinated by Czech patriots in May 1942. Retribution was swift and brutal. Of the inhabitants of the village of Lidice, all the adult males were executed, the women were transported to the concentration camp at Ravensbrück, and the children taken away to be 'Germanised'. The village was then razed to the ground. Marks had seen pictures of the place some years ago, and the whole episode was a chilling reminder of the ability of the human race to stoop to the depths of depravity. The term 'ethnic cleansing' did not exist during WWII, but its acts certainly did. This was all pretty dreadful stuff, but what did it have to do with him?

He flipped through most of the detail, and came to a slimmer file relating to one Kurt Daluege. This was the man charged by the Nazis with extracting revenge for the killing of Heidrich, a task which he carried out with enthusiasm. Apart from a brief summary of the man's military career and family history, there was nothing to connect him to the present, but Marks' attention was then drawn to three pages of handwritten notes headed up 'Rainer Guttman', together with a black and white photograph of a man in the uniform of an SS officer. He had served as deputy to Daluege at the time of the Lidice massacre, and pages one and two gave a biography from his birth to his execution following the Nuremberg War Trials at the end of the war. It was not until he turned to the third and final page that Marks let out a gasp of surprise.

Guttman had a son by the name of Mannfred, born in 1940, and amid all the confusion and movement of refugees at the end of the conflict, the boy and his mother disappeared. The notes claimed to have tracked them down to Oxfordshire in the 1960s, where she had remarried to one Maurice Roberts and the boy's name had been changed to Michael. He had been educated at the local grammar school, joined the civil service where he rose quickly in the hierarchy, and ended up working in the Home Office early in 1983. Marks read and re-read the name before him – Michael Roberts, and attached to the top of the page was a colour photograph which, if there remained any, removed all doubt from his mind that Roberts and Mannfred Guttmann were one and the same person. The consequences were obvious. If this news were to become general knowledge, the career and life of Michael Roberts would be utterly destroyed – he would surely go to any lengths to conceal it. The final and clinching fact for Marks was the signature at the bottom of the report - Thomas Weston! Had Roberts therefore either killed, or arranged the killing of, Weston to protect his own identity?

The fact that he was in possession of the file once again indicated that someone else had more than a passing interest in Weston. Marks decided to conceal the documents in a place known only to himself, and await any further contact from the mystery caller. Things were quiet for a couple of weeks as the department carried out its work on the latest homicide enquiry, but then a call out of the blue set him back on the track of Weston and Roberts. The voice was similar to that of the night at the phone box, and Marks transferred it to his private office, closing the door behind him.

"Marks?" It was a familiar voice, obviously muffled, and he could not say definitely whether it was male or female.

"Speaking."

"Get the file?"

"Yes. I've read it several times, but what has it got to do with me?"

"The links are there; you're a detective, aren't you? How can the son of a war criminal be working for the British security services?"

"What I am supposed to do, take on the whole of MI5 and MI6 on my own?"

"Roberts will know by now that it's missing, and the trail will lead to you. Weston got hold of the file and was blackmailing him; that's why he was killed."

"So you're putting me in the line of fire. Why can't you do it?"

"Too close to him, and I need to stay undercover until the matter's resolved. Look, when Roberts contacts you he'll want a meeting. Specify the place, insist that he comes alone, and call me on this number; it's untraceable and I'll know it's you."

The line went dead and Marks' head was spinning. How in blazes had he allowed himself to get involved in this? He was a copper, not a spy, and was now dealing with shadowy figures playing by rules that he didn't even know existed. The fact that he had the file again gave him no option but to play along with the caller's instructions. He was certainly on his own now, and there was nothing to be gained by involving George Groves any further.

When the call came from Michael Roberts, Marks noticed a definite change in his manner. The voice was hard and clearly threatening, and he spoke with a clipped tone. Gone was the friendly dialogue of their previous meetings, and a question regarding the secure nature of the line revealed his concerns for secrecy.

"I want that file back, Marks." This was the tiger stalking its prey, and it was imperative that the detective remain calm.

"I'm not surprised, but did you have to kill Weston for it?" This was a gamble, but it paid off.

"The old fool thought he could blackmail me, but in the end he had no idea who he was dealing with. Hand it over before you get hurt."

"And what if I do?"

"Then the whole thing goes away. The file gets destroyed and you return to your games of cops and robbers."

This nettled Marks, and he could feel himself rising to the bait. Nevertheless, he stayed in control and arranged a meeting for that evening at the intersection of Ramsey and Norris. Picking up the receiver again, he called the mobile number given to him earlier and the response was immediate.

"Marks?"

"Yes. Roberts has been in contact. The meeting's arranged for the same place as last time. What now?"

"I'll be in touch." Again the call terminated abruptly.

Later that afternoon, a call from the Chief Superintendent's office had him hurrying to the top floor of the building. In the room were the CS himself and two other individuals. One of them he recognised as George Watkinson; the other was a young woman who took him completely by surprise.

"Wallace, what are you doing here?" The DS from Marks' department smiled at his reaction.

"Wallace works for me." said Watkinson. "I'm sorry for the subterfuge, but it was vital in the circumstances. Look, we needed you to flush Roberts out after we discovered his secret. Weston had stolen the file and Roberts had him killed in an attempt to retrieve it. He must have thought Christmas had come when you handed it back. It was Wallace who returned it to you, and now we need your help to end the matter and rid ourselves of Roberts once and for all."

Much as he disliked all this cloak and dagger behaviour, Marks agreed to co-operate. He was wired with a listening device, and instructed to goad Michael Roberts into a repeat of the admission made earlier. Special Branch officers would be positioned to ensure that no harm came to him, but they had shoot-to-kill orders on Roberts if things got out of hand.

Aware that his movements may be under scrutiny, Marks made his way home and retrieved the file. He knew that Watkinson's men would be tailing him, and that he could be intercepted at any moment, but he made the location at the exact time agreed. The street was deserted, and it wasn't until a further fifteen minutes elapsed that he heard a distinctive click of footsteps in the darkness as someone approached from his right. Roberts stopped ten feet short, and pulled a pistol from the inside pocket of his coat – it was fitted with a silencer.

"Is that the one you used on my grandfather?" Marks steeled himself at this opening gambit.

"Weston was never your grandfather. That was a ploy to keep you from digging into the real truth of what you'd stumbled across; but yes, this is the gun. He was an easy target once he'd been located. Now, hand over the file."

Marks reached into his own inside pocket, and stiffened as Roberts levelled the gun barrel at him. Withdrawing the package, he reached out to his former benefactor.

"Put it down and step away." Roberts waved the gun to the right.

Marks placed it carefully on the ground and retreated a further ten feet, now wondering why Watkinson's people had not stepped in to arrest the man. He was alarmed to see Roberts raise the gun a little higher so that it was pointing at his forehead.

"My report will show, Inspector, that you rang me to set up this meeting and records will be arranged to support it. This gun has no serial number and in the struggle when I attempted to disarm you, the weapon went off, killing you. The only fingerprints on it will be your own, and the whole matter will be quietly forgotten – just one more corrupt policeman in a force which the public no longer trusts."

The 'pop' which Marks heard from behind left a single entry wound in the side of Roberts' head, and he collapsed to the ground. Several black-clad figures emerged from the shadows, removed the body and all evidence of the encounter, and disappeared. Dennis Marks was left standing alone as the rain started to fall, when he heard the now familiar sound of footsteps in the darkness. George Watkinson appeared before him and waved an arm towards the black Mercedes which had pulled up silently at his side.

"If you wouldn't mind please, Chief Inspector."

In a nondescript office somewhere in the city, they sat over coffee as George Watkinson revealed the full extent of the Michael Roberts story to the bemused detective.

"Thomas Weston was never your grandfather, and that's the only truthful thing which Roberts told you in the end. Gordon Marks was a highly decorated soldier killed in the line of duty, and really is buried in the churchyard at Roermond where you and your wife found him."

"Okay," said Marks, "But what about Walter Price? He saw my grandfather and swore that he was still alive."

"Money will buy the most convincing information at times, and I'm sure that Roberts paid him to say that. Sadly, I can't prove it now, as Price died six months ago from a heart attack whilst his daughter was out. Odd, isn't it?"

"But the medals and citations...?"

"Oh, they are real enough as far as your grandfather goes. They were there to lend credibility to the story, and suck you in." Watkinson shook his head.

"What about Weston?"

"A sad but ambitious man, totally out of his depth, completely unaware of who he was dealing with, and the danger into which he had placed himself. He was a minor operative who'd stumbled across Roberts' identity in the aftermath of the war, and routinely reported it along with other information which he'd collected. He later saw an opportunity to cash in, and stole the file, but the gamble cost him his life."

"So, that's it?"

"I'm afraid so. You've been terribly helpful, but unfortunately none of this can be officially recognised. You may, of course, rest assured that you and your family are now completely safe from harm."

Watkinson stood up, put on his coat, shook hands with Marks and left the office, his footsteps echoing in the darkness, along the corridor and down a set of stairs. As Marks prepared to leave, another figure stepped into the room. It was Wallace.

"I'll be leaving the department to return to MI5," She said. "Sorry for all the confusion, but it really was necessary."

Marks smiled and they left the building, together for the last time.

In a churchyard across town, the casket of Captain Gordon Marks was lowered, with full military honours, into its final resting place before a small crowd of family and friends. Funds had been made available by an unnamed source to relocate the remains from Belgium, and the headstone now bore the details of the man's military career together with the honours he accumulated during its progression. As the sun broke through a grey blanket of cloud, a volley of rifle shots split the air in final salute to a fallen hero.

Tuesday, 21st March 2006

Although Marlene Brough's fall had restricted her mobility, the injury sustained had not, on its own, been of sufficient concern to her doctor that it necessitated the attentions of her daughter. Pauline Spencer had decided, however, to take the opportunity, under the guise of helping her now retired parents through the recuperation period, to talk through a series of genuine concerns which she had been amassing about her marriage.

"So, what exactly is the problem, sweetheart?" Marlene instinctively knew that there was more to the visit than appeared on the surface. "Peter's a good man, you know."

"I know, Mum." Pauline sighed. "I just can't accept the same level of enthusiasm that he has for his job. It sometimes seems that there are three of us in the marriage, and I just can't compete with the entire Metropolitan Police."

"You knew where he was headed when you met him." Derek Brough leaned towards the fireplace and knocked his pipe out on the inside of the chimney breast. "You can't say that his progression's come as a surprise."

Pauline frowned. Her parents had welcomed Peter Spencer into their lives immediately the first day she brought him home and introduced them. Derek, in particular, got on extremely well with the young policeman, and their shared love of football cemented the relationship right from the outset.

"Surely you don't think that he has another woman somewhere." Marlene chipped in suddenly, searching her daughter's face for clues.

"No, Mum, although…" She shook her head and looked away.

"What? 'Although' what?" Pauline sat down at her daughter's side and moved in closer.

"Well, he works such long hours, and sometimes they stretch into weekends. It sometimes seems like I never see him from one day to the next. There are women in the same squad, and you hear things about…"

"Just stop and think, young lady." Derek leaned forwards in the chair opposite the sofa where they were sitting. "Put yourself in Peter's shoes and consider what you just said. He may just be having the same kind of doubts as you are.

How would you feel if he were to come to a similar conclusion about your side of the marriage?"

"I suppose you're right, Dad." Pauline sighed and shook her head. *"It's easy to see just one side of everything, but the only time I get him to myself is when I manage to pry him away to go on holiday, and that's an achievement in itself."*

She stopped short with the next part of the conversation in which she had been about to involve her parents. Telling them before releasing the news to her husband would have been unforgivable and she changed tack.

"His boss, Dennis Marks, has high hopes for Peter, and they do work very well together. Perhaps it's him that I should be jealous of."

The three of them laughed at that last line, and an otherwise difficult evening now eased into a dinner and fireside family event which harked back to the years of her childhood. Nevertheless, when she finally fell asleep that night, it was not before the very same concerns had resurfaced once more, and it was in the early hours of the morning before the arms of Morpheus finally enveloped her.

A few days later, when the two of them stood waving their daughter off, Derek Brough turned to his wife and remarked again on the conversation of earlier in the week.

"D'you think that something's amiss between the two of them?"

"No." Marlene shook her head. *"Peter's not like that. Shouldn't be surprised if there's some other family news just over the horizon, though."*

"You mean...?"

"Nothing, Derek Brough." She gave him one of her matriarchal stares. *"Nothing at all. Let's just say that it's woman's intuition."*

He left it at that. Something told him that the subject would remain closed until his wife had more concrete facts to go on.

Wednesday, 22nd March 2006

Back at home after the first sessions with Ron Greenaway, Dennis Marks was left to reflect deeper on the issues which were now confronting him. The list he had given to Peter Spencer represented only the barest details of what he now knew was being prepared against him, and he had to admit to himself that, were he in Eric Staines' shoes, the evidence which had been accumulated would look extremely damaging.

He rose from his armchair and poured himself another scotch. The strains of Puccini's opera 'Madama Butterfly' had moved into Act II, and Cio-Cio's plaintive lament 'Un Bel Die' brought a wry smile to his face as he slid back into the comforting leather of the upholstery. 'One Fine Day'... He scoffed. How ironic that he should be listening to that on this of all days. June chose that moment to enter the lounge, having finished tidying up after dinner – Marks had barely touched his meal.

"Dennis, dear." She turned down the volume on the CD player. "You need to eat. You've hardly touched anything since the weekend."

Marks smiled. She was a rock, and he nodded in agreement.

"Maybe tomorrow, June." He smiled back. "Just don't feel like eating anything at all right now, and before you say anything, I know that drinking on an empty stomach isn't going to do me any good either. You're as bad as Groves sometimes."

"Cup of tea would be better." She leaned over him, kissed his forehead and returned to the kitchen.

His thoughts moved on to Peter Spencer. His young DI would be putting his career on the line with what he had been asked to do, but with no other means of doing some digging around of his own, Marks had been forced into a corner. He thought back to his own days as a sergeant under Don Mullard, and wondered what his reaction would have been to a similar request from his boss. There had been some awkward moments back then, when the chain of evidence did not always lead them in the right direction. He wondered how much of his past would be dragged out into the open for the whole world to see and pass judgement upon.

Looking down at the now empty glass, his gaze wandered to the cut glass decanter on the drinks tray. The temptation to drown his sorrows was there, and his determination was sorely tested. The Goldblum case had pushed him in its direction once before, and he shook his head to clear away all thoughts of seeking comfort at the bottom of a glass. As if to reinforce his resolve, June reappeared from the kitchen and put her arms around his neck.

"All done, then?" She nodded at the empty glass.

"Yes." He smiled. "No sense in becoming morbid, is there? I'm going to need a clear head for the next few weeks, and a hangover is just the thing that I could do without."

He was asleep as soon as his head hit the pillow that night, and the exhaustion of the first few days of preparation had him sleeping like a baby within minutes. June looked sideways at him, put down her book, smiled, and turned off the bedside lamp.

Thursday, 23rd March 2006

The hand-written note through Groves' letterbox held no secrets from him. It was from Peter Spencer, and contained a list of seven names – Thomas Weston, Miles Thomas, Michael Grainger, George Riley, Susan North, Jennifer Yates and William France. Having pondered on the contents during the previous evening, he had now brought a further hand-written copy into the lab. The sense of the message was clear – he would have to re-examine all of the forensics and autopsy reports in each of the cases to make sure that any convictions based on that evidence were sound.

"Ah, Kevin. Just the person I was looking for." Groves smiled as his assistant entered the lab at the start of his shift.

"Something you want, Professor Groves?"

"Yes." Groves slid the piece of paper across the desk. "I need all of the files relating to each of those names, the cases involved, and all of the evidence boxes. I need to recheck the autopsy reports as well."

"Is this about DCI Marks?" Henson frowned deeply as he looked up from the note. "I didn't think we were supposed to get involved in IPCC matters."

"We don't answer to them, Kevin. You and I work for the Home Office, and Eric Staines, try as he may, has no authority over what's done in this lab." Sensing the apprehension in his young assistant, Groves continued. "In any case, you have no need for concern, as I'll be carrying out the re-examinations myself."

Putting all other work to one side, and delegating urgent tasks to other staff, Groves settled into the monumental task of trying to help Dennis Marks out of a hole which had been dug for him. With no-one within earshot, and free to voice his thoughts, a one-sided conversation played out at the end of the job.

"Weston – execution by a single shot to the head. Ballistics matched the bullet to the gun used by Michael Roberts in his attempt to silence DCI Marks. Taped evidence condemned the man on the spot, and there's nothing to indicate any connection to Marks' promotions."

He closed the file, placed the evidence box on the floor, and moved on to the next case. Giorgio Gasparini had beaten Miles Thomas, but the youngster's death had been at another's hands. The issue, Groves believed, had been the Italian's involvement in the death of Roger Preston.

"Nothing here, either. Sweat on Preston's shirt was a match to Gasparini's DNA, putting him at the scene. Fingerprints on the murder weapon came back to records held in prison files where he'd served time for a number of previous offences, and we found trace evidence of his presence in Preston's flat indicating that they knew each other."

The name of Michael Grainger, however, had him shaking his head. This was the case which had almost tipped Marks over the edge, and to this day neither of them could come up with any rational explanation for what had happened to the old Jew, Solomon Goldblum. All of the evidence had pointed to Goldblum's involvement in four killings, and the IPCC had been prompted to act based solely on the unreliability of DCI Marks following the events of the investigation.

"Scurrilous!" Groves closed the file angrily. "And totally irrelevant."

None of the autopsy evidence, and it was the only hard evidence that they had been able to obtain, cast even the faintest shadow across Marks' ability to investigate and close a case. In the end, the Jew's apparent suicide was all that they had on file, and a subsequent investigation had exonerated Marks from any blame in the matter.

"George Riley?" Groves scratched his head as he flipped through the file. "Ah yes, the ladder that Marks was supposed to have interfered with to secure David Farmer's conviction."

Running through the evidence box, he smiled at the lack of insight in raising the matter. The timescales did not fit, and neither Marks nor anyone in his team could possibly have had the time or opportunity to drill the weakening hole in the rung. This one was easy to rebut.

"Susan North." He mused. "Did the forensics on that one myself, and the lads on the scene never left any of the squad alone in the room after the bullet had been found. All the DNA evidence was solid, and the husband confessed in the end."

The pathologist shook his head, poured himself a coffee, and moved to the next name on the list – Jennifer Yates; the young girl who triggered the investigation into the Southgate Sisterhood. Alessandra Nelson had headed up a vigilante organisation bent on revenge for battered women whom the justice system had failed. He frowned – Marks and Spencer had been meticulous in their pursuit and prosecution of an intricate and complex case. In the end, it had been sheer doggedness and determination which unearthed the truth, but the turning point had been the death of Roger Nelson, Alessandra's husband. Groves himself had pointed Marks in the direction of the murder weapons, but it had been the DCI who had finally come up trumps with their discovery.

The final case, linked also to that of Alessandra Nelson, tied up the loose end which could have cost Marks his life, had the final member of Alessandra's society not been found. Bill France had been killed by a single blow to the head - his wife was found tied to a chair in an upstairs room. Forensics had won the day once more, and only when faced with incontrovertible proof had Margaret France broken down and confessed.

Once more, Groves' name was on the reports, and he stood back from his desk and smiled as he stretched after a long and arduous task. There was no doubt in his mind that Dennis was going to need all that the lab could provide in order to counter the charges which had been revealed at their earlier meeting. Groves was ready – all he needed was the call.

Friday, 24th March 2006

Any hopes which Eric Staines in particular, and the Metropolitan Police in general, had cherished of keeping the lid on the investigation into the conduct of Dennis Marks was blown wide open by the tabloid press.

Blazoned across all of the front pages were photographs of the DCI and a selection of pictures from the cases under review. At a hastily convened internal meeting, the Chief Constable sat facing Eric Staines and Ron Greenaway, Marks' legal representative.

"I shouldn't need to impress upon the two of you how serious this breach is." He began. "We may have to move DCI Marks and his wife to another location until the conclusion of the investigation."

"This can't have come from my department," Staines bristled. "All of the staff are hand-picked, and have been with me for some time. In any case, it's not in our interests to have DCI Marks in the spotlight right now."

"Gentlemen." Ron Greenaway frowned. "Neither does it serve our purpose to have the issues in the public domain. This can only further damage my client's credibility. I suggest we look at the instigators of the complaint before we go about an internal witch hunt."

"You may be correct, Mr Greenaway." The Chief Constable nodded. "Unfortunately, however, what's done is done, and the course of the complaint will nevertheless have to continue uninterrupted. I will, of course, be making a statement to the press defusing the matter and contradicting the leak as well as I can in the circumstances."

"Dennis, have you seen the crowd outside?" June Marks called to her husband from the side of the front widow.

The hammering at the door began almost immediately, and a series of flashes from the front garden told them both that they had the beginnings of a siege on their hands.

"I'm on the blower to Ron Greenaway now." He shouted from the hallway, struggling to make himself heard above the calls through the letterbox from the media camped outside.

June dropped the locking catches on the front door and retired to the kitchen to await her husband, only to be confronted by more of the press corps in their back garden, peering through the windows.

"What did he say?" She asked after they had both retreated up the stairs and into one of the back bedrooms.

"They have no idea where it's come from, but the Met are sending round a squad to clear the area. He's advised us both not to say anything to anyone until the entire matter is resolved – as if we would!"

"How can we live with all this going on? What about your meetings?"

"Calm down. They'll send a car for me when I'm needed, and all that lot out there will be told to clear off." He replied. "Other than that we're just going to have to tough it out now that the news has been leaked. I just hope none of it lands at Peter or George's doors – I'm going to need them if this sham of an investigation is to be made to go away."

Trapped as they were within the confines of their own home, the DCI and his wife need not have been concerned at the progress which Spencer and Groves were making. The leak had focussed solely on Marks himself, and had come from the office of Martin Ponsonby. Calling in a favour from one of the tabloid editors had done the trick, and a reminder of services provided in the past was enough to ensure that his name had not figured in the news release.

Saturday, 25th March 2006

Colin Barnes had read and reread the previous day's newspapers, and the inferences which had inevitably been drawn on the character and career of DCI Marks. Sympathies for the man ran deep in the aftermath of his collapse following the Grainger case. Barnes himself had suffered similar emotional trauma on the death of Stacey Richards, his fiancée. He and DI Harrington had been on the cusp of apprehending and charging the serial killer, Peter Tremayne, using eyewitness testimony that Stacey was about to provide. A speeding joyrider collided with the bus stop where she had been waiting, and she had been declared dead at hospital shortly after arrival.

Then he met Caroline Stenson, and his life turned around. They had met at one of his infrequent evenings out after Stacey's death – an evening into which he been dragged kicking and screaming by his mates. His mother had been the driving force, bodily forcing him out of the house and into the midst of a crowd bent on an evening at the local ice rink. That's where they bumped into each other – literally; the feeling had been electric, and he had never believed that anything so good could come around again. The date of Stacey's death had been etched on his memory for 28 years – Thursday, 5th October 1978, and now it seemed that he could finally put it all behind him. As if to dispel the mists of time, Caroline appeared at his side and kissed his cheek.

"Thought you were watching the game?" She said, glancing at the abandoned TV. "Can't believe you're staring out of the window instead of watching Spurs."

Barnes' affiliation for Tottenham went back to the days of his youth, standing on the Park Lane End terracing, watching Bill Nicholson's legendary team win the league and cup double in 1961. His curious behaviour today aroused the attention of his wife, and she knew that something must be very wrong to influence him in such a way.

"Oh, they're losing anyway, and I have something on my mind that just won't go away."

"Okay, so share. Come on, like you did with the Tremayne case. We cracked that one together, didn't we?" The smile and sly dig were enough to bring Barnes out of his reverie.

"Not this time, love. I shouldn't even have mentioned it at all."

"Is it the Marks case?" Perceptive as always, Caroline had put her finger right on the spot. "It was all over the papers, and I heard that the press had all but set up camp outside their house."

Barnes sighed deeply. It was hard enough at the best of times to keep work off the radar of his all-seeing wife, and he had, it was true, used her as a sounding board on a few occasions in the past. It did seem very hard to freeze her out at this point.

"I can't be specific. The Chief Constable's gagged the lot of us, and there was an extremely terse memo doing the rounds after the leaking of Marks' name to the press."

"Alright; no names, no pack drill." She sat down; this was not going to go away. "He's a good detective, yes?"

"Yes, and powerless to do anything to protect himself without help." He sat down at her side. "Look, this is so important – you mustn't breathe a word... "

"Colin!" The anger was real. "What on earth do you take me for?"

"Alright." He raised both hands in surrender. "I've been approached with some information which Marks and his team don't have, and I needed to take some extremely unusual action with it... otherwise I'm afraid he's a sitting duck."

"Needed? You mean that you're already involved?"

"Yes. It was last week, and now that the wheels are in motion, I can't stop them. The person coming to me has already put his neck on the block, and Marks' career is on the line. I couldn't refuse."

"Does his record stack up?" She was calmer now.

"Yes. That's what's in the file over there." He nodded to the armchair where he had been sitting. "It's exemplary, and apart from the blip with the Grainger case there's not a question which can be raised against him."

Caroline, like the wives of all senior officers, was privy to the events affecting those of similar rank to her husband and his own team. Consequently, news of Dennis Marks' near collapse had come to her ears shortly after it had happened. Sympathy ran deep and fast for the DCI, and the events now being related by her husband cast, in her eyes, an unworthy stain upon the record of an honest policeman. What she did not know, however, was the lengths to which he had gone in order to help. George Watkinson had already set in motion a chain of events of his own which, if successful, would not only save the endangered career of one of the Met's finest officers, but also put to rest the activities of a thorn in the flesh of the entire London police force.

Sunday, 26th March 2006

From his lofty perch on the banks of the river at Thames House, George Watkinson was able to take a dispassionate view of the events surrounding Dennis Marks, and would not, under normal circumstances, have taken too much interest in the activities of Eric Staines and the IPCC. As a matter of policy, he actively discouraged all of his staff from becoming involved in the day-to-day matters of domestic policing and its internal disciplinary mechanism.

This case, however, was different. Dennis Marks had been of invaluable help in flushing out the renegade operative, Michael Roberts, and had put his own life on the line in doing so. That he had carried the task out without the full knowledge of the strength of those covering his back had earned him a level of gratitude from MI5 not given to too many outside the agency.

Roberts was the son of a Nazi officer involved in the retaliatory action meted out by the SS in the wake of the assassination of Reinhard Heidrich. Czech patriots had ambushed the man, and his death sparked the elimination of the entire village of Lidice. Roberts and his mother, Maria, escaped after the war and set up home in Oxfordshire after she had re-married. The discovery and publication of Roberts' origins would have finished him in the security services, and he had committed murder to cover that fact. Marks had stumbled across the truth unwittingly, and Roberts' death had been the result.

Watkinson was in the DCI's debt, and repayment was high on his list of priorities. All that was needed was a call from the appropriate quarter, and he could take action. That call was not to be long in coming.

"Tea, sir?" The soft voice of Shirley Mann, Watkinson's secretary, shook him from his thoughts, and he smiled.

"That would be very nice, Shirley. Could you track down Barry Newman and ask him to come up here?"

"Very well, sir. Shall I bring an extra cup?"

"Yes, that'd be a good idea." He nodded. "I think he may be in here for some time."

Newman was knocking at the door of Watkinson's office within moments of being summoned, and the head of MI5 waved him to a couple of armchairs and a table where Shirley had left the tea tray.

"Take a seat, Barry." Watkinson took a deep breath. *"You need to clear your desk. I have a feeling that we are about to receive a call for help from a very important source."*

Monday, 27th March 2006

"Hello. Peter?" Pauline Spencer called out as she dropped her bag in the hallway.

A return home from her mother's came a day earlier than planned due to a quicker recovery from the fall which had temporarily incapacitated Marlene Brough. Hanging her coat over the newel post at the bottom of the stairs, she crossed into the lounge in search of her husband, convinced that he had fallen asleep in front of the fire. Standing in amazement at the threshold, she shook her head at the mass of paper strewn around the floor.

"What the..."

Walking across to the first pile of documents, she picked a piece up at random and started to read. Sitting down on the sofa, it quickly became clear to her that Peter had been doing a considerable amount of research into a set of old case files. As she moved steadily through them over the course of the next hour, one name cropped up again and again – Dennis Marks.

"My God, Peter, what have you got yourself involved in?" She said under her breath.

Like all wives of serving police officers, Pauline Spencer had a working knowledge of the perils and pitfalls of getting roped into investigations involving the IPCC, and had read of the fall from grace of a number of high flying career policemen over the years. She had read the newspaper coverage of the case against the DCI, and had seen the increasingly frenetic TV invasion of Dennis and June's private lives. That Peter had even considered playing a part in the drama appalled her.

"Peter!" She stood up again, papers falling from her knee and onto the untidy piles littering the lounge floor. "Peter! Where are you?"

She made her way upstairs, thinking that perhaps he had gone to bed after a lengthy and tiring trawl through the same files. He was not in any of the rooms, and returning downstairs in a state of some concern, rang his office number at The Yard. The duty sergeant picked up the call, but told her only that DI Spencer had left at his normal time. Running out of options, her next call was to the home of her parents.

"Calm down, love." Derek Brough was his usual, unflappable, self. "He's probably gone to the pub with a few mates from work. You are home a day early, you know."

"I know, Dad, but the house is in such a state, and it's not like Peter at all. What if he has got another woman?" She began to cry.

"Now look, he's a good bloke. You're overreacting." He sighed. "I'll get my coat, round up your mother, and we'll be up there in an hour or so."

"No, it's alright; I think he's back. That was the front door." She wiped away a tear. "I'll call you later."

Smiling now at her doubts and fears, she replaced the receiver and made her way out of the lounge and back into the hall. Peter was just closing the door as she came around the corner. There was a woman with him.

"Oh, Pauline." He said, caught off guard. "You know DS Wallace, don't you?"

The awkward silence as the three of them stood there seemed to last an eternity. Sandra Wallace; her position within MI5 and also, latterly, the Met, had given Peter Spencer a form of secure help with the proposition which he had laid before Colin Barnes. That Pauline has misread the situation was abundantly clear, and the DS broke the spell, excusing herself from a position of potential embarrassment.

"I guess I'll leave you two and head off home." She smiled at Pauline. "We'll catch up on the paperwork later, Peter."

Tuesday, 28th March 2006

Colin Barnes was, initially, unsure how to proceed with the information given to him by Peter Spencer. Aware of how quickly the IPCC tended to move, he had nevertheless taken a week to consider what options might be available to him. That the DI's job now lay on the line was beyond doubt, and the force could not afford to lose men of his calibre and integrity. Nevertheless, he had limited options available to him if he were to use what Spencer believed could free his DCI from scurrilous charges. Removing a small black notebook from his inside pocket, he ran his finger down the alphabetical list and stopped near the bottom. He made the call from his personal mobile.

"Yes." The answer was curt and impersonal.

"Barnes. Remember when you said that if I ever needed something, I was just to call you?"

"Of course."

"That time has come, and it has to be right away. Can we meet?"

"Out of town. Where's that pub you told me about in Essex?"

"The White Horse?"

"That's the one."

"Okay, but why there?"

"It's far enough away not to draw attention. This afternoon at two?"

"I'll be there."

This was a risk, more so than that taken by Spencer, but if the DI was prepared to go out on a limb for Marks he would need some clout behind him. Barnes looked at his watch – it would take an hour and a half to make the trip, even with a clear road. If he left now, there would be time to catch up with a name from his past.

The White Horse stands at the junction of Heath Road and Church Road in the Essex village of Ramsden Heath, in a typically picturesque country setting. Its history dates it back to the mid-19th century, and Dave Monk, the landlord, had run the place for a number of years. Dave was the son of Arthur Monk, the *sergeant who had given Barnes his step up into CID right at the start of his career. Barnes and his wife, Caroline, had been at the old man's funeral a few years back, and they had kept in touch over the following period. Sue, Dave's wife, spotted the Superintendent as soon as he set foot in the place.*

"Well, here's a sight for sore eyes! What'll it be, Constable?" Her eyes lit up as Barnes approached the bar.

"Orange please, landlady; I'm on duty." This interplay had become very easy between the two families in such a short time, and played out each time they met. "Is he in?"

"Dave!" She called over her shoulder. "It's the fuzz! You paid the road fund licence?"

Dave Monk emerged from the back room, sleeves rolled up and a towel in his hands. He was a big man, standing just over six feet two. His thinning hair still retained the curl of his earlier years at university, but an expanded girth, due in no small measure to the quality of his wife's cooking, was enough to ensure that he would never play for his beloved Spurs. The outstretched hand was the size of a boxing glove.

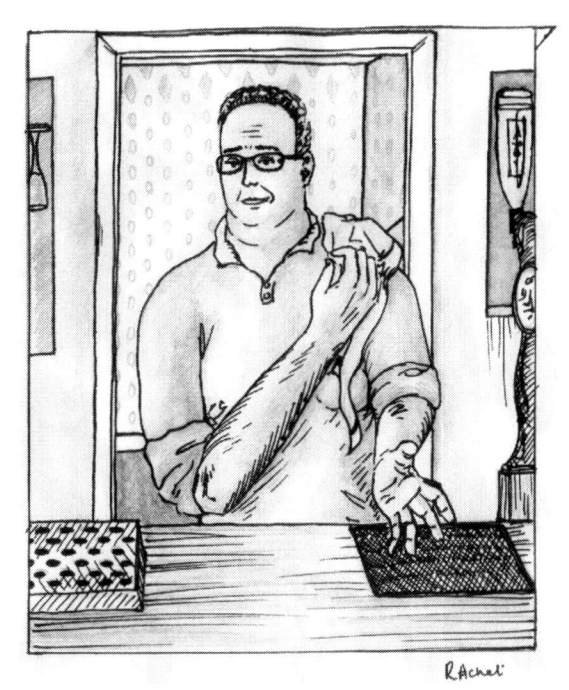

Dave Monk

"Colin. Good to see you again. Business or pleasure?"

"Just a spot of lunch with a colleague, in a nice, quiet place out of the way."

"Well now, let's see if we can find a table in a corner then, shall we?" He shepherded Barnes around to the left of the bar, where a small alcove held a single table and four chairs.

"This is just fine, Dave. My colleague should be here in around a quarter of an hour. Will you have a drink with me until he arrives?"

They chewed the fat for the following twenty minutes until a tall, distinguished-looking figure in a grey suit appeared at the door. Barnes spotted the newcomer immediately, and Monk picked up on the change in his demeanour. Rising from his seat, he shook the detective's hand, gave him the menu, and returned to the bar.

"Afternoon, Colin. I assume that we're safe from prying eyes." He glanced back at the bar.

"No need to worry about them. They're friends, and his dad was in the force. They're as discreet as they come."

"Good. Now, what is it that's so important that you have to drag me away from Thames House?" There was a smile on his face, but Barnes was left in no doubt as to the man's real feelings.

"It's delicate." Barnes sighed. "I, that is, we, have a senior officer under the spotlight of the IPCC, and certain facts have come to light which may cast doubt on the reliability of the proceedings."

"Isn't that kind of thing frowned on by the Met? I mean, if you were found to be in possession of anything to do with an ongoing investigation you could be in serious trouble."

"I'm acutely aware of the line I'm treading, but my source is convinced that the charges being made don't reflect the character of the officer in question."

"And the name of this officer?"

"DCI Dennis Marks." Barnes took a folder from his briefcase, and slid it across the table.

"Marks? I know him. Straight as a die. Who's muddying the water, then?"

Barnes, in reply, turned over a number of the papers, and pointed to a name halfway down one of the sheets. George Watkinson, for he was indeed the guest invited into the Essex countryside, frowned at the page.

"Michael Roberts? But he's dead. I was there on the evening he pulled a gun on Marks. Your DCI was entirely blameless, and, incidentally, was working for us at the time."

"Read on." Barnes tapped the page at a point further down. "There's another name that you may find familiar. We certainly did."

"Martin Ponsonby." He looked up. "Just a moment, didn't he end up on the end of some charges at a Law Society hearing?"

"Yes," Barnes leaned forwards, "and that was one of the results of a case being handled by Marks when he was a DI. Ponsonby is the brother of Roberts' widow. Now, that, to me, gives him one hell of a motive for mischief."

"There's more, isn't there?" Watkinson's instincts told him that the Superintendent had more up his sleeve than a mere case of revenge.

"Ponsonby is the solicitor representing Harold Shaw. Shaw was charged and convicted for dealing in class 'A' drugs back in 2003. His enforcer, Giorgio Gasparini, was also sent down in connection with those charges. They're both doing time in Wandsworth. He's handling their appeals, and any successful action against Marks is certain to raise serious questions about the safety of their convictions."

"So, what do you need from me?"

"I can't take this matter any further without compromising my own position. You, on the other hand, aren't subject to the same restrictions."

As their meal had now arrived, all talk of the case ceased and Watkinson was left to ponder the conundrum which Barnes had posed. With conversation now reduced to general chit chat, the germ of an idea began to take form, and by the time they said their goodbyes he had the basis of a plan to get Dennis Marks off the hook. Dave Monk and his wife passed more time with Barnes as he paid the bill, and nothing in his demeanour gave away the substance of the meeting which had just taken place. Nevertheless, Sue was not one to let the opportunity pass.

"What d'you make of all that then, Dave?" She cocked her head on one side as her husband came back from the till. There was a glint in her eye, and Monk knew he would not get away too easily.

"Dad always used to say that when coppers like Barnes have meetings in an out of the way pub, there's bound to be something going on. He always reckoned that the guy had potential, even when he was a raw recruit in uniform. Wouldn't surprise me if there was something amiss at a fairly high level. Anyway, it's not for the likes of us to speculate, especially when there's customers to serve."

A playful tap to the right buttock had her skipping away with a glint in her eye.

Marks, in the meantime, was going over the facts of the Weston Affair with Greenaway and Pierce, which they had left outstanding from the previous day.

"So, you see, there was absolutely nothing untoward in my dealings with Roberts. It was all very cloak and dagger, and I may have let my copper's nose get the better of me, but the man was dangerous. George Watkinson will tell you all you need to know about what he was up to."

"I'm sorry, Chief Inspector." Greenaway shook his head. "As I said before, we simply can't involve MI5 in any of this. Any references to Mr Watkinson are strictly out of bounds, I'm afraid."

"Well, how am I supposed to have paid for my promotion, then? Check my bank accounts – no money went his way."

"There's no reference in the charge to any financial exchanges. Did you provide any kind of services for the man?"

"No, and I resent the mere inference that I may have done. I simply followed my instincts, and the more he told me about my grandfather, the more the facts didn't seem to fit. It was purely a matter of investigating a dodgy story. That there was a family link is, to my mind, irrelevant."

Marks could sense that he was not scoring many points on the matter of Michael Roberts. With the man himself (and the only other witness, Walter Price) dead, it was unlikely, with the rest of the participants unreachable, that this particular case would save him on its own. Greenaway then turned back to the initial charges which related to the convictions of Harold Shaw and Giorgio Gasparini.

"The IPCC are taking very seriously the allegations from Mr Shaw's solicitor, Martin Ponsonby, that you manufactured and manipulated evidence to engineer their convictions. He's maintained his innocence throughout and, from what I can see in their submission, I'm afraid there do seem to be one or two inconsistencies in the procedures which took place."

"Alright then, why don't we go for the solicitor? He's Roberts' brother-in-law, did you know that? Couldn't you argue conflict of interest?"

"That would merely remove him from the case. The clients that he currently represents now have the scent of freedom in their noses. He'd simply be fired and replaced by someone else. The charges facing you won't go away just because we challenge his validity. It may actually put you in a more suspicious light."

"I'm afraid Mr Greenaway is right, Dennis. Eric Staines isn't a man tolerant of anything standing in his way," Jim Pierce chipped in. "I've seen this kind of thing before, and it did turn quite ugly in the end. You'd only end up regretting it."

"In that case," Marks sat back and folded his arms, much as he had done when questioning suspects in the past, "we could do worse than run the entire case from beginning to end. Then you'll see what really happened, rather than what some crooked dealer and his lawyer have to say. The whole thing kicked off with the murder of a young man by the name of Miles Thomas. Peter Spencer and I ran the investigation by the book, and you can check all witness statements to corroborate that."

"Dennis," Pierce chipped in, "Peter may, himself, be at the centre of a further investigation should this one turn out badly for you. It might be better not to include him right now."

"He is involved, and by the look on his face when I walked out of the office last week, he knows that. The team itself is under attack, and we need to use every piece of ammunition that we have. Peter and I have worked together for too long for there to be any possibility of a split in our relationship. Go and ask him."

It was a challenge which the DCI knew would go untaken. The Police Federation would not risk the attention which such an act would attract. Nevertheless, he wondered how far Spencer would have taken the information which he had posted through his letterbox. He was asking the young copper to stick his neck out when he really had no right to. He was jolted back to reality by the voice of Greenaway, as the solicitor opened another file. This was the one which had kicked off the entire matter. A young man deep in the murky world of drugs, and facing a trafficker ruthless enough to kill for the sake of protecting his turf.

Metropolitan Police

Case No. 611509250
Name: Thomas, M.
Date: 13-November-2003

Extract From the Notebook of DS Spencer

The House Manager, Mr Grant Thornton, has lived at the flats since their construction, and is responsible for the day-to-day running of the property.

He is familiar with each of the tenants in the block, and the position of his flat, at the entrance to the main stairwell, allows a clear sight of anyone entering or leaving the premises.

There is a keypad alarm which alerts him to the opening of the main front door.

He claims to know nothing of the circumstances surrounding the death of Miles Thomas, and remains adamant that he saw no-one enter or leave the premises on the afternoon in question.

He has no alibi for the time period, stating that he was alone and in his lounge watching the television all day.

His manner was nervous, and inconsistent with someone telling the truth.

Bodies of Evidence

1

Richard and Grace Thomas had not heard from their son, Miles, for several weeks. Whilst this was not unusual for the majority of young people at university, bearing in mind their busy social lives, for him it was completely out of character. He was one of life's spendthrifts, and constantly short of money for a variety of reasons. The telephone calls for emergency funding were regular and consistent, and despite their best attempts to rein in his extravagance, Miles invariably took no notice and they always capitulated to his demands. He was their only child and doted upon by his mother, much to the chagrin of Richard Thomas, whose reaction, gone unchecked, would have been to cut his son off and make him stand on his own two feet. That he never reached this point was down to the love he bore for his wife, a devotion which found its seed in 1976 and grew with each succeeding year. They had married after a brief engagement, and their son was born eighteen months later. Everything possible had been done to ensure that the boy received the best that they could provide, and he had drifted into further education at the University of London. There he obtained an Upper Second in Chemistry, a postgraduate Masters Degree, and further progress into studying for a PhD.

He was 28 years old and living alone in a privately maintained set of flats in Hackney - of this much his parents were certain. Beyond that, their knowledge was sketchy as Miles had limited contact via the use of his mobile phone, and had always been evasive about the address. All of their proposed visits had been discouraged, and on a couple of occasions actually forbidden. Calls to the university revealed that he had not been seen on campus for some weeks, but this was not unusual for PhD students who tended to research and work alone, only making appearances for appointments with their professors as and when they were needed. Nevertheless, Grace Thomas' concerns were deep enough for her to contact the local police to file a missing persons report, and two uniformed officers were sent to the university to obtain Miles' address.

Arriving at the location of the young man's home on Brenthouse Road, they were accompanied to Flat 7 by Grant Thornton, the house manager. When repeated knocking on the door received no response, master keys were used in an attempt to gain entry. When these failed, and it became clear that the lock had been changed, the house manager authorised the breaking down of the door. What they found inside resulted in the apartment being sealed off and a call put through to CID for a senior officer to attend. Dennis Marks arrived within half an hour to assurances from the two PCs that no-one had entered or left the building since they had gained access to the flat. The scene was one of chaos, with furniture overturned and broken items all over the floor. It was clear that some sort of feverish search had also taken place, and when he noticed the blood stain on the lounge floor, Marks called in the forensics team immediately. A statement had already been taken from Thornton, and Marks went through it with him. The man had heard and seen nothing untoward, but the detective felt that something was being concealed, and he asked Thornton for a list of tenants, telling him not to leave the premises. Peter Spencer, Marks' DS, arrived shortly afterwards.

"Anything for me, boss?"

"Not really until Groves' team arrive, but you could keep an eye on Thornton for me. He's hiding something, I'm certain of it. Get him to write out a list of tenants and we'll start on a door-to-door. Ask him what he thinks about all of them. You never know, he might let something slip."

DS Spencer disappeared down the stairway to the manager's flat as George Groves was arriving at the entrance to the block. They exchanged greetings, and the pathologist was pointed in the direction of the first floor where Marks was waiting. He smiled as Groves laboured up the final few steps.

"Age catching up on you, old man?"

"Less of that, Dennis; I'll take you on at squash anytime. Pulled a calf muscle yesterday evening and it's giving me hell."

"Need to see a doctor, then."

"Very funny." He nodded at the forced entry. "What's the score with this?"

"Missing persons report, and the lock to the apartment's been changed, presumably by the tenant," he consulted his notebook, "one Miles Thomas. The inside's a mess and there's blood on the floor, although no sign of a body. I'm the only one who's been inside - and before you ask, no, I haven't touched anything."

Groves smiled; this was always the first interplay at the start of any case and Marks had learned to get his retaliation in first. He was right though; there was broken furniture, clear signs of a struggle and blood near the settee, but no sign of forced entry. He gave instructions to his team of three who had just arrived, and they went over the scene with a fine-toothed comb. Marks hovered in the background, as was his habit, taking care to keep out of the way. He and Groves had been colleagues for some years, but the man could be very testy with anyone hampering progress, and he had witnessed firsthand the effect of reprimands meted out to the unlucky ones falling foul of forensics' routines. Peter Spencer appeared at the door with a sheet of paper in his hand; he gave it to Marks.

"There are nine tenants including the missing guy, but Thornton was very tight-lipped about any of them. It'll be a case of questioning the lot if we're going to find anything out about Mr Thomas. I see what you mean about him hiding something, though. I get the distinct impression that it's not all sweetness and light in this place."

They went back into the flat to find George Groves crouching over the pool of blood, busily cutting that section out of the carpet, whilst the rest of the team were collecting other evidence. He stood up at their approach.

"We're going to be a few hours yet, and this lot will take some sorting through. I'll call you when there's anything definite."

Marks nodded and they went back out onto the first floor landing, where a uniformed officer was approaching from the access stairway to the roof. Marks looked at Peter Spencer.

"I sent them up there to check the area out. Thomas has to be somewhere and that seemed to be the obvious place. Looks like they may have found something."

"Sir, you need to come up to the roof – there's a body up there."

From the description given by the house manager, this was almost certainly Miles Thomas. Marks sent for George Groves, but from initial observations it looked like the young man had taken a severe beating before suffering the fatal blow. Groves confirmed the cause of death and also reported that Thomas' kneecaps had been smashed, probably with the same weapon. This was not just murder – it was an execution, and someone must have heard something. The body was transferred to the mortuary where Groves himself would carry out the post mortem, but the pathologist's preliminary examination revealed an approximate time of death of between twenty-four and forty-eight hours earlier. It was now crucial that all of the tenants were interviewed without delay – one or more of them could be holding vital information and may even have seen the killer or killers. From the list of tenants, Roger Preston in Flat 8, and Jeremy and Alice Masterson in Flat 6, would be first to be seen – they were Miles Thomas' immediate neighbours. If anyone witnessed anything it was likely to be them.

2

At thirty-nine and single, Roger Preston was one of life's drifters. Having left school without much in the way of qualifications, he had wandered fairly aimlessly through a variety of professions before settling for a number of years into the role of a bouncer for the owner of a chain of nightclubs around the area. This line of employment had terminated as a result of a late night fracas with some out of town thugs, when he sustained severe head injuries causing unpredictable behaviour patterns. Mr Corrini, the night club owner, not wanting to appear ungrateful for Roger's years of service, put him on the lighter and less confrontational duties of general cleaner. All parties knew that this was only an act of sympathy, but it suited everyone to conclude the matter in such a way. On days when Preston was unwell due either to his recurring head condition or, as was more likely, an overindulgence in alcohol the night before, no-one questioned his absence from work and his wages were paid as normal. What he had not lost as a result of the injury, was a keen eye for detail and a good memory.

He rented the flat directly across from Miles Thomas, and was one of the first tenants in the building – he was there when the student first arrived, and therefore in a unique position to reveal details of his comings and goings. He was also the possessor of a short, and fierce, temper since his accident, and Marks knew that he would have to play the man very carefully if he were to obtain anything of value from him. These sketchy details had been elicited from Preston during the first fifteen minutes that the detectives had seen him, but now that his initial, confrontational, demeanour was beginning to ease, they began to push and probe, albeit gently, for more information.

"How was your relationship with Thomas, Mr Preston? I mean, were you on friendly terms with him?" Marks tested the water gingerly.

"Student, wasn't he? They're all the same; think they can change the world. No time for folks like me. Don't know they're born, half of them."

"Yes, but apart from that, did he ever speak to you?"

"Speak? Yeah, from time to time. Always on the go, though. In and out like a fiddler's elbow. Never stayed in one place for long enough to talk to properly, though."

"OK, what about friends? Did you see any strangers coming in and out with him?"

"Sometimes - mostly women, though, and I never saw many of them twice. There was a bloke who came regularly, three or four times a month, but I didn't get a clear look at him – he always had a hat on."

"Do you remember hearing a name?"

"No."

"Just one last question for now. Were there any regular times when Thomas was in or out of the flat?"

"Yeah, always going out around half past eight. I know that because it's when I go for my paper and I always see him leaving the front door. Takes me about half an hour by the time I've had a cup of tea at the café, and I hear him come back in at around ten."

Preston screwed up his face as if trying to concentrate, and rested his forehead on his right hand. Marks waited patiently, knowing that there was more to come but reluctant to probe in case the man gave up on it.

"Never saw nor heard anything then until the afternoon, around three, when he'd go out again and that would be until late at night, usually about midnight. Made so much noise coming in that you couldn't miss it."

"Alright, Mr Preston. We'll come back if we need to see you again. Thanks."

Outside the flat, Peter Spencer, who had remained in the background during the entire interview, looked at the notes which he had made and shook his head. If anything came to court, Preston would not be the most reliable of witnesses despite his remarkable memory – any defence barrister would tear him to shreds in no time. Still, it was a start and gave them the basis for a pattern of behaviour for the dead man. What neither of them had been aware of was the man listening on the other side of the kitchen door. He stepped out as soon as the detectives had departed.

"Very good, Mr Preston." The accent was not British. "Keep that up. Just do as I tell you, and we'll get along just fine."

Taking forty pounds from the pocket of his black leather coat, he dropped the two notes onto Preston's table and slipped away as Marks and Spencer entered the flat of Jeremy and Alice Masterson across the landing. The ex-bouncer picked up the money and pushed it into his trouser pocket. He didn't like lying. His dad had always warned him against it, and he knew that you always got caught out in the end. Still, it was easy cash, and if it weren't for Mr Corrini, life could be hard for a man like him. This guy had promised more money for his silence, and that would do very nicely for his evenings down at the Holly Bush, but he couldn't help wondering what it was exactly that Miles Thomas had been up to.

Roger Preston would insist that he was not an alcoholic; he did like his beer, and it was a well-known fact in the neighbourhood that once he'd had a few his tongue became very loose, and his reputation at the Holly Bush as something of a story teller was well established. Today was no exception, and the locals were so eager for gossip about the police activity, that the bank notes given to him earlier that day remained safe and sound in his pocket. Of course, it took more than a couple of pints to loosen Roger's tongue - he might have had a bash on the head, but that didn't make him stupid. He managed to string the sessions out very well until it looked as though his listeners were losing interest, and then he dropped his bomb shell. He had seen who was responsible for the body found on the roof, but the police wanted him to keep it quiet until they were ready to make an arrest. This earned him not a few extras, and he knew that, with a bit of luck, he could keep them all on the end of his hook for the rest of the week. What he hadn't seen, in the thickening mist of inebriation, was the man sitting quietly in the corner of the bar listening intently to every word that he said.

'Colly' Underwood was a snout. More specifically, Peter Spencer's snout, and had earned his nickname in a series of illegal bare knuckle fights in the East End of London some years earlier, where it was customary for cauliflower ears to be one of the traits of that trade. Having seen Roger Preston depart and wobble his way home, he finished off his pint and disappeared to make a call which should earn him enough for a few evenings to come. Spencer was at home with his wife when the call to his mobile came through from Underwood. He caught the usual knowing, but well-rehearsed, frown from his better half and went into the kitchen to take it.

"You're certain of this, Colly?" he said. "Okay, I'll see you at the usual spot in an hour, and don't be late. I'm in enough bother with the missus as it is."

Making the usual excuses to his wife, Pauline, he put on his coat and left to drive the thirty minutes to the station where he knew Marks would still be for the next hour or so. After comparing their recollections of the conversation with Preston from earlier that day, Spencer left the building for his meeting with his snout and Marks sat back down at his desk with a frown on his face. It was unusual to catch a break like this so early in a case, and he wondered if this was just Preston attempting to gain some local notoriety at their expense. Time would tell.

Underwood was at the meeting place when Spencer arrived, and briefly went over the events surrounding Preston's revelations at the Holly Bush. He hadn't intended being in that hostelry at all that day, but a short burst of heavy rain had forced him off the street and into a pint glass while it passed. From that point of view, Preston's remarks were ill-advised and unfortunate and, after the exchange of the usual going rate for information, both men returned whence they had come. Back at the station, Marks decided, after hearing Underwood's story, that nothing would be served by attempting to see Preston again before the morning – the beer would take care of that. An early call was scheduled for the following day and they left for their respective homes, completely unaware that the likelihood of Roger Preston making that meeting was reducing by the minute. Underwood was not the only person to overhear the conversations at the public house, and by the time the fading daylight gave way to early evening, the ex-bouncer had been lying in a blood-stained heap in the alley at the side of the flats for some hours. It was to have been his last session at the Holly Bush.

3

Jeremy Masterson's opening of the flat door nearly took Dennis Marks by surprise – it was almost as if he had been standing there waiting for the knock. According to Thornton's list, he had lived there with his wife, Alice, since the flats opened and, along with Roger Preston, they were the veterans of the block at 68 and 66 respectively. He was a retired businessman who had married his secretary and had lived happily ever after – until now. His dapper appearance portrayed him as something of a throwback to the 1950s, always clean shaven and sporting a shirt and tie – the kind of person dedicated to the maintenance of standards so sadly lacking in the modern hi-tec world. He beckoned the two detectives into the flat and introduced them to his wife, before offering tea or coffee. Marks was about to politely decline the offer, but Peter Spencer stepped in and accepted – he had noticed a tense look about Jeremy Masterson, a look which suggested that there was something which he needed to get off his chest. The acceptance of hospitality brought a sense of relief to the man, and they sat down whilst he busied himself in the kitchen.

Alice Masterson sat in an armchair near to the window overlooking the main street. She was bright and alert, but appeared to have limited mobility - a fact highlighted by her husband flitting about her like a bee around a jam pot. He was attentive to her every need, but whether this show was for their benefit only Spencer could not say. They settled into their respective seats, and Marks outlined what had happened to Miles Thomas. The Mastersons seemed deeply concerned at the death of the young man, as if the thought of a murderer lurking somewhere amongst the tenants worried them. Jeremy Masterson edged forwards on his seat and put down his cup and saucer.

"What do you need from us, Inspector?" he asked Marks.

"Apart from Mr Preston, you are Miles Thomas' nearest neighbours. If there were any disturbance in his flat, you may have heard it. I understand that he had a regular stream of visitors, and any one of them may have had something to do with his death. Is there anything that you can think of which may have appeared out of the ordinary over the past week or so?"

The Mastersons seemed to have been unnerved both by the question and also Marks' businesslike manner. This was a knack which he had developed quite deliberately over the years, and his habit of coming straight to the point without pulling any punches had caught many a suspect on the wrong foot in the past. Amid the slightly awkward silence, the DI had been consulting his notebook whilst Peter Spencer had left his seat and wandered around the room – actions which served to increase the tenants' state of anxiety. Sitting down again, the DS looked at Jeremy Masterson with a puzzled frown on his face.

"That's a very interesting fragrance, wouldn't you say, boss?" He looked at Marks, and then turned to the couple again. "Mr Masterson, if I'm not mistaken, it's the smell of cannabis. Now, why would an odour like that be present in your flat?"

Alice Masterson flushed noticeably and became quite agitated. Her husband sat in his chair clasping his hands and staring at his feet. Spencer had touched a nerve and it appeared to be quite a raw one. He pursued the question with a raised eyebrow as the husband's gaze met his own.

"My wife, sergeant, suffers from multiple sclerosis and used to go through quite severe bouts of pain from time to time. The cannabis has had a dramatic impact on reducing the effects of the condition, and in the absence of a suitable alternative treatment with the same results, we make no apologies for breaking the law."

His voice had gained in firmness and confidence during the confession, and he now met the inquiring looks of the detectives with renewed determination.

"Mr Masterson," said Marks. "It's not our intention to pursue or prosecute either you or your wife on the subject of the use of a class 'C' drug. We would, however, in exchange for immunity, like to know the name of the source of your supply. You have very little to lose because if, as we suspect, it was Miles Thomas, your dealer is no longer able to fulfil your needs. In any case your anonymity is assured, as we'll be questioning all tenants in the block."

Alice and Jeremy exchanged glances and she shrugged her shoulders. Miles Thomas had been supplying them, for almost a year, with enough cannabis for Mrs Masterson's use, and when Marks was told the price they had been paying he had to admit that the dealer hadn't done himself any favours – it was half that of the current street value. It would appear that the man had an altruistic streak in him which the detectives had not anticipated. These two had no motive for killing him. Indeed, it was in their interest to keep him alive and well. They were not the killers, and would not have been involved in any plan to dispose of him.

With the assurances given to them, the Mastersons' conversation widened to include what details they knew of Thomas' private life. There had indeed been a procession of young women in and out of his flat as Roger Preston had said, but what caught the interest of Dennis Marks was the mention of a regular male visitor two days before, seemingly intent on concealing his identity. The man was about six feet tall, of slim build, with a swarthy, Mediterranean complexion, and he always wore sunglasses, even in the semi-darkness of the stairwell and landing. The description approximated to that of Giorgio Gasparini, a small-time dealer with whom he had crossed paths early in his CID career. That had been ten years ago, and by the description of his designer clothing it was clear that he was now considerably further up the criminal ladder than before. It should not be too difficult to track him down, but it was a job that Peter Spencer would be better suited to than himself. Finishing their drinks, both thanked the couple for their time and left the apartment.

"Well, what do you think?" asked Marks.

"They remind me of a couple of church mice. Huddled together, scared to death of their own shadows, and just wanting to be left alone. They could be key witnesses to Thomas' abduction, but I wouldn't rely too heavily on them on their own."

"Peter, I want you to track down a guy called Giorgio Gasparini. He was a dealer when I knew him, and the Mastersons may just have placed him at the scene when Miles disappeared. It's important that you don't mention my name at this stage; he got off a drugs charge on a technicality when I was a DC, and you might scare him away. Get Wallace over here, and I'll carry on with the rest of the tenants with her for now."

Back inside the Masterson apartment, Jeremy was on the telephone in a hushed and troubled conversation with George Carlton-Smythe, the occupier of Flat 2 on the ground floor. His manner had reverted to one of nervousness and hesitancy, and his wife Alice was sitting at his side in tears.

"No." He insisted. "I told them just what we agreed – we were playing cards at the time you said, and you left our flat just before midnight. The Italian will get the blame and they'll think it's all drugs-related. I'm sure the Inspector knew him from the description I gave. Look, George, I can't get involved any more. This is having a terrible effect on Alice and she's got enough on her plate as it is. You're going to have to see this one through on your own."

He put down the receiver, and sat with his head in his hands as his wife placed her arm around his shoulder. They were in deeper than they expected to be at the outset, and things were becoming decidedly dangerous. Giorgio Gasparini was not a man to be trifled with. At the other end, George Carlton-Smythe sat drumming his fingers on the desk where he had been composing an anonymous letter to the police concerning the activities of Miles Thomas and Giorgio Gasparini. He had persuaded the Mastersons into co-operating after discovering Alice's dependency on Thomas for her supplies. The boy had become too big for his own good and needed taking down a peg or two. Gasparini was a thug, but Carlton-Smythe had not anticipated that he would take the matter so far.

4

Leroy Randall, the tenant of Flat 5 and final occupier of the first floor of the block, was 36 years old, single, and had been living alone since his stepfather kicked him out in 1985. He had come to Britain from Jamaica with his parents when he was just a baby, and his father had worked as a labourer for the council. It was low paid work which the average British male considered to be beneath his dignity. Like many West Indians, Jerome Randall had kept his head down and got on with the job. In the 1960s you had to put up with the racial abuse and taunts from the white residents where they lived in Bristol, but when the chance came to move to another area, he took his family to London where a job on the buses had come up. The early years in the West Country had taught young Leroy to watch out for signs of danger from gangs of white youths. He had become adept at looking after himself – joining a neighbourhood gym and learning to box had given him a certain amount of respect on the streets, and it wasn't long before the locals decided to leave him alone.

His father died in 1983 when the boy was sixteen and, for a while, he and his mother muddled along, albeit with steadily dwindling resources. Martha met Leroy's step-father, Gary, in the summer of 1984, and from the outset it was made clear that he was no longer welcome in his own home. Gary kicked him out within the year, and it was only due to the benevolent attitude of his employer that he got the flat on Brenthouse Road. He worked long hours, and his relatively high earnings were due, in no small part, to the shift premium for unsocial effects on his lifestyle.

By the time Marks was at Leroy's door, Detective Constable Wallace had joined him whilst Peter Spencer was tracking down Gasparini. Despite repeated knocking, there was no sound from within the apartment, and just when the two of them were at the point of leaving, a bleary-eyed Randall peered through the gap held by a security chain.

"Yeah? What you want, man?"

"Detective Inspector Marks and DC Wallace, Mr Randall. Could we come in, please? We have some questions that we'd like to ask you."

"Got any ID?"

They both held up their warrant cards, and after a prolonged scrutiny by the obviously sleepy tenant they were admitted to the flat whilst Randall disappeared to get dressed. He was back shortly afterwards, still not much better after a morning wash, and bemoaned the fact that he had only returned home from his shift four hours earlier.

"This is police harassment. I ain't done nothin', man."

Marks smiled at the stereotypical statement and made himself comfortable in an armchair by the fireplace.

"How could I possibly be harassing you, Mr Randall. We've never met before. Is there something that you're hiding? Something you'd like to tell us?"

Leroy sat down and Wallace followed suit. He rubbed the sleep out of his eyes and poured himself a glass of milk from the bottle which looked like it had stood on the table since the previous day. Marks grimaced at the thought of how it must have tasted, but then again he hadn't been at work all night. He continued.

"Your neighbour, Miles Thomas, was found dead on the roof of the block earlier today, and we're in the process of trying to ascertain his movements over the past week or so. Is there anything that you can tell us that might help in the enquiries?"

Randall jumped visibly at the detective's last statement and went into a tirade of denials.

"It wasn't me. I ain't got nothin' to do with it. Didn't even know the guy. I probably wasn't even 'ere either."

"Calm down, Leroy," said Marks. "We're just making enquiries. No-one's accusing you of anything…" and he paused "… yet."

Like Spencer in the Mastersons' flat, DC Wallace was scrutinising the room whilst taking notes of the conversation between Marks and Randall, but homed in on Leroy's hands where she noticed bruising on the knuckles of both. She nodded to Marks and he followed her gaze. Leaning closer to the man, the DI took a closer look.

"Been fighting, Mr Randall?"

Leroy pushed both hands into his pockets and leaned back in his chair, eyes flitting furiously between both of the officers.

"Boxing, officer. I go boxing at the gym. Been doing it for years. Ask anyone."

"We will," said Marks. "But for now, have you seen anyone out of the ordinary going in or out of Flat 7, or hanging around outside?"

"No, and I makes it my business not to. Keeps my 'ead down, I do. Ask no questions and nobody bothers you. Learn to do that quick when you stand out in a crowd. Know what I mean?"

Leroy was obviously nervous about something, and Marks decided to feed him a lie in an attempt to draw him out. Taking out his notebook and making a play of searching amongst the pages for some item of information, he stopped and tapped one of the pages. Looking up at Leroy, he smiled.

"According to Mr Thornton, you and Miles Thomas have had several altercations in the recent past. Isn't that strange behaviour towards someone that you don't even know?"

Leroy's face twisted in anger and he stood up, walked towards the kitchen, and then suddenly turned. Jabbing the air with a finger towards Marks, his tone was no longer that of the frightened, sleepy, shift worker awoken from a night's rest.

"That guy shoulda learned to keep 'is mouth shut for 'is own sake. Yeah; so me and Miles got history. So what?"

"So does that 'history' extend to a beating, or worse, a murder?"

"Listen, Mr Detective Inspector Marks, that Miles Thomas was one dirty operator. This was a nice block to live in before 'e turned up with his drug dealin' and lies. Talk to Carol Thorpe about 'er boy, Martin, and what Thomas did to 'im. Sure I thumped 'im, and yeah, that's what the bruises are about, but 'e 'ad it comin'. 'Im and his BNP mates don't belong 'ere. 'E'd been after me for a while, but I gave 'im a real pastin' last week, and 'e hasn't come near since."

Marks listened intently to this tirade and made no attempt to either calm Leroy down or ask anything further. Eventually, his rage blew itself out and Marks looked towards Wallace to make sure that she had everything written down. She nodded. Leroy was breathing heavily, had now resumed his seat, and was looking from one to the other as if waiting for some response. He got it, but it was not what he expected.

"Right then, Mr Randall, that'll be all for now, but we may need to talk to you again, so please stick around. In the meantime, thank you for talking to us – we'll let ourselves out."

Marks smiled as he turned at the door and closed it behind them, leaving Leroy still in his chair, and looking utterly bemused.

Leroy Randall

5

On their way back to the stairs leading to the ground floor, Marks and Wallace passed the flat of Miles Thomas to see George Groves and his team leaving the scene. Marks looked at his watch, and only then realised that they had all been at the flats for over four hours.

"Anything to report?" He asked, as the pathologist met him at the door. Groves smiled – this was typical Dennis Marks.

"I'll know more when we get all this stuff back to the lab." Came the standard response.

"What about the body?"

"Definitely dead." The man's sense of humour was... unique.

"Very funny. What about time and cause?"

"Odd, that. He'd been beaten and both legs were broken, but I think the beating itself occurred earlier than the rest of the injuries. Cause of death itself was a blow to the head with a wooden implement, probably something like a baseball or cricket bat."

"Anything interesting in the flat?" Marks pushed a little further as Groves started down the stairs.

"Apart from the blood stain, the place was covered in fingerprints, and we'll need to take samples of them and DNA from all the residents as soon as possible – I'll leave one of my staff to do that. We're checking the broken furniture for any missing pieces that could have been used as the murder weapon, but apart from that you're going to have to wait for my report. I'll get it to you as soon as I can."

"OK. There are four or five more people to talk to, so we won't be finished much before six. I'll catch up with you later."

Peter Spencer returned from his attempt at tracing Gasparini, and Marks assigned Wallace to assist in the fingerprint and DNA sampling. Giorgio had disappeared, and despite Spencer's visiting all his known haunts, no-one seemed to know where he could be found - a fact which did not surprise either of the detectives. They made their way downstairs to Flat 4 where, according to Thornton's list, the tenant was Carol Thorpe, who lived there with her eleven year old son, Martin. According to the notes which they had taken in his interview, Leroy Randall had made vague allegations to Marks and Wallace concerning the boy. Marks knew that he would have to tread very carefully if he were to find out just what that had involved.

Carol Thorpe was twenty-eight and a single parent who worked full-time for a local firm of chartered accountants. Her son, Martin, had been without a father figure since Eric Thorpe had walked out six years earlier when the boy was five. Despite her not coming home each day until around six, this had not been a problem as Martin had been collected from school by Audrey Welch, a friend of Carol with a boy of Martin's age. However, since they had moved away eighteen months ago, Martin and Carol's domestic routines had been disrupted quite badly. With time on his hands both before and after school, he had fallen in with a bad crowd and had become very disruptive both there and at home. Counselling had not really helped as the boy had simply clammed up and refused to co-operate. It was then that he came into contact with Miles Thomas.

At first, his behaviour seemed to improve as Thomas took an interest in him, but it was not too long before there was a dramatic change in his personality, and Carol began to notice items going missing from around the flat. When questioned, Martin denied all knowledge and became very aggressive - it wasn't until she found a syringe that she began to realise what was happening.

The detectives were admitted to the flat by Martin who looked at them both with deeply suspicious eyes. He shouted his mother and retreated immediately to what Marks supposed was his room, slamming the door behind him. They waited, front door still open, for Mrs Thorpe to arrive, and when she eventually appeared it was clear that she had been taking a bath when they called. Closing the door, she muttered something incomprehensible concerning her son's letting them in, apologised for her appearance, and retired to dress. Returning five minutes later, she invited them into the lounge and asked them to take a seat. She was an attractive young woman bearing the signs of ageing at an early stage, no doubt due to the responsibility of raising a child alone. Her smile, though welcoming, made Marks think she was nervous of their presence, possibly due to something relating to Martin.

"What can I do for you, Inspector? Is it something to do with my son? Has he done something wrong?"

This was a very defensive start, and they would have to be careful not to alienate the woman into concealing any information.

"No, nothing like that, Mrs Thorpe," said Marks. "We're making enquiries about Miles Thomas. No doubt you'll have heard by now that he has been found dead."

"Yes, my son said something to me an hour ago. On the roof, wasn't he?"

"That's true, but I'm interested in a statement made to us by one of your neighbours. Leroy Randall told us that there was a connection between Thomas and your son, Martin. Can you tell us what it was?"

Carol Thorpe paled noticeably at this statement and averted her eyes involuntarily, a clear sign that Marks had touched a nerve. She stood up and walked over to the window, staring out into the now cloudy and rain-filled sky. She turned back suddenly to the detectives as if she had steeled herself into action before she lost her nerve. Returning to her seat, she took a deep breath and opened her mouth to speak.

"No, don't tell them, Mum! They're coppers! It'll only cause trouble and they'll split us up – you know what Miles said, don't you?"

Martin Thorpe had entered the room without anyone noticing, and was now standing at the door with fists clenched and tears streaming down his face. He was shaking uncontrollably and his eyes flitted between the three of them with alarming speed. In the silence caused by his interruption he suddenly turned, ran to the apartment door, and vanished. They heard the front door to the flats slam as he evaded the officer posted there to ensure that no-one left the building. Marks cursed under his breath and made a note to reprimand the PC responsible. Carol Thorpe held her head in her hands. Marks guessed, from Martin's demeanour, that the boy's relationship to Thomas had been more of a commercial nature than anything else. It was anyone's guess, at present, whether it was restricted to merely supplying the lad, or, more seriously, extended into using him as a conduit for access to schools in the area.

It was a further fifteen minutes before Carol was sufficiently calm for them to continue with their questioning. Miles Thomas had indeed taken an interest in Martin some six months ago, and had supplied him with a range of increasingly powerful and dangerous drugs. The disappearing items from the flat were the boy's way of financing his habit, and when that ran out he was persuaded into dealing as a means of paying his way. Martin was now addicted to heroin, and despite Carol's repeated and increasingly vehement protestations to Thomas, the man had just laughed in her face. It had reached such a pitch that during one particularly belligerent encounter, Carol had been heard by other residents threatening to kill him unless he left Martin alone.

"I didn't kill him, Inspector Marks. I just lost my temper. It was only a threat - I was upset, and when he laughed in my face I just exploded. I'm glad he's dead, though; he was an evil man, but I didn't do it."

"Mrs Thorpe, whilst dealing in any prohibited substance is a criminal act, your son's addiction isn't our primary concern here. Whoever killed Miles Thomas may have done so for one or more reasons, and it's our intention to follow that trail wherever it may lead us. We'll be taking fingerprint and DNA samples from all of the tenants, and when Martin returns we'll need to speak to him. If you could ensure that he's here, I would be grateful."

"Odd, that." Spencer remarked when they were outside.

"What?" Said Marks.

"Thomas. Carol Thorpe referred to him as evil, and that he'd laughed in her face when she confronted him about her son's addiction. From what the Mastersons told us, he was cutting his own throat commercially with the price he was charging them."

"Don't forget, Peter, they were here before the Thorpes." Marks pointed out. "Personalities change under the influence of narcotic substances, and maybe he saw the old couple as some sort of parental figures. I don't know."

Marks left the flat with yet one more trail of enquiry to follow. They needed to find out more about the circumstances of Miles Thomas' enticement of Martin Thorpe and also the location of his supplies. This thing was expanding beyond the confines of the apartment block; they still had two more tenants to see and needed to re-interview the house manager, who had proved a little evasive when Peter initially saw him. There was, however, one passing comment which he had made, and this hinted at some sort of relationship between Carol Thorpe and John Fraser, the occupant of Flat 3.

6

At the age of forty, and an ex-boxer, John Fraser was a fine figure of a man who had earned his living in the brutal field of the professional arm of the sport for a period of fifteen years. A heart murmur had forced his retirement just when he appeared to be on the verge of a breakthrough, albeit at the relatively late age of thirty-two, and he had been pushed into a career change. He had used his former earnings to finance a legitimate coaching course in the sport, and now ran the largest of the area's three stables. In the eight years since retirement he had built up a very successful business, and would have no dealings with the shadier side of the game. To date, there had been no-one either brave or stupid enough to challenge those principles. Marks was intrigued by the allegation of a relationship with the Thorpes, and wondered whether this could have provided him with a motive for dealing with the problem of Miles Thomas.

"Come in, Inspector, I've been expecting you. No doubt Mr Thornton has pointed you in my direction – a strange man with the irritating habit of minding other peoples' business, but I suppose he's harmless enough really."

"Thank you, Mr Fraser, and yes, we have. If we could take a little of your time, there are one or two things we'd like to clear up. I gather you've heard by now about Miles Thomas."

"Yes I have. Not a pretty sight, I understand. He was involved in some dirty stuff and the world's better off without him, although I am very sorry for his parents. Please feel free to ask anything you wish, and no, it wasn't me who beat him up."

"We already have an admission from Leroy Randall to that, but we'd like to discuss your relationship with Carol Thorpe, please."

Fraser went on, at length, to elaborate upon Carol Thorpe's account of the breakup of her marriage to Eric. The man was a gambler, and although he provided a stable home background for their son, he was the cause of the family's chronic cash shortage. When he left, fleeing from his creditors, Carol was forced into supporting herself and Martin by going back to work. She had politely refused all Fraser's offers of financial help, and although a kind of understanding had been building up between them, he hadn't wanted to move too quickly into taking it to another level. There was also the added complication of Martin, and the boy had gone off the rails since the departure of his father. When Miles Thomas started to take an interest, Fraser's first thought was that he was making a move on Carol, but when it became apparent that the boy had started taking an interest in drugs, Thomas' motives became clear.

Without mentioning anything to Carol, he had lain in wait for Miles the evening before last when the dealer had returned from one of his periodic sales meetings. Pulling him into an alleyway, Fraser made his feelings and intentions plain to the man. It was a waste of time as Thomas was clearly high on something at the time, and any physical punishment would have had very little effect. Not to be thwarted, when their paths crossed the following day, a quiet reminder of the previous evening, and the consequences of ignoring any advice, were laid before Thomas, and this time Fraser ensured that his warnings were not misunderstood. The discovery of the state of the flat, together with the body on the roof, would have made him a prime suspect. There were no secrets in the apartment building, and he was sure that someone would have mentioned it to the detectives during the course of the day.

"Surprisingly not, Mr Fraser." said Marks. "But together with Mrs Thorpe's threats to Thomas, and your involvement with her, it does tend to put you into the spotlight. We don't yet have a definite time of death, but when we do I'll be returning to re-interview both of you."

"I wasn't responsible for his death, Inspector. I spend virtually all of my day at the gymnasium and have many witnesses to that effect. In the evenings there are intensive coaching sessions for a number of our brighter prospects, and I'm always there. Carol's complained about it in the past few weeks when I've stood her up."

"Have there been any unusual visitors to Mr Thomas' flat in the recent past?"

It was Spencer this time, using a tactic that he and Marks had developed to unsettle a confident suspect. Interruptions have the habit of surprising people into injudicious remarks which they would not ordinarily have made. It was not successful with Fraser, who was clearly not hiding anything.

"A number of women; rarely the same ones twice – he had stamina, I'll give him that. There was one man though, a six-footer and slim, always wearing sunglasses and a hat. He looked out of place, and I never heard him speak. He looked like he could be trouble."

"Did you ever go into Thomas' flat?" It was Marks this time, switching the point of the questioning.

"No. By the time I got involved with Martin's problems, I think Thomas was wary of being anywhere alone with me. If you're thinking that there'll be any trace of me in there, you're wrong."

"Well, we will need to take samples of your fingerprints and DNA in order to eliminate you, but it's just routine at this stage."

"That's alright with me; I've got nothing to hide. The man's gone and I'm pleased. Maybe now Carol can get her problems sorted out."

Marks and Spencer left the flat, and with only one more tenant to see they were no closer to an initial suspect than they had been right at the start. Their next call was at Flat 2, the home of George Carlton-Smythe, a retired colonel in the Green Howards.

7

Gaining access to Flat 2 was like attempting to break into Fort Knox. The door was different to all of the others and the original one, together with its frame, had been replaced with something far more robust and businesslike. The initial ringing of the bell had activated a spotlight trained straight downwards from ceiling height which flooded the area outside the doorway with an intense pool of blue/white light. The bulb casing itself was protected by a fully enclosed grille to prevent damage, accidental or otherwise. A voice emanating from a small intercom to the right of the door demanded to know the identity of the caller and his or her business with the occupant of the property. No details of the aforesaid occupant were forthcoming at this time.

"Detective Inspector Dennis Marks and Detective Sergeant Peter Spencer to see George Carlton-Smythe, please."

"That's Colonel Carlton-Smythe, for your information."

"My apologies." said Marks. "Detective Inspector Dennis Marks, and Detective Sergeant Peter Spencer, to see Colonel George Carlton-Smythe… please."

"Name and rank supplied. Where is your identification? Push your warrant cards through the letter box."

Marks sighed in frustration, and yet, after all the publicity instructing retired people not to admit strangers to their property without first supplying some means of ID, he couldn't really complain. Taking out their official wallets, they pushed them through the letter box and waited, and waited, and waited. Eventually, footsteps were heard approaching the door, and a number of security devices were disengaged allowing it to open. Before them, with a chin from which you could have launched a battalion of paratroopers, stood George Carlton-Smythe, sixty years old, and not looking a day over fifty. He was neatly dressed in a grey suit, white shirt, and what was clearly a regimental tie. He wore shoes that you could have used as a shaving mirror and, overall, made both of them look as if they had slept in their clothes for several nights.

Scrutinising both their faces for any hint of hostility, he waved them brusquely inside, and Marks almost expected to be marched into the lounge like some raw recruit on the parade ground. As they took their seats, Carlton-Smythe stood, in front of the fire, hands clasped behind his back, and rocking backwards and forwards gently on the balls of his feet. There was no doubt as to who would be trying to run the conversation, and Marks knew that it would be important not to let him dictate the direction of the questioning. Nevertheless, it was the Colonel who spoke first, in a clipped army style designed specifically to intimidate.

"Right then, it'll be about that good-for-nothing on the first floor!" He omitted the customary 'will it?'

"Could you tell me, please, Mr Carlton-Smythe, how long you have been a tenant in the apartment block?"

Marks completely and deliberately ignored Carlton–Smythe's opening remark, choosing instead to take a different route with the conversation, and also omitting the courtesy of addressing him as 'Colonel'. Whilst the man was still visibly irritated by this tactic, Marks pushed home the advantage.

"Sir? I asked you about the length of your tenancy here. Could you tell me when you first took up residence, please?"

The Colonel was so taken aback by this obvious lack of courtesy, that he automatically replied, and surrendered all control to the two detectives.

"Well, now, it must have been five or six years ago. Now, look here, Inspector..."

"So then, you must have arrived after Miles Thomas, because the university has him moving here in the autumn of 1992, at the start of his second year. Would that be correct?" Marks now had full control.

"Yes, I suppose so. He was no good, you know." Carlton-Smythe blustered. "No respect for others. Stint in the army was what he needed; that would have straightened him out!"

"Straightened him out? From what?" Marks frowned. "Was he involved in criminal activity of some kind? If so, who was he involved with, and could you provide names or descriptions?"

The Colonel conceded defeat at this point and sat down as the interview proceeded along more traditional police lines instead of the army court martial style that he had adopted. He had crossed swords with Miles Thomas on a number of occasions; mainly, it had to be said, on the subject of his manner and lifestyle, but more recently the issue of Martin Thorpe had come to his attention. Carlton-Smythe came from a background and time when youngsters were just that, and not some proto-adults hanging around street corners waiting for the next bit of trouble to come along. He liked the boy, and was sad to see his degeneration into the mire occupied by the likes of Thomas. There had been occasions when he had tried to intervene, and offered his services to Carol Thorpe as some sort of parental figure. The refusal was not a rebuff, nor was it treated as such, but the Colonel nevertheless felt that the woman was burying her head in the sand. He decided that direct action was the best course to adopt.

Waiting outside Miles' flat late one evening, and just out of sight, he stepped into the corridor as he heard the lock to Flat 7 turning. He took Thomas by surprise and pushed him inside, closing the door behind him. Whatever was said between the two men was never witnessed by anyone else, and the police had only Carlton-Smythe's account of events to go on. Harsh words were spoken and, according to the Colonel, Thomas made an intimidatory lunge towards him. It had been a mistake, as Carlton-Smythe turned the attack to his advantage and quickly had Miles on the floor, face down, with an arm pushed firmly up towards his shoulder blade. Lying prone, he was obliged to listen to the Colonel's words of advice regarding the Thorpe boy and his mother, which left him in no doubt as to the consequences of his ignoring them. A short left jab to the kidneys provided him with a reminder of what was in store should he choose to ignore it.

"That was all I did, Inspector. I had nothing to do with anything that happened after that; in fact you can ask the Mastersons. We play cards most evenings; Alice doesn't get out much these days and likes a game of Gin."

"We may well do that, Colonel, but for now that will be all." The alibi seemed a little too rehearsed, being practically word for word the one offered by Jeremy Masterson.

It had clearly been a bad week for Miles Thomas, as this encounter came on the very same day as his meeting with John Fraser. It must have left him with the feeling that the Thorpes were best left well alone, and there were no more reports of threats made to him by other tenants. That he may or may not have taken the advice offered to him, and thus have suffered the consequences, was a matter of some uncertainty. For Marks, there certainly appeared to be a number of people with a motive for doing the man harm, and any of them would have had the opportunity to vent their displeasure at his activities. The final appointment of the day was with the house manager, Grant Thornton, a man who had appeared evasive when questioned briefly by Peter Spencer some hours earlier. They headed in the direction of Flat 1 to learn that he had, somehow, left the premises during the day. This was the second instance of residents being allowed to slip through the net, and Marks vented his spleen to the uniformed sergeant.

"What's the matter with you?! I gave express instructions that no-one was to leave without my permission. We've now lost two potential witnesses for the day and I'm holding you responsible as senior officer! Clear?"

"Sir." Came the curt reply.

"Peter, get these guys together and spell it out for them in words of one syllable. For God's sake, they're only being asked to stand guard. It's not rocket science. I'll see you back at the station – I'm going to catch up with George Groves."

He stomped away still muttering curses under his breath; Spencer heaved a sigh and turned to the gathering uniformed group.

"Okay, gather round and listen carefully this time. I'm the one who has to work with him all the time – you aren't."

8

It was almost six o'clock when Dennis Marks arrived at the forensic laboratory, and George Groves was writing up his notes following on from the autopsy of Miles Thomas. The young man's parents had been informed of the situation, and had arranged to travel to London the following day to officially identify the body. The pathologist looked up from his desk as Marks entered the room and waved him towards the coffee percolator.

"Well, he was killed by a single blow to the back of the head, but it may not have been what the assailant had intended. There were significant other injuries to Thomas' body which lead me to believe that this was some sort of punishment beating which went wrong."

"What?" Marks had paused in the midst of pouring out drinks, now looking at Groves in some disbelief.

"Look here." They went over to a table where a number of photographs had been laid out. "Both kneecaps had been smashed, probably by the wooden weapon I mentioned to you at the flats, but the injury to the head isn't consistent with a premeditated blow to that area. It's almost as if Thomas was turning away when it landed."

"Would one person have been able to inflict all of the injuries alone?" Marks was struggling to come to grips with the reasoning.

"If that person were intimidating enough to get him up to the roof, then yes, particularly when you bear in mind that the blood we found in the flat belonged to Miles Thomas. The nose itself was broken, hence the bleeding onto the carpet, and the blows to the knees would have come as a surprise as Thomas would have been expecting more of the same once they were alone. The angle of attack suggested by the injury leads me to believe that Miles was turning away from whoever hit him as he was crouched on the floor."

"So this wasn't an execution as we initially thought."

"No, I don't believe so, although that's your department. However, I can tell you that the weapon you're looking for is neither a cricket nor baseball bat as looked likely at the start. We pieced together all of the broken bits in the flat, and we're a table leg missing."

He showed Marks the reassembled furniture broken in what they assumed was a struggle, and sure enough only three of the four legs of a coffee table had been recovered. The missing item was approximately two feet long, slightly oval in shape, and with a taper towards one end. Finding that would go a long way towards tracking down whoever had used it to kill Miles Thomas.

"We've compared the injuries to the body with one of the remaining legs, and they appear to match. Find me the weapon and I'll see what I can get from it."

As he left the lab, Marks wasn't sure whether to laugh or cry - they had identified the likely weapon. He was going to press for a murder charge despite what George had said, but where on earth was he going to start looking for it? The manpower required for an exhaustive search would be costly, and all senior staff had been schooled in the need for remaining within their budgets. He rang Peter Spencer to make sure that he had not yet gone home and told him to muster enough of the uniformed officers to mount a search of the area immediately surrounding the flats for the missing table leg. When he arrived at the scene a little later, it was to find an ambulance and George Groves already in attendance.

"What are *you* doing here, George?"

"Another body, Dennis. What are trying to do to me?"

In their search, one of the uniformed PCs had come across the body of Roger Preston. He had been clubbed to death and had been there for a while. Groves' initial estimate was two to three hours, with death caused by a blunt instrument, possibly the same one as was used on Miles Thomas. No sooner had he related this information to Marks, than a call went up from the back of the alley in which Preston had been found. In amongst the rubbish in a skip, and buried just below the surface, was the missing table leg from Flat 7. It bore traces of blood, and in the middle of one of the stains was a clear imprint of a finger or thumb. Groves bagged it immediately before anyone else could get their hands on it. Marks grinned from ear to ear – this was the case-breaker that they had been hoping for - and Groves shook his head in dismay; there would be no going home until Dennis had a positive identification from it.

There was no doubt as to the owner of the fingerprint once Groves had finished his examinations. Marks believed that Giorgio Gasparini had killed Preston, presumably as a result of his inadvisable conversations at the Holly Bush which were overheard by Spencer's snout. How he had come about that information was yet to be discovered, but the priority now was to find the man, and quickly, before he disappeared permanently. Peter Spencer stepped in at this point.

"Boss, it didn't seem all that important at the time, but I picked this up from a notepad in Carlton-Smythe's flat whilst you were questioning him."

It was a blank piece of paper, but when George Groves examined it closely there were the clear indentations of a message left from the original top sheet. Dusting it at the lab later with a dry ink powder, the text became readable, and it was clear that it was an anonymous message to the police linking Gasparini to Harold Shaw, a local businessman. It also gave details of Gasparini's visit to Thomas, the trip to the roof, and the time he left the premises. The case was now taking an altogether different, and more serious direction - Marks would need to obtain warrants to search both the home and the business premises of this new suspect. For the moment, the area was sealed off and all contact with the press or media forbidden whilst he and Spencer made urgent calls to higher authority.

The timing of the raids on both premises was simultaneous to prevent the loss of any evidence, and Harold Shaw was arrested on suspicion of drug dealing and murder. Without Gasparini, however, Marks knew that the murder charge would not stick, and a nationwide alert had been issued with all ports and airports being sealed off. The inspector had received his share of lucky breaks in the past, and another one came along just at the right time. Gasparini had left the capital after a meeting with Shaw following the disciplining of Miles Thomas, but was picked up by South Yorkshire police whilst speeding past the Woodall services on the M1. One of the motorway officers was quick enough to spot his resemblance to the bulletin issued by Marks and, detaining the Italian for questioning, transported him to headquarters in Sheffield from whence a message was relayed to Marks. He was transferred to the DI immediately, and by evening was sitting opposite him in Interview Room 3.

With Peter Spencer and the duty solicitor in attendance, Marks came straight to the point. Giorgio Gasparini had been identified as resembling a man leaving the flats on Brenthouse Road where the now deceased Miles Thomas lived. Furthermore, they had his prints on a weapon used to kill Thomas. The same weapon had been discovered in a skip at the back of an alley where Roger Preston, another tenant of the same flats, had been found dead. His injuries were consistent with this weapon and he was known to have been talking in a local pub about the identity of Thomas' killer. Marks told the now pale and nervous enforcer that there was enough evidence before him to ensure a lengthy jail sentence. However, should Gasparini choose to assist with police enquiries which were taking another direction, it was more than possible that a word in the appropriate quarters could ease the situation for him.

"I didn't kill Thomas. He was still alive when I left the roof. I'll admit to hitting him with the table leg, but that's all. You can't prove that I did anything to this Roger Preston and I don't know how the leg got into the alley, because I threw it down on the roof when I came down. I'm being set up."

Gasparini's denials were nothing more than Marks expected at this stage, but the detective had to admit that, without some corroborating facts, they would have a hard time convicting him for Preston's killing. If they could persuade Carlton-Smythe to formally identify Giorgio as the man coming down the stairs from the roof, that part of the case would be more or less airtight. He decided to try a bluff, and told the Italian that they had an eyewitness placing him at the scene at the time when forensics now say Thomas had died. His denials would be irrelevant in the light of this, and sentencing would be a formality. Gasparini looked at his solicitor for help – the man shook his head. There was only one way out.

"If I tell you who is behind all this, what will it get me?"

This was the case-breaking statement, and Marks nodded to Peter Spencer. The double act was about to kick in again, and keeping Gasparini off balance would be a key tactic in tightening the net around those ultimately responsible for the deaths of Thomas and Preston.

"Let's start with what you have to offer, and then we'll see what can be done as regards your case. If Thomas really was still alive when you left him, the charge may be reduced to a lesser offence."

9

Giorgio looked from one to the other and back again. He sighed and shook his head – it was now all down to damage limitation. They had him, and knew it. He had only one option and Shaw would have to pay the price. He began his story at his first meeting with Miles Thomas, a postgraduate without sufficient funds to continue his academic career. Gasparini saw him as an ideal supply line into the university campus and its student population. Harold Shaw had been only too pleased at a new avenue for the sale of the narcotics which he was importing from the Far East, and Giorgio's regular meetings with him ensured that sufficient quantities were directed towards Thomas to satisfy the constant demand from his customers. The problems started six months ago when Thomas became greedy, demanding a greater payment for his service.

A man like Harold Shaw had to be handled carefully. Like a modern day Dick Whittington, he had come to the area a penniless youth some thirty-five years ago. By a combination of sheer hard work, and the luck of being in the right place at the right time, he had made his fortune in the importing of textile products. His nose for an opportunity and a sound business brain allowed him to carve out a niche as a merchant, and he quickly made his name in a trade full of uncertainty in the mid 1960s. By the time the British textile trade began to crumble in the 1970s, he was well placed to take advantage of the expanding import trade from the Far East.

Then things started to go wrong, but it was not through the intervention of some unscrupulous competitor that his business began to fail. His increasingly lavish and hedonistic lifestyle placed higher and higher demands upon his skill in the market place. After a succession of inadvisable deals, and a run of pure bad luck, he felt his creditors closing in on him. He turned his attention to the murkier side of London's industrial sectors, and set up links with a number of East End gangs. In the aftermath of the arrest and conviction of the Kray Twins in 1969, the inevitable power vacuum enabled him to carve out a niche and establish a base. He traded in stolen goods, drugs, prostitutes and a portfolio of sub-standard properties. By the time that Miles Thomas decided to commence his campaign, Shaw was already the main supplier of a range of illegal commodities north of the river. His legitimate businesses, existing only as a cover, flourished as never before.

When Miles Thomas sought to muscle in on him, he did not take too kindly to the small-time dealer making waves in his organisation. He said 'No'. Thomas started withholding payments, and somehow managed to discover details of the foreign supply chain. Word got back to Shaw that attempts were being made to undercut him, but no more information was available as to the identity of the party involved. Gasparini was detailed to watch Thomas and report back on his movements. It didn't take the Italian long to discover Thomas' method of approach, and when Shaw had been informed, a disciplinary session was organised. This was the incident involving the roof of the flats and the table leg.

"Shaw told me to take care of the matter, make sure that Thomas understood who he was dealing with, and how far over the line he had stepped. He reckoned that a spell in hospital would set it all straight, and that it would end there. I didn't intend to kill him, and I'm sure that I didn't. Shaw is the man responsible, but you're not going to get me to testify against him in court."

Gasparini refused to say any more until a deal had been offered to him, and Marks had him locked up pending further enquiries. He told the duty solicitor that no charges would be raised at this point, but that they would be returning to the matter within the seventy-two hours allowed. Events now moved on at a faster pace, and with the required search warrants in his possession, the DCI's visits to Shaw would have to take place before news got to him about Gasparini's arrest in order to ensure the Italian's safety. Two teams of armed police arrived simultaneously at the business and private addresses, removing property and documents from both locations before sealing them off. Shaw himself was arrested on narcotics and murder charges and taken away to New Scotland Yard for questioning.

Sifting through the mountain of documentation seized from warehouse and home took some considerable time, but a picture was quickly emerging of a failing business which had rapidly turned around due to the injection of significant amounts of cash. Marks knew that they had to work quickly in order to be able to charge Shaw, and the following day evidence emerged that narcotics from the Indian sub-continent had been concealed within cones of cotton yarn delivered to the Shaw warehouse, where they had been removed prior to the cotton being repackaged for sale. The shipper had taken care to vary the shipping lines used together with agents, ports of loading and destination. Some of the consignments had even been trans-shipped and had lain in bonded storage for weeks prior to being moved on. Funds transferred had been laundered through a variety of innocent parties, but they all ended up in the same place – an offshore account in the name of Amanda Shaw, Harold's wife.

This was enough to tie both the textile merchant and his wife to the Thomas case, and they already had Gasparini's testimony that Miles' beating had been ordered by Shaw. Along with the drug trafficking, the man was looking at serious charges. Marks still wanted to make sure that the case was watertight, and in order to do that he would need Carlton-Smythe to confess to the writing of the anonymous letter. Returning to Flat 2 the detectives found no-one at home, but when their visit took them to the apartment of Alice and Jeremy Masterson on the first floor, raised voices were heard coming from inside. They stood silently at the door and listened.

"I told you before, George, we can't get involved any further. You have nothing to hold over us any more because the police know about the cannabis and aren't taking any action. You're on your own."

"You fool, man! They've already got the Italian for Miles' death so they're not looking for anyone else. All you need to do is hold your nerve and we'll get through this." Carlton-Smythe was becoming highly agitated.

"What does 'we' mean? You're the one who finished him off, remember? Don't forget the state you were in when you came down from the roof and cleaned up in our bathroom. Scared to death you were, and if you hadn't seen Alice smoking that joint we wouldn't be having this conversation now."

"He had it coming to him. Trash like that doesn't deserve to live amongst decent people. I did what any one of us would have done, and there's more than me taken issue with him; I can't be blamed if none of the rest of them had the backbone."

Marks had heard enough, and a sharp rap at the door brought complete silence from within. A second, louder, knock was answered by Jeremy Masterson in a state of some distress. The Colonel was about to leave when Peter Spencer barred the door and ushered him back inside. It didn't take long before the truth about the whole matter came spewing out from the Mastersons, leaving Carlton-Smythe high and dry.

Miles Thomas had been the cause of a good deal of bad feeling throughout the apartment block since his arrival, but the situation had worsened over the past twelve months. His dealings in drugs, and the stream of prostitutes in and out of the flats, had resulted in a number of complaints to the house manager. Grant Thornton failed to do anything about the situation, presumably because Thomas paid his rent on time. Apart from the brushes with John Fraser and Leroy Randall, Thomas had very little to worry about until he crossed swords with Harold Shaw. It was then that Carlton-Smythe saw his chance.

He had seen Gasparini on a few occasions coming in and out of the premises, and had witnessed the encounter on the day of Thomas' death which resulted in the two of them going up on to the roof. He followed quietly and hid behind one of the ventilator shaft covers, where he witnessed the beating meted out by the Italian. He picked up the discarded table leg, still covered in Miles' blood and bearing the thumbprint of Gasparini, and finished the job which Shaw's enforcer had left undone. Taking the weapon with him, he returned down the stairs where he met Jeremy Masterson coming home. It had been too late to conceal the facts from him, but when it became apparent that Alice was using cannabis supplied by Thomas, the Colonel used it as a lever to keep them both quiet. His alibi was thus complete, and the Italian would take the blame for the whole thing. It was only later that he had the idea of dumping the table leg in the alley to make it appear that Giorgio had thrown it there.

"George Carlton-Smythe, I am arresting you for the murder of Miles Thomas. You have the right to remain silent; but it may harm your defence if you do not mention, when questioned, something that you later rely on in Court. Anything you do say may be given in evidence. Do you understand?"

"Yes." The reply was resigned, and the Colonel could see his entire life evaporating before his eyes as he was escorted to the waiting squad car by the two detectives.

Back at the CID office Dennis Marks was carrying out the final review of the case with Peter Spencer. All of the pieces had slotted into place with the exception of the killing of Roger Preston. The DI frowned – damned loose ends, they were his nemesis. Giorgio Gasparini had denied any involvement, and had done so in such a cavalier manner that Marks was certain that he was responsible, but there was no proof. At that precise moment the telephone rang – it was George Groves.

"Dennis, have you charged anyone with Preston's death yet?"

"No, and I'm up the creek without a paddle on that one."

"Not any more. We found traces of sweat on the collar of Preston's shirt, and they weren't his."

"Go on, make my day – tell me you can match them up to someone."

"We took a swab from Gasparini when you brought him in, and his DNA profile is a perfect match to the sweat stains we found on the shirt. He was there at the time of the murder, so you should be able to charge him now."

Marks could have kissed the man. It was typical of the pathologist that no stone would be left unturned until all the evidence had been accounted for and cross-checked. It was the end of a perfect day. Peter Spencer noticed the change in his boss's demeanour.

"That it, then?"

"Absolutely. We'll pass on the information on the drug trafficking to the boys in narcotics, and let our friends at Customs and Excise deal with Shaw's business side of the affair. He'll be lucky to have two pennies to rub together by the time he gets out."

Wednesday, 29th March 2006

Martin Ponsonby closed and refolded the newspaper which he had now read countless times. The reports of the trial and conviction of Harold Shaw and Giorgio Gasparini were long and detailed, and gave him plenty of food for thought with the plan which he had been working on since the death of Michael Roberts. Shaw, like many a hardened criminal before him, had fired his legal team at the end of the trial in 2003, and had gone, still protesting his innocence, to begin the lengthy sentence at HM Prison Wandsworth which had been imposed upon him.

Ponsonby had seized the chance, and made an appointment to see Shaw at Wandsworth. The meeting, lasting only half an hour, was low key and brief in its content. Shaw's deeply rooted suspicion was not an easy thing to overcome, however.

"And just how do you propose to get me and Gasparini out of here?" He picked up on Ponsonby's look of surprise. "Oh yes; it has to be the two of us. My Italian friend has some very useful skills, and since you'll not be doing this solely for my benefit, there must be something in it for you. Do we have a deal?"

The solicitor was faced with no option but to agree. Revenge for the death of Roberts was his prime concern, and opportunities the like of which now sat before him did not come along too often.

"How are you going to frame the appeal?" Shaw leaned forward.

"If I can show that the evidence gathered from your premises was obtained illegally, it will be inadmissible in court." He leaned back and smiled. "A dodgy search warrant should do the trick."

"How do you mean?" Shaw was intrigued.

"Let's just say that I have it within my power to get the date on the document changed. If the search was carried out the day before, then all of that evidence will be tainted, and Marks will be held to account for carelessness in not checking the document."

"You can do that?"

"Mr Shaw, you wouldn't believe how much is possible when the correct amount of money changes hands. You just leave all that kind of stuff to me." He frowned. "It would be best if this conversation remained between just the two of us for the time being."

Later, back at his flat, Ponsonby made a series of telephone calls to a contact within the records department at New Scotland Yard, and the wheels were set in motion.

The young Martin Ponsonby had made his career decision at an early age. At school he had taken a keen interest in legal issues, particularly those involving crime. He became a member, and then the president, of the debating society where he was regarded as a formidable opponent.

When he succeeded in obtaining a first in law at King's College, London, he felt certain that he was destined for a glittering career as a barrister. However, reality hit him like a bolt from the blue, and failure at the Bar examinations came as a shattering blow to his dreams of one day appearing at The Old Bailey.

Not to be denied a career in the law, Ponsonby, through sheer perseverance and dogged hard work, obtained articles and qualified as a solicitor with Borrington Smythe and Headway, a medium-sized firm on Fetter Lane, where he developed a criminal practice which brought him into regular contact with the type of senior counsel he had once hoped to have become.

The death of his brother-in-law, Michael Roberts, at the hands of MI5 and the Metropolitan Police in the form of Dennis Marks, focussed all of his anger. Tackling the might of the security services was out of the question, but undermining the credibility of a serving police officer would be a much easier task to complete.

"Yes." He whispered to himself. "You'll do nicely, DCI Marks, and I think I have just the tool to use." He looked again at a picture of Harold Shaw and smiled. "Look out – here I come!"

Thursday, 30th March 2006

"Over here." Shaw nodded towards a corner of the exercise yard, and Gasparini followed. "Don't want any nosey screws getting wind of what I've got on the boil."

The two of them had been in frequent contact since their sentences had placed them within the confines of Wandsworth prison, and Gasparini had not fared well in the claustrophobic atmosphere of the jail. His nervousness had got him into a number of altercations with other inmates, and although none had come to the attention of the guards, his unpredictability had made him a man to avoid. Shaw appeared to be the only one able to wield any form of control over him, and knew nothing of the information given to Marks back in 2003 which had secured the search warrant.

"I can't stay in here much longer." The Italian rubbed his chin nervously. "Place is driving me up the wall."

"If you can keep a lid on it, we won't have to worry about that anymore." He glanced around the yard and, sure that they would not be overheard, continued despite the warnings from Martin Ponsonby to keep his mouth shut. "New legal team have come up with a plan to get the convictions overturned."

"What?!" Gasparini's exclamation of surprise was too loud for Shaw.

"Quiet, you fool!" He grabbed Gasparini's shirt. "If you want out of here, this has to remain between the two of us, capiche?"

"Okay, okay." He pushed Shaw away and straightened the shirt front. "What do we do?"

"Nothing. And I mean, nothing." He jabbed a finger in the air. "That means you staying out of the way of some of those hard cases that you've been rattling. I need you on the outside with me, not banged up in here. If this comes off, Dennis Marks will be finished as a copper, and you can have the pleasure of paying him a visit. Would you like that?"

Gasparini smiled for the first time. Yes, he would like to spend a few minutes alone with the DCI after three years inside, and would introduce him to his very good friend, pain. He nodded, but Shaw was not entirely convinced that the man meant business – a close watch would be needed for the next few weeks.

Friday, 31st March 2006

Rodney Patterson had been the governor of HMP Wandsworth for over ten years, and had crossed paths professionally with Dennis Marks on a number of occasions. To his mind, the DCI was as straight as they came, and he was amazed at the IPCC investigation which had resulted in the detective's suspension. He was also aware of Marks' role in the successful prosecution of Shaw and Gasparini, and personally saw no reason to doubt the verdict which a jury had unanimously pronounced.

Reports had come to him of the length and regularity of a number of recent meetings between the two inmates, and he had instructed a careful watch to be placed upon them. Shaw's apparent ease at not being either overheard or observed was not entirely justified. Patterson decided to split them up.

"Good morning, Mr Harris." He smiled at the entry of the chief prison officer.

"Good morning, sir." Harris stood rigidly to attention, as all his army training had taught him.

"Take a seat, please." He looked down at the two files on his desk. "There's a matter which I would like you to deal with right away."

"Sir."

"I want these two splitting up." He slid the papers across to the guard. "Put Shaw in 'A' Wing, and Gasparini in 'D'."

"Yes, sir." He rose to leave. "Will that be all?"

"For the moment, yes."

"Any particular reason, sir?" Harris paused halfway to the door.

"None that need concern you, Mr Harris." Patterson looked over the tops of his spectacles. "The less you know of my reasons the easier it will be for all concerned."

"Very good, sir." He left, mildly stung by the governor's brusque manner, but still smiling inwardly at the opportunity to poke a hard case like Gasparini in the eye.

Patterson leaned back in his chair. The decision would not be a popular one, and such action at other jails had sparked unrest in the past. Nevertheless, if what he believed was true, he may have foiled an attempt by Shaw to plan an escape. That he was just about as far from the truth as he could have been never crossed the governor's mind.

Shaw's reputation had gone before him when he arrived at Wandsworth, and there were a number of the more violent inmates who had associations with him in the past. That information, together with the weight which he could pull amongst the remainder of the jail's population, was about to blow up in the face of the entire prison staff.

Saturday, 1st April 2006

As far as prison riots go, this one was something of a damp squib. There had been a number of issues within the jail which had been fermenting for some time, but the lack of a catalyst to co-ordinate and set them off. Those in on the planning of the events of Saturday, 1st April were not to know at the outset how far they had overplayed their hand.

Andy Farrigan, a noted East End thug, had gathered around him a squad of like-minded hard cases and had tried, over the course of six months, to bait the prison guards into a series of confrontations. Tom Harris, the chief prison officer, had drilled his men well, and all attempts at violence had, so far, failed. Although a source of considerable disappointment to Farrigan, it had not stemmed his determination, and the reallocation of Shaw and Gasparini to different wings, one of which he controlled, left the way open for another attempt.

The trouble began relatively quietly, with a mealtime dispute over positions in a queue. Ordinarily intervention by one of the guards would have been sufficient to quell the argument, but this time it was not to be. In a matter of moments, the canteen was a battleground of flying cutlery and furniture as the guards on duty struggled to cope. Reinforcements were quickly on the scene, but the distraction had been enough to enable Farrigan and a few of his closest friends to overpower another guard, steal his keys, and make their way to the governor's office.

With Rodney Patterson in their power, the scene was now set for a stand-off while both sides gathered themselves for a confrontation proper.

In his new cell, Harold Shaw received the news of the start of the trouble with a worried look on his face. Without his involvement, it was highly likely that the riot would spread right throughout the jail, and he was forced into taking action to protect himself and Gasparini from becoming drawn into it.

"Here." He gave a note to one of the inmates in his pay. "Get this to Farrigan and tell him he'll answer to me if this thing isn't called off now. Get it?"

The messenger hurried away, acutely aware of the power which Shaw was able to wield both inside and outside of the jail. The uprising was over before it had properly begun and, faced with the wrath which would surely have descended *not just upon him, but also upon his family outside, Farrigan was forced to capitulate. He had counted on Shaw's support, but had seriously misjudged the attitudes of both him and Gasparini.*

Now restored to his office with both body and dignity intact, Rodney Patterson reflected upon the decision which had almost triggered a dangerous situation. Rescinding the original order, he had Shaw and Gasparini moved back to their original cells, and quiet descended upon the jail once more. Farrigan, for his involvement, was transferred to Dartmoor.

Back in his cell, Harold Shaw pondered on the events of the past few days. The near riot, allowed to escalate unchecked, would have seriously compromised his plans for release after the three years since the conviction. With freedom now a real possibility, he sent out word throughout the jail that any further disturbances would have severe consequences both for the instigators and their families on the outside.

Sunday, 2nd April 2006

In an office on Derry Street, W8, a tabloid newspaper editorial meeting in full swing was debating the issue of the media coverage surrounding Dennis Marks' present difficulties. Those present were by no means unanimous in their support for the spotlight which had been focussed sharply on the beleaguered DCI, and raised voices had been stilled on more than one occasion by Ian Phelps, the Editor-in-Chief.

"Look!" He yelled above the cacophony of voices. "This is getting the paper nowhere." The noise descended to an acceptable level. "We were the first out there with the story when it broke, and unless we stop all of this infighting, we're going to lose the advantage over the rest of the press."

The newspaper's contacts within New Scotland Yard had been quick off the mark with information relating to the suspension of Dennis Marks, but nothing since then had been forthcoming about the grounds on which the IPCC had framed the action. The paper's senior reporting staff had been amongst the first on the scene of the DCI's house but, like the rest of the media, had failed to penetrate the protective police cordon which had been quickly erected around the property. The silence had been deafening and public interest, after an initial bout of fascination and horror, was now beginning to wane as the latest scandal to hit football's Premier League surfaced.

"John." Phelps turned to his right. "We need to get someone from Marks' side to tell us what's going on. Ideas?"

John Barwell had been with the paper since his first job of running errands around Fleet Street in the old days. He had seen editors come and go, but Phelps seemed to have the golden touch – able to get to the nub of an issue in record time. He smiled grimly.

"We could get inside information from a variety of sources close to him if we used the correct methods."

"Go on." Phelps' interest was stirred, and the rest of the assembled group were stilled into silence, as they recognised the track down which Barwell was going.

"There are two people close enough to DCI Marks who will probably have all of the information that the IPCC are using against him." He paused, letting the *inferences sink in.* "We do have the technology to, shall we say, tap in to their lines of communication."

"Isn't that against the law?" *Phelps looked around the table for Terry Brightman, the paper's legal eagle. Barwell got in first.*

"Only if we get caught." *There was an almost inaudible gasp around the room.* "Face it, Ian; this is a good old fashioned scoop. Does the paper want it, or not?"

"So, you're suggesting that we... what? Tap their phones?" *Phelps frowned, knowing full well the difficulties of setting up such a venture.*

"No, nothing so crude." *Barwell snorted.* "Technologically, we're way beyond all that old crap. Think about all the mobile phone calls and e-mails which are out there in cyberspace. Intercepting them would by child's play for the right person."

"Hacking?" *Phelps' eyes widened in surprise.* "You can do that?"

"Not me, Ian. Too long in the tooth; I do, however, know one bright spark who would, for the right price, be prepared to help us along a little."

"I don't know. I'll have to give it some thought." *Phelps shook his head, but in the light of a dearth of other suggestions he had to admit, for the time being at least, that the thought of missing out on a story like this was extremely daunting.*

Back in his private office, half an hour later, and with Terry Brightman sitting opposite, he was mulling over the suggestions which Barwell had laid on the table once more.

"You didn't answer my question in there, Terry." *He twirled a pen in his fingers.* "Could we be in trouble?"

"Like the man said, Ian, only if we got caught." *He got up and walked to the window. He turned.* "Barwell's too savvy to get caught with his own pants down, but if it all went pear-shaped I guarantee that you'd be the one left holding the baby. Hacking into anyone's phones or e-mails is an invasion of privacy, and we've all been warned in the past about stepping over the line."

"Would you go with it?" *Phelps asked.*

"No, and if you do I'll be one of the first out of here." *Brightman's voice was flat, his stare icy.* "I have a code of ethics which, if stretched too far, will see me on the wrong end of the Law Society – that's a threat that I don't want hovering over my head."

"I'll give it some more thought."

Monday, 3rd April 2006

The week since Pauline Spencer's return had seen some radical changes in the couple's domestic arrangements. Unable to persuade his wife of the innocence of his appearance with Sandra Wallace on the evening of her return journey from the home of her parents, Peter had been forced to suffer a very frosty period of forty-eight hours before matters came to a head. When they did, it was with explosive results.

"Pauline." He caught her arm on the third morning as she was leaving for work. "Can we talk about this, please?"

"Oh." She replied, tartly. "There's something to talk about, is there?"

"Look." He sighed; she was not making things easy. "It was all totally innocent. Sandra's helping me with some stuff I need to dig out, and there's really no-one else I can turn to."

"And how long has she been 'helping' you? What else is there that's been going on behind my back?"

"Nothing. Like I said, it's all work related, and I need to keep a low profile."

"Alright." She put her bag down and folded her arms. "Tell me what it's about, then."

"I can't. I'm sorry, but we've all been warned about it getting out."

"So you can talk to Sandra Wallace, but not to me?" She picked up her bag again. "I don't think that we have anything further to say."

With that, she was through the door and heading for her car. Slamming the door hard enough to ensure that neighbours would hear, she gunned the engine and, with a screech of tyres, sped off. Peter was left standing at the still open front door, his head in his hands, and his marriage now hanging in the balance. Despite repeated calls to her office he received no answer, and when he returned home later that day, it was to an empty house. There was a message on the answering machine – Pauline had gone back to her mother's.

"Sandra Wallace." The voice was its usual cheerful tone.

"It's Peter, and I need your help urgently."

"What's happened?"

"It's Pauline. She's left and gone back to Ramsgate."

"Ramsgate?" Wallace asked, puzzled.

"Her parents live there." His voice began to tremble." I think she's left me."

"I'll be over in half an hour."

Peter's demeanour had changed dramatically since the telephone call, and when Sandra Wallace arrived it was clear that he had been crying. Dropping her coat onto a chair, she sat beside him on the sofa and took his hand in hers. Having worked together under Dennis Marks, there was a rapport between them which transcended what could have easily been mistaken for sexual attraction. Spencer was happily married, Wallace knew that, and their relationship proceeded on those terms. That Pauline had misunderstood was an event of potentially tragic proportions, but Sandra's presence now brought on a fresh bout of anguish, and he burst into tears, resting his head upon her shoulder.

Neither of them heard the key in the front door, nor the sound of it opening. Pauline's timing of a return following a twinge of conscience could not have come at a worse moment. Turning the corner of the hall, and into the lounge, the words died in her throat.

"Peter, I'm sorry, can we...?"

Their hurried disentanglement from the embrace which Pauline believed she had seen did nothing to dispel her renewed fit of anger, and this time it was directly squarely at Sandra Wallace.

"You!" She waved to the door. "Get out of here!"

"Pauline." Wallace shook her head. "It's not what you think..."

"How on earth do you know what I think?" She yelled. "You sit here, with your arms around my husband, and you think you know..." The tears began to flow, and she collapsed into a chair.

Peter took his chance and went to sit at her side. The story took some time to tell, and details of the case against Dennis Marks were omitted where he felt they could cause more problems, but gradually Pauline came to see what it was that Wallace had been trying to do. Sandra Wallace, sensing that she was no longer required, took a discreet leave and went home.

"So, why is all this such a secret?" Pauline sat back.

"Can't tell you the details, but I'm the only one who can stop something terrible happening."

Pauline looked at her husband long and hard. The events of the past week had been traumatic in the extreme, and she was still not entirely convinced of the innocence of what she had witnessed. There would be opportunity for Peter to step out of line again, and then there would be no going back.

Tuesday, 4th April 2006

John Barwell's confident assertion to Ian Phelps that he would be able, without too much trouble, to access information on Dennis Marks which had hitherto been denied them by normal channels was proving to be something of problem. His use of a university graduate keen to supplement an income below that necessary to fulfil his needs had, until now, been highly beneficial to both parties. Sums of money had changed hands, information had been forthcoming, and the newspaper hack had, disloyally, sold to the highest bidder under an assumed name. This time he was to be frustrated.

"What do you mean 'nothing'?" He growled. "I don't pay you to come with nothing."

"You pay me, Barwell, to come up with what I can. If there's nothing to come up with, then that's exactly what you get."

Raymond Calladine was a computer specialist. A first class degree, and years of sticking his nose in where it shouldn't belong as a youngster, had given him a taste for creating havoc and embarrassment wherever he could. Fed by Barwell's seemingly bottomless pockets and insatiable appetite for information, he was doing very nicely. Success, however, was never guaranteed, and this was one of those irritating occasions.

"I pay you to get what I want, young man." Barwell grabbed Calladine by the lapels of his coat and pulled him in close. "Don't mess with me – there's no more money."

"Back off!" Raymond broke the grip and pushed his assailant away. "If you listen to what I'm saying instead of going off on one, you'd see what I mean. These two..." He picked up the note which Barwell had given him at the start, "are a bit more savvy than the usual crowd you go after."

"Meaning?" Barwell pulled out a chair and sat down.

"Meaning that unless they actually communicate by e-mail, text, or voicemail there's nothing for me to hack into. I've trawled back for the past four weeks and I can't find anything relating to the subject matter that you gave to me."

"What?" Barwell looked in amazement. "Nothing at all?"

"Not a squeak, and unless you're prepared to pay out for some serious data manipulation, you're sunk." He paused, waiting for the carrot dangled to be taken – he was to be sorely disappointed.

"No. There's no chance of that." Barwell shook his head. "I've already been warned about overstepping the mark. I'll have to find another way of getting the results."

Raymond Calladine watched Barwell's departure from his first floor flat and, happy that the man was out of the building, dialled an unlisted number and waited.

"Yes." The voice was flat and impersonal.

"He's gone."

"Excellent. You managed to put him off the trail?"

"It wasn't too hard. Once I convinced him that our two friends are communicating by word of mouth only, he lost interest."

"But you could have led him further... couldn't you?"

"I could, and did make that suggestion." Calladine laughed. "You should have seen his face – he went quite pale."

"That's good. Now that we know what's involved, I think his editor will be getting one of our calling cards. Can't have the boys in the press stepping out of line. One of these days all this phone hacking is going to blow up in their faces."

"Anything else you need?"

"Not right now. We'll be in touch."

George Watkinson put down the phone and smiled. It was a smug, self-satisfied smile. Raymond Calladine would be an extremely useful asset outside of the confines of Thames House, and with links to the paparazzi would be able, with the help of MI5, to influence events to the benefit of his country.

Wednesday, 5th April 2006

Watkinson's position at the head of MI5 gave him much room for manoeuvre with the daily comings and goings of information gathering, and there was always a steady stream of newcomers willing to take up the challenges faced by the service. Raymond Calladine had been just one of them. Another, some years his senior, had already carved out a position of some importance.

Barry Newman's life had changed dramatically after a chance encounter with a beautiful French woman a few years earlier. Then in his mid-twenties, he had graduated to the Metropolitan Police via the tried and tested route of the Hendon Training School. Transfer to CID had come early after exemplary performances in uniform, and it was from this position that Watkinson had plucked him to work for the security services. He was brave and resourceful, qualities much admired by Watkinson, and which now gave the spymaster an opportunity to test the young man. He picked up the telephone.

"Sir?" The voice at the other end was curt and businesslike.

"Barry, step into my office, would you?"

"Right away, sir."

Watkinson had spent some time going through the files given to him by Colin Barnes, and although satisfied that there may be something odd in the matters currently facing Dennis Marks, he needed an independent take on the case. He had worked with the detective; Newman had not, and would see the files with an impartial eye.

"Take a seat, Barry. There's something I'd like you to take a look at." He pushed the file across the desk, and sat back whilst Newman skim-read the information. "This is the call for help I was telling you about a few days ago."

"A dodgy case?" Barry was quick to spot the problem, but was unsure as to what it was that Watkinson required.

"Perhaps, but the man I'd like you to take a look at is Martin Ponsonby, the solicitor acting for Shaw and Gasparini. There's a potential conflict of interest, and I need a deeper insight into the man's business dealings."

"Anything specific?"

Watkinson & Newman

"No. I don't want to influence you, but there's very little time to act. This is your only case until further notice, and I want it started right away. Use whatever resources you need – you've had the training, so you know what's required."

"Yes, sir."

Newman's training had indeed been thorough, and he had become highly skilled in the art of information-gathering, both officially and off the record. He had the feeling that this latest case was to be of the latter variety. Watkinson had stressed the timescale, and towards the end of the day he was in possession of Ponsonby's entire case load for the previous year. The Miles Thomas information was amongst it. By the time he went home that night, he had a raft of other data on the lawyer, both professional and personal. It was going to make for some interesting reading.

Marks sat at the table, tapping his fingers impatiently. The entire Miles Thomas issue had been a case swamped in detail, puzzling in the extreme, and with any number of potential culprits. That Marks and Spencer had managed, in the end, to identify Shaw and Gasparini as principal villains had been down to a stroke of luck in finding the weapon used by Gasparini, and their ability to follow the trail back to Shaw. What neither of them had realised until late in the matter was the personal enmity which Carlton-Smythe bore towards the young drug dealer.

"I see." Greenaway rubbed his chin. "This does put a different slant on things. If you're absolutely certain of all the forensic evidence, then it would appear that, between them, Shaw and Gasparini don't have the proverbial leg to stand on."

"Talk to George Groves. He handled all the analysis; in fact, it was he who found the DNA traces from the sweat stain on Preston's shirt. There's no way that I could have tampered with that kind of stuff."

"It is fairly certain that Mr Groves will be called to give evidence at some point in the proceedings, but I would advise you, in the meantime, to refrain from all contact with any officer who has had dealings of any kind in the cases before us. Anything remotely untoward could compromise everything that we're trying to do."

Marks frowned at this last comment. Groves would have been the ace up his sleeve, and could, single-handedly, have trashed any accusations which might be levelled at any of the investigations. However, Greenaway had specifically used the word 'officer', and that left Groves out of the equation. Spencer, however, was quite a different matter.

"Alright then, let's move on. There's a lot to get through, and if we're not careful we'll run out of time. What's next? The Great Train Robbery?"

"Chief Inspector, I must remind you that this isn't the time for levity." Greenaway's chastisement hit home. "These charges could well result in a prosecution and the end of your career. If they find a case to answer, you could be convicted and spend considerable time behind bars."

"Look, I'm sorry, but this is just so ridiculous. I'm not a bent copper – surely they can see that."

"The IPCC, as you well know, answer only to the guys at the top. They don't care who you are, or how good your record looks. The least hint of anything out of line and they come down on everyone involved like the proverbial ton of bricks. Now, the next file they've dug out actually casts some doubt upon your psychological health."

"How so?" Marks bridled at this suggestion.

"Well," Greenaway leafed through the list of charges, "It seems that you spent some months receiving psychiatric counselling following one of your cases..."

"Goldblum!" Marks interrupted. "I should have known they'd bring all that up again."

"Care to elaborate?" Greenaway put down his pen and folded his arms.

"Oh, it was a case I inherited from the archives. He was an old man with a beef against the police. It seems his father was killed way back in 1936, and the force was either unable or unwilling to bring the investigation to a satisfactory conclusion for him."

"So, why didn't you get in some expert help?" It was Pierce this time. "If you were in over your head, it would have been the sensible thing to do."

"Budgets." Marks snorted, keenly aware of the financial constraints placed on all within the Met nowadays. "If I'd even attempted to do that based on what I came to suspect, the boys at the top would have had me out of the door before you could blink."

"So you carried on regardless, despite the fact that there were things going on which were running out of control?" Greenaway again.

"I had no choice. Don't forget I was only a DI at the time, and with forensics unable to provide a shred of evidence against the man, I had to try to goad him into letting something slip which, in the end, he did."

Marks glanced from one face to the other, but it was becoming clear that Greenaway and Pierce hadn't the faintest idea of what had faced the squad. He had no alternative, painful as it might be, than to go over the events of the case in detail right from the beginning.

"It's a complicated story. I suggest you get some tea and coffee organised – this could take a while."

It had, indeed, been a traumatic sequence of events dating back to the mid-thirties and Oswald Moseley's black-shirted fascist movement. Marks had picked it up quite by accident, being the only detective available at the time

Goldblum made one of his periodic visits in an attempt to resurrect the case of his father's murder.

In the end, the Grainger killings had gone unresolved, as the entire matter took a series of completely unexpected turns, and pushed Marks to the brink of a nervous breakdown. It was a case which he had gone over time and again, trying in vain to make some sense out of the bizarre sequence of events which had him at the edge of a precipice. It was almost as if he had been staring into a pit, the like of which he had only read about in the writings of Edgar Allen Poe and Dennis Wheatley.

Metropolitan Police

Case No. 639612431
Name: Grainger, M.
Date: 29-May-2002

Case Notes of DI Dennis Marks

From recollections of a conversation with the Home Office pathologist, Professor George Groves, it would seem that there is a complete lack of any forensic evidence at the scene of the killing of Michael Grainger.

I am astounded by this revelation, and also by the fact that the lone civilian at the scene, a Solomon Goldblum, appeared unperturbed and unsurprised by the discovery of the body. I am also concerned at his manner.

My feelings are that he is aware of far more information than he is giving, and that he could, somehow, be involved in the crime. However, I have no hard facts to use as a basis for this conclusion at the present time.

Professor Groves can tell me very little at this early stage, apart from the fact that the body removed from the railings outside the synagogue on Heneage Lane was completely bloodless.

I have never come across a set of circumstances so bizarre in my whole career.

Full Marks

Neal James

Stick

1

The body impaled upon the railings opposite the Bevis Marks synagogue on Heneage Lane in London's East End was discovered at first light on Sunday morning when the army of street cleaners was approaching the end of its route. It was that of an old man. No, it was that of a very old man; a very old man who had been beaten and possibly tortured before death finally took him. The hygiene operative who found him had been so traumatised that paramedics called to the scene took him directly to hospital, and summoned a further vehicle to deal with the corpse. The ancient piece of humanity had been forced so firmly down onto the spikes that the fire brigade were compelled to cut through three rusting iron uprights before he could be removed and taken to the mortuary for examination. The forensics team scoured the sealed off area for clues but came up empty handed. That is to say, they didn't just find little of significance; there was nothing at all. It was as if the entire street had been surgically cleaned. Not one piece of evidence had been left to provide them with any guidance, and when they made a preliminary examination of the body now removed from its location, there wasn't a drop of blood to be found. It was almost as if he had been systematically drained, either during or after being killed.

The body had passed out of rigor, and now lay limp and emaciated on the mortuary slab as George Groves tried to make sense out of what was before him. All the internal organs had revealed a life of some hardship exacerbated by excesses of drink and tobacco and, in confirmation of earlier suspicions, it was without a drop of blood throughout its entire length. It was the oddest thing he had ever encountered, and as he stood back from the examination table the double doors at the end of the room swung open. Dennis Marks came to stand at his side.

"Any ideas, George?" Marks was the DI on duty when the call came in, and the initial report stirred his interest acutely.

"Morning, Dennis. Can't quite make this one out. He's in a bad way, and there are multiple fractures. Almost every bone in the body has been broken."

"So, where's the blood?"

"There isn't any. There was none at the scene, and every organ where you would expect to find it is completely dry. I can get enough tissue for a DNA sample, and fingerprints might reveal who he was, but I think you might have to check your missing persons records if you need any more."

"Where's the rest of the forensic evidence?"

"That's the strange part – there isn't any."

"What do you mean – 'There isn't any'?"

"We combed that street from end to end, and the search is still going on. There wasn't so much as a strand of hair. It was sanitised; you know the state of public toilets if you're the first in there in a morning? Well, that was how we found the street where the body was impaled."

"That's impossible."

"I would have thought so until today, but now I've seen everything. Scientifically speaking, we ought to have picked up something which could have been used to at least trace where the man had been, but…"

Groves shrugged his shoulders in resignation and continued with the autopsy. He was fairly sure that the cause of death was impalement, which meant that the poor man would still have been alive when he was forced down onto the railings opposite the synagogue. The whys and wherefores of the killing were immaterial to him – that was Dennis Marks' job, and he was more than happy to keep well out of it. With a shake of his head, the DI turned and left the mortuary to return to the crime scene; one more set of loose ends, and he hated them.

On Heneage Lane, Solomon Goldblum stood where he had been since the early morning discovery of the body of Michael Grainger. He was one of a growing number of ghouls who had come to the scene, passed their time in morbid curiosity, and left after an appropriate interval. He, however, as yet unique in his status of knowing the identity of the dead man, had remained. Watching eagle-eyed as the police and forensic teams went about their unproductive labours, he shifted his position from time to time in order both to retain some semblance of anonymity, and also to take the strain from his gammy leg. A serious injury at the Tilbury Docks in 1967 had seen him forced out of his stevedore's position with all of its lucrative spin-offs, and the break in his right leg had never properly healed. He was compelled to rely upon a walking stick to get around, and had acquired a noteworthy collection over the years. The locals all nicknamed him 'Stick', and the name had stuck, so to speak.

It was clear to him that the forces of law and order were having more than a few problems gathering evidence in and around the immediate area of the railings where Grainger had been impaled. The faintest glimmer of a smile flitted its way across his worn and craggy features, as he watched the uniformed police and the white-coated scientific team at work. They crawled ponderously up and then down the street and pavements in a fruitless search for anything which might link them to the body now on a mortuary slab. Finding himself now alone, he took out his pipe and tobacco and hobbled away from the striped tape which had cordoned off the area. He sat down on the first available bench, lit the old meerschaum, blew out a stream of pale blue smoke, and sighed in satisfaction. The arrival of Dennis Marks hardly caused him a flicker of interest, but it galvanised the uniformed squad now approaching the end of the street for the second time. Marks' reputation had earned him the respect of the divisional constables, and he was seen as fair but firm. Several young recruits had come unceremoniously to grief at his hands during the course of past investigations for their sloppiness in both dress and manner. He was not a man to take duties lightly, and those members of the constabulary now on site gathered round as he approached.

"Okay, so no forensics. We need to step up the house-to-house enquires; somebody must have seen or heard something during the early hours of yesterday morning between chucking out time and when the street cleaners arrived."

There was a low murmuring in the background, and Marks was quick to dispel any feelings of dissatisfaction.

"Look, we've got a pensioner who was rammed so hard down on to those spikes over there that it took three firemen to cut him loose, so I'm sorry if one or two of you feel a bit hard done to. I dare say the guy would swap places in an instant given the choice, so just get on with it."

The group dispersed amongst the neighbouring residential and commercial properties, leaving Marks alone on the street corner. He looked around the immediate area, and his glance came to rest on the figure of Solomon Goldblum, still puffing away contentedly on his pipe beyond the police tape. The man seemed to be alone, and cut an odd figure amongst the early morning carnage and police activity. Marks strolled over to the bench where he was sitting and took out his warrant card. Goldblum peered at it and smiled.

"Good day, Detective Inspector. Anything I can do for you? Very pleasant morning, don't you think?"

"For some, Mr…?"

"Goldblum, Solomon Goldblum, but folks around here call me Stick." He waved the ornate implement for Marks to see. "Yes, I suppose the unfortunate on the railings would have had a very different perspective. Nasty business from what I can gather."

"Indeed. Been here long?" Marks looked around for signs of anyone else in the area. "You seem to be on your own."

"All morning since your people turned up. I have very little to occupy my time nowadays, and the activity helps to pass the time of day."

For Dennis Marks, the man smiled way too much, and his manner was flippant in the extreme bearing in mind what had happened a few hours earlier.

"I don't suppose you could help us with our enquiries at all?"

"Well, if you mean do I know who the poor man was, yes I do; but as to how he came to be attached to the railings, then your guess is as good as mine, I'm afraid."

Marks took out his pocket book and noted down all the information given to him by Goldblum over the course of the next twenty minutes. He now had an identity and an address from this odd-looking man who seemed all too eager to assist in the investigation. That in itself was a little surprising for London's East End, where people tended to keep themselves very much to themselves. Closing the cover, he thanked Goldblum, taking care to note also an address where he could be found if needed any further.

2

Satisfied that he had given the retreating figure of DI Marks only sufficient information to allow him to find Grainger's home and the rest of his family, Solomon Goldblum nodded his head in satisfaction. Knocking out the contents of the meerschaum against the wall, he stood up stiffly, brushed the ash from the pipe off his coat and made his way to Aldgate tube station for the short journey to his bedsit in Whitechapel. Once inside, he detected a change in the atmosphere of the premises, and turning from the now closed front door he caught sight of the figure waiting for him in the kitchenette. The sudden cold made him shiver involuntarily, and moving into the small lounge he switched on the gas fire, rubbing his hands before its flames.

"The first part of our bargain has been completed, Solomon Goldblum, and no-one suspects your involvement. Once our agreement has been concluded I will return for the payment which you promised. Do not try to avoid your responsibilities; that would be a foolish and futile thing to do."

Goldblum had remained facing the fire during this statement and, turning slowly now, saw only the tails of a coat as the figure vanished silently beyond the lounge door frame and out of the place. He didn't even hear the front door close. He sat down and sighed. Michael Grainger, despite his frail and emaciated appearance, had been a difficult man to isolate and dispose of. With a close knit and self-preserving circle of friends, it had taken careful planning and not a little cunning to exact revenge upon the man who had got away with the most blatant case of murder which the East End had witnessed in many years. Solomon stared into the fire as memories from over sixty years ago resurfaced, and then leaned back in his chair as they played themselves out once more.

Grainger, in his early twenties, was a classic trouble maker on the lookout for an opportunity. That chance came along with Oswald Moseley and his Union of British Fascists, which fed all the man's neuroses and prejudices. He focussed on the Jews as the cause of all of Europe's ills, and with Moseley's rhetoric ringing in his ears, took an active part in the movement, becoming one of the notorious Black Shirts who formed its backbone. When his chance came to make an overt gesture at the Battle of Cable Street on 4th October 1936, he grabbed it with both hands. He was one of a small group of Moseley's parade which became isolated from the main phalanx in the confusion, and found themselves outnumbered by a large faction of counter-protesters. Prompt police action had prevented any serious trouble, but Grainger became personally involved in a verbal exchange with one of the Jewish section of the crowd.

Solomon Goldblum

As the confrontation subsided and the Jew walked away, happy that his small part in frustrating the march was complete, Grainger was still fuming at the manner in which his contribution to the effort had been nullified. He watched the man, and followed his every movement as the events of the day wound down. With order restored and the UBF marchers dispersed towards Hyde Park, he managed to slip away under the cover of a coat which he had stolen from a careless passer-by. Following the young Jew away from the area and down one of the capital's side streets, he ambushed him and rained down a series of blows onto his head with a piece of wood. As the man lay dying, he delivered a series of kicks to the recumbent figure and left for home.

That Jew was Abel Goldblum, Solomon's father. A number of arrests were made following the discovery of the body, and witness accounts taken of the confrontation between Goldblum and Grainger, but with the other members of the Black Shirt group providing the thug with an alibi, the police were unable to proceed and the case was dropped. Solomon was only eleven at the time of his father's death, and without the man's wages their family hit upon some hard times. Grainger, on the other hand, found an outlet for his political beliefs in the Spanish Civil War and fought on the side of the fascists who were the ultimate victors. He returned to Britain as something of a hero in the ranks of the UBF, and paraded his collection of medals openly in and around the pubs of the East End.

Throughout all of this, Solomon Goldblum's sense of anger and frustration grew by the day, and he swore vengeance on the man who had murdered his father and emerged unscathed. As the years passed however, Grainger disappeared from the London area for a time and did not reappear until the late 1980s. The intervening period had done nothing to cool Solomon's almost pathological fervour, and the sight of the now ageing Fascist in the summer of 1995 stoked it up to fresh heights. Although now in his seventies, and physically unable to extract his long-awaited revenge personally by reason of the injury to his leg, he was nevertheless determined in his quest.

Fresh enquiries with the police had elicited nothing more than initial mild curiosity which developed into irritation as Goldblum became more insistent. The case, they said, had been classified many years before as unsolvable, and he should go away and forget all about it. A deeply religious man, and orthodox in his beliefs, Solomon sought solace once more in the Talmud and the Hebrew Bible. He spent many hours at the synagogue on Heneage Lane in silent prayer as he asked for guidance and help from his God. That help, when it materialised, came from a very surprising quarter with a 100% guarantee of success; it did, however, have a price.

Goldblum had never married, and had only a few distant relatives to call family. He lived alone in a small bedsit (you could not call it a flat) and eked out his pension on the meagre lifestyle to which he had become accustomed. The stranger who had appeared at his front door late one evening brought a message from a man whom he referred to only as Nick. Goldblum should make his way to a named location in Whitechapel in one hour, and come alone. All would be revealed to him at that time and in that place; with that the individual turned and walked away. Goldblum never saw him again.

Solomon got off the tube at the Whitechapel station and made his slow but steady way to the corner of Court Street and Sheep Market. It was cold and dark, with a stiff wind blowing east along Durward Street. Pulling up his collar against the elements, the old Jew stepped into a doorway to await the arrival of Nick. The appearance of the tall, dark figure came suddenly and without a sound as the wind dropped; Goldblum jumped in surprise.

"No need to be startled, Mr Goldblum, you are quite safe…" There was a sinister pause. "…for the moment."

The voice was deep, with an edge to it, and yet strangely soothing. Solomon felt all his initial fears evaporating as the man continued his opening statement.

"I understand there is a matter to which you require a resolution, and which has been the cause of some personal unhappiness for quite some time."

"Yes." Goldblum tried to make out the man's features, but a combination of the darkness and the wide-brimmed hat pulled firmly down upon his head made the attempt impossible.

"In that case, we could come to some mutually beneficial arrangement, and if you agree to my terms I guarantee that all of your wishes in the matter will be fulfilled. How does that sound to you?"

"Too good to be true. What's the catch?"

"No catch. We each provide the other with something of value, and at the end of the deal accounts will be settled in full."

"So, do you know what I want?"

"That information has come to my attention, yes. Is there anything else that requires, shall we say, some resolution?"

Goldblum thought for a moment about this last statement. Until just now, he had never considered the full impact of the sins of the fathers being visited on the children, but the opportunity to extract vengeance on the whole Grainger clan was too great a chance to miss. He outlined a scheme for the removal of the entire immediate family of Michael Grainger, and the tall, dark figure nodded slowly in silent agreement. They shook hands on the deal, the only physical contact which was made, and the sensation sent a chill right through the old Jew's body. It was as if someone, or something, had touched his very soul, and for a brief instant he wondered at the wisdom of his involvement with Nick. The figure strolled purposefully down Durward Street, and Solomon realised for the first time that his footsteps had not made a single sound on the pavement.

3

Jane Morrison was forty-four years of age and married with one child, a son of twenty-four. She had been out for an evening with the girls, and as the hen night was coming to a close, became aware of the admiring glances from the young man across the bar. He couldn't have been that much older than her own Paul, and the thought of being fancied by someone of her son's age had never really crossed her mind until now. She headed for the toilets, secretly praying that he would still be there when she came back out. Freshening up what small amount of makeup was needed for these nights out, she pursed her lips and looked critically at the reflection in the mirror. It was true that, for someone on the wrong side of forty, she had held up pretty well these last ten years. Her husband was a jealous man, and would have taken a set of knuckle dusters to anyone making eyes in her direction. However, he was not here and this wonderful looking specimen was, just waiting (she hoped) back in the bar. Straightening the hip-hugging skirt, Jane turned her head to one side and then the other for one last crucial check in the mirror, and then stepped back into the room.

He was standing exactly where she had seen him, and staring intently in her direction. The smile on his face revealed nothing except intense interest in her appearance. As she walked back over to the table now being vacated by her friends, his eyes followed her like a pair of searchlights in the darkness. Jane made her excuses for opting out of the rest of the evening, and one or two of her crowd had noticed the glances between her and the man at the bar. Ribald comments were exchanged amidst a sudden outburst of raucous laughter, and they left. She gathered up her jacket and waved an empty glass at the barman; he nodded and went over to the row of optics. As she approached the bar, a cigarette lighter appeared and flickered into life. Jane had only just decided at that point to take the pack out of her bag, and yet this man, this stranger, seemed to know instinctively that she was about to. He smiled and lit up the room; yes, the entire room seemed suddenly so much brighter.

"Light?" The voice was like velvet, and melted away what remained of her inhibitions. She had already decided that she wanted him, and it was now only a question of when and where.

"Cheers, darlin'." She replied in that typically cockney tone made famous by countless actresses down the years.

As the drinks were brought over, there was a banknote already on the bar in payment. He picked up both glasses and walked away to a table in the corner leaving her to follow. 'Cocky bleeder.' she thought, but could not resist trotting after him. Three glasses and an hour later, they were at the door and heading out of the public house. The barman was the last person to see her alive as she walked away arm in arm with the young man.

Marks stood looking down at the remains of Jane Morrison with the taste of bile rising in his throat. He hadn't felt this nauseous since his days as a raw uniformed PC, when he had been called out to a house on a council estate. Neighbours had reported an unpleasant smell, and the sight of the woman hanging from the stairwell by a piece of curtain wire had turned his stomach inside out. That memory had come flooding back now like a bad curry.

The body (if that is what it could be called) carried no form of identification, but an early morning pedestrian out with his dog told police that she was Jane Morrison, and also indicated where she lived. Although not from the immediate area, the woman had acquired enough of a reputation for her name to be known around the borough. Like Michael Grainger, she had apparently been the victim of a particularly savage beating before being impaled on the same railings outside the Bevis Marks synagogue, and the irony in the name was not lost on the DI. With the similarities in the two killings, a link between them could not be discounted, but once again, house-to-house enquiries turned up nothing. Neither was Marks terribly surprised when George Groves reported the same sanitised state of the street area as before.

"Dennis, we've got a real weirdo on the loose here. Nobody, *nobody*, leaves a crime scene this clean." The exasperation in his voice spoke volumes.

Marks surveyed the area with a grim demeanour. He shook his head slowly from side to side as he watched the forensics team pack away their equipment. The place had remained sealed off to the public since the discovery of the first body, and a round-the-clock guard had been posted. The two coppers responsible for the night shift were now back at the station undergoing the mother of all interrogations. Both insisted that they had been awake and alert for the whole duration of the shift, but the fact remained that someone had taken the time and care to place – yes, place - a body onto the railings whilst they stood and watched.

"Damn!" Marks cursed, and punched the wooden fence at the side of the pavement, causing the uniformed crew at his side to jump.

"Temper, temper." The voice of George Groves, calm as always, sailed through his personal storm, and poured oil on the troubled waters. "That'll just get you an early ulcer."

Full Marks

Marks smiled through gritted teeth and looked down at his now splintered hand. Putting it in his mouth in an effort to ease the pain of the blow and its resultant slivers of wood, he glanced down the street. His brow furrowed as he homed in on the old figure reclining on the same bench where he had spoken to him only a day or so ago. Two killings in such a short space of time, and the same observer turns up in the same place. The detective walked deliberately over to the bench where the old man was sitting. There was an odd smile on Goldblum's face as Marks drew near.

"Good morning, Inspector. Another nasty piece of work? So soon after the other one too."

"Yes… tell me, Mr…"

"Goldblum, Solomon Goldblum. We met, when was it now? Oh yes, the other day."

He stretched out a hand in greeting. Marks declined the offer, choosing instead to feign attention on his injured fingers. The punch to the fence had not gone unnoticed by the old Jew, and his smile was not entirely benevolent.

"Well, Mr Goldblum, how did you know about the killing? I mean, it's early and you're sitting here as if it's the middle of the day. I'm told that the woman died in the early hours of this morning. Where were you at around one-thirty?"

"Oh, word gets around very quickly, Detective Inspector; you only have to keep your ears open. Oddly enough, I was with the Rabbi at around that time. You can check if you wish. There were some matters of a personal nature which I had to discuss with him."

"I will, and should I need to speak to you again, you'll be at the address in my notebook, will you?"

Goldblum nodded, and the detective walked back to find Groves' team leaving for the lab. The two of them travelled back to CID headquarters where a meeting was quickly arranged with DCI Harris, Marks' boss. The briefing lasted only half an hour, but Marks voiced several concerns at the lack of evidence at each of the crime scenes.

"There's something about these murders which I just can't put my finger on. This old guy, Goldblum, has turned up at each of the locations within a short time of the killings, and he's not like any of the normal ghouls we get. It's like he knows something we don't. I'm going to dig around in the archives for anything that links him to either of our two bodies. I'm sure that he's somehow involved."

Marks worked late into the night down in the gloomy depths of the archives. He never knew there was such a wealth of old case files, and many of them had never been committed to microfiche. He was just praying that the stuff he was looking for wasn't amongst those. Just as he was resigning himself to a protracted foray into the mountain of dusty files, his attention homed in on the aftermath of the Battle of Cable Street. Official reports indicated that there had been no fatalities following on from the violent clashes between the UBF and the army of protesters, but there, in a corner of the front page of the Daily Telegraph some two days after the event, was the account of the discovery of a body in an alleyway a short distance from Hyde Park.

Abel Goldblum had been identified by his widow, and despite a number of reports of a violent confrontation between him and a group of UBF black shirts, no-one had been arrested for his murder. There had been five of Moseley's followers involved in a scuffle, and one name leapt from the page and rang alarm bells in Marks' brain. Michael Grainger was in his twenties at the time of the march, and now here was a link to the present day and Solomon Goldblum. Removing his pocket book, the DI made a series of notes before filing a request for hard copies of the relevant pages. Switching off the dim light given out by the sixty watt bulb, he retraced his steps back to the squad room and the office of DCI Harris.

Harris had been in the division for over fifteen years, and had a nose for information. He had a near radar-like sense for anything happening on his patch, and would almost certainly be aware of any enquiries regarding Grainger during that period. He was still in his office when Marks returned; two divorces stood testimony to the man's dedication to his work.

"Dennis, still here? Not after my job yet, are you? Take a seat." Out of the bottom drawer of his filing cabinet, the customary single malt, along with two glasses, made its appearance as a prelude to departure. "What's on your mind?"

"Solomon Goldblum, sir."

"Goldblum, Goldblum... that name rings a bell."

"Hoped it might. I'm sure he's tied up in some way with these last two killings opposite the synagogue. What do you know about him?"

"Let me think. I started here in eighty-one, and he was already a regular down at the desk. That's it! Now I remember. He's been a persistent complainer about a lack of progress on his father's murder back in 1936. You'd have thought that he'd have let it go by now. Why, what's the connection?"

"Found him lingering at the scene of both killings. And I'm certain that he knows more than he's letting on."

"Got any ID on the bodies?"

"The first was an old guy named Michael Grainger, and the second was a female in her mid forties." Marks flipped the pages of his notebook. "Jane Morrison, local woman apparently."

"There's your link, then." Harris downed the remainder of his glass and replaced the malt in the cabinet.

"Sir?" Marks frowned.

"Morrison. She is, or rather she was, Grainger's daughter. That enough for you?"

"More than enough. Grainger was one of a number questioned over the death of Abel Goldblum. He was never charged because the UBF provided an alibi. The case is classified as unsolved."

4

Marks decided that he now had enough to bring Solomon Goldblum in for questioning in relation to the two deaths. However, he could not, for the moment, conceive of any way that a cripple in his seventies would have been able to inflict the types of injuries sustained by either of the victims. Still, with the old Jew's inexplicable appearance at the site of both killings, it was worthwhile rattling his tree to see what would fall out. He was on his way out of the station when a call from the uniformed desk sergeant had him back-tracking.

"What is it, Sid?"

"Think you need to take a look at this. Report's just come in of another body close to Heneage Lane."

Marks took the note from Sid Fretwell. The victim was Ray Morrison, forty-six and husband of the recently departed Jane Morrison. He looked at the duty sergeant in amazement.

"What is this, some kind of vendetta? Three bodies now, all linked to each other."

"Seems like it."

"Sid." Marks' brain switched up a gear. "See if the Scene of Crime Officer can get us a list of anyone watching what's going on. I'm on my way there."

By the time Marks arrived, forensics were well into the job, but it was becoming rapidly apparent that, like the two preceding scenes, there was very little for George Groves' team to work on. The chief pathologist came up as the DI got out of his car. He was shaking his head.

"Not a scrap of evidence, Dennis. This just shouldn't be happening; no-one is this good."

Marks scanned the street; there was a substantial crowd at the third killing – news had obviously got around about the link between the three victims. His sharp eyes missed nothing and there, in the background, puffing gently on his pipe, stood the figure of Solomon Goldblum. As he made his way down the street, the DI's appearance caught the attention of the old man, and he sat down on a nearby bench leaving room for the policeman to join him. As conversations between detective and suspect go, this one was far from one-sided.

"Here again, Mr Goldblum." A statement rather than a question, and the subtle difference was not lost on Solomon.

"Indeed, Inspector. Dreadful business, is it not? The poor man took quite a lot of punishment, I gather."

Marks' eyes narrowed. The old man seemed far too confident for his appearance to have been accidental, but his calm and relaxed manner could not be shaken.

"I was on my way to see you when the call came in, Mr Goldblum."

"Solomon, please." He smiled. "I feel as though we've become quite close."

Marks did not. "I'm a policeman, sir. We're not paid to be 'close'."

"As you wish. What can I do for you?"

"Answer a few questions, if you'd be so kind."

"Fire away."

"Not here; this is official. I'd like you to come down to the station. There are one or two details which have come to my attention, and it would be better served dealing with them in private."

Still the man retained his aura of inscrutable calm, and it was beginning to get on Marks' nerves. All the way to the station the faint smile never left his face, and it was almost as if the entire force was being led down a well-planned path to some destination known only to Goldblum himself. Once in the interview room, however, there was an almost indistinguishable change in the man's manner. Marks had the knack of detecting such small things, and this one had not gone without being spotted. The presence of a uniformed constable also unsettled him slightly – previous conversations had been on his turf, and under his control.

"Now then, Mr Goldblum." Marks smiled, but his eyes remained cold and focussed on the old man before him. "We have three bodies in quick succession, and you turn up almost immediately on the scene each time."

Goldblum opened his mouth to disclose some well-rehearsed speech, but the DI waved him down, and he remained silent.

"All of these victims are connected to you, and I find that very curious. Let's take Michael Grainger." He shuffled some papers which lay on the table. "Apparently he was involved in the inquiry into your father's death, but no charges were ever raised. I see from our files that you've raised a number of questions over the years relating to the case. Now, I understand the need for justice, but you have been informed of the status of the matter, and yet you persist in your quest."

"Inspector." Goldblum's face set, and his forehead suddenly resembled a ploughed field. "My father was an innocent protester in 1936, and was the victim of a violent and murderous man. Grainger was well known in the East End for his fascist and anti-Semitic leanings, and yet the police were either unable or unwilling to bring him to justice for the killing. He was heard bragging about the matter in the local pubs for months afterwards, and I have tried, down the years, to have him arrested."

"Yes, I can see from the file that you've made yourself well-known to the station…"

Marks' interview with Goldblum was interrupted by a knock at the door, and the face of George Groves as it opened.

"One moment of your time, Detective Inspector?" He retreated from the room and Marks followed, leaving a uniformed PC in attendance.

"What is it, George?" Now back on familiar terms without Goldblum present.

"I've been doing some digging around. The autopsies on the three victims we have indicate frenzied beatings prior to death in each case, and the injuries couldn't possibly have been inflicted by your man in there." He nodded towards the room vacated by Marks.

"But they're all linked," Marks responded, "and I'm convinced he knows all about it. I don't care how old or infirm Solomon Goldblum is, there's something very odd here."

They retired to the detective's desk where Groves laid out the pathology reports. The injuries to each body were extensive, brutal, and delivered with a considerable amount of force. Goldblum had provided an alibi for the time of at least one of the killings, his local Rabbi, and it may now be the time to check that story out. Returning to the interview room, he found it to be empty, and enquiries at the front desk revealed that Goldblum had been visited by a local solicitor, advised to say nothing further, and had been escorted off the premises whilst Marks had been in conversation with George Groves. Since the DI had no reason to hold the man, there was very little that could be done apart from berating the unfortunate PC left in charge of the man. Groves was still in the office when he returned.

"Dennis, there was one other thing, and it's going to sound pretty far-fetched."

"Well?"

"If you accept that Goldblum couldn't have inflicted the injuries which caused any of the deaths, then someone else did. If you believe that Goldblum was somehow in on each case, then you have to ask yourself what method of execution he could have used. The man's on the small side, and impaling bodies onto railings of the height of those on Heneage Lane would have taken the force of a single individual of approximately eight feet in height. I don't know about you, but I'm not aware of anyone around here who stands that tall."

"Just what are you getting at, George?" Marks asked.

Groves shuffled his feet. All of his training as a scientist had told him that there was a logical answer to every problem, and that just because it didn't stare you in the face did not mean that it was not there. You just had to look in a different place. He had no scientific answer to the three deaths in question.

"I've no evidence to give you which puts Goldblum at any of the scenes apart from your own statement that he was there very soon after discovery on each occasion. I'm going to hate myself for this, but the man is deeply religious. Have you thought of some kind of divine intervention…?"

Groves winced visibly at the look of amazement emanating from the face of the policeman standing before him. He sat down and Marks followed suit. Their voices hushed practically to a whisper.

"Are you serious? What are we talking about here? God? The devil? Demons? What…?"

"I knew you'd say something like that, but it's my duty to present all alternatives, however unlikely or preposterous they might sound."

Marks was about to reply, when a sudden commotion at the squad room door broke his chain of thought. A uniformed PC, whom he recognised from one of the early morning searches, rushed into the room and scanned it. Seeing the DI, he hurried over and whispered something into Marks' ear. The look on his face told Groves that they had another body on their hands. He was right.

"George, I think you need to get your staff together and meet me down by the river. We've got Jane Morrison's son, Paul, in the water with a six foot spike down the length of his body. He's dead, of course."

5

The body of Paul Morrison had been in the river for some hours, and initial examinations indicated that it had been placed there sometime during the previous night. The spike which impaled him had entered just below the left ear, and exited via the anus. It had pierced the heart with such accuracy that Groves' gruesome opinion was that it had been inserted slowly and with considerable force; he said that it was also very likely that the man had still been alive at the time. There had been no reports of any disturbance during the hours of darkness and, of course, no witnesses. One curious item was apparent however – Groves dropped a clear plastic bag into Marks' hand; it contained a button, brown in colour, and quite old fashioned in design. The DI had seen a coat bearing remarkably similar ones that very day – wearing it had been none other than Solomon Goldblum.

The convoy of police cars roared up to Goldblum's residence with much noise and flashing of lights. All doors were thrown open, and a team of armed officers covered every exit to the property. Marks was first to the door and hammered at its surface.

"Solomon Goldblum! Police – open this door!"

There was no sound from within the building, and Marks issued the same warning once more before the lock was smashed in, leaving the door hanging limply from its hinges. The tactical squad flooded the small bedsit, covering each room in a carefully choreographed manoeuvre. The place was empty save for Goldblum's cat, which regarded them all with an evil eye from the top of a chest of drawers. Their search of the premises was interrupted by a radio call from the station indicating that their quarry had just entered the building and was now waiting to speak to the DI.

He was sitting comfortably, quietly reading a newspaper, and puffing away on his now familiar meerschaum when Marks burst into the room. He smiled and folded away the paper, knocked out the pipe, and held both hands out before him in a gesture of surrender. They were alone.

"I believe you've been looking for me, Detective Inspector Marks. Well, I'm here now and you can arrest me; the job is complete, and I'm ready to face the consequences."

"Ready? For what? It shames me to say it, but we've no evidence linking you to any of the deaths apart from the last one." He dropped the button onto the table.

"Ah yes, I wondered where that had gone. It must have come off in the struggle. Young Morrison was stronger than we believed."

"We? Who is 'we'?" Marks was becoming irritated by this game of cat and mouse, but Goldblum's manner was unshakeable.

"Myself and an associate who was recruited with this series of tasks specifically in mind."

"And this associate, does he have a name and an address where we can contact and hopefully arrest him?"

"Oh, you've no need to worry unduly on that score. I owe him a debt and he'll be along soon to collect what was promised in settlement."

He smiled once again, and Marks could not understand the serene attitude which pervaded the man's entire being. It was as if he was awaiting some divine intervention – maybe Groves had been right after all. No. George was a scientist; this was outrageous, and Marks' police brain simply would not allow him to even consider it. He dealt in evidence, rock solid evidence, and provable scenarios. This was sheer fantasy, mindless, sense-numbing fantasy; he shook his head.

"No, you're just a murderer, a common killer of innocent people. You'll be judged and dealt with in the same way as countless others before you. Your accomplice, whoever that is, will be tracked down and placed beside you in the dock."

"My dear Inspector!" Goldblum laughed. "You simply have no idea what you're dealing with!"

Marks had only seen him smile before, but now he laughed. It was a spine-chilling laugh; a blood-curdler, and the DI held his hands to his ears as it penetrated his brain and brought him to his knees. He looked up at the glowing eyes of Solomon Goldblum boring down at him like two lasers.

"You failed me. You, and the entire system of law and order. You failed my father in 1936, and I've cursed you all for the past sixty years. My religion has failed me. All that I'd been taught by the elders of my synagogue and by the sacred texts of the Talmud have failed me. I prayed – how I prayed for justice, vengeance - VENGEANCE IS MINE SAYETH THE LORD! – but in my hour of need he didn't come. I was left alone, alone and desolate, with no-one to help me."

"This is insane!" Marks was now back on his feet but pinned to the wall by some unseen force.

"Insane? I'll explain insane to you. Insane is allowing the procreation of a genetic strand doomed to violence and the destruction of everything standing in its way. *That* is insane! The strain began with Michael Grainger and the death of my father. It grew with his offspring, and they were perpetuating his evil – that had to be stopped. I was the only one interested in the job, but my frailties stood in the way. When all seemed lost, a voice called out to me in the darkness and I saw retribution within my grasp."

Marks looked around for something to bring the man down. The windows to the office were clear, but nothing and no-one was moving outside. Everything was frozen in time – he was alone with this man. The voice ratcheted up a notch, and the laughter became almost demonic. He turned back to face Goldblum, his eyes wide in amazement.

"You see, Inspector, when all else failed me, this power was put into my grasp by the only force which showed any inclination to rectify the situation. Yes, I am a poor, old and lonely man, and no, I was not capable of inflicting the scale of injuries which your forensic teams discovered. I was there, though. I had to be. I had to witness the pain and suffering of those descendants of the man who had taken my father away from me. This is my revenge, and you can do nothing more to me; it's out of your hands!"

With returning calm, the serenity slowly came back to the old Jew's face and the pain inside Marks' head subsided. The force pinning him to the wall released and he lurched forwards to the table and sat down, breathless.

"I'm going now, Dennis Marks, but remember this. The force is now alive and has tasted the fruits of my fury. How do you think it will react at your next failure to bring justice to those who can't obtain it by legal means, and who cry out for vengeance in the night?"

There was a flash of intense white light, an acrid smell of burning, and then darkness.

The sound of running feet aroused Marks from his unconscious state, and the figure of George Groves was standing over him. The man's mouth was moving but no sounds were coming out of it. Slowly, the DI climbed to his feet and amidst a mumble of confused sounds, the voice of the forensic pathologist was becoming clearer.

"Dennis? Dennis! Look at me! Are you alright? Dennis!"

Marks focussed his eyes on Groves as all his senses kicked back in, and he started to make some sense of the riot of confusion which was running through the room outside. Goldblum was gone; for the second time they had allowed him to escape. So why was everyone looking out of the window on the far side of the office? He stumbled over there to see the smashed pane of glass.

"What the…?"

"It was Goldblum." Groves explained, still supporting Marks by the arm. "He crossed the room like someone possessed, and jumped right through the window."

"It's four floors down. What…?"

"He's gone, Dennis. He's lying in the car park on top of one of the squad cars. There's blood all around and it looks as if his neck is broken. What in God's name happened in there?"

Nick had been standing outside in the police station car park as Goldblum crashed through the window and plummeted one hundred and twenty feet to his death. Not one person saw as the black clad figure approached the broken body and took the soul which had been promised to him in full payment for his services. There were no eyes to see as he walked to the corner of the street. He smiled serenely, and removed a small black book from his inside pocket. Running a bony finger down the page he looked for his next appointment.

The official inquiry into the death of Solomon Goldblum revealed the suicide of an old man who had been helping the police with their investigations into the killings of four members of the same family. Evidence was produced to support the theory of Goldblum's involvement in the murders, and there were no suspicious marks on his body to indicate any mistreatment by the police. Dennis Marks was cleared of any blame for the old man's death, and in an office full of witnesses no-one saw the DI in the same room as Solomon as he burst through the place on his way to hell. In the light of all the evidence presented, a verdict of death by suicide was recorded.

Thursday, 6th April 2006

Of all the recent cases which Eric Staines' department had handled, Dennis Marks's was the one which had caused him more concern than any of the others. Sitting in the lounge of the home where he now lived alone, he had plenty of time to mull over the events of the weeks prior to the removal of the DCI from his duties. Policing the police was not the easiest of jobs which a senior officer was ever likely to face, and the choice of career which had taken him into the IPCC had, eventually, cost him his marriage.

Helen, his wife of twenty years, had withstood the demands which working for the Metropolitan Police had placed upon their marriage, and had been his rock on more than a few occasions. His move to the IPCC, the demands placed on their relationship by his involvement in the cases of the Birmingham Six and the Guildford Four, and his ensuing evolution into something of a social pariah amongst their police friends, had finally put the lid on the relationship. Fortunately they had no children.

Putting down the glass of single malt, he leafed through Dennis Marks' personnel file again and, not for the first time, wondered what it could have been that had set in motion the train of events which had brought one of New Scotland Yard's finest to his door. There had been corruption in the Met as far back as he could remember, and the Macpherson Inquiry into the murder of the young black teenager, Stephen Lawrence, had been the final wake-up call which had also lain a charge of institutional racism firmly at its door.

Too many questions – too few answers. He'd been through all of the case files which Martin Ponsonby had presented as part of the complaint levelled at the DCI and, on the face of it, there was a serious case to answer relating to Marks' conduct over the years. He shook his head – it was not his function to consider the whys and the wherefores; he had to face cold, hard facts and there were plenty of those amongst the papers – the solicitor had certainly been extremely busy.

Dennis Marks was in a tight corner, of that there was no doubt, and his isolation from the rest of his team should ensure that no backdoor help would come from that source. There was his DI, though – what was his name? Staines pulled out another file; Spencer – Peter Spencer. Spotless record since joining the Met, and with any sense he would keep it that way by staying out of the matter *completely. He nodded; that part of the case he could control, but there was another element to it all which could prove to be awkward, and he would have to tread very carefully. George Groves, unlike Spencer, did not work for the Metropolitan Police and, as such, would not normally fall within the sphere of influence of the IPCC.*

Picking up the whisky once more, he drained the glass and checked the time. Midnight – one more long day. He rubbed his tired eyes and decided to leave Professor Groves for later consideration. This was not the time for ill-considered decisions.

Eric Staines

Friday, 7th April 2006

Martin Ponsonby smiled as he reviewed the tactics outlined for the appeal against the convictions of Shaw and Gasparini. With well-paid contacts within the Metropolitan Police, he had been able to gain access to evidence material used in the trials of the two men. His assertion to Shaw of abilities in this area had not been that of a braggart – the search warrant used by Marks to gain access to the premises used by the drug dealer now bore a date twenty-four hours later than the raids themselves. Without that evidence, both would go free as much of the remainder of the data used to convict them would be deemed as tainted.

"Satisfaction at last!" He exclaimed out loud, safe in the privacy of his own office.

The solicitor's thirst for revenge, on the face of it derived from the death of his brother-in-law at the hands of those associated with the DCI, bore a further twist which rendered the vengeance personal and infinitely more satisfying.

Marks had been the senior officer, in his days as a DI, in a series of cases being run by Ponsonby. Then in the early stages of his career as a solicitor, he had taken a series of short cuts in procedure. Marks in general, and the CPS prosecutor in particular, had torn his case to pieces in court, and the three men whom he had been defending that day went down.

Were that not bad enough, his conduct subsequently came to the attention of The Law Society and, at a speedily convened disciplinary hearing, he received a severe reprimand. It had cost him his job at Borrington Smythe and Headway, where he had been carving out a niche for himself. Taking the first alternative position on offer, he had been obliged to step down several levels on the practioner ladder, coming to rest with one of the less choosy of the capital's legal fraternity. All hope of a career at the bar seemed well and truly gone.

"I'll make you suffer the way I did." He looked at the picture of Dennis Marks in the same newspaper that he had read many times before. "You really have no idea who you are dealing with."

The Shaw case, coming as it had out of the blue, was the proverbial gift horse which he simply could not afford to look in the mouth, and the files which Ponsonby had been able to collect had provided enough information on Marks for some serious muddying of the waters around the DCI.

He nodded; this was going to be like shooting fish in a barrel. By the time he was finished, Dennis Marks would be lucky to get a job sweeping the street in front of New Scotland Yard.

Saturday, 8th April 2006

With a break in the proceedings, Dennis Marks had taken the advice of his wife and was now sitting half way up in the East Stand at Tottenham Hotspur's White Hart Lane ground. They had, initially, been curious at the sudden departure of the press and other media from the camp which had been set up outside their home, but Marks had merely shrugged his shoulders and accepted their improved fortunes.

"You can't sit around here all day." She'd said to him earlier in the week. "It'll drive us both crazy. Go and watch Spurs; you know you always used to like it."

"I suppose you're right, but if Ron Greenaway rings, I'll have to go." He sighed. "I'd better keep my mobile switched on."

Tickets for the Manchester City game were going fast, and he'd had to take whatever he could. The corner section at the back of the seating area between the East Stand and the Park Lane End was the best he could manage, but granted at least a semblance of anonymity out of the main body of the crowd. He looked at his watch – 12.30; fifteen minutes to kick-off.

He never for once sensed the presence of the MI5 operative sent by Watkinson to watch over him each time he left home, and the individual concerned had been allocated a seat three rows back from the DCI's current position. His attention hardly wavered from the detective, and he witnessed nothing of the home side's 2-1 win.

For Marks himself, the entire event passed him by like a dream, and the roar of the crowd in celebration of Paul Stalteri's 44th minute goal in a 1-0 half time lead caused him only a momentary interruption from the thoughts surrounding the disciplinary hearing. Of more consequence was the stranger sitting next to him who had, like Marks, chosen to remain seated during the fifteen minute break.

"Cracking first half, eh?" He held out a bar of chocolate to the DCI.

"No thanks." Marks shook his head. "Gives me indigestion."

"Don't I know you from somewhere?" The stranger frowned in concentration.

Marks stiffened almost imperceptibly in his seat, and another figure, three rows

Full Marks

further back, took a sudden and intense interest in the conversation. Trained to lip read, the operative 'heard' everything that was said as the two faced each other, but Dennis Marks' final words were lost to him as the detective turned to face the pitch again.

"No, I don't think so." Marks cleared his throat. "Not unless you're from Coventry. I'm down here just for this game."

The lie was delivered with sufficient confidence as to allay any further suspicions which the stranger may have had, but did nothing to quell the concerns of the man sent to watch over the DCI. He decided to make his move shortly before the final whistle in order to get ahead of Marks and ensure that he arrived home safely.

With the game over, and the crowd of 36,000 slowly making their way out of White Hart Lane, Marks remained seated. His nerve had been shaken by the stranger's interest, and it took a number of questioning glances from the Tottenham stewards before he relinquished his place and followed the stragglers away from the stand.

The route from Paxton Road to the railway station on Love Lane is a distance of approximately four hundred yards, and Marks' steady stroll was paced to get him there in time for the next train. He picked up the sound of footsteps as soon as he turned the corner of Whitehall Street, and their speed seemed to match that of his own. Still concerned by the incident at half time, he slowed his step and waited for the individual to pass. When that had not happened by the time he reached the junction with Love Lane, he turned sharply to be confronted by a face he had never seen in his life before.

"Why are you following me?" He yelled, pinning the man against a wall. "Which of the scandal sheets are you working for? Why can't you leave us alone?"

"Wot!?" The exclamation of surprise was genuine. "Wot you mean, mate? Only tryin' to catch the train, ain't I?" Pushing Marks away, he hurried off down Love Lane and disappeared into the station.

Marks leaned against the wall vacated by the man, and breathed deeply. This was not the stranger inside White Hart Lane, and looking around the streets he checked his watch – 3.15pm; June would be expecting him home shortly, and she did not need to see him in his current state. Letting the earlier train depart, he put on his best voice and called her from his mobile. Another hour would not go amiss, and the platform would provide him with a place of refuge to gather himself.

The figure watching all of this from the corner of Whitehall Street, some hundred yards away, lit a cigarette in the cover of a doorway and followed the detective as he slowly approached the station. His position at the opposite end of the Love Lane platform would be taken to avoid any further concerns. Marks, for the moment, was safe.

Sunday, 9th April 2006

If the weekend had proven something of a rest period for Dennis Marks, the same could not have been said for Ron Greenaway. To the annoyance of the remainder of his family, he was now sitting at his office desk, reviewing more of the considerable pile of material which Martin Ponsonby had been digging up on the DCI. Sighing, he rose, stretched, rubbed his aching back, and headed for the coffee percolator currently brewing the latest of a number of batches. He looked at his watch – 3.30pm! He had been at the premises in Covent Garden since nine-thirty and nothing, so far, had jumped out of the files to grab his attention.

"Come on, Ron lad, you can do this." He muttered to himself as he returned with his latest mug of steaming liquid. "Ponsonby's not that meticulous."

Closing the file on the Weston Affair, he picked up the next one in the pile. The case of Miles Thomas was the one around which Ponsonby had framed an appeal against conviction for Harold Shaw and Giorgio Gasparini. As Greenaway leafed slowly through the contents, his attention came to rest on the search warrant which Marks had used to gain access to the business and private premises of the convicted drugs lord. Picking it up, he frowned and cocked his head to one side. He had been a criminal law solicitor for over twenty years, and a reputation for spotting things that others in his profession may have missed had gained him quite a reputation in London legal circles. The warrant felt wrong.

"Ron, you're missing something blindly obvious. Marks wouldn't have been so careless as to jump the gun. This date can't be right." He whispered to himself as he turned the document over, and held up against the light. "There!" He exclaimed, smiling broadly as he made his way to the window, and a brighter source of illumination.

The warrant had bothered him as soon as he picked it up, and at first he had thought that it was the thickness of the paper which was the problem. Digging out a printer's micrometer, he sighed in frustration as the reading corresponded to that of the regular quality which the justice system used, but that turned to elation when he saw the watermark.

"It's wrong! This damned thing's a fake!"

Greenaway's initial response to the discovery was to call Dennis Marks with the good news, but then he stopped and replaced the telephone receiver in its cradle. A nagging doubt inside his ever-alert brain told him that a face-to-face meeting would be the safest place to disclose the finding. Too many things about the case facing the DCI felt uncomfortable, and he had, on more than one occasion, wondered who was ahead of them in this game and how they had been obtaining their information. In the end, discretion got the better of him and he decided to keep the entire matter under his hat for the hearing itself.

"The last thing we need right now, is for some clever dick to find out what we know." *He nodded and finished his coffee.* "This thing's safe enough in plain sight, but whoever handled the switch in the evidence room is in for a few interesting questions."

As he left the premises in Covent Garden, Greenaway failed to spot the anonymous figure, sweeping the gutters some yards down the street. Dressed in typical council clothing, another of Watkinson's spooks removed the mobile from his pocket.

"Mathers?"

"Sir, he's just gone."

"You placed the document where he would have been able to find it, didn't you?"

"I did, and the original's here in my pocket."

"Good man. Pack up and get out of there now. Don't want an eagle-eyed supervisor spotting you. Some of them work Sundays as well."

Watkinson puffed out his cheeks. Another weekend of frustration for his dear wife, Marjorie, was over. The warrant faked by Ponsonby's contact had been a very good one, bearing all of the correct characteristics – watermark included. A less than perfect version of it, supplied by Solly Wiseman, a known forger in the 'care' of MI5, had replaced it in the file and was now in the hands of Greenaway and Marks' defence team. Time would tell whether it would be enough to free the detective from the clutches of the IPCC.

Monday, 10th April 2006

Back at home after the scare on the previous Saturday, Dennis Marks was left to reflect on his main protagonist in the matter – Martin Ponsonby. There being no call to attend any meetings at New Scotland Yard, he was sitting in his back garden on an afternoon of uncharacteristically good weather. With the initial hue and cry at the leaking of the case now, apparently, a thing of the past, the lives of June and himself had returned to a semblance of normality. She appeared, his guardian angel, from their kitchen bearing a tray laden with refreshments.

"I wish I knew what Ponsonby was up to." He remarked as she took a seat opposite him on the patio.

"What sort of man is he?" She passed a plate over to her husband. "Surely he must realise that a senior officer in your position just doesn't go around falsifying evidence."

"Depends who's paying him." Marks snorted. "He's had a bit of a chequered career, and our paths crossed some years back."

"What did he do?"

"Well, none of that is subject to the same restrictions as the rest of the case, so telling you won't do me any harm." Marks put down his cup and folded his arms. "He got careless with a fraud case about ten years ago, and three villains went down when it looked for a while as if they were about to get off. They'd set up a scam to con hundreds of people out of their life savings, and the contracts they'd sold were drawn up very carefully so as to give them a raft of penalty clause payments. None of the purchasers checked the paperwork carefully enough, and although the CPS brought a case against them, we were never that confident of a conviction."

"So what happened?" Now intrigued, June Marks leaned forwards.

"Ponsonby lost some documents crucial to the defence case, and it was enough to sway the jury. The three accused were convicted and got five years each." He shook his head. "When Ponsonby started getting threats, he asked for police protection. As senior officer on the case, it was up to me to make the call – I decided against it. We didn't have the resources at the time to provide the kind of cover that he was after, and he had to leave town for a while."

"But he's back now." June looked puzzled. "Is he safe?"

"Oh yes, quite safe." Marks replied. "The men in question were out in just over three years but, like all career criminals, tried to pick up where they'd left off. By that time another mob had moved into their territory and tempers got very heated. We pulled their bodies out of the Thames at Richmond Lock a month later. There were no clues as to who'd carried out the killings, and the case remained open. Ponsonby must have got wind of it and came back to his old stomping ground."

"And he holds you responsible for his own problems."

"Apparently so, although knowing that he's also the brother-in-law of Michael Roberts adds another twist to his sense of revenge. He blames me for the man's death at the hands of MI5. He can't touch George Watkinson, so I'm the next best target. The appeal against the sentences handed down to Harold Shaw and Giorgio Gasparini is just a blind."

"What about Ron Greenaway?" She switched the conversation. "Can you trust him to get the thing straightened out?"

"Greenaway's my representative, and will carry out the instructions that I give to him. If there's a way out of this, Ron will find it – I'm certain of that."

Tuesday, 11th April 2006

Martin Ponsonby was indeed a very bitter man. Not only had Marks been instrumental in his temporary demise in legal circles, but the man had also placed significant risk in his way over the convictions in the fraud case. Never for one moment had he blamed himself for the failure of the defence which he had considered so secure, and saw Marks in particular and the Met in general as conspirators in his fall from grace. Their refusal to provide him with the protection he had requested merely served to reinforce his belief that he had been hung out to dry.

With the enforced move from the capital, his wife, Melanie, had taken the opportunity to rid herself of the millstone around her neck which Ponsonby had become. A longing for the bright lights of London society on the arm of a successful and high profile member of the legal profession had proved to be a pipedream of gigantic proportions, and when the realisation of the humdrum future which lay before her finally came home to fulfilment, she was vociferous in her condemnation of her husband for his lack of ambition.

"You're just a little errand boy!" She yelled during one evening of drunkenness. "Running cap in hand to those thugs you work around!" The wine glass shattered into a myriad pieces as it hit the lounge wall.

"Those thugs, Melanie dear, are the ones who pay for your hedonistic lifestyle." He responded, having ducked quickly out of the way of the missile aimed in his direction. "You should be grateful that they come to me when they need help."

"Help?" She scoffed. "What do you know about help? You couldn't even help yourself when they had you up in front of that committee!"

Ponsonby sighed; this had been the way of things for some time now. Their lives had been descending into chaos for so long, that he had to admit to being unable to remember the last time that she had spoken to him in any other way. He had been able to withstand the rows at first – they had always blown themselves out and usually found a way of repairing themselves in the marital bed. However, as Melanie's bouts of drinking increased in volume and regularity, they brought with them a ferocious determination to resist any conciliatory overtures on his part. He began to seek solace in other directions, and that was when he and Suzanne met.

She and Melanie could not have been more opposite. Suzanne was brunette, warm and friendly, unsophisticated, and opened herself up to Ponsonby with his suave and smooth-talking manner. She was in his bed within a fortnight, and memories of his night time activities with his wife were becoming a set of fading memories. He should, by rights, have been pleased, but when one of the senior partners in the law firm took him aside one day, his manner changed.

"Martin, old chap." Stephen Lethbridge guided him towards one of the meeting rooms. "A word in your shell-like, my friend."

"What do you want, Steve?" Attitudes at the firm had always been relaxed, and Ponsonby's use of the familiar form of the name should not have been a problem. He never heard the subtle warning tone of Lethbridge's voice.

"What I want is not the issue, my dear chap." He closed the door and turned around. "If John Partridge finds out that you're screwing his bit on the side, there'll be hell to pay."

"What?" Martin stared in amazement.

"Oh, come off it." The senior laughed in his face. "Don't be so naïve." He paused. "My God! You really don't know, do you?"

"Suzanne is sleeping with Partridge? But he's old enough to be her father!"

"Indeed, and wise enough to fire you if he found out what you've been up to." He leaned against the wall. "Back off and get rid of her before this goes too far."

"Are you threatening me?" Ponsonby started forwards.

"Not at all." Lethbridge raised both hands. "Just trying to clue you in. I trust you do need the income to keep that wife of yours in a state of liquidity." He chuckled at his own joke.

Ponsonby had fumed for weeks but, in the end, had to heed the friendly warning. In the end it had been futile, as he came home one evening to a note left on the coffee table and a house now devoid of any of Melanie's belongings - she had left him. Another bullet had just loaded itself into the gun which he was now pointing at the head of Dennis Marks.

Wednesday, 12th April 2006

It had been several weeks since Martin Ponsonby's initial representation of Harold Shaw. Not only had DCI Marks and the team been fortunate in bringing down a major drugs cartel in 2003, but the combined forces of New Scotland Yard and HM Revenue & Customs had been able to pass on information to their European counterparts, and shock waves were still rippling outwards from the Caribbean to the poppy fields of Afghanistan. Full of a measure of self-congratulation, all were oblivious to the workings of the mind of the now highly motivated Ponsonby.

The disgraced solicitor's approaches to Harold Shaw had, initially, been greeted with significant measures of disbelief and open ridicule, but as Ponsonby's overtures became more and more insistent, Shaw was becoming increasingly inclined to cut the man a break – after all, what had he to lose?

Martin Ponsonby himself, his ambition fuelled by a thirst for revenge and an overbearing belief in his professional resurrection, had not been aware of the dangerous waters into which he was, once more, sailing. A near fatal brush with the London underworld had singularly failed to stir in him the voice of caution which ought to have alerted all of his senses of self-preservation.

Harold Shaw's influence both inside and outside of prison was well-known in criminal circles, and the recent altercation with Farrigan was just the latest example of the man's ability to flex his muscles. Ponsonby's naïveté in a plot to use the drugs baron in his quest to bring down Dennis Marks was ill-advised at best, and deadly at worst.

Shaw had become more and more fascinated by the solicitor's confidence where others had failed in the past, but saw him and his employer as a way of circumventing the reaches of the law in the future; all he needed was a legal way out of the incarceration which was starting to threaten his empire. The wolves would soon be gathering, and his boys on the outside would not wait forever.

"Let's put it this way, Martin – I can call you Martin, can't I?" He smiled. "You and I could go places once I'm out of here, and who knows... you may even be able to set yourself up in a law firm all of your own. Now, how would you like that?"

The words had rung out time and time again in Ponsonby's head since that day and, unaware as he was of the forces now beginning to range against him at MI5, he saw no danger in taking the criminal at his word. After all, they both knew that Shaw was as guilty as hell, and that Gasparini was a psychotic killer on the lookout for his next piece of entertainment. He saw only the advantages which had been denied him in the past, and the hunger for success burned as fiercely now as it had years before. They shook hands on the deal, and his fate was, from that moment, sealed.

Thursday, 13th April 2006

George Watkinson flipped through the dossier of information which Barry Newman had laid before him as soon as he set foot in his office at Thames House. He suppressed a whistle, and merely shook his head in surprise. The depth of the data which the young man had obtained went far beyond anything that he had expected. He removed his glasses and looked across the table. Newman sat there stone-faced.

The young copper's attention to detail throughout his training at Hendon had stemmed from a childhood steeped in mathematics – a science which provided him with a perfect grounding in the computer techniques which were to enhance his later career. Reviews at every stage of his short stay in the force had been highly complimentary, and it was these which ultimately brought him to the attention of MI5; that, and an act of great courage in rescuing Danielle Moreau, a beautiful French NATO agent, had sealed the deal which now found him on the other side of the desk at the headquarters of one arm of the security services.

"This is quite a story, Barry. Where did you get the information, or would it be better that I didn't know?"

"Quite easy, really." Newman smiled for the first time, now sure that he had not overstepped the mark. "A group of us at university set up our own IT network, and it sort of went from there. I seemed to have the knack of being able to get into places where I could find interesting stuff."

"I see." Watkinson frowned. "Can I assume that none of this appeared on your CV when you applied to Hendon?"

"Yes, sir." Barry grinned. "It isn't the sort of thing that you admit to if you're looking for a career in the police."

"Alright then, well you'd better run me through some of this – I haven't got the time to read it all in detail. The IPCC don't hang around when they get their teeth into someone."

"Very well. If we look at Ponsonby's earnings over the past six years, you'll see a steady pattern of income. Now, if you cross reference that to his bank balance... there," he pointed, "you can see that there seems to be rather more than could possibly be earned in the normal run of things."

"Yes, I see. So, where do you think that the extras come from?" Watkinson knew where this was going, but carried on regardless.

"He's clearly got some form of supplementary cash flow from somewhere, but I haven't been able to pin that down yet. All the additional deposits have been in cash, so they're untraceable unless we know the serial numbers of the individual notes, and that's out of the question."

"How have you managed to pull out this information?"

"I was hacking from my mid-teens, and none of my digging left any trace on the servers I was scouring. It's simple once you know how."

"So, is there anything that we can use to bring the man to heel? Marks is running out of time, and it'll have to be something pretty damning to stop this case moving."

"Well, there is this." Newman pulled out a piece of paper from the back of the file, and watched as Watkinson's eyebrows shot up.

"Are you absolutely certain?" His demeanour had changed dramatically as he read it.

"Yes, sir. He's been a member for over ten years now, and there's a note of the address where they meet right at the bottom. I even managed to extract a list of members, and a little snooping around their bank accounts flushed out a corresponding set of withdrawals which matched the deposits made by Ponsonby. I think you might find the name of the man interesting. He's..."

"Yes, I can see that. My God! This is dynamite. You're certain that no-one can trace this back to you?"

"Absolutely sure, sir. The signal was bounced off servers all across the globe, and none of them left the IP address which I was using at the time. It's a dynamic as opposed to a static one and changes with each transfer."

Watkinson read the last page once more. Dropping this into the mix would certainly derail the entire case against Dennis Marks, and he would need to handle the matter personally. Barry Newman had surprised him; the young man was going to be an enormous asset.

"Thank you, Barry. That'll be all for now. This is a most impressive piece of work, and you may just have saved the career of one of the best detectives in the Met."

Watkinson waited until the door had closed, and then told his secretary to take the rest of the morning off. The phone call which he was about to make was not *for the ears of anyone else. He picked up the receiver and keyed in a private number. The voice at the other end was cold and businesslike.*

"PM's office."

"George Watkinson, MI5. Get me the Prime Minister right away."

"So, you see, the case of Abel Goldblum still remains open. The Met are no closer now than the police were in 1936 to solving the case."

Marks shook his head. The case had certainly shaken him, both physically and psychologically, and the nightmares were slow to recede. This charge on its own could seriously undermine his credibility as a serving officer. That no-one else in the entire office appeared to have witnessed the events of that day between him and the old Jew was disturbing to say the least, and Marks' memory of the whole conversation was as clear now as it had been at the time. There had been times in the night when, had it not been for the intervention of his wife, June, those nightmares may well have pushed him irretrievably over the edge. He was snapped back out of his reverie by Greenaway.

"Yes, I appreciate that, but the charge against your ability to carry out the duties of the rank is still a strong one. Allied to the other matters we've already discussed, it makes worrying reading. Shaw's solicitor has certainly been busy digging around into your background. Are there any other matters that I should be aware of?"

"Look, all of my staff will tell you that there's nothing wrong with the way I operate. You need to talk to them."

"All in good time, Chief Inspector. It's important, first, to go through all of these files, one by one, and assess them for the impact they might have on your defence. We'll come around to corroborating testimony later."

The day, for Marks, dragged on in similar vein for what seemed an eternity without much in the way of progress becoming apparent. He knew, deep down, that Greenaway and Pierce were fighting his corner as hard as they could, but without the assistance of others as close to the case files as he was, there appeared to be no light at the end of a dark and lengthening tunnel. Home was a haven that he desperately craved each day, and a place to which he willingly retreated at the end of each session.

Friday, 14th April 2006

"You did what?!" Pauline Spencer, having only recently been partially convinced of her husband's innocent behaviour with a colleague, was confounded at the news of his meeting with Colin Barnes which Peter had just revealed to her.

"Dennis needs all the help he can get, love." Peter, sensing his wife's less than enthusiastic demeanour, sat down on their sofa and patted the place at his side. She remained standing.

"Have you not considered for a single moment what effect this could have on your career and our income?" She rammed the point home.

"Yes." He sighed – this was not going the way he had planned. "Dennis is a good copper, and something about this whole thing just isn't right."

Peter Spencer had thought very carefully about how to explain to Pauline the events of the preceding days, and he had believed that she would appreciate what he was trying to do. Clearly he had misjudged her reactions completely. He was somewhat relieved when she eventually sat down.

"Peter. Listen to me, and listen carefully. Dennis Marks is big enough to fight this case alone. If the IPCC get wind of what you've done you'll be on the wrong end of some similar charges."

"I know that, Pauline, and I'm sure that he wouldn't have asked me for help unless it were absolutely necessary – it had to have been his last resort."

The Spencers' marriage had survived the long hours which Peter had been obliged to spend at his job – it went with the territory. Pauline realised that, and had known her husband since his early days in the force. As a young married and, until now, childless couple, it had not presented too many problems. Her mother's unfortunate accident, now fortunately behind them all, had nevertheless brought both of their careers into sharp focus and she was looking forward to the change in their lifestyles, news of which she had been about to divulge to him when the matter of DCI Marks' suspension came up.

"You have to pull out of it, Peter."

"I can't." Spencer shook his head. "I went to see Superintendent Barnes and he's looking into the case as well. He needs all the information that I have to give Dennis even a fighting chance of survival."

"Oh my God!" She buried her head in her hands momentarily. "You fool! Where will you find another job if it all goes wrong? It's not just the two of us any more..."

"What?" He sat back. "What do you mean?"

"I'm pregnant, you idiot. That's what I mean." She wiped away a tear. "This IPCC investigation's come at completely the wrong time for us."

"Look." Spencer was struggling for words now. "Barnes promised to keep my name out of it; we'll be alright. I swear it."

"You'd better hope so, Peter; for your own sake as well as mine." With that she rose, left the room, and went upstairs.

Spencer was left to ruminate over the events of the past half hour. He had believed that Pauline would be firmly behind the actions that he had taken. The news of her pregnancy now introduced another element into a very fragile situation. The first seeds of doubt were beginning to germinate and undermine his hitherto solid confidence.

Saturday, 15th April 2006

The unexpected news of his wife's pregnancy had set Peter Spencer back. They had always planned to have a family, but the timing of Pauline's announcement, delivered in the manner which he had experienced the day before, resulted in a sleepless night for both of them. Rising earlier than his customary six-thirty, he was met in the kitchen shortly afterwards by his bleary-eyed wife. Taking another mug from the cupboard, he turned to be faced with a more conciliatory Pauline than had been apparent the previous evening.

"Peter, I..."

"No need, love." He pulled her to him. "I should have thought it out more clearly. I'm sorry; I should have asked you first."

"Look." She said, sitting down at the table. "I know how you and Dennis Marks work together, and I was wrong to go off the deep end. Without your help he's probably going to lose everything."

"I could go and see Barnes again. You know, just to make sure that he keeps me out of it."

"No." She said. "That would probably make things worse, and you've already got Sandra Wallace on the case as well."

"There's nothing going on between us, you know." He got in quickly, sensing that the unfortunate situation was still unresolved. "She's just a colleague."

"I know." Pauline smiled. "That's another thing I got wildly wrong. I've got a fence to mend there, and it will need to be sooner rather than later if she's to be of any help to you. When's the hearing?"

"About a week away. The IPCC gave Dennis a month to get his defence sorted, and I don't know too much more beyond that list of names he gave to me weeks ago. I haven't dared try to get in touch with him."

"What about George Groves?" She asked. "He doesn't work for the Met, does he?"

"No, but I'm staying away from him as well. Knowing Dennis, they'll have been in touch, and George will be doing as much as he can. Staines has no authority over anyone in his department. He'll be alright."

"So that's it, then? Just a case of wait and see?"

"Afraid so." There was a pause. He looked at his wife's tear-streaked face. "Pauline; once this is over, I think I'll put in for a transfer."

"Are you sure?" She looked at him in surprise. "The Met's been your whole career. Won't Dennis take it badly?"

"No, I'm not sure." He replied. "But we have to start thinking about what's right for us and the new addition. London might not be the best place to be bringing up a family. There are always opportunities in other parts of the country."

With a sense of peace now restored to the Spencer household, Peter's day proceeded along more routine lines as he and Pauline parted company to their respective jobs. The thought of what he had said to his wife, however, remained with him during his shift, and the more he considered the implications of leaving the Met, the more he became convinced that it would be the right thing to do. Timing his announcement to Dennis Marks would be the tricky part, but the DCI would have to accept the situation – perhaps they had worked together for too long.

Sunday, 16th April 2006

With little more than a week to go before the commencement of the IPCC hearing, Martin Ponsonby was feeling extremely confident. All was now in place to take down one of the Met's most highly regarded detectives, and the spin-offs for completing his act of vengeance would be considerable.

Once Shaw's appeal had been successfully completed, there would, he was sure, be a rash of other cases making their way to his door. Every villain put away by the DCI and his team would then be baying for retribution against the Met, and Ponsonby's future would once more be looking brighter.

Re-sorting the files for the final time in order to ensure that everything was in the correct order, he came to the copy which he had taken of the search warrant used by Marks to raid Shaw's premises. He held it up to the light, leaned back in his chair, and smiled. Getting the faked copy, with its altered date, into the secure evidence depository had been a masterstroke. Marks' reputation for meticulousness would, on the basis of that alone, now be seriously compromised. He stood up, crossed the room, and opened his briefcase.

Taking a plain brown envelope from one of the rear sections, he listened at the door to make sure that he would not be interrupted. He sat down once more and removed a single piece of paper from within it. He laughed silently to himself as he placed the fake and the original on the desk before him, side by side. The copy was perfect and, had the dates upon them been the same he would not have been able to tell them apart. He rubbed them between his fingers – they even felt identical, and Marks' defence team would have an impossible job casting doubt on the evidence which he had presented.

He stiffened, suddenly. In a moment of random doubt, he took them both to the window and held them up to the light. No, there was nothing to worry about. Looking through the fabric of the paper, there was nothing that he could see which would cause anyone to doubt the authenticity of the warrant he had engineered. Sighing in relief, he returned the original to the place where it had lain since the documents had been swapped. It was the sole place where he could be certain that it would never be found – the briefcase never left his side.

The watermark had gone undetected, and Ponsonby's moment of doubt had passed.

Monday, 17th April 2006

That MI5 owed Dennis Marks a debt of gratitude for the DCI's involvement in the Michael Roberts affair was, to George Watkinson's mind, beyond doubt. Without his participation, the rogue operative would have remained in place, untouchable, for many years. Any leaking news relating to the grandson of a Nazi war criminal working within the British security services would have therefore been catastrophic.

Substituting Ponsonby's faked search warrant with one of his own was Watkinson's only way of helping Marks out of the hole which had been meticulously dug for him by the solicitor. With plans already afoot to render the man ineffective in the future, he put on his coat and headed off across town for Whitehall and a meeting at the highest levels of government.

"Shirley." He pressed the button on his phone linking him to his secretary.

"Yes, Mr Watkinson."

"I'll be out for the rest of the day. If anyone asks, you have no idea where I am."

"Of course, sir." She said conspiratorially, knowing full well where her boss was going.

The drive from Thames House, even allowing for the heavy London traffic, was not a long one, but still gave Watkinson time to consider the heights to which the case of Dennis Marks had reached in political circles. The man he was about to see would wield the final sword which should remove the scurrilous charges from Marks' record and prevent an illustrious career from being consigned to the scrapheap.

The Cabinet Office, on Horse Guards Road, is the department of Government responsible for supporting the Prime Minister and Cabinet. It is composed of various units that support Cabinet committees and which co-ordinate the delivery of government objectives via other departments. Watkinson was shown into one of the side rooms on the first floor, and walked to the window overlooking Whitehall. With no political affiliations to cloud his judgement, service to a progression of First Lords of the Treasury had been consistent enough down the years to gain him the unquestioning trust of each new PM passing through the doors of Number 10 Downing Street.

Had Dennis Marks been aware of how highly he was regarded within the corridors of power, he would have been truly amazed. His name was well-known to those on both sides of the despatch box at Westminster, and the capital could ill afford to let his name go through the mire of an IPCC investigation.

Watkinson's musings were dispelled by the sound of the door catch, and he turned to face the smiling features of the most powerful man in British political circles.

"Alright, George, what is it that's so important that you drag me out of a meeting with the Foreign Secretary. It had better be good, for your sake."

"Prime Minister, I must warn you that a series of events has come to my attention that require your immediate attention."

"Oh, for God's sake, can't you spooks keep things under control? There simply isn't anything more important at the moment than convincing the British public that we are their best hope for riding out the current economic difficulties."

"Sir, I beg to differ. If I could show you the information, you may wish to revise that opinion." *He opened his briefcase and placed the file which Barry Newman had prepared in front of the PM.*

The First Lord of the Treasury huffed in derision, and scanned the papers now laid out before him. A very quick reader, he was soon to the point where Watkinson wished him to be, and stopped abruptly, looking up at the head of MI5.

"What does this mean?" *The question was delivered with the first hint of uncertainty that Watkinson had seen from the man.*

"It means, Prime Minister, that there appears to be a link between a member of your cabinet and the solicitor named. Ponsonby has a less than honourable reputation in legal circles, and the minister mentioned seems to have been one of the sponsors clearing the way for his joining this organisation." *He pointed a little further down the page.*

"Yes, yes." *The voice was becoming extremely testy.* "I can read, and I am familiar with the group. There's nothing wrong in being one of its members as far as I am aware."

"Indeed, sir. It would, however, stir up quite a lot of trouble in the media if it got into the tabloid press that a solicitor representing two violent criminals in a case against one of the Met's finest had links to a member of your government... would it not?"

Full Marks

The Prime Minister leaned back in his chair and shook his head. The political wolves had been gathering for a while, and a recent series of exposés had badly shaken both the party's and his own personal standing. Already facing calls for another ministerial sacking, the matter which Watkinson had just revealed, together with enquiries into his use of RAF transport for political purposes would be a major embarrassment after the 2005 general election where the government's majority had been reduced by almost one hundred seats.

"Alright. What do we do about it?"

"Sir, the minister concerned should be encouraged to dissuade the aforementioned solicitor from continuing in his action."

"Just a moment, George; we have laws against that kind of thing in this country. How do I know that the policeman in question really is as good as you say?"

"Because, sir, I took the liberty of bringing along his record with the Metropolitan Police for you to peruse. You'll note that he's received a number of commendations in the past, and was at the heart of one particularly awkward situation a few years ago, when we unearthed the son of a Nazi war criminal working for the very security services which protect you."

The PM read the file from beginning to end and, closing the final page, nodded in agreement. He pressed a button on his telephone. A female voice answered.

"Yes, Prime Minister."

"Julie. Get me Tom Williams, and tell him it's urgent."

"Very good, sir."

Watkinson had strolled over to the window of the cabinet office, and was looking out over Whitehall. He was familiar with all of the corridors of power, and had served governments of both political persuasions. They all meant the same to him; transient politicians strutting their hour on the world stage, most of them completely oblivious to who it was that actually ran the country. He turned.

"I'll leave it in your hands then, Prime Minister." He picked up his briefcase and headed for the door before the man summoned was due to arrive. "No point in scaring the life out of him, is there?"

"No. I can do that for the two of us." His face remained set. This was not going to be a particularly tasteful piece of work. Williams would carry out the task designated, and then the minister concerned would tender his resignation – it was the only way of avoiding another banana skin.

Tom Williams had served the party well for over thirty years, and had occupied cabinet posts in the past. His integrity had never been called into question, and the PM considered him to be perfect for the job in hand. His current position as Chief Whip gave him considerable power, and the minister concerned dare not fail to carry out the instructions which would be passed down to him.

"Come in, Tom. Take a seat." He waved towards a pair of leather armchairs. "Drink?"

"Not just now, Mark. A little too early for me, thanks." Williams sat down. "Where's the fire?"

Mark Barrowman showed him the file left by Watkinson, and his eyes opened wide in amazement.

"Blackmail?"

"Seems like it. From the figures on those bank statements Ponsonby can't possibly have earned that kind of money in so short a time. I want you to find out, and fast, what's been going on. I need an answer this afternoon. Watkinson also gave me this." He passed another piece of paper over. "The guy there is the Grand Master of the lodge where they both belong. Get on to him and bring some pressure to bear. This thing needs killing - we've got enough problems with the press as it is."

"Okay, Mark. I'll sort this out. This afternoon, you say?"

"Yes, and make sure that it's done discreetly. I don't want any of the tabloid hacks getting wind of it."

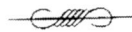

"Alright. How many more of these files are there that they're looking at? It seems like we've been doing this for ages, now." Marks sighed yet again.

"There are still four left, and with your hearing scheduled very soon, there's no time to waste. We'll be working at them all week and over the weekend, I'm afraid."

The next file was that of Samuel North, a dubious character whom Marks had had in his sights right from the outset. The case appeared to be an open and shut matter, and the discovery of the incriminating evidence by Peter Spencer had been the turning point in the whole investigation.

"So, what are they saying with this one, Mr Greenaway?"

"The allegation here, Chief Inspector, is that you manufactured the evidence when it wasn't there. Specifically, that you switched the bullet found at the scene with one which you could prove came from the gun."

"What? That came from in between a studded partition in the Norths' home. How the devil could I have switched it?"

"That's not for me to answer, but they go on to say that you smeared blood from that bullet onto the one you submitted into evidence in order to frame Mr North. Presumably, according to them, you would have disposed of the actual bullet."

"That's nonsense. North had plenty of reasons for wanting his wife out of the way and ample opportunity for doing it. There was enough circumstantial evidence to arrest and charge him without the bullet in the first place. Finding it was the bonus that wrapped the case up. Listen, I'll tell you exactly what happened."

Metropolitan Police

Case No. 684287714
Name: North, S.
Date: 12-July-2002

SOCO Report 08-July-2002

The body of a middle-aged woman was found lying in a ditch at the side of a secluded country road at approximately 6.00am by an early morning jogger.

Preliminary indications are that she had been shot at fairly close range, wrapped in a length of plastic sheeting, and rolled off the road.

There were no clues in the immediate vicinity, and the road and its adjacent area have now been cordoned off.

Despite an intensive fingertip search, nothing had been retrieved to provide clues to her identity at this stage, but more staff have been drafted in to extend the hunt.

It is likely, at this stage, that she was killed in another location and that this is simply the dump site for the body. Any tyre tracks from a vehicle will have been washed away by the heavy rain of the previous week, and preliminary findings indicate that she may have been lying at the site for a period approaching a fortnight.

Full Marks

Neal James

Marks on the Wall

Full Marks

1

The Audi pulled off the A111 Cockfosters Road and turned right onto Ferny Hill. At three in the morning, the likelihood of encountering another motorist was remote, and this was precisely what the driver was counting upon. Having killed the lights, he pulled up a mile along the road past Ferny Hill Farm and switched off the engine. Moat Wood lay to his right and he sat momentarily with the window slightly down, listening intently for any sounds of movement. Rain had started to fall as he made the turn off the main road, and now began to strengthen into a steady downpour. He smiled grimly at the forces of nature which were set to make his task so much simpler. He got out of the car.

Standing in the open, he listened once again. The road was unlit, and there were no lights visible from the farm in the distance. Heavy cloud obscured a full moon, giving just enough light to carry out the task which lay ahead. Opening the boot, he reached inside and dragged a bundle from its depths. She was light – lighter than he remembered, and rolling her into the ditch at the roadside took minimal effort. Wrapping her up in the plastic sheeting at the outset had been more of a problem, and he would take care of any traces remaining in the boot later. He stopped and listened – silence has a sound all of its own, and the call of a distant owl was all that broke its grip on the night. He wiped his hands on a cloth before closing the boot lid, and returned to the driver's seat.

The rain had now increased in intensity, and surface water flowed freely along the road. The tyre tracks which he had left in the mud at the roadside were quickly washed away as he turned the vehicle around and left the scene. With headlights still off, there was nothing to betray his presence, and the barking of a dog as he passed Ferny Hill Farm once again was the only clue that he had ever been there.

"So, what are we looking at?" Dennis Marks strode across from his car to the cordoned off area where George Groves was busy examining a body retrieved from the side of the road.

"Well, my guess is that she's been here for at least a week." The pathologist stood up from the squatting position he had adopted. "The recent warm weather's speeded up decomposition, and there's no ID."

"I know what you're going to say, but I'll ask anyway." Marks sighed. "Cause of death?"

"Oh, that's easy." Groves smiled – he loved these games. "Single gunshot to the head – there, look." He pointed to the body.

"Presumably a body dump." The DI looked around.

"Yes. No signs of any kind of a struggle, and I can't find the bullet although we haven't searched the entire area just yet. I would imagine that she was shot somewhere far away from here – no sign of the weapon either. There are no other marks on the body, not even to the hands or arms. I think she was taken by surprise."

"Who found her?" Marks looked towards the patrol car further up the road.

"A chap out jogging at six this morning." Groves nodded in the same direction. "Your uniform boys are taking a statement."

"Tyre tracks?" A sense of frustration was beginning to settle around the DI, and he strolled up the side of the road, looking down at the ground.

"Sadly not." Groves followed close behind. "Last night's downpour would have taken care of anything left by a departing vehicle."

"What about witnesses? There's a farm over there." He pointed at Ferny Hill Farm in the distance.

"You'll have to check with your boys, but I think they've already been over there." Groves replied. "By the looks on their faces, I don't think anything positive came from the visit."

"Typical!" Marks exclaimed. "A body with no ID, advanced decomp, no weapon, no witnesses, and we can't even identify a vehicle."

"That's about the size of it." Groves began to pack up his kit. "However, she'll still be able to tell me more once I get her back to the lab, so don't go beating yourself up too much... yet."

"Susan North." Groves smiled as DI Marks entered the lab on the following morning.

"That was quick, even for you. Friends in high places?"

"No, Dennis." Groves smiled. "Pure chance. It would seem that our customer has a police record – we have her DNA on file."

"What?"

"Shoplifting." Groves fetched a folder from a table at the side of the room. "It seems that she was caught at one of the Bond Street stores in London in 1999."

"It says here that she was put on probation for six months." Marks frowned. "Seems a bit light to me."

"Well, that's your department, but the judge would appear to have been influenced by her previously clean record."

"Either that, or she hadn't been caught before." Marks closed the file. "Anything more?"

"Peter Spencer has the report – he was in here about half an hour ago. It's all in there."

Marks' DS was poring over the file when he arrived in the squad room; he slid the documents over the desk to his boss and went to get a drink. He returned moments later to find the DI frowning in puzzlement.

"It says in here," Marks pointed to a sheet at the back of the file, "that Susan North had originally been bailed to appear at the Crown Court, but there's no record of a trial date being set."

"No." Spencer said. "I checked into that, and it looks like the charges were reduced and she was allowed probation instead."

"I'm sorry, I don't..."

"Looks to me as though Daddy had some friends in high places, and he pulled a few strings. I did some further digging, and it seems as though the North's marriage wasn't all sweetness and light." Spencer leaned back in his chair, took a mouthful from his mug, and continued. "There were a number of instances where neighbours reported loud arguments coming from the property. I've sent uniform to bring in the husband, Samuel North. They should be back soon."

A call from the desk sergeant confirmed Spencer's statement, and the two of them made their way down to an interview room where North was sitting with his solicitor. Over the course of the following half hour, Samuel North kept his mouth firmly shut, and had clearly been advised to say nothing to the police beyond confirming his identity and address.

"Very well, Mr North." Marks said at last. "We'll be holding you in connection with the death of your wife. A search warrant will give us access to your property, and we'll be taking a detailed look around. You'll be held here, as I'm sure your solicitor has told you, for a maximum of seventy-two hours, after which I will make a decision whether or not to charge you with her murder."

2

Dennis Marks sat in the lounge and looked around the room. He was convinced that Samuel North had killed his wife, Susan. Everything was there. He had motive, opportunity, the weapon, and there were enough people who knew that the marriage was going through serious problems to put the man firmly in the frame. Despite all of this, the DI had nothing concrete to place North at the scene during the period that the pathologist estimated to be the time of death. If they went to trial based on what evidence was currently available, he may be acquitted – on the other hand, the Crown Prosecution Service may not even agree to go that far. Susan North had been shot, her body wrapped in plastic sheeting, and dumped at the side of an isolated country road. According to the post mortem report she had been dead for at least two weeks.

North had married into money, becoming an essential part of his father-in-law's business, and inheriting a share of the company when the old man died. His wife, Susan, obtained controlling interest when her mother passed away, and became the driving force with her sixty per cent share to his own forty. Their marriage, although happy enough at first, had never been one of undying love, and when disputes over the future direction of the company became more prevalent it descended into an acrimonious business relationship.

This suited Susan, leaving her free to explore her own social life whilst still keeping the brakes upon Samuel's ambitions, but when he found out about her affair with the tennis coach at her country club, their relations disintegrated. Susan's golfing partner, Abigail Marshall, reported her missing to the local police when she failed to appear for her regular twice weekly round without informing her. Susan had always been meticulous in her contacts with friends, but when Abigail's follow ups revealed little progress, her next call was to another friend - the wife of the Chief Superintendent.

Dennis Marks received instructions from his boss to take a personal interest in the case, and keep him informed of all developments. It was always frustrating when workloads were disrupted by requests from on high, but sometimes you just had to get on with it, and this case had something about it which he just could not put his finger on. Based on forensic evidence leading back to North's gun, a search warrant was obtained for the family home, and Samuel North was arrested on suspicion of murder.

The police team had been all over the house with a fine-toothed comb, but nothing else connecting the place with the murder had come to Marks' attention – there was a loose end here somewhere, and he hated them. He decided to go home and review the case file in the morning. Picking up his coat, he looked around once more – it had been done here, in this room; he was sure of it, and all he needed was the final piece of evidence to put North away.

He was in early the following morning, and well into the case file when Peter Spencer made an appearance. The detective sergeant had been Marks' right hand man for a few years, and their ability to bounce ideas off each other had led to some successful prosecutions in difficult circumstances in the past. He fetched a coffee for them both and sat down opposite his boss.

"Anything new?"

Marks leaned back in his chair and scratched the back of his head – it was a habit he had when the blindingly obvious seemed to be lurking just out of his reach.

"No, and I've been at this for over an hour now. As I see it, we have a couple of suspects; the husband, Samuel North, and this tennis coach – what's his name?"

"Mark Collingwood – but he has an alibi. At the time the pathologist says Susan was killed, he was in France with another one of his pupils, and they were there for a fortnight for some coaching." He laboured the final word. "I cross-checked with the hotel manager where they were staying, and he corroborates the story."

"Well, that just leaves us with North. The problem is we can't tie him to the scene. We know from the autopsy report that Susan was killed by a bullet matching the type in his gun. The gun is licensed to him and is used at the local firing range, so evidence that it was recently discharged doesn't prove a thing, and his are the only fingerprints on it. Witnesses at the range place him there regularly during the period when she was killed, but we can't pin any of them down to a time, and no-one heard any shots coming from the home at the time of death. How long have we been holding North?"

"Forty-eight hours up to last night." said Spencer. "That gives us just one more day before we have to either charge or release him. What about bringing Collingwood in? He may be able to tell us more about the Norths' domestic situation."

"We could do. He may be holding something back. Let's go back to the North house first – there's something there that I'm missing and it's driving me up the wall."

The house was still sealed off from the press and public, with uniformed officers covering front and rear entrances. Marks and Spencer walked the entire property for the third time during the case, and sat down in the lounge where the DI was convinced that the murder took place.

"There's something about this room that bothers me, and I can't make out what it is." he said to Spencer. "Take another walk around and see what you think."

Spencer walked around the room, stopping periodically, deep in thought; when he sat down opposite Marks, his words grabbed the DI's attention.

"Well, I'd certainly sack the decorator."

"What?"

"The decorator." He nodded over to the other side of the room. "Anyone with the North's money would be entitled to expect a better wallpapering job than that."

Marks was out of his chair in an instant and at the place indicated by his sergeant. He looked back at Spencer with a broad smile on his face - the first time that had happened during the case.

"Look at that, Peter." He pointed to a join in the paper. "June and I had our lounge redecorated, and the decorator started in the middle of the wall, and worked outwards to the corners. I think somebody's replaced this whole drop, but it's just too wide and there's an overlap. Get forensics back in here; I want that entire length removing in one piece – let's see what's behind it."

They both sat with bated breath whilst the forensic team painstakingly removed the eight foot strip of wallpaper. One of the team turned to Marks.

"There's something here you should see, sir."

The lack of spatter had bothered Marks from the start of the investigation - now he knew why. Had Susan North been shot in the middle of the room there would have been blood everywhere, and it would have been almost impossible for her killer to clear up the mess.

"Peter. If I am pointing a gun at your head from about six feet away, where would you go?" He raised a finger to simulate the shot.

Spencer involuntarily took three steps backwards and, as his boss approached, continued until his back came up against the wall.

"Now I've got you pinned, and a shot from here would only stain the area immediately behind your head. Turn around."

There, on the bare plaster, was the trace of a blood stain which had been covered by a fresh piece of paper, and in the middle of the mark was a patch of filler covering a hole. An attempt had been made to clear the area of spatter, and enough had been removed to ensure that there was nothing to soak through the fresh drop. Marks tapped on the wall and smiled once more.

"A studded wall. I reckon the bullet will be at the bottom of the partition." He turned to the forensic team. "Let's get this section of the wall removed."

The team cut the entire area of plasterboard away for testing, and on the floor in between the studding was a blood-stained bullet. Marks put on his gloves and removed it with a pair of tweezers. Holding it up to the light, he pointed out the blood and traces of flesh to his sergeant.

"He knew exactly what he was doing. Forcing her back to the wall reduced the spray of blood to the area immediately behind her head. He could have worked out that he would have to replace only one strip of wallpaper, or at worst, two. What he failed to account for was the fact that the bullet would be lost in the partition wall, but he must have thought that filling the hole and covering the area with a fresh drop would conceal the facts."

Marks & Spencer

"Back to the lab then?" said Spencer

"Yes, and if forensic tests show that these traces carry Susan's DNA, North will have a hard job explaining it together with a match to his gun. We've now got him at the scene. Put that together with both her affair with Collingwood and control over the company, and that's motive for murder. Good job you spotted that wallpaper, Peter."

Samuel North's solicitor was at the station when the two detectives returned late that afternoon. He was on the point of demanding they release or charge his client when Marks raised a hand and ushered him into an interview room. North was brought in from the police cells, and a smile crept across his face when he saw his lawyer. That disappeared rapidly when Marks dropped a small polythene bag onto the table. In the bag was the bullet removed from the wall in North's lounge, and accompanying it were the forensic and ballistic reports matching it to his gun and Susan's DNA. Marks inserted two new cassette tapes into the interview recorder and switched it on.

"This interview is timed at 16.05 on Tuesday the 16th of July. Present are DI Marks, DS Spencer, Mr Samuel North and Mr Paul Firth, his solicitor. Samuel North, I am charging you with the murder of Susan North. You have the right to remain silent; but it may harm your defence if you do not mention, when questioned, something that you later rely on in Court. Anything you do say may be given in evidence. Do you understand?"

Tuesday, 18th April 2006

Robert Hampson, Grand Master of the Freemasons' Hall, frowned as he read, once more, the note on the desk before him. He had recognised the handwriting on the envelope immediately, and did not need the heading announcing its despatch from the Chief Whip's Office to know the identity of the sender.

Communication from the Whip's Office for anyone in government was concern enough, but to an outside organisation it raised questions of quite a different manner. The lodge had managed, over the years, to remain aloof and quite divorced from any potential embarrassments which could arise from conflicts of interest. Its members were all acutely aware of the penalties for bringing the organisation into disrepute, and the communication gave no clue as to the matter in question or the identities of any of the parties to it.

Tom Williams was an MP of considerable experience and standing within the Houses of Parliament, and had served a number of party leaders and heads of government in his lengthy career. A northerner, his manner was brusque and businesslike with a gritty edge which barely concealed a ferocious temper. That temper was, fortunately for Robert Hampson, of no use to him whatsoever outside of the Palace of Westminster. However, a cautious approach would be the order of the day until the reason for his request became apparent.

He rose from his ornate oak desk and strolled over to the window overlooking The Mall. There had been a few occasions where he had seriously considered taking the gold-plated pension to which his position entitled him, and, at sixty next year, his wife had been making overtures in that direction for some time. Having survived the enquiries around the uncovering of Anthony Blunt, the fifth man in the now infamous case of the Cambridge Five, he had nevertheless trod a wary road since the man had been stripped of all his state honours. A thorough investigation into the backgrounds of all serving at the Palace had ensued, and had made for some very uncomfortable months.

With that all now behind him and, he believed, consigned to the past, this fresh request had come at an inconvenient moment. Planning for a royal visit to Norwich had been completed, but experience had taught him to be prepared for all eventualities. He had not allowed for anything of this nature, and careful control would be required to keep the matter out of earshot of the Palace grapevine.

"Sharon." He buzzed his secretary. "I'll be out for a while. Make sure that no-one panics while I'm gone, would you?"

"Of course, sir. When will you be back?"

"A little after lunch." He replied. "Oh, and you'd better make a note. I'll be late in tomorrow. Ten thirty or thereabouts."

Wednesday, 19th April 2006

Hampson was not accustomed to being questioned by outsiders in what was considered to be inviolate premises. He had listened carefully to everything that Tom Williams had said, but had remained stoical in defence of his members.

"We are an organisation which stands firmly behind the interests of those of our membership who find themselves in, shall we say, difficulties."

"Even if those difficulties contravene the law of the land?" Williams was not a man to be trifled with, as a number of MPs had come to realise down the years.

"Mr Williams." Hampson shifted in his chair – the movement was picked up by Williams, and he smiled. The man was clearly becoming uncomfortable with the information which had been divulged. "I am fully in support of the laws of this country, but my hands are tied."

"In that case," Williams smiled, "I understand that there are plans in progress for the expansion of this building. I may have to see what influence I can bring to bear on the matter; we have to be so careful about the standard of construction work permitted in the centre of the capital."

"I see." He sneered. "So this is your subtle form of blackmail, is it?"

"Not at all; merely a restatement of what the borough's policy happens to be."

"Alright, then." Hampson sighed in resignation. "What exactly is it that you need?"

"Not much, as it happens. The minister and the solicitor require encouragement to bring their little arrangement to a close. We can, of course, take independent action on the blackmail, but the PM feels that it could be counterproductive, if you see what I mean."

"Expulsion from the lodge is out of the question, you know. After all, you haven't provided me with conclusive proof. There's no way of finding where the money actually came from."

"I'm certain that you can handle the situation without any further help from me." Williams smiled again and Hampson winced. "I look forward to the case being dropped. I'll see myself out."

With no other alternative, a brief note was made and sent out to the individuals concerned. A special meeting of the officers of the lodge would be held immediately, and the entire matter wrapped up before it got out of hand.

"Damn and blast!" He thumped his desk in frustration.

"So, does that make any more sense than the bilge that they've been feeding to you?"

As the case had progressed, Marks was getting the feeling that it would not matter one iota how much he could come up with to rebut the charges against him; Staines would have his way. Things were now wearing very thin in his opinion.

"Yes, I have to say, it does." Greenaway replied. "You couldn't possibly have had the time to switch the bullets as they say, and since your sergeant was with you during the entire episode, he would have surely noticed if you had tried. His testimony is going to be very important on that score."

"Thank God for that! Peter's one of two people who I can rely on utterly."

"However," Greenaway cautioned, "as I said before, if this all fails to persuade the tribunal of your innocence he could end up going down with you."

"Has anyone spoken to George Groves yet?" Marks leaned forward.

"That'll come later, when we get to the actual hearing, Chief Inspector. For now, we must finish the review of the case files which they are going to try to use against you."

"What's next, then? My wife's beginning to wonder who I am these days. I'm spending most of my time here with you, when I should be at home. She's worried sick."

Ron Greenaway was not entirely unsympathetic to Marks' domestic case. His own spouse had been making similarly strident noises in his direction since the outset of the case, and he was wanting to wind the matter up as soon as possible. It was, in his opinion, beginning to look more and more like a witch hunt than a properly constructed investigation, and there were one or two holes beginning to appear in the charges. He wasn't about to tell Marks that at the moment, though. There would be no point in building the man's hopes up at this stage, only to have them demolished at the hearing.

"David Farmer, a double glazing salesman whom you arrested for the murder of three men last year. The break in the case seemed to have come when you *found a ladder which had been tampered with at the home of a woman by the name of Cecily Harris."*

"And just what are they saying there?"

"That you, or someone in your team, tampered with the ladder after it had been used by the woman's husband. They maintain that the death was, in fact, accidental and not arranged by David Farmer at all. The inference is that you falsified the facts to suit your need for a conviction."

"You mean the hole we found in one of the rungs?"

"Exactly. The charge indicates," he consulted the file, *"that you are responsible for its appearance, after the death of Mr Harris, thus securing the conviction of David Farmer."*

Dennis Marks smiled sadly and shook his head – he was doing a lot of that at the moment. This was another of the tricky cases which always seemed to find their way into his hands. It had been a fairly typical matter of circumstances getting out of the control of the perpetrator once he had taken the next step, a step which took him beyond doing a favour for a beautiful woman into something approaching a full-time job. The man had made mistakes, it was as simple as that, and those mistakes led to his downfall.

Neal James

Metropolitan Police

Case No. 709143665

Name: Riley, G.

Date: 23-September-2004

Extract from the Yorkshire Echo 1st June 2004

The body of local businessman George Riley was pulled from the wreck of his car at Sutton Bank yesterday morning after fire crews had been summoned to the scene of a road traffic accident.

Roulstone Scar, as the incline is locally known, has been the site of numerous accidents over the years, but fatalities have, fortunately, been few and far between.

Mr Riley was seen running out of control in his car by a walker approaching from halfway down the hill. Mr John Dempsey, a retired schoolmaster, indicated that the driver appeared to be fighting for control as his vehicle careered through the roadside barrier and into the adjoining field.

The car, he said, came to an abrupt halt when it crashed into a tree about fifty yards away. Mr Riley was pronounced dead on arrival at hospital later that morning.

Sources on site discounted alcohol, or any other form of intoxicant, as a contributory factor, but did indicate that fractures to the vehicle's brake pipes would have rendered it uncontrollable in the circumstances.

Enquiries, we are told, are ongoing.

Full Marks

Foot in the Door

1

It had begun to cross the mind of Dennis Marks that the trickier the cases were, the more likely it was that they would end up on his desk. He should really have taken this set of circumstances as a compliment - the team that comprised him, Peter Spencer and George Groves had acquired the type of reputation inclined to send the shivers down the backs of the criminal fraternity. Nevertheless, none of them seemed to have much in the way of a social life these days, and the respective wives had become vociferous in their opinions on the matter.

"Don't you get the easy ones any more?" June had asked on one of their rare evenings together. "I mean, aren't there any other coppers in the Met these days?"

"June, dear…" He winced at the expression these words produced on the face of his long-suffering wife, "it goes with the territory. Criminals don't take time off, and we all have to be on alert all of the time."

"Really." She scowled, but could never hold onto anger in the face of her husband. "Ever since the promotions you got after all that nonsense with Michael Roberts, and the involvement with that George Watkinson chap, there hasn't been a single weekend that we've had entirely to ourselves."

The dialogue continued in this vein for the whole evening, and it did come as a relief for Marks to realise that Groves and Spencer were probably experiencing a similar going-over on the first free evening that any of them had enjoyed for quite some time. There was no real malice in anything that June said, and he always took it on the chin and let her blow off whatever steam had been building up. It invariably dissipated reasonably quickly.

He smiled at the recollection of the evening as he began to plough his way through the latest batch of case files which had arrived on his desk. Sighing, Marks sifted through them looking for something that would grab his attention. Something out of the ordinary, they needed it after the recent rash of bloodcurdling homicides. He, they, needed a case to stir the puzzler's instinct, one that might even beat them for its ingenuity. One which - wait a minute. He put the rest of the files to one side, and started to leaf through a set of documents which had been forwarded to the Met by the North Yorkshire Constabulary.

A colleague in the Scarborough force, Frank Collins, had lost track of a suspect in an insurance case. The company had paid the claim in full, finding nothing to alert them to any untoward circumstances, but the copper's 'nose' had told him that it all seemed just too convenient. Marks dialled the phone number on the inside flap of the file. A familiar voice greeted him from the other end of the country.

"Dennis. Long time no see."

"And just what can the Met do for you boys up there, Frank?" Opening banter of this type had been common all through their training at Hendon, but the two had taken different paths in the progression of respective careers.

"I assume you're looking at the Riley file." Collins replied.

"I am. What's the problem?" Marks, having now forgotten the grumbles which had been rumbling around his mind, was scenting something interesting.

"It's too easy. Everything seems to be tied up so neatly that there just has to be a catch somewhere. According to one neighbour, and the insurance company never even went down that road, the marriage had been on the rocks for a while."

"So, there's your motive." Marks interjected.

"Right, and there were sightings of an unidentified younger man at the house on a couple of occasions. The Rileys had all their windows and doors replaced, and I managed to track down a salesman by the name of David Farmer."

"Did you pull him in?"

"Not enough evidence to even think about it. On the surface it looked like a straight business transaction, and that's presumably why the claim was settled without a fuss."

"So, what do you need me for?" The DCI was now puzzled, but with his interest stirred, he was getting in deeper by the minute.

"Farmer's now left the area. He and a colleague resigned from the company, Surebright Home Improvements, and set up their own firm down your way."

"So, you reckon he had something to do with George Riley's death?"

"Can't prove it, and the accident was put down as being due to worn brake pipes leaking fluid. The car ran off the road down Sutton Bank near to Helmsley, and that was that."

"Looks open and shut, then. What can I do?"

"Dennis, it's not in the file, but David Farmer's father was a mechanic, and the lad spent a lot of his time around cars. I found that out by digging around. It's possible that he and Jennifer Riley had something of a relationship going, and she persuaded him to bump off the old man."

"Alright, is there an address for the new company? I can have a good sniff around the area and see what I can come up with."

"Yes. Towards the back, and we also know where he's living down there. Sorry to dump this one on you, but you always did like a challenge, didn't you? Let me know how you get on with it."

"Okay, Frank. I'll talk to you when I've assembled the team."

2

There was the bare minimum of information in the file sent from North Yorkshire, and what there was gave precious little in the way of leads for Marks to follow up on. The address would, of course, be the place to begin, but the rest of David Farmer's background was a complete mystery to him. Had the DCI known then of the details of the meeting with the Rileys, the man's greed-fuelled spree would have been stopped before it had gained the momentum to continue.

David Farmer had always wanted to be a salesman, and despite all the advice from the teachers at school, he was adamant that his career path would take him down that road. Leaving at sixteen, he took the first job he could find in a sales office, and his enthusiasm, coupled with a willingness to learn, landed him a place sponsored by his employer at a commercial college. He excelled in the subject, passing all the exams with flying colours and moving up the albeit small corporate ladder with a rapidity which surprised all of his colleagues. Inevitably, with further progress hampered by more senior staff, the time came to move onwards and upwards. His next job, for a much larger company, was in the area of home improvements - specifically the double glazing field.

Again he applied himself diligently and got to know about the industry. Single, and in his twenties, he had what he thought to be the perfect job. Perfect, that is, until one morning in late May in the North Yorkshire coastal resort of Scarborough where he made the acquaintance of Jennifer Riley. He was well up with his sales targets for the month, so wasn't trying particularly hard to gather in extra business, and this calmness in demeanour was one of the secrets of his success, making him appear less pushy than competitors in the industry. Nevertheless, he was always on the lookout for anything that appeared to be an easy sell, and number fourteen Walsingham Gardens fitted the bill exactly. The house was large and in a quiet cul-de sac, but the wooden windows and doors had seen better days, and were starting to let the rest of the property down.

Straightening his tie in an almost ritual way before facing a customer, he walked up the gravel drive, put on his best smile, and rang the doorbell. The woman who eventually opened the front door took his breath away, and for the first time ever he was momentarily lost for words as she returned his smile. She was a brunette, with hazel eyes and a stunning figure. At about five feet eight, she was slightly shorter than him, and had the kind of hands which had never seen a day's manual work in their lives.

"Yes, can I help you?" She had a voice which could charm the birds down from the trees.

David Farmer & Jennifer Riley

"Good morning, Mrs…?"

"Riley, Jennifer Riley."

"Good morning, Mrs Riley. My name is David Farmer from Surebright Home Improvements. Would you be interested in replacing your existing frames?"

She looked him critically up and down, stepped out of the porch, and gazed at the windows and door with a frown on her face.

"They do look rather tired, don't they? Why don't you come inside and let me take a look at your brochures – perhaps we can come to some arrangement."

Over coffee, they spent the next hour exploring every aspect of Surebright's portfolio, and David was left with a quotation to prepare for a complete refit throughout the property. The job was larger than any of those he would normally have dealt with, and would earn him a tidy commission. As he rose to leave, he noticed a change in her manner and she appeared to be crying. Unsure of how to deal with the situation, he extended a hand and placed it upon her shoulder. She was in his arms immediately and dissolved into floods of tears, as she began to explain the position in which she had found herself. She had been married for fifteen years, and over the past five had known of her husband's affair with a woman in Thirsk. Jennifer had attempted to discuss the matter with him, but all efforts had been brushed aside and she was now left alone most of the time, as he always seemed to be away on business. There was no love left in their marriage, and if she could find a way out of it there would be no regrets.

David remained there for the rest of the afternoon, comforting her in the only way he could think of, and assuring her of a return in a few days with the figures which she had requested. There was no shame in his mind relating to a brief affair with an unhappy, attractive woman, even though she was his senior by about ten years, and he was looking forward to their next meeting. George Riley was at home when he made that call, and you could have cut the atmosphere between Jennifer and him with a knife. He glanced at the quotation in a cursory manner, and with a wave of his hand told his wife to please herself. Picking up his golf clubs from the hall, it was clear where he intended to spend the rest of that day and probably the majority of the evening. Left alone together, the formalities of the paperwork were completed quickly, and David returned the signed contract to his briefcase.

"Do you see what I mean?" she asked. "He's like that all the time, and it's come to the point where I would be better off without him. If I could find some way of freeing myself I'd do it in a flash. I wish he were dead."

David was at a loss for something to say in a situation which he had never encountered before, but was sure that there was more to Jennifer Riley than met the eye. He was not to be disappointed.

"What should I do? If I file for divorce, he'll fight me all the way and then move in with his fancy woman. He's extremely wealthy, and employs lawyers who could keep me tied up in court for years. Even the insurance policy only covers accidental death."

"What if he *did* have a fatal accident?"

"In that case, everything goes to me. There are no other beneficiaries in his will, and he has no family." She paused. "What are you suggesting?"

Full Marks

For a moment Farmer thought that he might have overstepped the mark, and turned to stare out of the back window into the large well-kept garden. She continued.

"If I could find someone who could arrange for him to somehow accidentally suffer fatal injuries, there would be a considerable amount of recompense for that kind of service. Do you have anyone in mind?"

He was now getting in too deep to pull out without facing embarrassing consequences. Knowing that George's mistress lived in Thirsk, and that he called on her regularly, the route would probably have to take him along the A170 from Helmsley, and down the dangerous incline of Sutton Bank. A brakes failure along this stretch of road could have serious consequences for any unwary driver, and it would not prove too difficult to engineer some wear to the fluid cables underneath the car. David's dad had been a mechanic, and so all of his teenage years had been spent in and around the series of vehicles which occupied their drive and garage. It was time to take the bull by the horns. He stared at her intently.

"If a person knew the likely timing of the next visit, arrangements could be made to modify the reliability of the brakes on George's car. A fractured brake pipe could be lethal in a place like Sutton Bank, and if a payment for that service were to be made in an untraceable manner, no-one would be any the wiser."

Jennifer looked at him long and hard, turning the matter over and over in her mind. She had only known this man for a matter of days, and had poured out her life to him in that time. Were they to go ahead with this, there could be serious consequences for both of them, and yet the alternative for her would be a lifetime of misery and loneliness. She asked him straight to his face if he would do it. For David, this could be no more than a business transaction, and whatever had happened between them so far would have to stop. She said she understood, and that all contact would cease, just as it would following the completion of the double glazing installation.

The driveway to the house front was long and isolated from the roadway, giving cover from prying eyes as Farmer quickly worked on the brake cables three nights later whilst the Rileys were out. He knew how to make fractures look like accidental damage done by a loose brick, and had even taken the precaution of providing one as evidence. Laced with brake fluid and left lying in the road outside the house with a trail leading up the drive, it would ensure that any accident investigator came to the correct conclusion. Regular as clockwork, George departed the next day and headed out of Scarborough, with David following him at a respectful distance as far as Helmsley. Now he and Jennifer simply had to bide their time and carry on as normal.

She called his mobile two days later, confirming that George had been taken to hospital after leaving the road unaccountably halfway down Sutton Bank. He was pronounced dead on arrival, and after a consoling visit from the local uniformed police, she was left as sole beneficiary, inheriting everything. The payout from his insurance policy should net £1.5 million, of which £100,000 would be sent to him, in used banknotes, in payment for the service. At more than double his annual salary, this amount placed David in a situation of some comfort, and he returned to his normal lifestyle convinced that he would hear no more from Jennifer Riley. How wrong he was.

3

By August, David Farmer had left Surebright, along with Roger Harding, to set up their own business, and initial deals indicated that the company was moving quickly in the correct direction. They had set up in London, far away from any contractual restrictions imposed by their former employer, and David was relaxing at home after a meeting with the bank when his mobile phone rang. Usually it was from Roger to remind him of commitments for the following day, but the number displayed did not look familiar. The voice at the other end made him sit up with a start.

"David, it's Jennifer. Look, don't worry, there's no cause for alarm, but I have a friend who could be in need of the same sort of service to the one which you provided for me earlier this year. The installation would be similar, and she is flexible with regard to contractual terms. Are you interested?"

Farmer was dumbstruck. He was a salesman not a fixer, and the job for Jennifer had been as much out of sympathy as it was with regard to financial reward. Now here, out of the blue, was an opportunity to expand what could become a pension fund for his old age. Jennifer had told him over the phone that no names had been mentioned at this point, but that the woman was in a similar position to that which she had occupied a few short months ago.

He bought himself a new mobile on a Pay As You Go package, and told her never to call him again on his normal number. She gave him details of the friend, and he agreed to call and set up preliminary discussions. Telling Roger that he would be away on a sales trip, he set out across the M25 for South Mimms and a service area meeting with Rosemary Davidson.

The facts were almost identical to Jennifer's situation, and the fee for completion and method of payment were the same. It was almost too easy to believe – the man (David declined the offer of his name, preferring to remain anonymous) worked in the City, and after parking his car always made the final leg of the journey by tube. From an earlier trip, David knew that the underground was always packed, and that it would be quite easy to engineer a terrible accident for someone caught up in the crush of passengers for an approaching train.

The job was over and done with minimal planning involved. Farmer simply positioned himself two rows back from his target and stumbled into the man in front of him under the weight of a *heavy* suitcase, apologising profusely for his clumsiness. Instinct forced this passenger into breaking his forward movement by placing a hand upon the back of the person in front, who in turn pushed Rosemary's husband into the path of the approaching vehicle. By the time of the impact, David was away from the scene with all other eyes on the horror unfolding before them. Back in his car, he called her with the result of his action. Three months later, with the insurance claim finalised, he was £100,000 richer and back on the road in his normal business. He called Jennifer to ensure that no more recommendations were likely, and chose to believe that he would hear no more. He didn't; at least not from her.

News of the death of Rosemary Davidson's husband, Paul, had not reached Dennis Marks' ears until some time after it had happened. It was only when two witnesses came forward much later, reportedly seeing a man with a suitcase hurrying towards the tube station exits, that he started to take an interest. The insurance claim made by the grieving widow had, as with that of Jennifer Riley, been paid out without much of a delay. There was, at the time, nothing suspicious to alert the claims department.

The general description given had fitted that supplied by Frank Collins for David Farmer. Marks and his DI, Peter Spencer, were soon at the premises of the company set up by Farmer and Harding in Pinner.

Farmer was not there at the time, and his partner, Roger Harding, was very vague on the subject of his appointment schedule. Marks and Spencer, in their turn, were not about to reveal the subject of their interest and run the risk of spooking the suspect into flight. They returned to base empty-handed.

"So, you think he's bumping off the husbands and making some rich widows very happy?" Spencer was becoming an expert at getting to the nub of a case.

"It wouldn't be the first time, and I'm not ruling out further interest of a personal nature either. If he is up to some extra-marital stuff, that could be what'll bring him down."

"What next, then?"

"Well, we know where he lives. I suggest we stake out the home, and tail him when he shows his face. I want to find out where he goes next. Draw up a rota, and let's get on it straight away."

The business set-up with Roger Harding was progressing very nicely, but David's accountant partner was becoming aware of the lack of paperwork relating to recent business trips. At one of their weekly meetings he broached the subject, and, finding himself in a corner, Farmer lamely explained that he had paid expenses on his personal credit card, and that recompense could take place at the time of their annual bonuses. Roger frowned and let it pass, deciding instead to file it for future reference, but also to keep an eye on his associate's movements from now on. A phone call to his new mobile a few weeks later had David hurrying out early one afternoon with a vague 'see you in the morning' parting line.

Accountants are curious creatures by nature, and Roger was soon in David's private office looking amongst the papers on his desk. There was nothing of unusual interest there, but his partner had, surprisingly, left his laptop switched on and logged in with just the cover pulled down. He had obviously forgotten about it in his haste to leave. Raising the cover, Harding was faced with a set of files which he had never seen before, one of which contained a list of passwords – he printed a copy of it. The eyes nearly popped out of his head when he came across David's offshore bank account details and the amounts of cash it contained.

Like all partners, they knew the details of each other's remuneration package, and these figures could not possibly be any part of that. Within his hands he held much of Farmer's private wealth, and the means to acquire it without leaving a trace. He used the passwords to access all the files and, satisfying himself that he had full and complete control over all funds, closed the computer down for the day, tidied up, and went home to consider his next move. At the same time, David was on his private mobile to Rosemary, the mystery caller that afternoon. Like Jennifer before her, she had a friend who required the help of someone discreet and willing to benefit by a six-figure sum for certain services. He tried to explain that this was not something which he had ever intended to carry out on a regular basis, and that he would, regrettably, be unable to offer any assistance. After a muffled conversation at the other end, during which time he deduced that the friend was present, Rosemary relayed the message that the fee would be double his usual charge.

Leaning on his elbow and with head in hand, David tried one last time to dissuade both women from the course of action which they were pursuing, but when the final offer of £250,000 came back as a reply, he couldn't refuse. This, he stated, was to be the final job, and no further recommendations were to be made to any more deserving individuals. Both women agreed, and arrangements were made to meet with customer number three to discuss details. Claiming to be on his way to another business trip, a ruse which Roger accepted rather easily, David wondered where all these women were coming from and was sure that, somewhere, a smart detective would make a connection of some kind to link him to all three events – or was he just becoming paranoid?

4

With his attention focussed blindly on the task in hand, David Farmer was completely oblivious to the team of detectives now watching his every move. Marks picked him up as soon as he left home, and was certain that another husband was soon to meet his fate, when his quarry's car took a very different turn to the one which would normally have taken him to work.

"There we go, Peter. Looks like our fox is about to go rabbit hunting again. Seems like we're off for a trip round the M25." They pulled out, following at a discreet distance.

The meeting with the customer, Cecily Harris, lasted all of half an hour, and Spencer was able to get a number of very clear photographs of the encounter. Now they had the source of the information as well, tying Farmer down to the rest of the killings would be quite a simple matter. They did not have to wait too long for the inevitable accident to happen.

When an overweight man falls from a ladder forty feet up the side of his house and dies as a result of a massive skull fracture with no-one else anywhere nearby, there is not usually much cause for suspicion of foul play. For David, this was an unexpected bonus as it was not the method which he had planned to use in disposing of the unwanted husband. Since he had not informed the wife of his chosen technique it really made no difference, and in the course of time he collected his fee for a job well done. He became a little uneasy some time later when a call came from Cecily (the beneficiary of his latest assignment) informing him of a visit to the house by the local CID. A neighbour had reported seeing an unknown man at the house during the days immediately prior to the fatal accident, and further enquiries had revealed the name of his company on an advertising sticker in the rear window of his car.

Back home, he had no option but to sit tight and wait for the enquiries to hit a dead end, but when Dennis Marks made a connection from Cecily back to Rosemary, and then Jennifer, things took a turn for the worse. Farmer received a visit soon after from Marks and his DI. Questions as to his relationship with Jennifer Riley and Rosemary Davidson were detailed and lengthy, but any real evidence beyond that of a business deal for double glazing was circumstantial at best, and the detectives left with nothing more than when they had arrived. Still, Marks was now convinced that there was more to this than some randy salesman and a few desperate housewives. Like all criminals Farmer would slip up - they all did in the end - and it would just be a case of putting the pieces together.

David decided to take the rest of the week off, and left a message for Roger at work to say that he would be back in on the following Monday. When that day came he returned to the office to discover that Harding had, himself, decided to take a leave of absence but had left no indication as to his proposed date of return. Initially this was no cause for concern, but when he switched on his laptop and accessed the private files, Farmer got the shock of his life. His online offshore account had been emptied of its entire contents including the newly received funds from Cecily – a total of £450,000 - and a call to Roger's flat was redirected to the House Manager's office where he was informed that Mr Harding had vacated the premises without leaving a forwarding address.

He put the telephone back down in its cradle as his attention had now been drawn to flashing blue lights outside the office window. Two police patrol cars had pulled up behind an unmarked vehicle from which DCI Marks was exiting with a smile on his face. They entered the salesman's office to find him sitting at his desk with his head in his hands.

"They all screw up in the end, Mr Farmer. Overconfidence breeds sloppiness – what made you think that a hole drilled through a ladder rung wouldn't be spotted? I'm sure that the power drill we found in your victim's garage will match it. I said to my DI that it would only be a matter of time. You'd better be coming along with us." He looked to the nearest uniformed PC, and inclined his head towards Farmer. "Cuff him please, constable."

As he sat in the squad car on its way back to the station, David pondered upon the irony of being caught as a result of the only death of the three for which he was not responsible. He wouldn't even have the comfort of knowing that he had £450,000 waiting for him when he eventually did come out of jail.

For Marks, this had been one of the easy ones which he had been dreaming of right at the start. It had not been without its challenges, though, and there was a moment when he wondered whether Farmer would, once again, slip through the net. Picking up the telephone, he dialled a Scarborough number.

Thursday, 20th April 2006

"Professor Groves. Do you have a moment, please?" Eric Staines, timing his arrival to perfection, had entered the forensics laboratory when no-one else was there.

George Groves looked up from the report on which has had been working, and frowned. He stood up and walked past the figure of the superintendant; opening the door into the general office, he looked up and down for his assistant, Kevin Henson. He was not there. He turned.

"What are you doing here?" The question was flat, impersonal, and intended as a rebuke.

"I was hoping for a quiet chat." Staines sighed. "But I see that I may have caught you at a bad time."

"I wasn't aware that there was a good time to be visited by the IPCC." Groves retorted. "Can we cut to the chase?"

"Very well." Staines leaned against a cupboard – it was clear that he would not be invited to sit down. "I was hoping to get your agreement not to become involved in the matters surrounding the suspension of DCI Marks."

"I see." The beginnings of a smile flitted across the pathologist's face. "How uncomfortable that must feel."

"Professor, I am asking out of politeness." His voice chilled. "Anyone becoming involved without the sanction of the IPCC could face some very awkward repercussions."

"That sounds like a threat." The smile vanished.

"Take it as you wish. I'm running this investigation, and I will not tolerate any hindrance."

"Listen to me!" Groves stabbed the air. "You can please yourself how you flex your muscles at New Scotland Yard, but it won't work here. My staff and I work for the Home Office and, as such, do not answer to you or your department."

Staines opened his mouth to reply, but then thought better of it. He looked Groves in the eye, frowned, and then turned towards the door. He stood for a moment, hand on the handle before turning back.

"If I find out that there has been any attempt to influence the course of my investigation, I promise you that I will take every step possible against those responsible – and that includes you and your department, Professor Groves." With that final riposte he was gone.

Groves stood speechless at the side of his desk. Kevin Henson chose that unfortunate moment to make his appearance.

"Kevin!" Groves exploded. "Where have you been?"

"Out, Professor." Henson was dumbstruck – it was highly unusual for his boss to lose his temper. "Superintendant Staines told me to go out for a while."

"You take your orders from me!" Groves shouted. "Staines has no authority over this lab, and you should have known that! Get out of here!"

Henson left the lab, face red with the admonishment which had been meted out to him, and Groves was instantly regretful for the way that he had reacted. His anger, nevertheless, was still burning fiercely, and had not abated by the time he arrived home that evening.

"What on Earth's the matter, dear?" Alison Groves took her husband's coat and hung it on the rack in the hall.

"Eric Staines!" He fumed. "Just who does he think he is!?"

As good a sounding board as anyone, Alison listened patiently to the events of the afternoon as her husband vented his spleen at the activities of the IPCC. In the end, to her, the solution was a simple one.

"George, dear." She smiled. "Who do you work for?"

"What?" He shook his head in puzzlement.

"Your boss – who is your boss?"

"Well." He paused, thinking. "I work for the Home Office, so I suppose that it's the Home Secretary... of course! Alison, you're wonderful. I'll just be a moment, and we can be off out for dinner.

"Hello, George." The voice at the other end was pleasant and friendly – they had known each other for some time.

"Home Secretary. I..."

"Home Secretary? How long have we been on formal terms?"

"Very well... Charles. I need your help, and it's official business."

"Alright, spit it out. Who's bitten you?" The man's insight knew no bounds, and put Groves at ease with what he was about to do.

Suitably reassured at the end of the conversation, and now completely confident in the stance which he had taken with Eric Staines, he and his wife made their way out to their favourite little Italian restaurant in Knightsbridge.

Friday, 21st April 2006

There were now only three days to go until the date of Dennis Marks' hearing, but Eric Staines had seen and heard nothing to shake the conviction he held that the DCI's days as a detective with the Metropolitan Police could be over. His team had been thorough, and he had personally overseen every aspect of the work done in preparation for the day. He shook his head – they never learned; every one of the men who had appeared before his investigations had believed that the rules could be bent to suit themselves. Dennis Marks' record had been exemplary, it was true; however, it took only the smallest of temptations to sway even the straightest of coppers, and they all had their price.

"That's it, sir." The young sergeant placing the last of the files on his desk smiled at Eric Staines.

"Wipe that grin off your face!" He growled. "It's someone's life you're handling there. We might think he's guilty, but until that hearing he's still entitled to some respect."

"Sorry, sir." He backed away sharply, and left the room.

Staines sighed - he should not have chewed the youngster out. Perhaps his wife had been right all along. The job had to be done, but the price for all such as him was high. Seen as necessary by those in political and social circles, IPCC staff were regarded as social outcasts within the confines of the police force.

There had been much initial media interest and, like the rest of the Met hierarchy, he had wondered at the leak of the information. The IPCC should have been able to locate the source, but had failed to find a single lead. Staines had been considering retirement for a while, and the case surrounding the DCI had taken the edge clean away from his enthusiasm for the job. This, he had decided, was to be his final act. Win or lose, he would move on to pastures new.

He looked again at the terse note from the Chief Constable and winced. A slap on the wrist from that height was always a matter of significant pain, and told him that his calculated gamble in approaching George Groves had not paid off. The man's contacts at the Home Office clearly valued the pathologist's independence, and Staines had been left in no doubt that he had, on this occasion, overstepped the mark. The ringing of his private line was to be the bearer of further cause for concern.

"Staines." The caller ID gave him the information he needed. "What is it, Barnes?"

"Just thought you'd like a piece of information that might save you and your department time and trouble." The relaxed tone had all of Staines' senses on alert. "Wouldn't want you making fools of yourselves, now would we?"

"Get to the point." He was in no mood for games.

"Very well." Barnes continued. "Just trying to smooth the way."

The conversation, one-sided as it became, lasted no longer than a few minutes, but during that time Staines' eyes widened in surprise. With the ground now opening up beneath the entire investigation, Dennis Marks' team appeared to have pulled a rabbit out of the hat at the last moment.

"A fake?" He gasped in surprise. "I don't believe it."

"You can take a look for yourself, if you wish." Barnes sat back in his chair. "I have it right here."

"Don't go anywhere."

Staines' presence in Colin Barnes' office at New Scotland Yard did not go unnoticed, but the smile on the face of the Detective Superintendent relieved the concerns of all those who witnessed his arrival. Behind a closed door, but visible to the outer office, Barnes slid a piece of paper across his desk and watched as Staines read its contents.

"Told you so." He said, once the scrutiny had finished. "Puts a different spin on everything, doesn't it?"

"Where did you get this?"

"Come on, Eric." Barnes laughed. "And you'd reveal your sources to me, would you?"

"Had to ask." He shook his head.

"Without that, your case won't hold much water, will it?"

Staines left. That Marks had friends in high places was not a secret within the Met, but just how far they reached had not, until right now, been apparent to him. Returning to his office, he summoned the rest of the investigating team and broke the news to them.

Saturday, 22nd April 2006

"Well, I can see both sides of this one, I'm afraid, Chief Inspector. We have no clear indication, according to your testimony, who could have drilled the hole in the ladder rung. The evidence, from that point of view, seems to be entirely circumstantial, and we have only your investigative techniques which forced a confession out of Mrs Harris."

"Oh, come on!" Marks' temper was starting to get the better of him, and he thumped the table in frustration. "It was there for all to see in the end. A golden opportunity for Farmer to line his pockets, and three lonely women prepared to pay handsomely to rid themselves of their husbands. What more do you want?"

"But you had no financial evidence at the end. There was no proof, apart from the confession, that Farmer ended up with any financial reward at all."

"Look, Mr Greenaway, the account was a numbered one with a Swiss bank, and you know as well as I do what they're like for disclosing information. It was our opinion at the time that Farmer's partner, Roger Harding, had made off with the money, having discovered where it was. He merely impersonated Farmer, used his passwords, and shifted the lot."

"That may well have been the case. However, the IPCC are wanting a more robust account than that, and they are alleging that you took a number of shortcuts to secure the conviction. That being said, we need to press on – there are only a few days left to formulate some kind of defence."

"Is this the last one? Are we any nearer getting these trumped-up charges dismissed?"

"I'm afraid there are two more, and it did surprise me to find that they were linked."

"Alright, who have I stitched up this time?"

"That's just the kind of attitude which the investigating team will use to discredit you. I suggest that we stick to facts, and cut out the attempts at levity. These people are serious – they don't have a sense of humour."

"Very well, let's move on."

"The Southgate Sisterhood. You had a very curious set of circumstances with this one, and the allegation is one of lack of attention to detail. I'm afraid *they've bundled this one up with an old case that you worked on with Don Mullard. Neither of you came out of the earlier case smelling of roses, and the investigation thinks you were too concerned with burying the original case for good, rather than focussing on the truth."*

Marks laughed. This was turning into a farce, and the whole matter of Alessandra Nelson and her activities was in danger of being derailed from what it actually was – a vigilante taskforce bent on extracting justice outside of the law.

"There were more things going on in this case than it appeared on the surface. We were badly let down at trial, and then had to face a number of bodies turning up out of the blue."

Marks carried on with his version of the case, completely unaware of the wheels which were beginning to turn in the background.

Martin Ponsonby was totally out of his depth and he was perspiring freely, a clear indication of the nervousness he felt at being summoned to a meeting of the lodge council. These gatherings normally meant only one thing – expulsion. Those feelings were exacerbated by the presence in the same room of the very man that he was blackmailing. How the Grand Master had come by that information he had no idea, but the opening of the Grand Chamber door dismissed that thought from his mind completely.

"Come in." The command, for that is what it was, shook him, and the two of them trod their way like some French aristocrats on the way to the guillotine.

Robert Hampson sat in his ceremonial chair on a raised dais at the far end of the chamber. Normally the room held no fears for members, but on this occasion it was considerably more solemn that usual. The silence was deafening. When the Grand Master rose to speak, all eyes turned in his direction – a chill ran down Ponsonby's spine.

"Certain matters affecting the two of you have been brought to my attention, and considerable pressure has been brought to bear upon me and this lodge." The voice boomed out in the stillness of the chamber.

He paused for effect, and heads turned in all directions as if in search of additional information from fellow members present. He continued.

"The fact that this has reached the ear of those in government concerns me deeply, and I will not allow the sanctity of this place to be violated by outsiders. You," he pointed at Ponsonby, *"are the cause of that act of trespass, and you'll be held to account for the behaviour which has compromised the lodge."*

"Me?" Ponsonby swallowed hard.

"Silence! You'll be allowed to speak when it's appropriate. The lodge ordinarily takes no interest in the outside activities of its members, but that trust has been broken. The criminal activity will cease immediately; failure will result in severe penalties for the both of you. I'm sure that your respective employers would take a dim view of it becoming public."

He paused again; a master not only of his lodge, but also of the dramatic and its effect on those under his spotlight.

"I have also been enlightened on the matter of some legal proceedings which have been instigated against an officer of the Metropolitan Police. That must also cease, and you will ensure that any charges are removed on a permanent basis. Do you understand?"

He glared at Ponsonby, who was now beginning to shake under the scrutiny of the entire chamber. The man at his side had, throughout the entire proceedings, said absolutely nothing, and that, in the solicitor's mind, merely served to isolate him further.

"Yes." The reply was weak, almost silent, but in the still of the chamber was audible to all present.

"You can go." Hampson waved his hand, and Ponsonby was shown to the door, his trial over.

The rest of the members present made their way silently through the same door, leaving only two figures in the chamber. The second man had remained. With the sound of the door closing, he turned his eyes to the dais. Silence returned as the Grand Master removed his robes and came across the floor. It was clear that the proceedings were over, and that the next conversation was to be of an altogether different nature.

"My office, Trevor?" Hampson asked, an arm indicating the way. The door closed behind them, and the two men sat down. "Good Lord, man, why didn't you tell me? What is it that he's got on you?" The voice was exasperation in the extreme; the face showing a total lack of understanding.

"A mistake. A simple mistake. An error of judgement in showing someone around the House of Commons when I believed that there was no-one else there to see."

"Someone?" Hampson's face bore a deep frown. "Who exactly would 'someone' be?"

"A friend. A young man keen to see the trappings of government outside of the daily hurly burly of activity. Ponsonby was in the central lobby as we were *coming out and saw us together. I tried to get the young man out of the way, but it was too late."*

"You fool!" He shook his head slowly in a clear show of disgust.

"I know, I know. The next thing was a phone call asking for a meeting. I had no alternative. If my wife found out she'd divorce me; it would be all over the press and I would have to resign my seat. The effect on the government would have been very serious."

"It's gone beyond a simple matter of your own personal circumstances now. You may have to resign anyway. That'll depend on the PM and the Chief Whip. I'm more concerned about the lodge. If Ponsonby carries out the instruction I gave, you'll be safe within it, but if he defies me... well, you know what'll have to happen then."

"I do, and I'm truly sorry."

"Well, there's nothing further to be gained at the moment." The Grand Master stood up. "You'd better get back to work before someone starts asking questions."

Robert Hampson returned to the desk. He had been Grand Master for more years than he cared to remember. It had been a delicate balance keeping his position at work and his role at the lodge separate. That had been successful... until now. He drew in a deep breath. The fact that MI5 were aware of a possible conflict of interest was a matter of grave concern, and the entire situation now hinged on the actions of a less than scrupulous solicitor.

Dennis Marks' position was one which he desperately needed to rectify. The man was clearly too good an officer to lose, and the fallout likely from any conviction was too awful a situation to contemplate. Putting on his coat, he closed the door behind him and made his way back across London to The Palace.

Full Marks

Metropolitan Police

Case No. 730224019

Name: Yates, J.

Date: 25-November-2005

Transcript of Emergency Services Call

'Emergency. Which service do you require?'

'Ambulance - quickly! My daughter's tried to kill herself!"

'Give me your name and address, please, madam.'

'Yates; Doreen Yates. Quickly! She's turning blue! I don't know what to do. Please help me... please!'

'Stay calm, madam. Where are you?'

'Twenty-eight, Leigh Hunt Drive in Enfield. The bastard's going to pay for this!'

'Ambulance is on the way. Excuse me, madam, what did you say?'

'Michael Partington-Smith. He's the one responsible. I'll kill him if it's the last thing I do. My Jennifer didn't deserve any of this!'

'Madam, calm down. Help is on the way.'

'Help? Where was the help when my daughter needed it against that animal?'

The Southgate Sisterhood

1

The clerk to the court looked up from his papers, glanced at His Lordship Martin Wiles, who nodded back, and turned to face the waiting jury. A hush descended upon Court 2 of the Royal Courts of Justice, and Dennis Marks held his breath as the official addressed them.

"Would the foreman of the jury please rise?" He glanced back down at the indictment before him. "Have you reached a verdict upon which you are all agreed?"

"We have." A murmur of anticipation ran around the courtroom like an unruly child.

"Silence in court." The voice of Mr Justice Wiles was enough to halt its progress any further.

"On the charge of rape, do you find the defendant, Michael Partington-Smith, guilty or not guilty?" He looked up from his papers once more.

The atmosphere was electric as the foreman took an eternity to issue forth the finding. When it came, it was as if a dagger had been driven into the heart of Doreen Yates.

"Not guilty."

The eruption of noise within the room was considerable, and Marks held his head in his hands as Mr Justice Wiles called for order again and again until some semblance of silence had been restored. Jury members looked at each other in consternation as the clerk resumed his address.

"On the second charge, that of causing actual bodily harm, do you find the defendant guilty or not guilty?"

"Not guilty."

A second disturbance arose, more muted than the first, but of equal hostility. Once more Mr Justice Wiles was compelled to restore order. He raised his eyes to the dock, where the figure of Michael Partington-Smith had been standing, stone-faced, throughout.

"Michael Partington-Smith, you have been acquitted of the charges brought against you. You are free to go." The statement was delivered flat, in clear disagreement with the verdict, but from a man powerless to offer any solution.

"You bastard! You evil, conniving, bastard!" The court stilled as the voice of Doreen Yates resounded like a death knell from the public gallery, her red hair flying behind her as she approached the balcony edge, knuckles contracting and turning white as she clasped the rail. "You raped her, you bastard! You deserve to rot in hell!"

Any further diatribe was stifled by the groan which took her downwards into the arms of surrounding friends. Partington-Smith allowed himself a small smile as he left the dock to rejoin his brief and his family. Outside the courtroom, and in the fresh air which he had not expected to breathe again so soon, the young aristocrat faced a barrage of cameras and reporters on the steps of The Old Bailey. He was not allowed to answer any questions, as the Rolls Royce containing his parents pulled across the road and whisked him away.

Doreen Yates and her daughter, Jennifer, emerged some time later, on the arms of two friends, and with the prosecuting counsel beside them. Dennis Marks met them all, his face lined in concern.

"Mrs Yates, I'm so sorry. We had him." He turned to the daughter. "What happened to you in there, Jennifer?" She was not given the chance to reply. Doreen erupted once more.

"That smartarse barrister! All that stuff he brought up about her. That was years ago! Caught us all by surprise, it did. She never had a chance once he got going on that, and what about the eyewitness? Where did *she* get to?"

She was ushered away, with her daughter in tow, to a waiting taxi. As she was about to get in, a hand stayed her progress and Doreen turned to face a woman she had never seen before. Suddenly, her right hand was clasped by the stranger.

"He shouldn't be allowed to get away with that. There are other ways of obtaining justice." With that she was gone, and once inside the cab Doreen looked down at her hand where a neatly folded piece of paper had been planted. The wording was clear and straightforward – 'Call me', and it was followed by a number.

Completely oblivious to the scene which had just been played out, Marks turned to Roger Harobin, the prosecuting counsel, and shook his head in disbelief.

"What the devil went wrong in there? I thought we had him. She picked him out on the ID parade, and with his record it should have been a piece of cake."

"Inspector, you know as well as I do that it's never as straightforward as that. The DNA evidence was never disputed, your only independent witness failed to show up, and from that point on it was only her word against his. Yes, she picked him out of a line-up, but when defending counsel rattled her, she caved in. That kind of thing is enough to sway a jury, and the burden of proof is 'beyond reasonable doubt'. From the instant they brought up her past, I knew we were in trouble. We should have been made aware of it."

"His past record counts for nothing, then." It was a statement, not a question.

Both men were familiar with the criminal activities of Michael Partington-Smith, and the jail term from which he had recently been released. That information was never divulged to the jury during the trial, and their deliberations were based solely on what they saw and heard in the courtroom.

The evidence presented told the story of a party thrown by a friend of the accused, to which Jennifer Yates had been invited by a group from the place where she had only just started work. At twenty-two, and eager to fit in, she had readily agreed to the idea, and had freely indulged in the food and drink which was laid out in abundance. As the evening drew on, she was approached by a good-looking man of a similar age to herself and, flattered by his attentions, succumbed to the charm which he used upon her. That young man was Michael Partington-Smith; as he plied her with alcohol, her inhibitions dissolved and she became more and more amenable to his suggestions.

Jennifer Yates was no shrinking violet and, whilst sober, was not unaware of the dangers posed by strangers. This part of her past had been used by the defence counsel to rattle her composure and assurance in court, and had been instrumental in sullying her character in the eyes of the jury. As she slipped deeper into a state of inebriation that evening, Partington-Smith steered her upstairs to one of the numerous bedrooms in the house. Here she was completely at his mercy, and it was not until he had begun to remove some of her clothing that the reality of what was about to happen kicked in, and she began to resist.

Michael Partington-Smith was strong and fit, far stronger than Jennifer even when sober, and she stood little chance of fighting him off. Her struggle, ineffectual as it was, fuelled his passion, and he set about her with his fists. Her screams and pleas for mercy went unheard as the noise of the party downstairs drowned out any possibility of rescue. The rape was brutal, and he left her in the room some half an hour later in a state of severe distress, returning to waiting friends at the party below. He had been seen going back downstairs by a young woman emerging from the bathroom. She spotted the bloodstains on his shirt, and had initially come forward to testify to the fact. That she had failed to turn up on the day of the trial was the result of the financial muscle wielded by the

Partington-Smiths. She had been paid off, and was currently lying on a beach in Trinidad.

No-one had missed Jennifer, the group she had come with having moved on, and she was left alone to minister to her injured body and mind, as she redressed and made her way home.

Partington-Smith admitted having sex with Jennifer Yates that evening, thus rendering any DNA evidence irrelevant. He had, however, strenuously denied the use of any force before, during, or after the act, and the prosecution had been unable to shake his version of the events of that night. There had been no trace of blood on his hands, or the clothing into which he had changed, to substantiate a beating of any kind, something which Jennifer had stated was due to his wearing of gloves. This fact was ridiculed by the defence and, at that stage of the trial, raised a smile on the faces of a number of the jurors.

His alibi for the rest of the evening came in the form of a group of his friends who had seen him steer Jennifer up the stairs to the beginning of her ordeal. Their testimony had also proven to be unshakeable, and he was depicted as the innocent victim of a young woman giving herself freely to any man who came her way. From that point onwards the case began to collapse, as defence counsel relentlessly destroyed the young woman's credibility before a judge powerless to prevent it.

2

It had been three weeks since the trial, but Dennis Marks had been unable to put the case behind him. The absence of the key witness, Sandra Davies, had been the pivotal incident in securing the accused's acquittal, and she had apparently vanished without a trace. Peter Spencer chose that moment to enter the office, and knew in an instant from the look on the face of his boss that the case notes on the desk were not yet going to be consigned to records.

"Not letting this one go, are you, sir?" He sat down.

"Too right I'm not! That young thug got away with it just because his parents had the wherewithal to buy off our only witness. God knows where she went! Or for how much."

"No luck with his previous either."

"No. Pity the defence never tried to portray him as squeaky clean. If they had, our brief would have had the chance to attack his character. Too damn clever for his own good, that Jeremy Battersby. How he manages to sleep at night I can't imagine."

"No point in crying over spilt milk, then." Spencer sighed. "I see what you mean, though."

"It still grieves me that the little swine got away with it this time. He'd only been out of Wandsworth for three months after a two-year stretch for sexual assault. He got out in a year and a half, and now he's at it again."

"Any news on the girl? I mean, it can't have been easy for her."

"Last time I heard, no-one had seen her out since the trial. Christ knows how they're coping."

Marks' words were prophetic to say the least. Since the fateful day of Partington-Smith's acquittal, Jennifer Yates had not moved outside the confines of the family home on Southgate's Leigh Hunt Drive. She had, in that short space of time, become withdrawn and depressed. Doreen watched her like a hawk, but could not avoid leaving the house for essential purposes. It was on one of those trips that Jennifer took matters into her own hands. On her return,

Doreen found her daughter hanging from the banister – she had torn up a bedsheet and tied it around her neck.

Jennifer was the only daughter of a largely loveless marriage, Frank Yates having walked out before the girl had reached school age. Consequently, Doreen had been forced to bring up the girl alone. There were no grandparents, and life had been very hard. Hard, that is, until the lottery win which transformed their lives. Half a million had been more than enough to make them comfortable, and the future had all seemed to be so bright. They had moved from the two-up, two-down terrace into a four-bedroom house on Leigh Hunt Drive, and all their problems seemed to be behind them. Now this. She was on her way to the funeral parlour to make arrangements when she found the piece of paper in her coat pocket – the coat pocket where she had shoved it, and then forgot all about the woman outside The Old Bailey.

There it was. 'Call me... 369 1714' – a local number. Time for that later; she was going to be late.

Doreen Yates arrived at the office of Nelson & Nelson (Funeral Directors) on Crown Lane fifteen minutes later. The half mile walk from home gave her time to think through what she would do with the note which had been half-forgotten. Events were to render that option somewhat irrelevant as she stood before the board outside the premises and stared in surprise at the telephone number displayed upon it. Taking the slip of paper from the depths of her coat, she read out what was written on it...0208 369 1714.

"The same number." She said to herself, almost in a whisper.

"Mrs Yates?" The question came from a man in his fifties, getting out of the driver's side of a black hearse.

Doreen snapped out of the daydream brought on by the number, and turned to face the owner of the firm, Roger Nelson.

"It is Mrs Yates, isn't it?" He held out his hand in greeting. Doreen took it.

"Yes. Mr...?"

"Nelson, Roger Nelson. I believe we have an appointment."

Roger Nelson stood a shade over six feet, had warm, brown eyes, and a full head of steel grey hair. His upright posture bore the hallmark of a military man, and he had, indeed, served Queen and country in a variety of trouble spots in the world, achieving the rank of Major before retiring on a full pension. He had met and married his wife, Alessandra, some years earlier and they were partners in the thriving, if somewhat morbid, trade of funeral directors.

Rachel

Roger Nelson

Stepping into the reception area from a day of bright sunshine, Doreen was initially unaware of the female figure sitting at a desk in the corner of the room, but as her eyes adjusted to the comparative gloom, she stepped forward automatically to greet the woman she last saw on the day of the trial. A small, almost imperceptible, shake of the head from Alessandra Nelson halted her in her tracks. Roger, having turned to close the door, had been unaware of anything out of the ordinary, and now ushered Doreen into the room.

"Would you like some tea?" He smiled, and waved her towards a table and chairs.

The two of them discussed the arrangements for Jennifer's funeral over the next half hour, and at the conclusion of their meeting Nelson rose to leave.

"I'm terribly sorry to rush off, but I have a home call to make. My wife will sort out all the paperwork, if that's alright with you." He smiled once more and was gone, leaving the two women face to face for the first time in almost a month.

Alessandra Nelson rose from behind the desk where she carried out the administrative side of the business which she ran with her husband. At 45, she was ten years his junior, and exuded an air of calm efficiency. A brunette with shoulder length hair and pale blue eyes, she stood five feet seven to Doreen's five feet six. The smile was warm and welcoming, but once the pleasantries and the business side of the visit were over, her demeanour hardened. They were two women with much in common.

"The number on the piece of paper..." Doreen began.

"Is the same as ours. Yes, but I never expected to see you like this. Roger doesn't always keep me updated with appointments. He's a lovely man, but a little scatterbrained sometimes."

"So, what now? Why such a cryptic message?" Doreen frowned.

"Mrs Yates..."

"Doreen."

"Doreen. You shouldn't have suffered in the way that you did, and I was so sorry to hear about what happened to your daughter. The legal system may have let you down, but there are other ways." She waited for a response.

"What do you mean? How can this be put right? She's gone now; nothing can replace her, and he walks free." Doreen had begun to cry, and Alessandra was quick to move in.

"My point precisely. Why should that be? To all intents and purposes, Michael Partington-Smith is responsible for the death of your daughter. Why should he not pay for that?"

"I don't understand."

"Doreen." Alessandra took a deep breath. "I can arrange for things to turn very nasty for his family if, that is, you so wish."

"How?" Interest suddenly aroused, Doreen was now all ears, and ripe for the proposal which had been on Alessandra's mind some weeks earlier.

"There is an organisation - no, a society - which is dedicated to rectifying such miscarriages of justice, and all that will be needed from you is an agreement to take part. We, that is, it, can remove that man from society because, make no mistake, he will do it again unless he's stopped."

"How do you fit in with it?" She sat back, suddenly concerned for what she may be getting herself into. Alessandra sighed. It was now or never.

"Your situation is very similar to mine. The only difference is that my Wendy was only eight when a pervert took her away from me. We had a witness too. Unfortunately I didn't realise until the trial that the woman was an alcoholic, and the defence barrister made her look completely unreliable when it came to court. She was the only one who saw my baby taken, and the man who did it walked free."

"So what did you do?"

"I waited. I grieved. Then the grief turned to anger, and that changed into a determination to have my share of the justice that had been denied. I killed him. I waited one night until I saw him alone, and I killed him. That was *my* justice."

"You got away with it?" Doreen's interest dawned once again.

"Oh no. I waited for the police to come. I called and told them what I'd done. I wanted the whole world to know that he couldn't get away with what he did to my baby. They locked me away of course. Three years I served. You might think that's not long enough for taking a life, but the court was sympathetic. I still don't understand. I thought I'd be away for life."

"How does this affect me?" Her interest was now fully aroused.

"I can help. It'll have to be done secretly of course, and you'll have to join the Sisterhood. I started it when I got out of prison."

"Does your husband…?"

"Roger knows nothing of what goes on outside of the company. As far as he's concerned, our little gatherings are something in the way of a Women's Federation."

"What do you propose? I mean, your note…"

"Destroy it. There must be nothing to link you to what I have in mind. Come to the next meeting and I'll put the rest of the girls in the picture."

Doreen got up to leave, but then turned. Alessandra Nelson was smiling; smiling as if she knew what the next question was going to be.

"Sorry, Alessandra. I'm still not entirely clear. What *is* going to happen? I mean, what do you have in mind for Michael Partington-Smith?"

"Oh, I'm afraid I should have explained, and please call me Sandy. It's quite simple really - an eye for an eye, do you see? He took something away from you, and now he must be made to pay. He must die. We'll kill him. That will be your revenge for the suffering he inflicted on your Jennifer."

3

It was 6.30am when Marks' breakfast was interrupted by a call from his DI. Peter Spencer was not normally given to acts of sudden urgency, and that in itself had him out of the house in the space of a few minutes. He was at the eastern end of Broomfield Park in less than half an hour; Spencer and George Groves were already on the scene and standing outside a small tented area on Palmers Green. Uniformed officers were in the process of sealing off the immediate area.

"Alright, George, where's the fire?" Marks had become accustomed to some cryptic messages from the pathologist, but there were still occasions when the man's addiction to the crossword mentality caught him off guard.

"I told DI Spencer that you needed to see this right away." He grinned. "You didn't have to burst a blood vessel though. Don't want *you* on one of my tables."

The man's penchant for the macabre was well known throughout the Met, and both detectives had been on the receiving end on a number of occasions. However, the smile faded as the atmosphere returned to some state of normality. The three of them stepped inside the tent.

"I think you may well be acquainted with this one." He pulled back the sheet covering the body, and Marks let out a low whistle.

"That's…"

"Michael Partington-Smith, or what used to be the young gentleman. Had him at The Old Bailey only a few weeks back, didn't you?"

"A double charge of rape and actual bodily harm. Neither stuck and he walked free. Key witness let us down at the last minute." Marks moved closer. "What's *he* doing here?"

"No idea, but he's dead alright. More specifically, murdered." Groves pointed to a spot on the young man's neck.

"What's that?"

"Cause of death, Dennis. Puncture wound, entering here…" He turned the head to the right, "… exiting there," and then to the left.

"Can't be a gunshot injury."

"The exit wound's too clean and precise for that. A bullet would have made quite a mess of the other side of the head. No; this is small, five millimetres maximum. It pierced the carotid artery, and he literally bled to death." Groves waved his hand at the surrounding area of crimson grass.

"Any idea as to the kind of weapon we're looking for?"

"Something long and strong. Rigid enough to penetrate muscle and go right through the neck. A screwdriver would do it, but it would have to be thin, thinner than a normal one. You'll struggle to find one that would do this kind of job and still leave such a neat exit wound."

"Do you have a time yet?"

"Give me a chance. I won't know that until we get him back to base. He was out all night though – he's covered in dew."

Their conversation was halted prematurely by a radio call from a uniformed PC across the park at its western edge.

"Sir! We've found another body. It's up near Powys Lane."

"Alright, constable." He turned to Spencer. "Who found this one?"

"Chap out walking his dog this morning. He's over there." He nodded in the direction of a squad car where a middle-aged man was talking to another of the uniformed police.

"Okay, you make sure that they get all of the details." Marks turned to the pathologist. "George, let's go and see what's going on at the other end of the park."

Broomfield Park covers an area of over fifty acres from Powys Lane in the west to Palmers Green in the east. Marks and Groves were on the scene of the second discovery in a matter of minutes, to find that another tent was in the process of being erected around a body already covered by a sheet.

"Sergeant?" Marks addressed the senior officer present.

"Sir, this is exactly how we found him. No-one's touched a thing." He glanced at Groves, acutely aware of the dangers of moving a body before clearance had been given.

"Alright, we'll take it from here." He lifted the sheet, and stepped back in surprise.

"Friend of yours?" Groves put down his bag and moved in for a closer look.

"You could say that. This is Jeremy Battersby, and we now have a link to the body down there." He nodded in the direction from which they had just driven. "This was the chap who got our boy off the rape and assault charges a few weeks back. Now they both end up dead in the same place and at the same time."

"Let's leave the timing to me when I get them taken back to the lab, shall we? I'll carry out a preliminary examination, and we can get him moved. I'll get some more of my team down here to go over the entire area. You will make sure that it's *all* sealed off, won't you?"

The look on Marks' face told him all that he needed to know. It was a cheap shot really, and just the kind of banter which the DCI should have expected.

Back at the mortuary some hours later, George Groves had the two bodies side by side, and had commenced his autopsy on Michael Partington-Smith when Marks walked in with his DI.

"How's it going?"

"Well, I've only just begun, but there are one or two things which immediately grabbed my attention."

"Go on." Marks shook his head. Groves was good at this. He'd been watching too much television.

"Well, look at this wound. The precise nature of it puzzled me at first. A spontaneous attack would have been inaccurate at best. This, however, hit one of the major bleed points in the human body – the carotid artery."

"What's your point then, George?" The DCI sighed.

"Your killer knew exactly where to strike to cause maximum effect. Once the weapon had hit its target and had been removed, the man was as good as dead. He'd have no chance of stopping the bleeding by himself, and couldn't possibly have called for help."

"Why?" Marks frowned.

"The wound also punctured the windpipe. He'd be drowning in blood as well. Someone's done a really professional job here."

"So, we're looking for… what?" Peter Spencer had been taking notes up to this point, but joined in the discussion.

"Or who." The pathologist 'grew' inches as he delivered what he considered to be his *coup de grace*. "Someone with a detailed knowledge of human anatomy. A doctor or a nurse, perhaps. This was carried out with a precision that no ordinary killer would possess."

"Alright, what about the other one – Jeremy Battersby?"

There, on the second slab, was the lifeless form of the former Queen's Counsel, Jeremy Battersby, who had been instrumental in destroying Jennifer Yates's testimony in court. The very man who had brought aspects of her earlier years to the attention of the jury, and thus seriously damaged her credibility in their eyes. Marks took a closer look. The wounds were almost identical and, according to Groves, he too had bled out.

"Any guess at the time of death?"

"Well, based on liver temperature, and I've done them both, I say that the two of them were killed between eleven and midnight last night."

"What, both? At the same time?"

"I'd say so. You could be looking for different killers."

"Are you linking these two bodies?"

"Come on, Dennis. I'm the pathologist, I just present the facts and make suggestions. You're the detective; it's up to you to draw any inferences. All I can tell you is that the killings bear a remarkable similarity to each other. Beyond that is out of my remit. Sorry."

"Thanks very much, George." Marks smiled ruefully. He should have expected no less. "It's strange, though, that these two should turn up there, at the same time, and with comparable wounds."

"I'll give you that, Dennis, and you're probably looking for a similar weapon as well."

Back upstairs, Marks and his DI continued to mull over the preliminary findings of the pathologist. Two bodies, linked by a case dismissed three weeks earlier, and which now turned up at the same location, at the same time, on the same evening.

"I think, Peter, that we need to pay a call on Doreen Yates. There's something decidedly odd about this whole thing, and her family is the only link I can come up with for our two corpses downstairs."

"There is something else, sir."

"What's that?" In the time that they had worked together, Marks had grown to trust the instincts of his young detective, who had developed a keen sense of hunch for his years.

"Since the trial, and bearing in mind your interest in this case, I've been doing some digging around and I've come up with a couple of interesting things."

Full Marks

"Go on."

"Well, Jennifer Yates's funeral was a week last Saturday, and as it was my day off, I decided to go along. I know, 'shame I hadn't something better to do with my time' and yes, I did get some flack from the missus as well, but I wondered if there could be anyone else there who might seem out of place."

"And was there?"

"This is where it gets a bit tenuous. During my digging around, I came across a kind of organisation in the area, known as the Southgate Sisterhood. They put themselves out as a sort of support group for women; women like Doreen Yates who've suffered at the hands of violent men."

Peter Spencer was acutely aware of the shakiness of the argument that he was about to propose, but carried on with it anyway. Marks had done no less during the time that they had worked together.

"I traced the group back to its meeting place, and they tend to get together regularly each month or so. They meet up at the home of a woman by the name of Alessandra Nelson. Alessandra Nelson is the other half of Nelson & Nelson, Funeral Directors."

"Nothing wrong with that, Peter." Marks was struggling to see where Spencer was going with this.

"Yes, but if I were also to tell you that Alessandra Nelson has a police record, would that arouse your interest?"

"Maybe… what was it for?"

"Murder. She killed the man acquitted of abducting, raping, and killing her eight year-old daughter. He got off because a key witness let the prosecution case down. Sound familiar?"

"Alright. There are similarities, I'll grant you that, but what is there that links the two women beyond what you've just said?"

"The guy she killed was Donald Swinson."

"My God!" Marks' eyes widened at the disclosure.

"Yes, sir. Her name then was Sandra Benway. You were the arresting officer on the case, but Swinson got off when your key witness, June Blount, proved unreliable."

"I remember now. That must have been twenty years ago. Blount was a recovering alcoholic. She'd been clean for almost a year, and then inexplicably went back on the booze the week before the trial. We suspected that someone had got to her, but couldn't prove it. The case collapsed. Don Mullard was running the show at the time, but when it fell apart, the details of what had been done to that little girl got to him. He never came back to work."

"No." Spencer continued. "His death was attributed to a suicide by the coroner, brought on by depression. The thing is, Doreen Yates has been seen at the home of Alessandra Nelson, and one of those occasions was at the latest meeting of the support group. There are a number of ex-cons amongst the members as well."

"So, what are you suggesting? A society which takes the law into its own hands when it feels like it?"

Spencer never got the chance to answer as Marks' phone rang out, and the voice on the other end had them down in George Groves' lab within minutes.

"You've got something, George?"

"Maybe. Remember when I said that the murder weapon would have to be something strong and thin?"

"Yes, so what?"

"How does a knitting needle make you feel?" Groves pulled the bodies of the two victims from the range of cold storage drawers.

"A what?"

"Five millimetre, number six, steel. Here, take a look." He produced an implement similar to the one he had just described, and pulled back the sheet covering the body of Michael Partington-Smith.

Inserting the knitting needle into the right hand side of the young man's neck, it was a perfect fit, and exited smoothly from the opposite side. He repeated the operation on the lawyer, Jeremy Battersby, with the same result.

"I'll admit it's a leap of logic…"

"No, it's perfect." Spencer chipped in. "Think about what I said upstairs, sir. How unlikely would it be that anyone could believe a group of women capable of killing anyway, and with a knitting needle as well."

"You have a theory?" Groves looked, nonplussed, from Spencer to Marks and back. "Thought I was the one with the off-the-wall ideas."

Marks stood for a moment, trying to rationalise what his DI and the pathologist had both come up with. He had no alternative explanation and, outrageous as it sounded, Peter Spencer's proposition was the only working theory available. He shook his head. They had considered a doctor or a nurse as the professional having sufficient anatomical knowledge, but a funeral director or his staff would also present a good even bet.

"Alright then. Peter, cancel the trip to Doreen Yates; let's keep her for later. I think it's time we took a look at Alessandra Nelson."

4

Alessandra Nelson had come to Southgate with her husband, Brian Benway, when she was twenty. They had lived in Widnes with her parents, but when he was made redundant in 1982 they sought a better future and a fresh start. Their daughter, Wendy, had been on her way home from school when she was taken from the street of the London borough of Southgate by a man, initially identified as Donald Swinson, driving a white van. The tragedy of the little girl's murder split the couple up, and she later met and married Roger Nelson.

The Nelsons had lived in the detached house adjacent to the business since their marriage, and although he was aware of the background to her earlier life, Alessandra's husband had no idea of her involvement in the darker side of the Southgate Sisterhood's activities. She had made it her intention to keep it that way.

The smile which greeted Marks' ringing of the doorbell was genuine enough, and she had always taken great care to extend the same hospitality to any stranger who came to the door. The displaying of police ID cards had no effect on her demeanour at all – in fact it was quite the opposite.

"Good morning, Mrs Nelson. I'm Detective Chief Inspector Marks, and this is my DI, Peter Spencer."

"How quaint. Marks and Spencer. I'll bet you get some leg-pulling about that." She beckoned them inside as they exchanged glances.

"No, Mrs Nelson, I don't believe we do." Marks couldn't disguise the feeling that she was far too much at ease.

"Now then, Chief Inspector, what can I do for you? I don't think I have any unpaid parking tickets." Another smile, almost as if she knew the game and was certain that he was onto a loser.

Marks wondered whether she recognised him. It was a long time ago when their paths first crossed, and it had been Don Mullard leading the investigation into the death of her daughter. He decided to keep that quiet for the moment.

"No, Mrs Nelson, nothing so trivial, I'm afraid. We're looking into the deaths of two people in the area." He opened his notebook.

"Can't help you there. I have no idea who the two gentlemen were."

Marks stopped. No mention had been made of the sex of the victims – how could she possibly have known that? There had been nothing in the press except for the revelation that two bodies had been discovered in Broomfield Park. He looked up at Alessandra, who had quickly realised the hole that she was descending into. Her correction was instantaneous.

"My husband had been driving down Alderman's Hill and someone told him about the discovery."

"I see. He will, of course, confirm your version of events?" His gaze returned to the notebook, but Peter Spencer was watching her every move.

"Yes, but unfortunately he's out at the moment." She held her breath for the next question. It was not long in coming.

"Do you know a woman by the name of Doreen Yates?" Their eyes met once more.

"Doreen Yates..." She frowned, more in hope that this was an easier line of questioning than anything else. "Ah, yes. She was the one whose daughter was... oh dear..."

"Yes, Jennifer Yates took her own life about a month after the trial. Tell me, how did you make Mrs Yates's acquaintance?"

Alessandra Nelson had been aware that Marks was leading the case against Michael Partington-Smith, and it was more than likely that she had been seen talking to the woman as she got into her cab that day. She decided to tread carefully.

"I approached her outside The Old Bailey and gave her a slip of paper with our organisation's contact details. I told her that we may be able to help her and her daughter."

"Exactly how, Mrs Nelson?" Marks had stopped writing, and now looked into her eyes for any hint of a lie.

"We're a support group for battered wives and suchlike. You'd be amazed at how many there are inside Holloway Prison. Women, just like I was, failed by the justice system and punished when they took out their own revenge."

"So, how many of your group are ex-cons?"

"Inspector, we don't keep membership lists. The women come and go as they please. Sometimes they don't return after a single visit. I can't remember their names."

"I see. Well, I think that'll be all for now. If there is anything that you remember, please feel free to give us a call." The DCI handed over his card.

He smiled. It was a cold, hard smile, and the point was not wasted on Alessandra Nelson. She was not out of the woods yet, and was quite aware of Marks' reputation. Whether he remembered their previous encounter she was not certain.

Back at the station, the two detectives sat comparing notes of the meeting which had just taken place. Alessandra Nelson was certainly a cool customer, and apart from the one slip, had covered her story extremely well. There would be no point in speaking to her husband, as Marks assumed that he would have been in on whatever she had been involved in, and would corroborate her version of events. Peter Spencer had gone to the canteen and now returned with two coffees and a smile on his face.

"Alright, stop looking like the cat that got the cream. What is it?"

"Remember when we were coming back in the car, and you asked what could possibly have got the two men out in the same place at the same time?"

"Yes. Well, what is it?" The smug look on his DI's face was reminiscent of his own when he was the same rank.

"I've been keeping an ear open for anyone who might be coming back into the country after, shall we say, a holiday abroad." Spencer waved a slip of paper in front of his boss.

"Give it here." Marks took the note, and his eyes widened in surprise. "Sandra Davies?"

"The very same. Came through immigration a week before our boys were found dead. Now why would she come back when she knows that we'd be on the lookout for her?"

"Only one reason I'd take the risk. Whatever the Partington-Smiths paid her must have run out. My God! She's come back for more to keep quiet."

"That's what I thought, sir, but she's gone to ground. No trace for the past week or so. Mind you, if she was trying to blackmail Michael Partington-Smith, wouldn't it be more likely that she'd be the one we'd have found? And what reason would she have for wanting either of those two dead?"

Marks shook his head and took a long pull from his mug. There was no doubt that Sandra Davies would have been taking a considerable risk if she had, in fact, returned and attempted to extort more money from Partington-Smith. But why kill him? And what possible motive could she have for wanting the QC dead as well?

Full Marks

A call from the desk sergeant had the two of them heading for the door.

"Sir, we have reports of a body at the Muswell Hill golf club. Mr Groves says to tell you he's already on his way."

The young woman had been strangled. That much was clear from the marks around her neck. George Groves was in the middle of his preliminary examination when the two detectives arrived. Sandra Davies had lain covered by a layer of sand in the bunker at the edge of the fifth green, adjacent to Alexandra Road. Heavy rain during the previous week had caused the postponement of any activity on the course, and the head greenkeeper had discovered her as he carried out a survey of conditions prior to reopening.

"George?"

Groves stood up from his squatting position over the body. It would take a while to clean her up and draw any firm conclusions as to her fate but, as usual, he had pulled sufficient forensics at this stage to give Marks something to begin with.

"I've taken some scrapings from under her fingernails. Looks like skin to me, so we should be able to get a DNA profile. I can tell you that she wasn't killed here, though. She put up a struggle, and there isn't enough of a disturbance in the immediate area to make me believe that it happened here. This was a body dump."

"Timing?" Marks had to ask, and always got the same reply.

"Not at this stage. She's been outdoors for a while though, and the road over there would have been a perfect place to stop a car, make the drop and leave quickly, even allowing for the length of time it would have taken to bury her. Might be worth your while checking the membership list at the clubhouse; the person doing this would have needed to know the best time to carry it out, and also the layout of the course."

"Alright, George, I'll catch up with you later at the lab." He turned to Spencer. "Come on, Peter, let's talk to the greenkeeper and track down the club secretary."

The greenkeeper, Peter Lucas, could tell them no more than he had already given in his statement to the uniformed officers. That area of the course lay right at its perimeter, and was easily accessible from Alexandra Road. Had it not been for the rain, the body might have been discovered earlier, but it had been buried close to the edge of one of the sand traps around the fifth green. Most shots landing there inevitably ended up in the centre, so it could have lain relatively undisturbed for a while longer. The club secretary, William Blythe, was less forthcoming.

"I'm afraid I cannot release a list of members to you, Chief Inspector. We are covered by the Data Protection Act, and our subscribers are entitled to that level of privacy."

"Mr Blythe." Marks' frustration was evident from his tone of voice. "May I remind you that a body has been found on your golf course, and that we are in the middle of a murder inquiry?"

"That is your concern, not mine." Blythe bristled at the officialdom which he saw as a challenge to his authority. "We will make the course available to you and your officers, but without a court order our records must remain private."

Back in the car, Marks instructed Peter Spencer to process an application for the seizure of the golf club records, whilst he followed up the discovery of the body of Sandra Davies with George Groves. He was in the pathologist's lab within half an hour.

"News?" He was straight to the point, and Groves held up a finger, beckoning him over to a table where the clothing of the late Sandra Davies was being examined by another member of his staff.

"She was killed in relative comfort, Dennis." Groves had become a master of the oblique statement, and over the years it had been something of a challenge for the DCI to work out.

"You've really lost me this time, George."

"Look here." He picked up a pair of shoes. "See the fibres trapped in the heel? They're Axminster, and very high quality as well. You won't find carpet like that on the lounge floor of too many houses around here, and there'd be a limited number of outlets selling it."

"Alright, so what are we looking for, someone with enough money not to need to kill for it, but who does so anyway?"

"Or…" Groves raised a finger, "someone who is being blackmailed, and who decides that enough is enough. Know anyone like that?"

"Hold on, she was our key witness and vanished. We suspected that the Partington-Smiths may have bought her off. Maybe she came back for more from the father and mother and they, or he, decided to end it once and for all."

"Maybe, and there's also this. It was in her hand." Groves handed Marks a plastic evidence bag containing a button. "It's also high quality, and probably off the kind of jacket that a member of a golf club would wear. Here, I've pulled off a list of suppliers using that very one."

"You, mate, are a star."

"Yes, I know. I'll need that back when you've been to see… you know…"

"Thanks, George, I know exactly where our next call will be. As soon as Peter gets back, we're off to that golf club again, and if a certain name turns up on the membership list, I think Miss Davies' killer will be safely in the net."

5

With a warrant secured, Marks' investigation into the golf club membership list proved highly fruitful. There, halfway down the second page was the name of Donald Partington-Smith, together with home address and telephone number.

"I'll need a copy of this, please, Mr Blythe." Marks handed the papers over with a satisfied smile on his face. "Oh, and could you let me have sight of one of the blazers that your members use?"

The button supplied by George Groves was a perfect match to those on the coat which the secretary himself wore and, now armed with a mounting pile of evidence, Marks was off to the home of the parents of Michael Partington-Smith.

Initially, Donald Partington-Smith denied any knowledge of Sandra Davies, and Marks went along with the man's statements far enough to allow him to dig a hole from which it was going to be impossible to escape.

"That's a rather nasty looking scratch on your face, sir. Mind telling me how you came by it?"

"Ah... yes, I did it whilst shaving. Rather careless of me." Partington-Smith fingered the mark on his right cheek.

"Indeed. Well, I have another theory. You see, we recovered this from the scene of a murder today, and it matches those from the blazers worn by members of your golf club. Would you mind if I took a look at yours? You are a member of Muswell Hill, aren't you?"

Once faced with the button found in the hand of the dead girl, however, Partington-Smith capitulated.

"She came here asking for more money, Chief Inspector. The filthy little gold-digger. Yes, we paid her off so that Michael would escape jail. He wouldn't have survived another term in one of those hell-holes. I tried to reason with her, but she wouldn't budge. Stood there sneering at us – who did she think she was? We struggled and she scratched me. I had my hands around her neck, and before I knew what I was doing, she was on the floor, and no longer moving. I tried to resuscitate her, but it was too late."

"So you killed her… just like that. No thought for the fact that she had a life."

"What was I *supposed* to do? Keep fuelling her greed? She would only have come back again."

Marks shook his head. There was nothing more to do. The man had admitted the murder, and with DNA samples certain to match those found under Sandra Davies' fingernails, a conviction would be a formality. With his son gone, there was probably very little meaning to the rest of his life anyway.

With one murder investigation now closed, there did remain the matter of the other two corpses still in Groves' refrigerated store, and they were currently no closer to solving those killings than they had been at the start. His initial thoughts of Sandra Davies luring both men to their deaths now seemed a remote theory, and he was back to the only link which he had at the beginning – that of Doreen Yates to Alessandra Nelson. The postponed visit to Mrs Yates now became his number one priority.

The news of the killings of both Michael Partington-Smith and Jeremy Battersby had rattled the already fragile composure of Doreen Yates. Her initial show of outrage in the courtroom had subsided prior to the suicide of her daughter, and its re-ignition had stalled when the full realisation of what Alessandra Nelson had said came to pass. She had spent days churning the consequences over and over in her mind, and was convinced that there could, at any moment, be squads of police beating down her front door. There was only one thing to do - she put on her coat and made for the Nelson home.

"Doreen. This is unexpected. Come in." Alessandra looked up and down the street as she ushered the anxious form of Doreen Yates into the hallway.

"Are you alone? I mean, can we speak freely?"

"Of course. Roger is out playing golf at the Muswell Hill course. He won't be back for ages."

"Look, when you said that Michael Partington-Smith should pay for what he did, I never took you seriously when you said he had to die. Now there are two bodies that the police have found, and the other one was his lawyer."

"Calm down, and stop worrying. There isn't a thing that they can use to tie those two in to either of us. I made certain of that."

"How? How could you possibly get rid of all the evidence? I mean, there would have been blood all over the place, wouldn't there?"

"Look, you have a motive for killing him, but no opportunity. I have neither, and none of the members of our little group can be placed at the scene at the time that the killings happened. The police have no weapon, and they probably haven't a clue what it was that was used anyway."

Roger Nelson chose that precise moment to return from an abortive attempt to avail himself of a walk with friends whilst sinking a few golf balls. He was in an excited mood, and after stowing his clubs in the store cupboard under the stairs, came into the lounge and poured himself a scotch. He had been unaware of Doreen's presence, but smiled a greeting as he turned to face her.

"Mrs Yates. So nice to see you. Not here on business, are you?" He laughed at his own sense of the macabre.

Doreen hesitated, unsure of how to reply, bearing in mind the conversation which had been taking place not moments before. Alessandra stepped into the breach.

"Doreen just called in to ask about the next meeting of our little group, dear. Didn't you, Doreen?"

Doreen nodded nervously. With no other way out of a potentially awkward situation, she was compelled to follow the lead. She had no need to be concerned – Roger was full of the news which had come out of the secretary's office at the golf club. He sat down with his second whisky and told the two women of the events of the day. Unconcerned at the apparently anxious state of their visitor, he ploughed on with the tale of the discovery of a body near to one of the greens, relating the indignant manner of William Blythe when the police returned with some official piece of paper and took away a set of records relating to the club membership. He had, he said, overheard the mention of a name.

"What the devil was it, now?" He rubbed his chin and frowned. "Parsons… Parton… Patten… no, Partington. It was that Partington-Smith fellow. Thinks he owns the damned club. Wasn't it his son who was involved in that rape case malarkey at the Old Bailey?"

"Couldn't possibly say, dear. Are you dining out tonight, or shall we have dinner at home?" Alessandra's attempt to steer the conversation into calmer waters appeared to succeed.

"Might as well stay in. I say, Mrs Yates, care to join us? I'll open a bottle of Chateau Neuf du Pape."

"No! Thank you… er… I have some things that I need to do. I'm sorry to be abrupt but I really do have to be going."

"Damn shame. Well if you must, you must." He turned to his wife. "Going up to change, Sandy dear."

He was gone, and Doreen Yates breathed a sigh of relief. The news of another killing only served to heighten her already fragile state, and Alessandra knew that she would have her work cut out to stabilise the woman if she were to be of any use at all to the aims of the group. Her turn would come to repay the debt which she had incurred, and there was already a target in mind when the time came.

"Doreen. Go home and stay there. Just carry on as if nothing has happened. The police may wish to interview you because of your connection to Michael Partington-Smith through the case. That's all they have; they can't link you to the killing because you weren't there, were you? You did go out that night as I told you to, didn't you?"

"Yes. Yes, I did. I was at the cinema with Rosemary, a friend, and I did what you told me to do. The chap at the ticket office will remember me because I made a fuss about losing my purse."

"Good. That gives you a clear alibi for the entire evening. Did you go straight home afterwards?"

"No. Rosemary suggested a meal, so we went to a little Italian restaurant in Southgate. I used to go there with Jennifer, so the manager knows me."

"Even better! Just tell the police that if they call, and they may not even bother. Just be ready, and stay calm. You have nothing to worry about. Let me take care of everything else."

With the door now closed behind the retreating form of Doreen Yates, Alessandra had the seeds of a doubt about the plan that she was about to set in motion. A plan that would wreak full vengeance on those who had remained untouched by the tragedy of her little Wendy. Then, and only then, would she be satisfied that her little girl would be able to rest in peace, and of course there would be nothing to link the unfortunate Doreen back to her, beyond her attendance at the innocent-sounding Southgate Sisterhood.

6

Marsha Tully had made a point of frequenting the White Hart on Chase Side for more than a month. Just around the corner from Southgate tube station, it was easily accessible from her home in Langford Crescent near the terminus of the Piccadilly Line in Cockfosters. It was also the local of Daniel Emmanuel.

Emmanuel was a serial wife-beater, and had been in and out of Wandsworth several times over the past few years. His convictions were not for offences of a domestic nature - his wife Emily was far too scared to involve the police in that. They had consisted of burglary and assault, the second of which he practiced with regularity on his family to varying degrees. The last of the punchbag sessions had consigned her to hospital for a period of six weeks while the wounds healed, and despite concerted pressure from Social Services, she had refused to make any form of complaint.

Tully had been in Holloway at the same time as Alessandra Nelson, and had quickly become fascinated by the woman's outlook with respect to the lack of justice for those women suffering at the brutality of their partners. The small group which surrounded the then Sandra Benway quickly fell in with her philosophy of dealing out retribution once they were outside the confines of the women's prison. Contact details were secretly exchanged and, once freed at the end of their respective sentences, they all met up once more.

Tonight was intended to be the last time that Danny Emmanuel would ever contemplate another assault against either his wife or his family. That Marsha was known to him made the revenge which was about to be inflicted all that much sweeter. Emmanuel, for his part, saw her as simply one more piece of skirt to fuel his inflated ego.

"You on yer own tonight, babe?" He swaggered up to her end of the bar, eyeing her lithe, scantily-clad body with a greed which came directly from an overactive libido.

"Could be." It was hard to disguise the revulsion that she felt, but success tonight depended heavily upon her ability to at least act the part which he expected her to play.

"Yeah, okay, here's how it's goin' down." He smiled, cupping her chin in his hand as he leaned in. "Me an' you's gonna have a little fun, an' if you're really lucky, I might let you see me again."

"Suits me. Anywhere special in mind?" She could feel the bile rising in her throat as his other hand caressed the top of her leg.

"Let's go, an' I'll show you exactly what Danny can do for a lucky girl like you." He grabbed her by the hand and led the way to the door. Not a head had turned in the entire room – a fact which she believed would weigh heavily in her favour after the act which was about to be performed.

Outside the pub, they left The Bourne and entered Grovelands Park from Queen Elizabeth's Drive. Emmanuel led her to a small stand of trees close to the boating lake, and pinned her roughly to the trunk of one in the centre of the cluster. The leer on his face set the hackles rising at the back of her neck. No, not yet; she had to be prepared. A false move at this stage could ruin the entire plan.

His large hands were all over her as she squirmed and giggled under his rough caresses. Once free of the grip around her arms, all thoughts for her own safety were gone, and she reached inside the right leg of the knee-length black leather boot which hid the weapon.

"You filthy bastard!" Her whispered insult went almost unheard as he worked to remove what clothing she was wearing. He never saw the needle as it rose to puncture the left side of his neck.

Alessandra's training had been precise. All members of the Sisterhood were instructed carefully as to the exact point of entry which would cause maximum damage with minimum effort, and Marsha's aim was almost perfect. Almost, but not quite.

"What you done, woman!?" He screamed, wrenching himself free from her clutches, and preventing the removal of the knitting needle, an action which would have instigated a flow of blood so rapid as to have him dead in minutes.

"You're a dead man!" She had misread the situation, and was now retreating without finishing the job. Panic had set in; it was not supposed to have ended like this. She had to get away.

Emmanuel, far from being able to pursue her fast-disappearing form, turned back to the main road in search of help. He collapsed in front of an approaching motorist on The Bourne, and was soon surrounded by a growing crowd of onlookers. Within half an hour he was in the Accident and Emergency department of the Barnet General Hospital, the needle still where Marsha had inserted it.

The call to Dennis Marks came from the duty sergeant, and he was at the reception desk of the A & E with George Groves at his side within the hour. They were kept waiting for a further half hour until the surgeon was located.

"No Spencer?" Groves looked around for the DI.

"Peter's up north for a few days doing some digging around. The governor at Holloway is a friend of mine, and we managed to get our hands on a list of Sandra Benway's little group whilst she was on the inside. He's checking out the last known addresses of some of them who came out around the same time as she did." His attention was suddenly drawn to the end of the corridor. "Ah, looks like we could be in luck."

"DCI Marks? Roger Bream." Roger Bream, the surgeon, stood over six feet and towered over him. "You're here about Mr Emmanuel, I understand."

"Yes. When will I be able to question him?"

"You won't, I'm afraid. He lost too much blood and there was nothing we could do. The needle initially staunched the flow, and it was touch and go for a while, but in the end we were too late to save him."

"Did he say anything before... you know?"

"I'm sorry, Chief Inspector." He shook his head. "Your man was unconscious all of the time he was here."

"Do you have the weapon?"

"Yes, here." He produced a plastic bag. "No-one apart from me has touched it, and I was wearing gloves. I assume you'll want it for forensic testing."

"Mr Bream, I'm George Groves, Home Office pathologist. Can I see Mr Emmanuel to take a look at his hands?"

"Of course. We bagged both of them anticipating your request, and I did notice something under his fingernails. If you'll both follow me, I'll take you to him." He turned as they moved off.

"That's a real shame." Marks said as they walked away. There was something in the surgeon's manner which didn't quite fit, and Emmanuel's death seemed all too convenient.

As he watched Marks and Groves leave the hospital, Roger Bream wiped the metaphorical sweat from his brow. There was all to lose by letting Emmanuel talk to the police after the cash he'd been making from their arrangement. He'd been able to cover up the missing stocks of diamorphine, but an investigation into the young man's affairs may well have revealed everything. The concealment of the missing drugs had been very skilfully carried out, and no-one at the hospital would question his notes after the *unexpected* rupture of the carotid artery. There was nothing that Marks would be able to do now to prevent disposal of the body in the normal manner.

Back at the lab, the DCI paced up and down as Groves processed the needle and the samples of skin and hair which he had taken from Danny Emmanuel. The hair had been recovered from his right fist, and it was clear that a struggle had taken place during the attack.

"Here's the DNA profile. Whoever did this will have quite a mark across the skin somewhere, and it matches the results from the hair. You're looking for a single attacker. I also managed to pull a partial print from the end of the needle, so I reckon you ought to be able to identify whoever did this if they came out of jail recently."

"I'll cross-check them with the paperwork I got from Holloway. If this ties in with one of Alessandra Nelson's little group, we could be well on the way to finding our Broomfield Park killers."

7

Marsha Tully had panicked. For someone who had served jail time, she should have been able to cope with the task set for her by Alessandra Nelson.

"Just isolate him, and once he's distracted shove the needle right through his neck. Aim for the carotid like I showed you, and you should be able to take out the trachea as well."

The words had seemed so straightforward when Alessandra had been showing her what to do, but once it came down to the time and the place, things just seemed to move so fast, and there was no chance to be as precise as she had been instructed. Danny Emmanuel had fought back in a way that she had not been prepared for.

"Don't worry about him." Alessandra had said. "He'll grab for the needle in his throat, and won't have time to be concerned about you. Just make sure you get to it first, pull the thing out and run like hell. He'll bleed to death in minutes and you'll be away."

Alright, Marsha got the needle in there, but it failed to penetrate all the way through to the other side of the man's neck. He grabbed for her instead of the weapon, and had her by the hair. It was only the kick to the groin which finally freed her from his grasp. The needle remained where she had planted it. The darkness covered her escape and she made it home on foot without being seen. The bloodstained clothing was burned once she had changed, but the fact remained that she had left evidence back at the scene which would surely bring the law knocking at her door pretty soon. She needed help, and Alessandra was the only person she could think of.

"Marsha!" Alessandra pulled Tully inside the door, looked up and down the street, and closed it. "What are *you* doing here? Have you forgotten what we agreed?"

"I didn't know where to go. He fought back and grabbed me by the hair. I …"

"The needle! Where's the needle?"

"I couldn't get it out again. He…"

"What? You fool! That thing will have your fingerprints on it, and they'll trace you through your prison record. My God! They'll track you down here. What have you done?"

"I'm sorry. I didn't know where to go."

"Your clothes. What did you do with the clothes you were wearing? They'll have blood on them."

"I burned them before I came here. Alessandra, you've got to help me."

"Where did you leave him?"

"Grovelands Park. He was heading back to the road. I ran in the opposite direction."

"Alright. Look, you can't stay here. He'll probably be at the Barnet Hospital. Go home, pack a bag and leave London. Here, take this to tide you over." Alessandra gave her a wad of money from her handbag, opened the door and pushed her back out into the night.

This put an entirely fresh complexion on things. None of those charged with the tasks that she had given out were to contact her under any circumstances. Success was always assumed from the instructions given out, but any failures were to be treated as precisely that. The group members were to disappear back into their ordinary lives, and nothing should have been left at any of the scenes which could link anyone to her.

"Damnation!" Alessandra thumped the hallway wall in frustration. Her husband chose that exact moment to make an entrance.

"You alright, old thing?" Roger had the oddest turn of phrase at times, and it usually brought a smile to her face. This was not one of those times, and she erupted.

"No, I'm not! Why can't people just do as they're told, instead of…" She stopped, now aware that her husband was staring at her in complete surprise. He had never seen her like this before.

"Steady on. What on earth's got into you?"

"You wouldn't understand. I have to go out." She put on her coat and left.

Roger frowned. He had been aware, unbeknown to Alessandra, of his wife's outside interests for quite some time, but had kept his own counsel at the types of women coming to and going from their home. It had started to make him uncomfortable, and the appearance of Doreen Yates, shortly after a court case involving her now deceased daughter, had led him to make a number of enquiries following the closure of the golf course. Those enquiries had brought him back to the discovery of the bodies in Broomfield Park, and the identities of the two men. He decided to follow his wife.

Alessandra's course took her in the direction of Leigh Hunt Drive, and the home of Doreen Yates. Now that there was a clear possibility that the Sisterhood's cover had been blown by Marsha Tully's clumsiness, it was important that she, like Weston, be persuaded to disappear. Focussed on the place of her destination, she was completely unaware of the figure trailing her at a distance of some fifty yards.

"Alessandra." Doreen Yates was taken aback by the appearance at her door so late in the evening. "Will you come inside?"

"No. I have no time. Look, there's been the most awful cock-up, and you have to leave London. Take this and leave town. We're all compromised now, and if you don't get out the police will have the lot of us locked up in no time."

A similar wad of cash changed hands together with a slim manila file, and she turned to leave. Roger had been standing, concealed, at the bottom of the pathway and she almost caught him by surprise, but Doreen halted the initial progress.

"How long for? I mean, is this permanent? What's happened?"

"No time to explain. Just do as I've said." She was gone, and having allowed her to pass, Roger emerged from his hiding place and stood, dumbstruck in the darkness.

It was now clear to him that illegal activities of a serious nature had been going on right under his nose. Their years of apparently blissful marriage were now left in some disarray, and he decided to confront Alessandra with what he had seen and heard as soon as he arrived back home.

8

"So, what did you find out?"

Peter Spencer had returned from his three day trip up north, and was now updating his boss with the results of his trawl through the records in a number of the county police forces.

"You were right. Three cases. Two in Yorkshire and one in Manchester. These women…" He dropped the Holloway Prison files on the table, "were released a couple of weeks before three unsolved murders. One in Leeds, another in York, and the last one in Manchester's Moss Side."

"Any connection to our current bodies?"

"They all served time with Sandra Benway, and the victims were three men released from jail after serving terms for a range of sexual offences."

"Addresses?"

"There." Spencer pointed to a separate file containing up-to-date personal details. "We can pick them up at any time once warrants have been issued. There's enough to arrest them all on suspicion, and we can then move in on Alessandra Nelson."

"Alright. Get on with that, and make sure that we have them down here by the end of tomorrow. I'm off to pay a call on the Nelsons. It's time we rattled a few chains in that direction."

Leaving his DI to arrange the necessary paperwork to tighten the net around the now sinister looking Southgate Sisterhood, Marks was at the door of Roger and Alessandra Nelson within the hour. The blood on the doorknob had him reaching for a pair of latex gloves from the inside pocket of his coat. Repeated knocking failed to elicit an answer, and taking care not to smudge the stain he stepped carefully inside. Roger Nelson was lying at the bottom of the stairs, his head turned at an unusual angle. Even to Marks' untrained eye, it was clear that his neck was broken, and that he had been dead for some time. There was no sign of his wife and, summoning backup and forensics, he carried on with a preliminary search of the house.

Nothing in the downstairs area caught the DCI's attention, but there were clear signs of a struggle on the landing at the top of the stairs. Several items had been disturbed, and large pieces of broken pottery littered the area. Looking at the body of the funeral director once more, it was fairly clear that death had been caused by the fall and not as a result of any injuries inflicted prior to its happening. That, however, was for the pathologist to determine, and George Groves chose that exact moment to put in an appearance.

"Looks fairly straightforward to me. Broken neck…" He looked up the stairs. "…marks on the wall where the head probably made initial impact on the way down, and this pool of blood on the bottom tread. Did he fall, or was he pushed?"

"Very funny, George. Boot's on the other foot now, is it?"

"Come on, Dennis. Makes a change for me to hassle you for an opinion. Looks like your boys are here at last." He nodded beyond the open door towards a squad of uniformed figures on their way up the path.

"Right." Marks gathered them together. "I want this place taken apart. Anything out of the ordinary, you shout for me straight away. Work in pairs and make sure that you don't miss anything."

"Sir." Peter Spencer appeared at the door. "Yorkshire and Manchester police will pick up our three suspects first thing tomorrow. Did you know that the Nelsons' car is missing?"

"No. Have we got the registration number?"

"Already circulated. She won't get far. I've alerted all ports and airports as well. It's just a matter of time."

"Good work, Peter." Marks' day was just about to get a whole lot better. A voice from upstairs had him taking them two at a time. "What is it?"

"Sounds like a hidden panel in one of the rooms, sir."

It took Marks and Spencer a while to work out the method for releasing the catch to the partition wall, but when they did a hidden doorway opened to reveal a small office space within one of the bedrooms. The cubicle - it was no more than that - held a filing cabinet and a small desk, nothing more. It was clearly some kind of administrative space kept quite separate from the main family business, and one which Marks doubted Roger Nelson knew anything about. Once opened, the cabinet and its drawers revealed the full extent of the activities of the Southgate Sisterhood.

"Let's get this lot packed up and down to the station. I'll get George to go over the place for any forensics…"

"Sir. You need to see this." Peter Spencer was standing with one of the manila files open.

Marks took the papers from his DI. The file was labelled 'Wendy', and Spencer had pulled it from an archived section of the cabinet marked 'Specials'. The information within it related to the daughter Sandra Benway had lost when Donald Swinson had been arrested for her abduction and murder. His picture was pasted to the inside cover, and a thick red marker pen had been used to cross his face out. The fact that Alessandra Nelson was responsible for his death had not even required any proof, but Spencer's low whistle brought Marks back to the present day.

"My God, this is serious. It seems Alessandra was compiling a set of files for members of the group to take care of. Danny Emmanuel has one in here, and the designated member was Marsha Tully."

"Okay, so that's the end of that one then. Once we have her, the case should be open and shut."

"Yes, but look at this next one. It's still in the process of being finalised, but there's no member name on the inside cover."

"That's alright. Maybe she never got around to organising it."

"No, sir. That's not what I mean. The picture inside the file… it's…"

"It's what, Peter? Come on, don't mess me about."

"It's you, sir. You're the target. Looks like she's given someone the task of eliminating you. There are notes in here relating to Inspector Mullard, but he's dead. Seems like she's holding you responsible for Swinson's release."

Marks was stunned. He had sent officers to the address in Leigh Hunt Drive, but Doreen Yates was gone. Neighbours reported her getting into a taxi the day before, taking suitcases along with her. No-one seemed to know where she had gone, and the taxi dispatcher only had a dropping off point at Kings Cross station. It was perfectly clear to him now that she was the one charged with his elimination.

"Sir." A call came from one of the squad cars in the street at the front of the house. "We've picked up Mrs Nelson. She was pulled over on the M1 just north of Derby. She's being brought back to London."

That, at least, should enable Marks to close the book on the Sisterhood. Once all the forensics had been collated, those responsible for the vigilante killings would all be behind bars, but it still left the maverick factor of Doreen Yates. There was no way of knowing how deep ran the woman's commitment to the

Sisterhood. That Alessandra Nelson had been instrumental in taking out Michael Partington-Smith and Jeremy Battersby now seemed obvious. There was always payback in situations like that, but the hardened outer shell of the policeman within him had Marks shrugging off the risk as just one more factor to be taken into consideration with the job he had to do.

9

"Are you sure you're alright, sir? I mean, surely we can put a round the clock watch on your home."

Peter Spencer was more than a little concerned at the change in Marks' demeanour since the discovery of the file at the Nelson home, and the DCI had been uncharacteristically quiet during the intervening hours.

"Not necessary, Peter. Doreen Yates is long gone. We've circulated her description, and she's quite distinctive in appearance. Even then, I doubt we'd be able to hold her on any substantive charge. What could we say? She won't be out there for long, and arresting her in possession of a pair of knitting needles won't go down too well with the CPS. I'm more bothered about the lack of weapons with these current killings."

"Meaning?"

"Well, they, and it has to be 'they', *must* be somewhere. I can't believe that the same needle was used in all of the attacks, even though George Groves couldn't be certain about it."

They had talked all around the subject for over an hour, when Spencer suddenly brightened.

"Wendy Benway."

"What?"

"The little girl, Wendy; Sandra's daughter."

"Alright, you've lost me again. Why?"

"Might be worth while taking a look around the grave. What better place to hide them if you're used to being seen there, say, putting fresh flowers in a pot on a regular basis."

"I suppose it's worth a shot. Do you know where it is?"

"Yes, it's another bit of digging around that I've been doing. We'll need a warrant." Spencer was all smiles and it served to lighten the mood which had descended over the case.

Southgate Cemetery is situated on Brunswick Road, and the two detectives were shown to a plot in the northwest corner of the grounds. There, neatly trimmed and with fresh flowers in a white marble pot, lay the memorial to Wendy Benway. They stood in silence as the caretaker moved off, and an elderly woman approached from across the pathway.

"Comes every other day, she does. Haven't seen her for a few though. Puts fresh flowers in each time, and does a bit of gardening as well. Such a shame about the little girl, and I remember them laying her to rest. Was really glad when the pervert got his just desserts as well."

She wandered away towards the exit, and Marks waited until she had disappeared before taking a penknife out of his pocket. He looked around before squatting beside the plot. He hadn't been poking the grass for too long before the blade came into contact with something hard and metallic. From out of the sod, and pushed far enough down so that it was not obvious, he extracted a knitting needle.

"Look at that. You were right, Peter. Let's see just how many she's stashed here."

In all, there were fourteen single needles, none of them making up a matching pair. Fourteen weapons from fourteen crimes. They were aware of six – three up north and the rest in the Southgate parks. That left a further eight about which they knew absolutely nothing. Bagging each one separately, they returned to Groves' lab and handed them over for testing. Coming back past the duty sergeant's desk, Marks was met by the figure of Alessandra Nelson as she was escorted into the station by uniformed officers.

"We meet again, Mrs Nelson. I think the game's up this time." He turned to the desk. "Sergeant, I'd like Mrs Nelson taken to interview room one, and you'd better alert the duty solicitor as well."

Alessandra Nelson sat stone-faced in the room as Marks entered, with Peter Spencer close behind. The duty solicitor was already there, and after two tapes had been prepared and inserted into the recorder, the interview began.

"For the record, this interview is timed at 1815 hours, and those present are DCI Marks, DI Spencer, Mrs Alessandra Nelson, and Mr Barry Fry, the duty solicitor. Mrs. Nelson, would you care to explain what happened at your house?"

"Is Roger...?"

"He's dead. A broken neck, but you probably knew that the moment you got to the bottom of the stairs. What did you do?"

"It was an accident, Chief Inspector. I didn't mean to kill him. He wouldn't let go…" She stopped, the duty solicitor's hand upon her arm.

"I see. Did he find out what you and your girls were up to?"

"No." She shook her head at Barry Fry. "I need to tell them." She turned back to Marks. "I went to see Doreen Yates, and he must have followed me. When we got home, he just kept going on and on about something he thought he'd heard."

"And what *did* he hear?"

Alessandra could sense that she was being cornered and needed to think quickly. She decided to keep to the facts about Roger, but try to distance herself from the Southgate Sisterhood's activities. She was about to be outmanoeuvred.

"A private conversation. Doreen had been calling on me regularly after those two bodies were found in Broomfield Park. She was worried that, somehow, she might be held responsible."

"But you knew that wasn't likely, didn't you?"

"When I got back home, Roger began pressing me about the support group. He thinks… thought… that it was something more than that."

"So you killed him."

"No, well, yes… look, it's more complicated than that. He followed me up the stairs, and we argued at the top. He grabbed me by the arm and spun me around to face him."

"And that's when you pushed him down them." Marks leaned forwards in his chair.

"No. I raised my arms to break his hold, and he stumbled. He fell backwards and knocked over the vase that you probably saw on the landing."

"And then…?"

"His foot was on the edge of the top step, and he lost his balance. I reached out to grab him, but he was already part of the way down the stairs. The sound when he hit the bottom was sickening."

"So you just left him there?"

"I checked to see if he was still alive, but his head was... you know. I knew he was dead, and there was a pool of blood around it. That's why you probably found my prints on the door handle. I didn't mean to kill him, Inspector. It just happened."

"We could probably charge you with manslaughter right here and now, but there's a more serious matter to resolve." Marks paused, and the atmosphere in the room chilled considerably.

Alessandra Nelson shifted uncomfortably in her chair, and the body language was picked up very quickly by the DCI. She was beyond the control of the duty solicitor by this time, and Marks sensed the endgame was about to be played out.

"The bodies in Broomfield Park… you knew who they were when we first questioned you. Of course we can no longer check your version of those events, since your husband is now dead."

"I have no idea what you're talking about. As I said, someone told Roger when he was on his way home."

"Yes." Marks sat back. "But, you see, my DI has been on a trip up north, and it would appear that three unsolved murders of amazingly similar style were committed up there. Trouble is, they never found the weapons involved."

Alessandra smiled inwardly at this revelation, but Marks picked up on the small, involuntary movement which turned up the corners of her mouth.

"I say *they* never found them, but we did." Onto the table, and in true dramatic style, the DI dropped fourteen plastic bags. Each one contained a knitting needle, and they were all the same size.

"Where did you…?" She stared down at the table. The reaction had been automatic, but when the truth dawned, her eyes flared at the two detectives sitting opposite. "Wendy! My little Wendy! You bastard! You desecrated her grave!"

"Chief Inspector." It was Barry Fry this time. "That evidence is inadmissible unless you have a warrant."

"You mean one of these?" Peter Spencer waved the paper in his right hand, and Alessandra looked at her solicitor with tears in her eyes.

"Yes." He turned to his client. "I'm sorry, there's nothing I can do. This all seems to be in order."

"So, Mrs Nelson. Fourteen needles, fourteen sets of fingerprints and fourteen DNA profiles. Once we've compared them to prison records, and we will, all of our killers will be soon be behind bars. Now, I wonder what stories they'll tell us. Plea-bargaining, the Americans call it, and they'll certainly put the Southgate Sisterhood's head of operations right under the spotlight."

There was no way out. Alessandra was completely boxed in. Friends in Holloway they had certainly been, but they'd all save their own skins when the chips were down.

"I'm saying nothing more." There was a defiant tone now to the voice of Alessandra Nelson, and there remained only one more matter to resolve. Marks went in for the kill.

"Where is Doreen Yates?"

"Doreen?" She smiled. "Why, can't you find her? What a pity. Why would you be interested in her, I wonder?"

"We know that you gave her a file." Spencer had been taking notes up to this point, but changed the point of the attack.

"Do you now? Well, you see, now I'm just a funeral director, and you're the detectives. I suggest you go forth and detect."

That was all that Marks and Spencer were to get from Alessandra Nelson. With the evidence amassed there would be no way out of a prison sentence for her. No doubt she would be treated with the same reverence as before by the inmates of whatever institution she was sent to. She had been seen as something of a messiah in Holloway, and that status would surely follow her around.

Now back at the office, Spencer drummed his fingers on the desk as Marks appeared with coffee from the canteen.

"Just one final thing, boss. What could possibly have lured both Michael Partington-Smith and Jeremy Battersby into Broomfield Park at the same time, and on the same evening?"

"Simple, Peter." Marks smiled, his turn to get one over on his DI. "Sandra Davies."

"Davies? But wasn't she already dead?"

"Certainly, but what you have to remember is that neither Michael nor Jeremy had ever actually spoken to the woman. It was the senior Partington-Smiths who paid her off. So, when a phone call came through from someone claiming to be her, and threatening to blow the whole matter wide open, they both reacted."

"So, Battersby was in on the bribe?"

"I shouldn't be at all surprised if he knew about it. He'd sailed very close to the wind on a number of occasions in the past."

"Alright." Spencer persisted. "But how would Alessandra Nelson have known about Davies being back in the country?"

"Contacts, Inspector, contacts. Those ex-con friends of hers had look-outs posted. One of your three from up north has already spilled the beans on that."

It seemed that Marks would have to be content with things as they had turned out, but a call from the desk sergeant was to change that perception considerably.

"Sir. Graham on the desk. There's a lady down here says she needs to see you right away."

"Who is it?"

"Says her name's Doreen Yates."

The two detectives were there in minutes to find a somewhat flustered and apprehensive redhead seated opposite the desk. Once inside the same interview room recently vacated by Alessandra Nelson, Doreen Yates took a deep breath and began her story.

"I just couldn't do it, Inspector." She placed a manila file onto the table. "It doesn't seem right. I'm not a killer, and I don't think taking another life will do any good now that my Jennifer is gone."

"Thank you, Mrs Yates." Marks sighed inwardly with relief as he took it from the table.

"I suppose you'll be wanting to charge me with… something." She sat before them, a crushed expression on her face.

"No, I don't think so. You've broken no law as far as I can see, and this file was never ours until right now. You are free to go."

"But what about Mrs Nelson? I mean, she gave me that and I was supposed to kill the person in there as part of the bargain for her killing… you know."

"Did you know that at the time that Michael Partington-Smith and Jeremy Battersby died?"

"Well, no; it was much later that she told me what I would have to do."

"That's it, then." Marks smiled as he held the door open for her. "There was never an agreement of any kind. We won't be charging you."

Back in the office once again, Marks sat down with a huge sigh of relief, and dropped the manila file onto his desk.

"Looks like I'm in the clear now, Peter. I'd say a celebratory drink is in order. Shall we say The Crown and Anchor at clocking off time?"

Peter Spencer was not smiling, however. He had picked up the file and was browsing the contents. After two passes through the pages, he shook his head.

"I think, boss, that we still have a problem." He dropped the file onto the desk, open at the first page, and pointed at the picture.

"But that's not…"

"You. No, it isn't. We can stop this guy being eliminated…"

"But there's somebody out there with a file with my name on it, and my picture inside."

The Southgate Sisterhood were to have the last laugh for now. Marks would, without doubt, eventually isolate all of the members of the group, and it was more than likely that whoever had the file would merely dispose of it once the news of Alessandra's arrest became public. However, knowing the typical profile of those women coming out of Holloway, particularly those with misandrist tendencies, he would never be sure of complete safety until all the files had been recovered.

Sunday, 23rd April 2006

This was a meeting to which Martin Ponsonby was not looking forward. Harold Shaw had been involved in the drug trafficking trade for quite some time, and news of his arrest and conviction had been a matter of considerable public interest. Ponsonby had left it until the media spotlight had moved on to approach the man. He could, he had said, appeal against the convictions of both him and Gasparini on the basis of fabrication of evidence and mismanagement in a number of other cases. Shaw had shown not a little interest. That had been three months ago, and much careful preparation had gone into digging out enough detail to put Dennis Marks at the end of some very awkward charges.

"Dropped? What do you mean 'dropped'?" Shaw was halfway across the table before the prison guard restrained him, forcing him back into his seat.

"I mean, Mr Shaw, that I can no longer represent either you or Mr Gasparini." Ponsonby was shaken by the man's violent reaction, notwithstanding his earlier reticence at the thought of this meeting.

"You promised that we'd get off once you'd stitched that copper up." Shaw's voice quietened almost to a whisper, and the menace in its tone sent a shiver the length of Ponsonby's spine. "Now you come here and just drop the both of us back into this rat hole?"

Ponsonby glanced nervously at the prison guard standing silently now, in the corner of the room. Shaw picked up the look and laughed openly.

"Don't worry about him; I own quite a few in here. He'll stop me hurting you though. Wouldn't do to be damaging visitors, now would it?"

"I'm sorry. This has all got out of hand, and forces much higher up the food chain are now taking an interest." He rose to leave. "I have other matters which require my attention."

"You can't just walk out on Harold Shaw, you pencil-pushing little weasel!" He jabbed a finger through the air. "Keep looking over your shoulder, Ponsonby. One day, there'll be a knife sticking out of your back."

He was still shaking when Shaw had left the room, and the guard came over to where he sat.

Full Marks

Martin Ponsonby & Harold Shaw

"You alright, sir?" There was no real concern in the voice and Ponsonby knew it.

"Yes. Yes, just a chill. I'll be fine as soon as I'm out of this place."

Outside Wandsworth prison, Ponsonby hailed a cab on Heathfield Road and made his way back to the office. Shaw's threat had to be taken seriously, and a career outside the capital was now becoming a very attractive possibility. Once back at his desk, all papers relating to the action instigated against Dennis Marks would be destroyed, and the complaint registered with the IPCC withdrawn. He would then disappear. Shaw, on the other hand, was not one to let the small matter of a betrayal pass by so easily. Afternoon leisure time saw him and Gasparini in close conversation over a game of draughts.

"So, he's just walked away after telling us that he could get the conviction squashed?"

"Quashed, you stupid idiot, quashed!" Useful as he was, Gasparini was not the sharpest knife in the drawer. "We need to get you out of here."

"Me? I thought we was stuffed."

"I'll find another bent lawyer, but you, my friend, have a job to do. I want Marks taken care of, and then you can disappear. I'll make sure that you have enough to get you far away from London once you've done what I need - savvy?"

Gasparini smiled. The thought of extracting revenge on those who had put him inside gave him an enormous amount of pleasure. He would take great care in selecting the correct method, and would ensure that pain was involved in substantial quantities. It was what he did best.

"Are you sure that all of the evidence will stand up to re-examination, then?" Greenaway looked up from his papers.

"Positive." said Marks. "We had Alessandra for the accidental death of her husband, and the whole thing started to unravel from that point onwards. The case is solid. No short-cuts, and certainly no attempt to brush Don Mullard's investigation under the carpet."

"Okay. We'll leave that one then. This final item sort of ties up a loose end, but again, the charge is that you were too intent on covering your own back, and that you let the evidence get the better of you."

"I would just like to point out that I had a sword hanging over me at the time. We had clear evidence of someone out there with a brief to take me out of circulation on a permanent basis!" Marks snorted.

"Are you certain that this wasn't the result of you taking your eye off the ball?"

"Positive. I'm a professional. Danger comes with the territory; you just learn to live with it. There were enough people around covering my back anyway. What is this final file?"

"William France. The man killed by a ball of ice. A ball of ice? How realistic is that?"

"As realistic, Mr Greenaway, as forensics made it out to be. All the evidence was there, and we merely put it together. Everything fits - there were no loose ends, and no false suppositions."

"The underlying tone in all of this, Chief Inspector, is that you are a man under considerable pressure. You've been on the verge of a nervous breakdown, and that persuaded you to make it some kind of crusade to keep your good name and maintain a reputation for getting results."

"No!" The DCI thumped the desk. "I'd never do that! This last one just shows how far I'll go to get at the truth, however carefully it has been concealed. Margaret France is a devious, clever woman, who saw an opportunity to get out of a very difficult situation. The fact that we managed to tie up the last loose end in the Sisterhood case came as a bonus."

Metropolitan Police

Case No. 754391678

Name: France, W.

Date: 19-January-2006

Memo

From: Charles Brandridge – Senior Crown Advocate
To: Det. Chief Inspector Dennis Marks
Date: 26-January-2006

Subject: William France (Deceased)

Based on the information which you and your team have supplied on the above matter, I have reviewed the case and have come to the following conclusions:

1. There is no doubt in my mind that we would be able to secure a conviction against your prime suspect.
2. Based on witness testimony and forensic evidence, I believe that the charge of murder, as you indicated at the outset, is the one which should be pursued.
3. The defendant's plea in mitigation, and willingness to accept the lesser charge of manslaughter, should be dismissed.
4. Your suggestion of proceedings against the third party on a charge of collusion will not, in my opinion, result in a conviction, and should be dropped.

Of course, should any further corroborating evidence arise with regard to point four, the Crown Prosecution Service would be prepared to reconsider the matter.

Full Marks

A Woman Scorned

1

With the case of the Southgate Sisterhood now behind him, and its architect, Alessandra Nelson, behind bars, Dennis Marks was able, as well as he could with the threat of a hidden assassin lurking in the background, to carry on with the CID's current case load. There was never any shortage of criminals freely plying their trade, and the variety of scenarios which frequently confronted him and his DI, Peter Spencer, never failed to amaze either of them.

Today was no exception; as they stood in the kitchen of a house in Tooting, Marks was faced once more with a riddle which was going to take some unravelling. The body of William France lay face down in a pool of blood, and it seemed, to the two detectives now staring down at it, that the man had died as a result of a blow to the back of the head. George Groves was of a similar opinion.

"The point of impact is here." The pathologist said, pointing to an area just off centre at the back of the skull. "Looks like death would have been quick, if not instantaneous, and there appears to be a large section of bone embedded in the brain tissue."

"What sort of force could cause that?" Marks squatted down for a closer look.

"Wouldn't take that much, Dennis. Some skulls aren't that thick, and can be as thin as an eggshell in places. This one isn't too robust, and the blow was at right angles, so the force of the impact would have been quite considerable."

"You know what I'm going to ask now, don't you?"

"Yes, yes. Time of death. First estimate puts it at about eight to ten hours ago, but I'll know more once I get him back to the lab."

"That would make it..." Spencer looked at his watch, "around dinner time yesterday evening."

"Very good, Peter. We'll make a detective of you yet." Groves smiled at the easy opportunity to crack a joke.

"Who found the body?" Marks looked around the room.

"His wife's sister. She called this morning and rang emergency services from her mobile. The front door was open and it seems to have been forced. Mrs France is upstairs; she'd been bound and gagged, but apart from that hadn't been touched. Looks to me like a break-in that went wrong, but then that's your department isn't it? Uniform took a statement from her. Look, I'm going to tidy up here and get all the stuff back to base. You won't go touching anything, now will you?"

"The sister." Marks ignored the remark. "Where is she now?"

"I think she left just about the time you arrived."

"Anyone get her name?"

"One of your uniforms, I think."

Marks and Spencer went upstairs to find Margaret France in a state of shock. Now freed from the confines of the gaffer tape which had been used to bind her to a chair, she was sitting on the bed. A WPC was by her side; she rose to leave.

"No, Marshall, stay where you are." Marks waved her back to her position. "Mrs France may be in need of some female company."

He looked around the room. Furniture had been disturbed, possibly indicating that a struggle had taken place before Margaret France had been subdued, but the woman herself appeared to be free of any injuries or bruising.

"Mrs France, I know this may seem very upsetting, but it's important that we get some information whilst it's still clear in your mind. What happened?"

"Bill… my husband, I heard noises from downstairs. Is he alright?" The tears flowed, and Marks was instantly on the back foot.

"I'm afraid he sustained some serious injuries, but we're taking care of him." As facts went, this was accurate, and he tried to sidetrack further questions. "It's vital that we find out who did this. Can you give a description of whoever attacked you?"

"He was wearing a ski mask, so I couldn't see his face. He wasn't that tall; about the same height as me, but he took me by surprise. The next thing I knew I was up here and strapped to that chair." She pointed across the room.

"Alright. Did he say anything? Could you tell if he was local?"

"No, he never spoke at all. I just heard sounds from downstairs, and Bill call for help. Then it went quiet. I thought he was going to come back upstairs for me, but I heard the door slam, and knew that he'd gone."

"Alright, we'll get you down to the station while our forensics team take a good look around here. Someone will take a statement from you there, and I'll see you again a little later."

Now that both the husband and wife were off the premises, Marks and his team were able to go through the house from top to bottom in a search for clues. George Groves was standing in the kitchen at the side of the bloodstain where William France had lain. The frown on his face told Marks more than words could ever have done.

"Something tells me that you aren't a happy bunny."

"Hmm? Oh, yes, well it doesn't quite fit. You see, the body lay here," Groves pointed to a spot in the middle of the floor, "but the blood has spread further than I would have expected if he'd simply fallen to the ground."

"You mean he was moved?"

"Quite possibly. Almost as if the scene were being prepared for us in advance. By my reckoning, and going by scuff marks on the floor tiles, he was struck over there by the door. There's no way that he would have landed over here and have made those marks."

"So, we're looking at a setup then. Question is, by whom. The wife was bound and gagged upstairs, so I don't see how it could have been her." Marks frowned.

"Let's go and take a look then, shall we?" The pathologist was off and halfway up the stairs before Marks had moved.

The place was empty now that Margaret France had been escorted to the station, and Groves was able to get a full picture of what he might be up against. He walked around the room with a puzzled expression on his face, and came to a stop at the side of the bed.

"Is this the cloth that was used to gag her?" He picked up a strip of material from the bed.

"Yes, according to the uniformed officer who was first at the scene, the wife's sister removed it when she found the two of them."

"I'll bag it along with the gaffer tape. This piece looks as if it was used over the mouth, and the rest would presumably have been what kept her in the chair. We might be able to get some prints from it."

"The phone's on the floor and off the hook – looks like she might have been trying to call for help." Marks donned a pair of gloves and picked up the receiver. "Let's see what the last number dialled was."

The memory was clear of calls logged. That puzzled him, and he replaced it in the cradle. Groves, meanwhile, had emerged from the other side of the bed with a cardboard reel in his hand, and it was empty. Holding it against the ends of one of the pieces of gaffer tape, he looked at the DCI with raised eyebrows – it was the same width.

"A match?" Marks walked across the room and took the object. "Why should there be an empty tape roll in the room?"

"Saw it once on TV." Peter Spencer had entered from the top of the stairs. "You need to look for something that fits inside the centre."

"Meaning?" Marks frowned in puzzlement.

"Look, if I sit in this swivel chair where she was presumably bound, I can place the reel onto…" He looked around, "…this bedpost." He pointed at the corner of the bed. "Then, if I stick one end onto my coat, sit in the chair and swivel it, I can give the impression of being bound to it by another person."

"Yes, but why go to all that trouble?" Groves was as stumped as the DCI.

"If you wanted to murder your husband and make it look like a break-in, you would." Spencer smiled, and it was another one of those looks which meant that he knew something that Marks didn't.

"That's a bit of a leap of logic, even for you."

"Not if she'd taken out an insurance policy on him, it isn't." He held up a set of documents. The Frances had indeed taken out a policy on the life of William, the husband, and it was dated nine months earlier.

"So, what's the motive? Greed, I suppose."

"No, according to these credit card statements that we found stuffed down the back of one of the lounge cupboards, Margaret France was deep in debt. That's motive for murder in my book."

"Right, Peter, we'll get off to the station. George, can you bring me up to date when we're all back at base? Mrs France has some very awkward questions to answer. Oh, and let's get the name and address of the sister. Seems she vanished as soon as she set eyes on me."

"Maybe that's just the effect you have on people, boss."

2

Margaret France was in one of the interview rooms when Marks arrived back at the station, and a WPC was sitting with her, having supplied the customary cup of tea to distraught victims of a crime. She looked up and smiled weakly as he came through the door.

"Mrs France, my DI here will take a statement from you, but could you let us know the name and address of your sister, please? It appears that she left your house before we had a chance to speak to her."

The DCI left instructions with Peter Spencer to take his time with the statement. He was more than a little curious as to the motives of both women, and it concerned him that the other one had disappeared so quickly after the arrival of the squad cars at the France house. There seemed to be no-one at home at the address given by Margaret France, and a neighbour reported a hurried departure from the premises about two hours earlier. The woman, a Mrs Brenda Pollock, had not told anyone where she was going, but had taken luggage with her. Clearly she was not intending to return in the near future.

With a name and description, Marks returned to find Peter Spencer still taking notes from Margaret France, and headed off to check the name given to him against police records. What he found came as quite a surprise.

"You certain about this, Sergeant?" He asked the officer in charge of records.

"Yes, sir. She was in Holloway between those dates." He pointed at the computer screen.

"Known associates?"

"Here." He switched to another screen, and one name which astounded Marks was there for all to see – Alessandra Nelson.

Even with a two hour start, Brenda Pollock had only got as far as Euston, and had boarded the first train heading north. The ticket clerk remembered her, and she was intercepted at Birmingham New Street. Now back in London and in the hands of CID, she started when Marks entered the second interview room at the station.

"Mrs Pollock, I'm very curious to know why you vanished so quickly from your sister's home this morning. As you may be aware, you could be an important material witness in our search for whoever killed your brother-in-law."

Brenda Pollock refused to make an official statement, and would only confirm verbally that she had found the body in the kitchen, before freeing her sister from the chair upstairs.

"I understand that you were in Holloway at the same time as Sandra Benway."

"It's on record."

"You know, don't you, that, as Alessandra Nelson, she was the head of the Southgate Sisterhood."

"I've got nothing to say about that."

"I see. Well, we have a warrant to search your house, and if there's anything there linking you to that organisation's activities you could be in serious trouble. Did you know that she was responsible for the deaths of at least six people?"

"What?" A look of genuine surprise flashed across her face.

"Did she give you any documents?"

"No comment." She folded her arms and sat back in the chair. "I want a lawyer."

"Alright." Marks nodded, and sent for the duty solicitor. Peter Spencer appeared at the door and beckoned him outside.

"Look what we found in Mrs Pollock's luggage." He handed the DCI a slim manila folder, and Marks froze. Opening the cover, he breathed a sigh of relief.

"Right, so we now have what I hope is the last of that damned woman's hit list, and it looks like I'm in the clear." The folder contained the details Brenda Pollock would have needed to carry out the killing, and Marks was the intended target.

"Do we charge her in connection with the Nelson case?"

"Yes." The DI handed the file back. "I don't want to spend the rest of my life looking over my shoulder. Let's make sure that it sticks."

"There's still her involvement with the France matter to look into. Shall I question her, or will you?"

"Hold her for now until we've done with the wife. I'm going to see Groves and check what he's managed to dig up."

The pathologist was just cleaning up when Marks arrived, and the body of William France now lay in the refrigerated compartment alongside other unfortunates who formed his clientele.

"Cause of death, not surprisingly, was a single blow to the back of the skull." Groves wiped his hands as he turned from the sink.

"Okay, what am I looking for?"

"Something round - no, spherical - and very hard. I found traces of fluoride in the wound, so I think we could be talking about a ball of ice."

"Ice?"

"Perfect. Use it and then run it under a hot tap. Bingo! No more murder weapon."

"But how does it get to be spherical?"

"That's where you come in, Dennis. Have you checked her refuse bin for anything out of the ordinary? She would need to have used a mould, so you'll be looking for something round and soft, maybe a small ball like a child's toy. She could have filled it with water and then have cut it away once the ice had formed."

"A ball?"

"Perfect for the job, and easily disposed of without anyone giving it a second thought. Anyone apart from me, that is." He smiled, and Marks was out of the lab in minutes, heading for the France home. If his instincts were correct, today was the day the local authority refuse collectors paid their fortnightly visit.

He and Peter Spencer were back within the hour with the contents of the green bin provided by the council. Groves emptied them out onto a large plastic sheet on the floor, and smiled once more in triumph.

"What did I tell you?" There, in the midst of all the rubbish, were the two halves of a small rubber ball.

"Now what?" Peter Spencer had not been in on the earlier conversation, and Marks had merely told him that they needed to get to the France home quickly.

"Now, Inspector, I check this for fingerprints and traces of DNA, make a mould of the two halves and fill it with water. You come back in, say a couple of hours, and we see what has turned out. My money's on a perfect match for the wound in the back of William France's skull, but let's not jump to conclusions, eh?"

With Margaret France still in the interview room, the two detectives returned to confront her with the latest findings. Faced with the unravelling of the plan she had so carefully prepared, her demeanour changed from that of the grieving widow to one of a cornered rat. She demanded legal representation, and they left her alone with the second solicitor summoned that day. Brenda Pollock, having had time with her own representative, was not in a mood to negotiate.

Groves, Marks & Spencer

"My lawyer says that I've done nothing wrong, and that you're going to have a hard job making anything stick." Her defiance was now complete.

"Mrs Pollock." Marks' attitude hardened. "The Southgate Sisterhood was a vigilante organisation set up to kill. Alessandra Nelson gave you a file with my details inside it because she blamed me for the failure of the case against the man who killed her daughter. I'd say that puts you at the centre of a conspiracy charge, irrespective of what you may have been told. You could be looking at some serious jail time. Now, I'm not an unreasonable man, but it looks to me as if you are up to your neck in this current case as well."

"Bill France's death is nothing to do with me. I went to the house like I said to Margaret I would. We always go out on the same day each week, and when no-one answered the front door, I went round the back. That's when I found the place open, and Bill in the kitchen. I didn't kill him."

"No, I know that. You ran away as soon as you saw me though, and that makes you a suspect. I can make a case for implicating you in the murder purely in circumstantial terms, and it might be enough to sway a jury into convicting you along with Margaret."

"Margaret? What do you mean? She was tied up!"

"Yes, now let's think about this. You did that between the two of you. Bill was insured, and a lot of money was involved. You probably decided to bump him off and split the proceeds."

"No! You might be able to set me up with Sandy Benway, but I'm not coughing to this one."

"Very well, Mrs Pollock. We'll be back in here once we've charged your sister."

The interview with Margaret France was conducted in quite a different manner now that Marks had his potential assassin on the ropes, and she was calm and collected. The DCI laid before her the scenario which he believed fit with the facts and circumstances which had been found at the scene earlier in the day.

"You killed your husband. You hit him on the back of the head, strapped yourself to the swivel chair upstairs after taping a gag to your mouth, and then sat and waited for your sister to arrive. You'd already forced the back door to make a burglary look the likeliest explanation, and then you simply disposed of the weapon. Brenda, I believe, knew nothing of the plan, and it was important from your point of view that she remain what she is - an independent witness to the scenario you created."

"What weapon?" Margaret France smiled and leaned back in her chair. She knew that, without a weapon, it would be impossible to tie her to the crime.

"The ball of ice which you made from the mould which we found in your refuse bin. Once we have the fingerprints and DNA traces you left on it, the case will be open and shut. Our lab boys are, as we speak, making an identical weapon from the two halves, and once compared to the wound at the back of your husband's skull, it'll be enough to convict you."

"I have no reason for wanting Bill dead." The first signs of uncertainty flickered across her face as she fought to regain control of the situation.

"We found the credit card statements, Mrs France. You're heavily in debt. The insurance policy you took out would have solved all of that, and Bill's death at the hands of an unknown burglar would have ensured the payout."

Margaret France sat stone-faced when confronted with the facts Marks had just outlined. The timings had been so tight once Bill had been dealt the fatal blow, and it had taken nerves of steel to carry it out and stay in the house all night with a corpse in the kitchen. Once the following morning came around, preparing the house for Brenda had taken up all of her resolve. She had almost forgotten about the ball, and threw it into the bin at the last moment, knowing that the refuse collectors would dispose of it for her. The fact they were late on this particular day had ruined the plan. Had they been on time, the mould would have been lost forever and she would have been in the clear. Peter Spencer entered the room, and placed a file on the table. Marks opened it and smiled.

"Well, it looks like the final pieces are now in place. The ball of ice we made, Mrs France, fits perfectly as I thought it would. Fingerprints lifted from the mould match those which we took from you earlier as part of our elimination process, and there were traces of DNA from your hands on its surface. I'd say that puts you at the scene, and with the motive suggested by your debt problem, we'll be charging you with the murder, and your sister with conspiracy on another matter. Looks like a really bad day for the family, doesn't it?"

"He was cheating on me, Chief Inspector." Her resistance collapsed. "Bill wasn't aware that I knew, but he was planning to leave me. I couldn't allow him to get away with that after all the years we'd been married. Yes, I was heavily in debt, and without his income I would have been in quite a mess. Just when I was at the point of sorting it all out, it looked as though the rug was about to be pulled out from under me."

"And this was your only solution?"

"You'd be amazed at how easy it is to take out an insurance policy, and it seemed like manna from heaven. I forged Bill's signature on all the documents, and they didn't even ask for him to be present. If I hadn't acted now, he would have been gone in a week. You must think me very bad."

"Sad rather than that. There's always another way of finding a solution to a problem. Too late for you now, though."

The two detectives watched as Margaret France was taken away to be charged and held in police custody pending a magistrates hearing the next day. Peter Spencer shook his head.

"One dangerous woman, Margaret France."

"Well, you know what they say." Marks added. "Hell hath no fury like a woman scorned. Seems her husband hadn't read that one."

Monday, 24th April 2006

With the case reviews now complete, Marks could not hide the nervousness he felt at the prospect of the hearing which was about to take place. It was now Monday morning, almost a month after the initial suspension meted out by Eric Staines, and as his wife shepherded him to the door, they looked into each other's eyes.

"It'll be alright, Dennis. You'll come through this. There's nothing that they can pin on you."

"I know, June. What worries me is that they don't. I've seen good coppers go down the drain after hearings like this. Even if it all comes to nothing, there are always people in the background mumbling away about 'no smoke without fire' – you can't win. I may end up having to resign either way."

"Forget all about it, then. Just tell them the truth, like you always have done. If you leave the force we'll be alright." She smiled. "Now go and give them hell!"

Those final words from his wife instilled a fresh sense of purpose into the flagging spirit of DCI Marks, and he entered the halls of New Scotland Yard with a defiant air and his head held high. Let them give it their best shot; he'd dealt with their kind before. His mood was undaunted as he came face to face with the man who had set all of this in motion, and after the briefest of courtesy nods, they took their places before the tribunal which was to decide the DCI's fate. Marks could not derive the slightest hint from the stone face of the Chief Constable chairing the hearing, and as he took his seat at the side of Ron Greenaway, he was completely unaware of the figure now taking a place at the back of the room in a seat reserved for other members of the Metropolitan Police.

Superintendent Colin Barnes had watched the previous month's events with mounting interest, aware of the pressure which was building on Dennis Marks. He had carried out his own, covert, enquiries into the allegations made against the DCI, and had come to the conclusion that there were forces operating about which the detective knew nothing. With his contacts in the security services, he had been able to ascertain that the solicitor at the centre of the allegations, Martin Ponsonby, was the brother of Michael Roberts' wife. Once that link had been established, a number of facts began to fall into place, and the lawyer had been put in a position of being struck off the Solicitors' Roll were he to persist with the case against Marks.

A private word in the ear of George Watkinson had those responsible for the malicious accusations under the spotlight, and ready to withdraw all complaints. Marks was, of course, unaware of any of this.

"Are you ready to proceed, Superintendent Staines?" The Chief Constable looked up from the papers before him.

"Sir, the IPCC is satisfied that there is no case to answer against Detective Chief Inspector Marks. We withdraw all charges against him." Staines resumed his seat.

Marks' head snapped round to face that of his tormentor, but Staines sat stone-faced and remained looking straight ahead.

"In that case, this meeting is over." The Chief Constable looked at Marks. "Detective Chief Inspector, you are reinstated with immediate effect."

As they all started to leave the room, Marks turned to Ron Greenaway, who merely shrugged, packed his briefcase and tagged on at the end of the line now vacating the room. One figure which did not follow was that of Colin Barnes. He waited until the room was empty save for himself and Marks, and then made his approach.

"A satisfactory conclusion, Chief Inspector."

"Sir." Marks' puzzled look was met with a smile from Barnes, who waved him to a chair.

"You're clearly wondering what on earth just happened."

"Something like that, yes."

The facts relating to Martin Ponsonby were now laid out before the bemused detective, and his anger started to rise.

"You mean to tell me, that with a little bit of digging, the IPCC could have knocked this on the head right at the start?"

"Don't be too hard on them. They have a job to do, the same as you or I. Theirs is not a brief to answer questions but to ask them, and ask them of the correct people as they see it. You're in the spotlight as soon as your head pops up above the parapet, and they'll pursue you to the ends of the earth if necessary. Don't worry; the truth would have come out in the end."

"I understand that, sir, but the wife and I have been through hell since this thing started."

"I'm afraid it goes with the territory, Dennis."

"Who put the brakes on it? It couldn't have been you."

"No. As an officer in the Met, that would have been impossible. It's not, however, outside the reach of the security services, and the people that they lean on usually take notice pretty quickly. Come on, we have an appointment at Thames House."

"MI5? Why are they involved?"

"Because, Dennis, Mr Watkinson has a matter that he would like to discuss with you. I understand that the two of you have already met."

"We have, sir. It was his people who roped me into the affair involving Michael Roberts. I'd say he owes me a favour."

"Chief Inspector." Barnes smiled. "It's never that easy with our friends over there. When they say they'd like to see you, it usually means that they hold all the cards."

"Any idea what it is that they want from me?"

"Haven't a clue, I'm afraid. I was just asked to escort you over there for a chat once this nonsense today had been put to bed."

"Ah, gentlemen, so good of you to call." It was clear that George Watkinson had been expecting the imminent arrival of the two detectives, and they adjourned to a private office on another floor of Thames House.

Safe in the knowledge that the building was free from any external listening devices, Watkinson came straight to the point of the requested visit.

"Chief Inspector, I regret the ordeal that you were forced to endure. It was none of our doing, but there is a matter to which I would like you to devote some attention."

Marks smiled. He knew from past experience that these 'matters' to which Watkinson referred were never quite as straightforward as they appeared to be. He tried a diversionary tactic.

"What will happen to Martin Ponsonby?"

"Ah, yes, our delinquent lawyer." Watkinson, not in the least sidetracked from his true intentions, was nevertheless inclined to cut Marks a little slack. "Oh, he'll go back to doing what he ought to do, without treading where he doesn't really belong. He was in over his head, and now that he knows that I don't think there'll be any trouble from his quarter in the future."

"We should focus on what MI5 want from the Met." Colin Barnes pulled the conversation back onto the track which Watkinson was treading.

"Indeed, Superintendent. This..." he pushed a photograph across the table to Marks, "is a man in whom we would like you to take an interest."

"Who is he?" Marks stared at the snap, and frowned.

"Christopher Morse, and that's all you need to know right now. I'll make sure that a file is sent to you within the next few days."

"Not one of yours, is he?" The DCI suddenly stiffened, acutely aware of the problems of becoming involved in the undercover world of espionage.

"Not any longer, and he's started to carve out a name for himself in the criminal fraternity. You'll find all you need in the files."

"Very well." Marks' tone was reluctant, but he realised that he had few options. "I'll need to take my own team into the investigation with me, and they'll have to be properly briefed."

"That's fine by me." He turned to Barnes. "Superintendent?"

"No problem from the Met's point of view." He shook his head and turned to Marks. "Who did you have in mind?"

"Peter Spencer – he's my right-hand man. I'll need a DS as well. You took Wallace back from me, remember, Mr Watkinson? She was a good sergeant."

"I do, but she never really worked for you. Any names I should be aware of?"

"Just one, and she has a first rate pedigree. Came through Hendon and transferred to CID very soon after joining the Met. I've heard very good reports about her."

"It'll have to be cleared with her superior, but I'm sure Superintendent Barnes will be able to help there. What's her name?"

Now it was Marks' turn to smile, and he played the hand with the ease of a seasoned poker player. The name, when it was announced, caused eyebrows to rise on the faces of both men.

"Chloe Warner."

"Chloe Warner?" Watkinson looked at Barnes. "Isn't she...?"

"My sister." He smiled. "Yes, she is, and I'm sure that she'll be delighted with the compliment. It'll have to go through the proper channels, though. We've always kept our careers quite separate, for obvious reasons."

"I'll take that as arranged then, shall I?" Marks was happy at having the final word.

The telephone ringing on Watkinson's desk cut the conversation short, and his face became grave at the news being divulged to him.

"Thank you, I'll pass that information on." He looked at Marks. "It seems that you may have a problem on your hands, Chief Inspector."

"Meaning?" Both detectives were aware of Watkinson's aptitude for the understatement.

"It would appear that Giorgio Gasparini has escaped from Wandsworth prison. It happened this morning."

"Gasparini? Wasn't he the one..." Barnes never got the chance to finish.

"Who threatened to kill those responsible for putting him away. Yes, he did, and that puts three of us in the frame. I have to warn Peter Spencer and George Groves before he can get to either of them."

Monday, 1ˢᵗ May 2006

Shaw had been as good as his word, and Gasparini's escape from Wandsworth had been an act of pure simplicity. The correct amount into the appropriate hands, and he was a free man. The Italian now had to work fast and get out of London without delay once the task set had been completed. He looked at the three names on his list. Marks would be the hardest target with Spencer close behind. The pathologist, George Groves, would be the one to take out first, and the address was just below the name. Gasparini smiled at the resourcefulness of Harold Shaw.

George Groves and his wife lived south of the river in Bexley. The four bedroom detached house on Hurst Road was within walking distance of the railway station and the short journey into the centre of the capital. Gasparini had been sitting at the end of the road in the car he had stolen, waiting for the pathologist to come home at the end of his day. Groves arrived at five-thirty, and the hit man was close on his heels as he opened the front door.

"Keep moving!" He hissed as he shoved Groves inside and closed the door.

The gun pulled from his pocket ensured silence in the house, as Gasparini waved his captive down the hall and towards the kitchen.

"Close those blinds!" He barked out the command, and Groves obeyed automatically, never once taking an eye off the gun. "Now, sit down!"

"What do you want?" It took Groves a moment to recognise the man, but then his whole demeanour changed. "You better make the most of this. Marks will get you once he finds out that you're free, and he won't be unarmed this time."

"Shut your mouth! It's him I want, but you'll do for starters."

As if on cue, blaring klaxons cut through the late afternoon air as a fleet of armed response vehicles blocked either end of Hurst Road, effectively cutting Gasparini off from escape. Now he was cornered, and consequently became far more dangerous. There was an eerie silence before the voice of the DCI boomed out through a megaphone.

"Giorgio Gasparini! Come out with your hands raised! We have the place surrounded, and you're going nowhere."

Full Marks

"See?" Groves raised one eyebrow as Shaw's enforcer turned to face the front of the house. He sat down as he had been ordered. It was now over to Dennis, and he had seen the man in action too many times to have any doubts over the outcome.

"Come with me!" Gasparini grabbed him and dragged him into the lounge. Holding the gun to the pathologist's head, he pushed aside the net curtains.

"Marks! See this?" He pulled Groves close to the window pane. "He gets it unless you clear the way out of here!"

"Now, sir?" The marksman at the DCI's shoulder had Gasparini in his sights.

"Not yet, sergeant. George is too close and Gasparini's a psychotic. You'll spook him if you miss, and George Groves is more valuable to me alive than dead. Send a team round to the rear of the property, and we'll try to get through the back door."

"Sir."

There was a tense, silent period, with Gasparini and Groves moving constantly from the front of the property to the rear, and back again. It was impossible to get a clear line of sight on the gunman. A call came over the radio receiver from one of the marksmen.

"Sir, I'm on a garage at the back of the adjoining property, and it overlooks the kitchen. If we can keep them both in there, I might be able to take your gunman out."

"Right. Keep me posted." Marks turned to three of the squad. "You, you, and you, take up positions behind the front wall, and make sure that Gasparini sees you. I want him moved to the back."

"Anything I can do, sir?" Peter Spencer arrived at Marks' side.

"Peter. Hold the fort here. I'm going round to the back. Maybe Gasparini will give us a better target if he sees me out there."

Marks made his way along Hurst Road, turning left into Manor Way. A series of lock-up garages gave him cover as he approached the end house where Groves lived. The trees at the bottom of the pathologist's garden provided cover as he took up his position. A wave to the marksman atop the end garage was enough to indicate his presence, and a call over the radio held the man's shot for his command.

"Gasparini!" Without the megaphone, Marks was attempting to give the impression that he was alone.

The blinds at the kitchen window moved to one side. Marks looked up at the sniper, who shook his head. Not enough for a clear sighting. He needed the Italian out in the open.

"Me for Groves. How's that for a deal?" *He waited.*

"Out into the middle of the lawn, Marks! I want you where I can see you!"

The DCI edged forwards, one step at a time, delaying the exchange, hoping that Groves would understand what it was that he needed to do. Inside the kitchen, the pathologist knew the signals, and prepared himself.

"Open the door, Gasparini. Let Groves go. I'm on my way – look, I'm not armed."

There was a click as the key turned in the lock, and the marksman on the garage roof hunkered down to line up the shot. Like gunfighters in a Wild West street, Marks and the two emerging from the kitchen stood facing each other. There was sudden movement as Gasparini levelled the gun not at Groves' head, as previously, but now over his shoulder and lining up with that of Dennis Marks.

Groves had seen the marksman on the garage roof out of the corner of his eye as they emerged, and moved first as Marks dived to one side. The action caught Gasparini momentarily off balance, and as his shot rang out there was an accompanying 'crack' from the top of the garage. The enforcer collapsed to the floor, a single bullet wound to his right temple. Armed units flooded the house and garden as the area was sealed off. In the ensuing confusion, George Groves had not noticed where Marks had gone. When the smoke from Gasparini's gun cleared, he saw the form lying face up on the left hand side of the lawn.

"Dennis!" *Groves rushed over to the side of his colleague.*

Marks lay where he had fallen after the shot from Gasparini's gun. His eyes were closed, and he lay spread-eagled on the ground.

"Dennis." *The call was quieter now, and said almost in disbelief at what seemed to have happened. Peter Spencer rushed through the house and into the back garden.*

"The boss?" *He called out to Groves, who nodded.*

Spencer walked over and kicked Marks on the left leg.

"Come on, sir. No messing about. We got the bad guy." *Marks stirred.*

Groves stood wide-eyed as the DCI sat up, unbuttoned his coat, and removed the body armour. He smiled at the pathologist.

Full Marks

"Good bits of kit, these. You should try one someday." He handed it over.

"You swine! I thought you were a goner, there." Groves scowled.

"What? You thought I'd be daft enough to face a madman like him without a vest on? You must be losing it in your old age, my friend. Come on, since I'm now officially reinstated thanks to Peter's digging around, I'll buy the two of you a coffee."

Tuesday, 9th May 2006

Peter Spencer fingered the envelope in his inside pocket nervously as he strode through the squad room. Marks was already in his office, and had been there since before eight. He stopped at his own desk and sat down momentarily. He and Pauline had been over and over the scenario many times the preceding week, and it was only now that he had summoned up enough nerve to go through with the plan which they had been discussing. His transfer request was burning a hole through the jacket, and his mouth was drying by the second.

"Peter!" The DCI had spotted him through the glass, and was waving him into the office.

"Good morning, sir." Spencer smiled as he opened the door.

"Well, sit down, man." Marks frowned. "You look like you've got the troubles of the whole world on your shoulders."

"Thank you, sir." He took a deep breath. "There's something..."

His well-rehearsed speech was interrupted by the shrill buzzing of the telephone on the desk, and Marks smiled and held up a finger as he picked it up.

"Marks." He paused. "I see; where was this?" He grabbed a notepad from his drawer and began scribbling furiously. "We'll be there right away."

"Sir..." Spencer began again.

"It'll have to wait, Peter." He was out of his chair. "Come on, it would seem that we have a dead teacher at the Lainsford Grammar School in Edmonton. You can tell me about it later; will it keep?"

"Yes, sir. Of course."

Spencer sighed, and followed in the wake of DCI Marks as he led the way at a fast march down to the garage area. Pauline's plans for a better life outside the capital would have to be put on hold for a little longer.

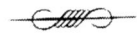

The scruffily-dressed, middle-aged man checking into the ex-cons' hostel off the Bayswater Road bore nothing which would attract the casual observer's attention, and that suited him perfectly. He took the room key from the chain-smoking, unshaven guy at the front desk, along with a letter which had been delivered for his attention a day or so earlier. His reservation was on the second floor of a dingy boarding house which had been taken over by the prison service for just such as him.

The room was small, contained a rudimentary bed, a small chest of drawers which had seen better days, and a wardrobe with one door hanging loose. There was a dirty sink in one corner, and he had the use of a shared toilet and bathroom. Light was provided by a single, dirty, sixty watt bulb. The entire room was the epitome of neglect. He was not bothered in the slightest, and had no intention of sticking around to make any complaints to the landlord.

Throwing his case on the bed, he took out a packet of Silk Cut, lit up, and leaned back against the pillow. It was the first proper cigarette he had seen in quite a while. Taking three long draws, he blew out the blue smoke at the light bulb and sighed. He sat up. Tearing open the envelope collected from downstairs, he tipped the contents onto the bed. It contained one piece of paper and a photograph. The message was clear and unambiguous.

'Don't miss. £10,000 now, £10,000 when it's done. Don't even think of double-crossing me.'

There was a safety deposit box key taped to the note - the first payment and the weapon needed would be there. He looked at the photograph; he knew the man well. He should do - the guy was responsible for the five year stretch from which he had just been released.

The face of Dennis Marks looked back at him from the picture. He smiled – this was going to be good. Revenge and a payment at the end to put cream on the cake. Doubtless the gun supplied by Harold Shaw would be untraceable, and the Thames was a very large river. Shoving the case under the bed, he rolled over and closed his eyes.

Thursday 13th July 2006

Harold Shaw crossed the exercise yard at Wandsworth prison, and fellow inmates parted in silence as he made his way to the bench on its far side. His incarceration of over three years had done nothing to quench his thirst for revenge. Giorgio Gasparini's failure to eliminate Dennis Marks had, it was true, been extremely disappointing – he had thought better of the Italian. He sighed as he turned and sat down in the afternoon sunshine, and unfolded The Daily Mail, a copy of which was hand-delivered to his cell by one of his cronies every morning.

Dennis Marks could live a little longer, but the full weight of Shaw's fury had been expended upon the overconfident Martin Ponsonby. The solicitor had believed, quite wrongly, that with Shaw confined he was now relatively safe notwithstanding the man's threats. His naiveté was to prove fatal. Harold Shaw smiled grimly at the inside front page story. There were no pictures save for a headshot of the solicitor – that would have been tacky even for one of the red tops – but a full report of the lawyer's demise was provided in graphic detail. It made no difference; the drug baron knew exactly what had happened, since he had orchestrated and paid for the execution.

Looking up from his newspaper and across the yard, he laughed openly as those inmates who had been watching turned their heads away – it did not pay to incur the wrath of Harold Shaw; even inside Wandsworth his influence reached too far for safety to be guaranteed.

"Blackfriars Bridge, wasn't it?" DCI Marks said, as he and Groves entered the lab.

"It was." The pathologist replied. "Virtually in the same place as they found Roberto Calvi in June 1982."

"Calvi?" Marks frowned. "Wasn't he the Italian banker linked to the Masons?"

"Yes, and that's where the comparisons to Ponsonby get interesting." He walked over to the table where the solicitor's body lay. "Look here."

"His throat's been cut."

"And from left to right in Masonic style. This starts to look like an execution going back to the Middle Ages." Groves remarked. "The hanging of the body from a bridge, according to Masonic rituals, symbolises the killing of someone who's betrayed the organisation."

"So, we could be looking at Robert Hampson as our prime suspect. He's the master of the lodge where Ponsonby was a member according to a whisper I heard from our friends at MI5."

"Perhaps." Groves hesitated. "That all feels just a little too cut and dried for my liking. He'd had his slap on the wrist – why kill him?"

"Shaw!" Marks shook his head.

"Pardon?"

"Harold Shaw. He sent Gasparini after me and used you as a decoy." They moved to a side table and sat down.

"Yes, but we could never trace the Italian back to him." Groves pointed out. "The gun was untraceable, and Gasparini is dead."

"Ponsonby screwed up his appeal, and Shaw's not a man to take that kind of thing lying down."

"There you go, then." Groves smiled. "Go after him for the killing of the solicitor and close the case."

"Not so easy. There'll be nothing to lead back to him, and the chances of getting anyone to grass on him are zero." Marks sighed. "I think this is one that we can't win. If there are any forensic traces on the body, they'll simply lead back to whoever committed the actual murder, that's all."

"Do you think that you're safe?" Groves became suddenly concerned.

"I don't think Shaw will come after me again following Gasparini's death. That might be a step too far, even for him." Marks shook his head and rose to leave. "It's another blasted loose end, though – how I hate those damned things!"

Other Books by Neal James

A Ticket To Tewkesbury

Julie Martin is the most unlikely of heroines in a struggle for supremacy which reaches to the very pinnacles of power within modern Britain. The letter, found amongst her recently deceased aunt's belongings, sets in motion a chain of events which had their roots in the death throes of Nazi Germany in 1945.

Roger Fretwell and Madeline Colson, two young lovers at the end of hostilities, are in possession of a set of files which fleeing survivors of the Third Reich would rather had lain buried. Now exposed once more, the secrets which they hold put their very lives in peril, and set in motion a chain of events from which there could only be one winner.

Set against the idyllic backdrop of the West Country, Roger and Madeline's love story weaves its way into the dark and troubled waters of espionage, as competing forces will stop at nothing to gain control of a situation so vital for the future of democracy in modern Britain. The breathless pace of the storyline is unrelenting, as the chase over the length and breadth of the country comes to a shattering climax on the platform of Nottingham's Midland Station. The final solution to the drama leaves a surprise ending for the reader to ponder.

Short Stories Volume One

How would you write to God for clarification on matters of the utmost urgency? Find out how Moses might have done it.

Dry your eyes after a heart-rending tale of Aunty Rose, and the tragic story of Liz when she finds the father she never knew. Shake your head at Mike's naiveté in dealing with a stranger in black, and share with Dave his hidden guilt when Tommy Watkinson returns to talk to his son, Paul.

Fly into the realms of fantasy with James Taylor as he gets lost in a place that he knows only too well, and try to sympathise with Ray when the old couple ask him to save humanity.

Follow Dennis Marks in a trilogy which brings the book to its close as he searches for the truth about his grandfather. This collection of little gems will expose every emotion on the rollercoaster which you are about to ride.

Two Little Dicky Birds

On Saturday 8th April 1975, in a fit of rage, Paul Townley took the life of his father, Harold. The significance of that single event was to affect the rest of his life, as he resolved to make it his mission to rid society of the kind of person that the man had become.

The first killing took place six months later, and over the following fifteen years seventeen more were to follow, as the trail of devastation left by a serial killer covered the length and breadth of England.

Detective Chief Inspector Colin Barnes looked down at the letter which lay on the desk before him. An icy hand gripped his heart as he read once more the details of the eighteen murders. Murders which had come back to haunt him from his past as he realised that he would, once more, be faced with the serial killer who had called himself... Petey.

Follow the chase for Petey, two and a half decades after his first appearance, as its climax takes you across the Atlantic to New York's JFK airport and into the arms of Detective Tom Casey of the 113th Precinct, in a plot so intricate it will leave you breathless.

Threads of Deceit

George Carter is a man with problems – big ones, and of the financial kind. Accustomed to getting his own way, he rules his roost at Brodsworth Textiles with an iron fist.

James Poynter is a young man out for revenge. Set up for a crime which he did not commit, and by someone whom he believed he could trust implicitly, his sole focus becomes one of retribution against his former boss and the firm which he is defrauding.

His future at Brodsworth Textiles disintegrates one Friday evening prior to his wedding, when conscientiousness overtakes him and he returns to the factory after work to rectify an administrative error.

What he learns in that moment sets off a chain of events which sends him spiralling downwards, and out of a job which had promised to propel him to senior managerial level.

Murder, deception, drug trafficking and embezzlement combine to derail the futures of everyone connected to the company, and set off a Europe-wide chase for the man at the centre of a plot so intricate that the forces of law and order in several countries are thwarted at every turn leading to a stunning climax at Bristol Airport.

About Neal James

Neal James, an accountant from Derbyshire began writing in 2007 when one of his short stories made it into the top ten of an international competition. He realised that he had a wealth of factual information at his fingertips which he could convert into fiction.

His background is that of a miner's son. Educated through the state system to degree level, he found work after college in accounting and that is where his qualifications lie. However, a broad industrial working life has provided him with sufficient data to mould a number of plotlines into novels.

Neal James is the author of "A Ticket to Tewkesbury", "Short Stories Volume One", "Two Little Dicky Birds" and "Threads of Deceit".

There has been coverage of Neal's work in the local press. The Derby Telegraph, the Nottingham Evening Post, and the Ripley & Heanor News have all run features on his growing portfolio of writing. He has appeared on BBC Radio Derby and BBC Radio Nottingham, as well as a number of Book Chat shows both in Spain and the USA.

Connect with Neal James

http://www.nealjames.webs.com/

http://www.goodreads.com/user/show/6864216-neal-james

http://www.facebook.com/neal.james.125

http://www.linkedin.com/profile/view?id=116462215&trk=tab_pro